ry.

THE SOUTH AFRICAN

THE
SOUTH AFRICAN

Paul A Taylor

Book Guild Publishing
Sussex, England

First published in Great Britain in 2009 by
The Book Guild Ltd
Pavilion View
19 New Road
Brighton, BN1 1UF

Typeset in Baskerville by Ellipsis Books Limited, Glasgow

Printed in Great Britain by CPI Antony Rowe, Chippenham

A catalogue record for this book is available from
The British Library.

ISBN 978 1 84624 367 7

To Shirley, forever my princess
For 'poppy' with whom life has so much meaning.
Thank you for everything.

Prologue

South Africa, 24th March 1974

The woman pulled the animal skins tight up around her neck, and snuggled into her husband's back for more warmth, the red-hot embers of the smouldering fire not adequate enough to contend with the cold African night. She knew that there would be no sleep tonight: the child growing within her was becoming restless, it would soon be time.

Beside her on the dirt floor of the hut her firstborn, David, lay sleeping soundly, oblivious to the falling temperature, and as she turned to make sure he was well covered the pain arrived. Short and sharp, she cried out loud, awakening her husband, who knowingly rose and left the hut, returning minutes later with two women and a wizened old man.

The old man kicked the dying embers into life and then fed the hungry flames with twigs and placed a tin can of water on them. Taking a goatskin pouch from around his neck, he poured the contents of herbs and spices into the liquid and began to chant. As the woman's efforts became more intense he scooped up a ladle of the now steaming water and began to dance around the birthplace, sprinkling the contents over her body and the child's head as it appeared. Then he took the newborn out into the cold night air and, holding the naked baby high above his head, he turned round and around, praying as he offered the child to the stars and the universe.

When he returned the child to the hut he found the woman

1

lying there tired but smiling contentedly her firstborn now beside her under the skins clinging to his mother, bemused but not frightened by the events of the night. He placed the protesting new arrival in her arms and she put him to her breast, immediately silencing him. She had given her husband another son and his pride and love was there for all to see as he stood looking down on his family. 'This son, my wife, we will call Paul.'

London, 24th March 1974

The girl had stood for what seemed an eternity outside the big wooden door set in the wall, the rain pouring down incessantly upon her, still uncertain as to whether she was doing the right thing. She didn't want a child but the teachings of the church were planted deep down inside her soul; abortion was not the answer, she couldn't deny giving life to someone. She was cold and soaked through and had gone over and over in her mind who else she could turn to, then the stirring inside her made the decision for her.

Summoning up her courage she reached for the bell pull and heard somewhere far off a deep resonant sound. Almost immediately the large wooden door creaked open and she was greeted by a smiling nun, which instantly calmed her fears.

'Come on in out of this rain, my child. You will catch your death of cold out here.'

Taking the girl by the arm, she led her into the hospice, its warmth immediately enveloping her, further calming the butterflies beating about her now trembling body. She was led into a sparsely furnished bedroom and told to strip off her wet garments, the nun returning soon after with towels, dry clothes and another nun.

'I'm Sister Mika and this is Sister Ruth. How may we help you, my child?'

The girl spoke for the first time; her speech had an Italian accent. 'My name is Donna,' and she looked down sheepishly to the slight swelling that was her stomach.

'How long have you to go, Donna?'

'I think six weeks, I don't know.'

'You have no family, no one who can help you?'

The girl shook her head then gasped and grabbed her stomach, her face creased with pain. The two sisters took hold of her before she could fall and laid her on the bed as the girl gasped again.

The birth was quick, the tiny boy very premature but in no danger. The sisters wrapped him in towels and offered him to the girl, who turned her head away and refused to take hold of the baby.

'I don't want to see him, I don't want to touch him. Please, no council home for him, find him a good home where he can have every chance in life and christen him Mario Barolli.'

The two nuns nodded knowingly and took baby Mario away, leaving the exhausted girl to sleep, certain that after rest and time to reflect she would change her mind. When they returned two hours later she was gone, leaving behind her £200 on the bedside table.

1

South Africa, October 2003

Dawn's first rays were breaking over the surrounding hills, the expectant silence that accompanies each daybreak hanging heavy in the air. Almost immediately the tranquillity was broken as the slow, throbbing beat of drums rose out of the earth and reached for the sky, their haunting significance echoing around the valley.

Instantly, smoke rose up from the kraals as dormant fires were replenished and the sound of hungry, crying children combined with the murmuring voices of an awakened people joined the birdsong carrying on the breeze.

As the drums increased their urgency, David's big, broken body was taken from its sacred resting place and arranged on a pallet of dried saplings woven with vines and adorned with orchids, then anointed with palm oil. The rising sun shone down from a crystal blue sky, illuminating the naked ebony corpse as they covered it with a lion's skin and placed a spear in his hand. He was ready for the ultimate journey.

All around him the villagers stood, silently paying their homage. Only one man showed any emotion in his face as the women began wailing their sorrowful farewell. Blinking heavily, Paul fought back the tears, then, as the incessant drumming reached a crescendo, the tribal elder put his flaming torch to the pyre, the women ceased their weeping, and the whole valley filled with the sound of joyous song.

London, September 2003

Amanda Nicholson was seventeen years old going on forty. Another product of a violent and broken marriage, she had run away from home when she was fifteen, having met Sonny. After a lifetime of tears and no love she had found him one day, during a break in lessons, leaning against the perimeter fence of the school smiling at her and saying nothing.

Despite her questions he remained silent, still smiling warmly at her, and then he pushed through the fence a piece of paper with an address and telephone number scrawled across it. She grabbed it from him and ran across the playground and back into the classroom, her mind and body aroused with the excitement of it all. She didn't call him immediately she got home, or the next day either, and just when she thought she could hold out no more she found him waiting for her outside the school the following day.

Despite the differences in colour and culture, Amanda had found the love she craved and, regardless of the warnings from her friends, she moved in with Sonny. London became her oyster and for three months her life was a carousel, a non-stop world of parties where she was made to feel like a queen as Sonny showed her off to everyone.

She started smoking hash and drinking heavily and, as the partying became more frenzied, her young body's needs became more demanding and she started snorting cocaine. The trips got heavier but the cravings within her could not be satisfied and very soon she discovered the world of heroin.

During this time Sonny had turned into a vicious monster and she found herself in her mother's shoes as the violence returned to her world, a world from which there seemed no escape. One day, after yet another beating, he told her that he could no longer afford to feed her habit and threatened to throw her out on to the streets.

Amanda begged for mercy. She didn't want to go back to her

parents and had no one else to turn to: Sonny controlled her life totally, he bought everything, paid all the bills, she didn't have a penny in the world to call her own. So Sonny relented, telling her that there was only one route she could take, only one solution if she wanted to stay – and so the men arrived in her bed.

Fat, thin, young, old, ugly or handsome, black or white, Amanda had no idea most of the time who she was sleeping with as, night after night, the endless stream flowed through her bedroom, violently abusing her young drugged body.

Despite the lateness of the hour it was still sweltering, the Indian summer a bonus for the pavement cafés as they teemed with people who usually, at this time of night, would be long gone. He was 6' 3' and black, and thankful for this unexpected bonus as he threaded his way through the milling throng. Most of the time he stood out a mile but in this multi-cultural melange that was London at night he was almost indiscernible.

To all and sundry he appeared to be just another guy soaking up the atmosphere, looking for a good time but, behind the tinted glasses, the eyes were darting everywhere and the body was tensed, coiled, ready to react to the first hints of danger. After half an hour of fruitless searching he realised that his luck wasn't in, she wasn't in any of her usual haunts so, ignoring the warning voices in his head, he decided to abandon the easy option and go for the dark side.

Leaving the bright lights and safety of the crowd, he ducked into a side street and immediately took refuge in the first doorway available, glancing back through the filthy glass window to make sure he hadn't been followed. All around him the cardboard city that housed London's down and outs was settling down for the night, while below them the tube trains rumbled by, emitting their welcoming warmth as the temperature rapidly fell. They all knew him or knew of him in this nether world, and pretty soon the grapevine would reveal his presence to interested parties, so time was not on his side; he had to find the girl and find her quickly.

As always the message she had left on his mobile was almost incomprehensible, her speech slurred and broken, but one name had rung out loud and clear through the jumble, a name which had stirred his every emotion. Abdul Karim. A ghost from the past, a dead man, so why should this poor creature suddenly phone and mention his name?

Her information in the past had always been reliable, and had credited him with much success, although he knew her motives were only materialistic and feeding her habit any which way was her sole motivation in life. He always hoped that she would use the money he gave her to nourish the wafer-thin body with something other than heroin but that was a wild dream. He had met so many like her and knew that the odds on saving her life were infinitesimal but his job allowed him no sentiment in this, results were the only thing that mattered to him and finding her tonight was a priority.

Someone called out a greeting so he crossed the street to acknowledge the person and have a chat, knowing that this was a dangerous move but one that was unavoidable. Leaving a fiver in the old man's hand, he quickly moved on, the girls of the night, young and old, accosting him playfully as he passed them by, their respect for this man total, but there was no sighting of the one he sought.

He was certain by now that the word would be out on the street so he needed to find her quickly if he was to greet the dawn, there were too many around here who would relish this golden opportunity. She could, of course, be turning a trick but he couldn't hang around all night waiting for her to reappear. He really hadn't thought this out properly, rushing in blindly, ignoring all his training, breaking all the rules, the obsession totally dominating his thinking. Then he spotted the pimp. If he was in the vicinity it was collection time.

He had to take the chance and wait a little longer. The girl's residence was just around the next corner so hopefully she would show soon. He knew this piece of shit well, a woman-beater who

8

ran a mile if a man came anywhere near him and, as he slipped into the shadows, he watched as this loathsome creature menacingly gathered his ill-gotten gains from his other women.

The girl appeared just as the pimp's patience was running out, his frenetic pacing up and down had been punctuated by the punching of walls and the smoking of several cigarettes and, on seeing the girl, he grabbed her wrist and threw her against a wall, slapping her face repeatedly. The man in the shadows held himself in check as the scene unfolded in front him, resisting the urge to intervene and teach him a lesson he would never forget.

'One day, Sonny, one day soon,' he murmured under his breath as he watched the girl hand over the money and receive in turn a little package which she grabbed from the man's hand, a gesture which caused him to laugh out loudly.

As she ran off on unsteady limbs a car pulled into the kerb and the pimp was gone. Checking that it was safe, he emerged from his hiding place and took off after the girl, certain of her destination.

He found the pitiful creature as he had expected, huddled under the bridge in the shelter of the iron stanchions, frantically injecting the killer substance. She was unaware of his presence and as he saw the craving inside her beginning to subside he gently whispered her name.

'Amanda, it's me, don't be frightened.'

She started at the sound of her name and turned, then broke down in tears as he approached her. He took his jacket off and placed it around her shivering shoulders, then sat down beside her and took her in his arms.

The silence was temporarily broken as a train thundered across the bridge, then returned as it departed, and she clung on to him until all her demons had receded. She was in a mess, the bruising in her face was beginning to come out, the blood from her nose congealed on her top lip, and he reached into the pocket of his jacket and took out a handkerchief and some mini Mars bars. As she ravenously ate the chocolate he went to the water's edge, dipped his handkerchief in, and returned to wipe the blood from her face, then held the soothing cold cloth to her swelling cheeks.

They continued to sit in silence, the man knowing that the clock was ticking, but he patiently waited until the girl was ready. When she finally spoke it was with some difficulty, the swollen, cut lips hurting like hell as she looked up into the kind face that always brought her comfort.

'How come you're here, my black knight in shining armour?' She stared longingly into the eyes of the one and only light in the dark that was her life and nestled closer to him. 'You always appear when I need you most.'

'You left a message on my mobile last night, don't you remember?'

'No, what did I say?'

'Most of it was gibberish but you kept repeating a name: Abdul Karim.'

Amanda blanched, the fear returning to her face and he placed his hands on her shoulders, steadying her, as she started to shake once more.

'Amanda, tell me about him.'

'He's vicious, far worse than Sonny. He's Sonny's source and, whenever he's around, I have to be available for him all the time.'

The girl shivered again at the thought. At least the heroin he brought with him meant he was soon beyond anything physical or sexual but, up to the point of unconsciousness, he was the most perverted man she had ever known.

'I know this is painful for you but have a look at this photograph.'

She recoiled at the monstrous image in front of her, and turned her head away, but it was nothing compared to the shock waves running through his body. How could this be possible? More importantly, where was Abdul Karim now and where did he go from here? He had to push her further.

'I'm sorry to press you on this, but did you ever see this man outside of your flat?'

'Only once, about a fortnight ago when Sonny took me to see a doctor in the Fulham Palace Road. I had a skin reaction to the injections that wouldn't go away and Sonny and the doctor were talking about the Arab when he arrived. That's when I learnt his name. They were obviously well known to each other and the meeting was planned.'

'What did they talk about?'

'I wasn't really interested so I didn't pay them much attention.'

'Try and think, Amanda. Anything you recall could be important.'

'Sonny and the Arab went out of earshot while the doctor examined me, but odd snippets came through the partitioning as he got more heated.'

He looked at her intently, willing the words from her mouth.

'There was some problem with the distribution of a shipment, I think. The Arab was angry because someone called Uncle Freddie had refused to help him. I'm sure that was the name because he repeatedly cursed him but, as I said, I wasn't really listening. All I can remember is that he was beside himself: I've seen him in this mood and it isn't pretty but, thankfully, he had left before the doctor had finished with me.'

He hid his elation at this further piece of information as he helped her to her feet, putting a £20 note in her hand.

'Promise me you will go and have a good meal with this and not buy any more shit tonight.'

'I promise, honestly, thank you so much.'

Taking her head in his hands he bent down and kissed her forehead.

'Amanda, it's not too late you know I could get someone to contact you who could help.'

She stared long and hard up at him, the pleading in her eyes giving him the answer then, as he turned to leave, another thought came to mind.

'Tell me, do you remember the name of the doctor by any chance?'

11

She laughed for the first time and he immediately knew the answer.

'Silly question, right: there was no plate on the door, no receptionist, no surgery.'

She nodded agreement, still smiling at his back as he slipped into the night.

2

London, October 2003

The South African Airways 747 hovered like a giant bird as it made its final approach to London Heathrow. Then it swooped down out of the mist, hitting the runway with a triumphant roar, and taxied to its allotted stand. The ground services hurried to attend, but the passenger in seat 163 was oblivious to all that was happening around him.

He did not unbuckle his seat belt when the plane stopped or make any attempt to move, despite the requests of his fellow passengers. A combination of jet-lag and grief enveloped him, his mind shut down, his body was too exhausted to respond. The emotion welled once more in his eyes as a stewardess, sensing that there was a problem, approached him.

'Excuse me, sir, are you all right?'

He did not reply immediately, so she shook him gently as she unbuckled the belt. With half-glazed eyes he mumbled an apology and stood to retrieve his hand luggage. Still in a trance he drifted through Immigration and Customs but as he entered the Arrivals lounge he was jolted from his reverie.

'Paul Mackenzie.' A deep, resonant voice, a sound from the past penetrated his being and, turning, he saw the unmistakeable figure of Michael Mamtoba. A giant of a man in every sense, the schoolteacher to whom he and his brother owed everything stood there looking as if the march of time had passed him by.

Proud and erect, not even a trace of grey on the noble head, his warm smile a welcome sight.

The memories came rushing back as Paul fought his way through the noisy crowd towards a man whose patience and guidance had enabled firstly his brother, and then himself, to escape the poverty and violence that was their destiny. They had been the lucky ones. In a country so divided by hate and colour very few got the opportunity, but they had had a university education and a chance of a future thanks to him.

His love and gratitude for this man knew no boundaries and, as the years apart dwindled into minutes, he felt as ever his inner strength returning in the presence of Michael Mamtoba.

The two men embraced, holding one another fiercely for what seemed an eternity until Paul realised the presence of two women. One he remembered meeting a long time ago, Michael's wife, Helen. He apologised as he turned to greet her and, in turn, was introduced to a tall, elegant women with beautiful honey-coloured skin who really needed no introduction; he would have recognised her anywhere. Frances Johnson, his brother's girlfriend: David had never stopped talking about her the last time he came home and he could now see why.

However, this was not the time for talking so, after the usual short pleasantries, a silence descended upon the party as they found Michael's car and then made the slow stop-start journey through the early morning rush-hour traffic to London.

It was the first time that he had left his native country but, for Paul, there was no feeling of excitement, no wonderment at this new and different culture, only a huge void that even the presence of his friend and mentor could not compensate for.

'Here we are, Paul!' Helen's voice broke the gloomy silence. They had pulled up outside a row of terraced houses that he instantly recognised from photos David had sent him.

'We have a room ready for you if you would like to stay or we can take you to your brother's flat later.'

'Thank you. I think a shower and some breakfast would be nice at this moment, but haven't you all got jobs to go to?'

'Only I've got to go to work today but I should be home by seven-thirty if you do decide to stay at the flat.' Frances spoke her first words in over an hour. 'These two have managed to take the day off but the hospital is so short-staffed it wasn't possible for me. There are two bedrooms, and you won't have any difficulty in knowing which one is mine, and there is plenty of food in the fridge.'

'Thank you, you have all been so kind.' Paul wasn't quite sure what he wanted to do at this precise moment. 'I would like to spend some time with Michael and Helen obviously, but maybe a few days of solitude wouldn't be a bad idea.'

'I haven't tried to find somewhere else to live yet, Paul. I hope you don't mind if I continue to stay at the flat, it's as if David is still protecting me.'

'Of course I don't mind, it's your home. If I do decide to stay I promise I won't get in the way, you'll hardly know that I'm around.'

'Michael has a key, just make yourself at home.'

Paul felt for her as she said her goodbyes and left. Like them all, Frances was living a nightmare, still unable to accept that David was gone.

Feeling a lot better after a long hot shower, and a change of clothes, Paul went down to the kitchen/diner where he found the table laid for a feast.

'Helen, this is magnificent! Do you normally eat this much for breakfast?'

Michael laughed, and again that deep sound that Paul remembered so well seemed to rebound off the walls.

'To the English, breakfast is like a religion and it must be given due reverence daily. It gives you a good start to the day and Helen and I never miss out, then we have a light lunch and dinner in the evening. I'm just so sorry our first meal together in years is in such terrible circumstances. What happened?' He hadn't

15

wanted to broach the subject so soon but he could not contain himself any longer.

'I have read the police report, which told me absolutely nothing, except that David died from injuries sustained in a fall, and the coroner's verdict was accidental death. What was he doing 100 miles from London lying at the bottom of a cliff face and not wearing any climbing gear? We all know that David was a careful, experienced climber who would never take any risks. He was fanatical about safety, checking everything twice, and he would never undertake any climb without the appropriate equipment.'

'I agree with what you are saying, Paul, I had to identify the body.' Michael's voice faltered as he relived that awful moment. 'The only rope burns were on his wrists and, although there was massive damage to his upper body, there were no broken limbs or skin abrasions.'

Paul fell silent then as he reflected on Michael's words for he too had noticed that they were the only burn marks and, up to now, he hadn't given them a second thought. David had had two close encounters with death whilst climbing, and on both occasions he had sustained broken limbs and severe abrasions, only his ropes saving his life.

'You know why he was in England and what he was investigating. Did he ever mention any people's names, places that he had visited, or is there anything else you can remember that could give me a lead?'

'Paul, as good a friend as I was with David, he never discussed his day's events, although at times I felt he wanted to. Yes, I know why he had come to England and why he had stayed, and that you two were determined to eradicate the human trafficking of drugs between here and Durban, but that was it. I never asked questions although I did notice a change in him these last few weeks: he appeared to be very preoccupied and incommunicative, even Frances confided in us that she was worried about him.'

The conversation drifted to Paul and Durban, and he started to relax a little as he recalled tales about their homeland, but the nagging doubts had resurfaced and would not go away, so when Helen suggested after breakfast that he went and lay down while she cleared up he declined. Although he was very tired the adrenalin was pumping once more and he was beyond sleeping,

'Thank you, but I think I'll go for a walk if that's all right with you two, try to clear my head a bit and digest that wonderful breakfast.'

3

Paul soon found himself alongside the river and immediately his thoughts returned to Africa, to the round grass hut that was school, and Michael Mamtoba was teaching them all about England and its capital London, which stood on the river Thames. How it was from there that all the great explorers and traders had sailed to the African continent in search of fame and fortune, their dreams often floundering in the mighty oceans. He then mesmerised them all with his tales of treks into the vast hinterland, the battles with the inhabiting tribes, and the discoveries of strange animals and places. It was also the day that Michael Mamtoba became their surrogate father.

Running home from school, their hearts and minds racing with thoughts of the new world that had been opened up to them, they plunged into the river that half encircled their village and swam and played until they were nearly exhausted. Dragging themselves from the water, they then climbed one of the giant trees along its banks where, tired but joyously happy, they sat and surveyed their home. They watched the animals in the kraals, the smoke gently rising from the huts, and began discussing the day's lessons. They were soon sailing the high seas, fighting off pirates and, having discovered a small island, they made camp, caught giant fish and searched for buried treasure.

Suddenly, they became aware of gunshots and the ground shuddered beneath them as, thundering down the valley towards the village came what seemed to them a hundred horsemen carrying flaming torches and shooting at everything in sight. The two boys sat holding one another tightly, unable to move as they saw their village and their beautiful home go up in flames then, as quickly as the rebel bandits had appeared, they were gone, stampeding the village cattle in front of them. For what seemed an eternity the brothers watched the smouldering ruins then David, as the elder, helped his little brother out of the tree and they ran hand in hand towards the charred remains, screaming out loud for their parents. They found Michael Mamtoba cradling the body of their dying father. Their mother, lying a few feet away, was hardly recognisable.

A cold wind came off the river, breaking Paul's thoughts and, glancing at his watch, he saw that he had been gone for almost two hours. Concerned that Helen and Michael would be starting to worry he quickly retraced his steps back to the row of terraced houses and there, sure enough, he found the schoolteacher pacing up and down outside looking for his errant pupil.

'Sorry, Michael, I got carried away out there. There are so many thoughts and memories that bind us all together.'

'I know, Paul. Would you like to see David's flat now? It's only ten minutes away and Helen has got things to do in the house, so we would be better off out of it.'

The flat occupied the top floor of a terraced house similar to Michael's, and although David had sent him many photographs, nothing had prepared him for this: the flat was a shrine to Africa. From the ochre of the walls and the raffia mats on the floors to the many paintings hanging everywhere, it was home, it was where he wanted to be.

'Michael,' Paul began, but Michael was already ahead of him.

'It's all right, Paul, I understand. I knew the minute you saw this place you would want to stay here. I'll drop your bags around later.'

Left to his own devices Paul wandered from room to room, marvelling at his brother's taste although he suspected that Frances had been a big influence. Fighting the fatigue, he lay down on the spare bed and stared at the photographs of himself and his brother that adorned the chest of drawers, the painful memories flooding back.

Cold, it's so cold! Paul stirred and on opening his eyes realised it was also pitch black in the room. Switching on the bedside lamp he glanced at his watch: it was one o'clock in the morning and he'd been asleep for twelve hours. Undressing quickly he slipped beneath the bed covers and was soon asleep again, awakening some six hours later to find a note on the bedside table.

Working 7am till 3pm today. Glad to see you are staying, your cases are in the kitchen. Love Frances

As the fog in his head lifted and his mind began to clear, his first thoughts, as ever, were for his dead brother. Then he felt the anger and pain resurfacing, so, donning David's tracksuit and trainers, he left the flat and began pounding the streets of Battersea, soon finding the park.

Thankfully, there were less people in here, which allowed him to increase the pace as he exorcised his demons, releasing the tensions from his mind and body as he fell into his daily training routine. Back at the flat he retrieved his cases from the kitchen, unpacked, and took a shower. After fixing himself a more modest breakfast than the day before, he settled down in the living room and took out his mobile.

'New Scotland Yard, good morning.' The girl's London accent was familiar in his ears.

'Detective Chief Superintendent Carlisle please, my name is Paul Mackenzie.'

The DCS answered almost immediately. 'Welcome to London, Sergeant, I've been expecting your call. How can I help you?'

'Could we meet please, sir? There are one or two things I would like to discuss with you regarding my brother's death.'

Paul expected to be fobbed off on some lesser ranking officer, so he was taken by surprise when Carlisle said, 'Is ten-thirty tomorrow morning in my office OK for you?'

'Thank you, sir. I look forward to meeting you. David often spoke about you.'

'All good I hope, Sergeant. I'll see you in the morning,' and the DCS hung up.

4

Matthew Simon Richardson, Earl of Turnford, only child of the Duke and Duchess of Rushtington, had had a base in life which was calm, orderly and very loving, a firm foundation from which he had prospered. His parents, whilst being eternally thankful for this wonderful gift, had strived hard not to spoil the child, and from his first day at school their efforts had been rewarded, his tutors instantly recognising his exceptional attributes: coupled with his kindness and consideration for others there was a firmness and purpose of mind which made him a natural leader.

He was not pushy, he just somehow stood out from the rest, and his parents proudly watched his progression through his formative years as their son was made captain of the school rugby team, senior school prefect, and achieved academically from an early age results which meant he was destined for a very sound future.

His father was an avid huntsman, and a master shot, and it soon became obvious that his son and heir was following in his footsteps. Matthew's natural ability with a gun astounded the old timers who thought they had seen it all, and by the time he was thirteen he had become a living legend amongst the country folk in the county. Also, like his father, he commanded the respect of people without ever seeking it and when he went on to Eton everybody, including his parents, was of one opinion: the young Earl was tailor-made for the political arena.

However, it was not what he wanted and after many an hour of soul-searching he confounded everybody by choosing the military, and went on to Sandhurst, only he knowing the real reason for his decision. No other vocation in life would give him the opportunity to release the pent-up emotions that he had fought to suppress since his childhood. There had always existed another person within, a dark and violent soul that cried out for release. He wanted to taste extreme danger, to walk the thin line between life and death, he wanted to go to war.

He quickly adapted to military life: the discipline, the comradeship, the pomp and ceremony, it all came so naturally to him, as did the thought of killing a fellow human being. His name came very quickly to the attention of the commanding officer as his leadership and natural military skills soon became apparent, and he was flagged as one who could go right to the very top of the British armed forces.

Women played no part in his life, and had never really interested him; they were an unnecessary distraction and sex was something he could live without, his one and only lust was the thrill of the chase and the kill that followed. His regiment specialised in black operations: they would enter countries illegally, sort out the problem and get out before anyone realised what was happening, at least that was the theory.

One day he was summoned to the CO's office to be told that he was to lead an incursion into a tiny African state that, like a lot of others, was torn apart by civil war and governed by a manic despot. The irony of it all was that the man had been educated at Eton and had received his military training at Sandhurst.

His orders were to remove 'permanently' the offending General, allowing the choice of the people and the British Government to take over but, unfortunately, their intelligence had been false and the supposed local sympathisers were non-existent. They were led into an ambush which left many of his men dead, and although his natural reaction was to stand and fight, common sense prevailed and he managed to escape with the remainder of his troops.

23

There followed an international outcry at the behaviour of the British Government and, although no blame was attached to him, he resigned his commission. Despite the pleadings of his parents and the military hierarchy he stuck by his decision, only he knowing the real reason behind it. He had received a telephone call offering him a six-figure sum to remove the offending General on his own, and so his new career had been born.

Central Africa, March 1999

As he wound his way up into the hills, and closer to enemy territory, he was more than conscious that the engine noise of the old Land Rover could be heard above the raging storm, signalling his presence, but it was a risk he had to take. A journey across country, on foot, was out of the question in these conditions, although for how much longer he could continue like this he was uncertain.

The incessant rain fell from the sky with a deafening roar, the windscreen wipers of the vehicle no match for this endless tide of water that swamped them, and he knew that this was one battle he wasn't going to win. Visibility was down to zero and to his right the steaming ravine was trying to drag him closer and closer to his maker. The road was now a river awash with all kinds of debris and as another tree, its fronds bent double by the wind, tried to claw the canvas awning from the rear of the Land Rover, he knew it was only a matter of time. He would have liked to have got closer to the frontier but, if he was not to die in this godforsaken jungle, he would have to abandon the vehicle soon and do it the hard way.

The decision was taken from him moments later. The engine started to splutter, then died, as the water finally penetrated its heart, and he rolled back off the road into the dense brush. His luck was in: there were no hidden ditches or tree stumps and, after covering the vehicle with branches and leaves, he began the long foot-slog for the border.

Keeping the road as his guideline he picked his way through the trees, ever mindful that he could run into a border patrol but, knowing the enemy as he did, he was sure that these soldiers would be tucked up somewhere warm and dry. They were some of the most undisciplined troops in the world: they killed at will and were usually stoned out of their minds on drugs and drink or, as in this instance, missing from their post, and he crossed the frontier without any problems.

From his previous experience here he had learnt the hard way that these were a fickle people whose only allegiance was to the punda, the local currency; whoever paid the most had their unswerving loyalty. The tribal differences which had decimated the African continent over many centuries were quickly forgotten when money was laid on the table, so this time he would seek the help of no one, he would wait, observe and choose his moment. The arrogance of this self-styled General, and the total lack of authority surrounding him, meant that he would have an opportunity very soon.

He thought back then to that terrible day and the bloody rear-guard action they had fought as he had led his depleted troops in retreat. They had taken refuge in an old abandoned mine-shaft, to assess the situation and tend to the wounded, and there they had stashed their excess weaponry.

He had decided to bury it in there rather than let it fall into the hands of the rebels if they were captured, a decision he now reflected that was meant to be. Except for the hunting knife strapped inside his left leg he was unarmed and, if he were captured, he would be at the mercy of a people who did not know the meaning of words like civilised and humanitarian. Some were still cannibals and as the General had expelled most of the white people from the country, or placed them under house arrest, he could not afford to be spotted by anyone.

At least the rain afforded him some sort of cover as his instincts, and the familiar landmarks that appeared, took him ever closer to the mineshaft and hopefully a shelter for the night. If the cache of weapons had been discovered he would have to abort this attempt and think again – there was no way he would be able to source the things he needed without word getting around very quickly. But his first priority was to seek the safety of the pit head, from where he could reassess the situation.

Cautiously making his way around the outskirts of the capital, he noticed that life here seemed to be going on as before and did not appear to be affected by the civil war that ravaged the rest of the country. The street markets were teeming with people, despite the weather, and the buildings appeared not to have suffered any battle damage. Despite the efforts of the UN, and various other world bodies, trading sanctions did not seem to have had any effect because there were other equally rebellious nations within this vast continent willing to do business with its leader.

He reached the mineshaft without encountering any problems and was relieved to find it as he had left it: the boulders blocking the entrance appeared not to have been moved, although they were now covered in thick vines, which was something he had not bargained for.

Cursing his luck he began hacking away at them, ever mindful that he was too exposed out here, the nerve ends jangling as he constantly looked out for signs of trouble.

Finally, he managed to prise loose a couple of the rocks, the hole only just large enough for him to crawl through, and as he gratefully fell into the old shaft the smell of rank, trapped air and dead vermin hit him.

Fighting the nausea he blindly felt his way along the tunnel until he was sure it was safe to light the torch and was greeted by the horrific sight of two skeletons, their bones picked clean by the inhabiting rats. He remembered these two young men vividly, their injuries so bad they were beyond help, their plaintive pleadings leaving him no alternative. He had sent his men on ahead then shot them both like the wounded animals they were and, as his anger mounted at the thought of the local treachery that had nearly killed them all, he said a prayer for all those who had perished that day.

There was no chance of lighting a fire but at least he was out of the rain that had managed to penetrate through to every part of his body and, after removing his sodden clothes, he began exercising his cold, lifeless limbs, the circulation gradually reaching the dead extremities.

Thankfully the weapons were still in place and, as he settled down to eat his cold but welcoming rations, he started to relax and began reflecting on the tragic events of the past few months which had turned his whole world upside down.

The slow, lingering death of his adored mother had been the first real heartbreak of his life: only fifty-five years old, she had been diagnosed as terminally ill some months earlier and he and his father had never left her side till the end.

It had left his grieving father a broken man and he had been reluctant to leave him to come on this mission but, in the end, he had had no choice. His paymasters, although full of sympathy, were losing too much money a day whilst the offending General was in power, so he had told his father that he had a business opportunity in Africa which wouldn't take too long to conclude and that on his return the two of them would try to rebuild their lives together. Unbeknown to Matthew at the time, they would be the last words he ever spoke to his father.

5

London, October 2003

Frances arrived home just after 4pm and the two of them hit it off at once. It was as if they had known one another all their lives, but both knew the real reason: David.

She showed Paul all the things they had bought together, including the African artefacts that were part of a heritage of which David was so proud, and then she told him all about her West Indian background, her job, her parents, her love of London, her love of David.

Here she broke down and Paul went to comfort her, the two of them bound together by death as the tears arrived. He had spent the past three weeks in a self-controlled coma that he needed to break free from and here with the love of David's life was the right time and the right place. They clung to one another, saying nothing, just allowing their grief to flow as the memories of David flooded through their minds.

Suddenly it was dark in the flat as the cold October evening quickly drew in and Frances got up to pull the curtains and switch on the lights. As if by magic the sadness was immediately banished, the warmth of the wall colours and the lanterns hanging everywhere brightening the mood and lifting the gloom as Paul rose to go to the bathroom.

'Would you mind eating out tonight, Paul? I don't feel much like cooking and there is a super trattoria just around the corner.'

'Sounds like a good idea to me: would it be OK with you if Michael and Helen joined us?'

'I would love that. They have been so good to me these past three weeks and I think a night out would do them good as well. I'll phone them now.'

'One other thing, Frances. Could you organise a taxi for me for 10am tomorrow? I have an appointment with DCS Carlisle at New Scotland Yard and I wouldn't have a clue how to get there.'

'No need. I start work at 11am tomorrow so I can drop you off on the way. The hospital is just across the river from the Yard.'

Later that night Paul lay in bed mulling over an evening that had been a happy occasion despite the giant cloud that hung over them all. From the reception they had been given by all the staff, through the wonderful Italian meal, to the company of that gentle giant of a man and his wife, it had been one of those nights that he would always remember. The laughter had returned to their lives and, feeling more relaxed than he had in a long time, he soon drifted into sleep.

He was awakened by the knocking on his bedroom door and that wonderful Jamaican accent. 'Breakfast in ten minutes.'

For the first time in weeks Paul felt alive as he showered and got dressed in one of David's suits – unfortunately, all the clothes he had brought with him were far too lightweight for the London climate. It fitted and felt fine, as he knew it would; he only hoped that Frances wouldn't mind too much.

'Wow!' was her first reaction on seeing Paul, immediately relieving his worries.

'I hope it's OK with you, Frances, but none of my clothes are suitable for this cold, damp weather.'

'You look superb! David would be very proud of you. Now sit down and eat up, you are going to need all your energy today.'

She dropped him off around the corner from the Yard. Since the terrorist attacks on the twin towers in New York, on 11th September 2001, the British Isles had been on constant alert,

29

and security was at a maximum. However, Paul was expected, and he received a warm reception from both civilian and uniformed staff as he was subjected to a quick body search and then led to the third floor office of the DCS.

Martin Carlisle was forty-seven years old and had been the youngest ever to attain the position of Detective Chief Superintendent. His spectacular rise through the ranks had been attributed to his man-management skills and his brilliant record of crime solving, but those who were closest to him knew that there was a third and more important reason. Known throughout the criminal fraternity as 'Mr Clean', his integrity was invaluable to a police force that had taken more than its fair share of knocks over the years.

As Paul entered the office, Carlisle was momentarily taken aback by the uncanny resemblance to his elder brother, then he rose to greet his visitor and shook him warmly by the hand.

'Sit down, Sergeant. Would you like some tea or coffee?'

'No thank you, sir, I'm fine.'

'Right, before we have a chat I'd like you to sign this.' He tossed across the desk a buff-coloured form that Paul recognised instantly. 'I've cleared everything with the Commissioner in Durban. The last thing I want is for you to be charging around London like some headless chicken stirring up a hornets' nest. I'm also short of good detectives so this way we may be able to help each other.'

Three weeks of planning how he was going to investigate his brother's death had suddenly gone out of the window: it was being offered to him on a plate. He had only known this man for five minutes but he had instantly recognised the qualities that had made his brother so proud to serve under him. Signing, without hesitation, he handed the form back.

'Good, welcome to the Met, Sergeant. Now I suppose you want to know where we are in the investigation into your brother's death. The short answer to that is nowhere. There was no official police inquiry opened into the "South African's" death.'

Carlisle smiled as he saw the reaction to this title on Paul's face. 'Forgive me, your brother was known in every nick, club and pub and by everyone on both sides of the fence as the "South African". He was an exceptional man and a brilliant copper who, without trying, commanded so much respect from everybody who came in contact with him, good and evil. I'm sure you don't need me to tell you all this.'

Paul smiled, fighting his emotions, and just shook his head. All his life it had been the same where David was concerned and for him to have died so young was unforgivable: someone somewhere was responsible and would have to pay, of that he was certain.

'As I was saying, there is no official investigation as the coroner's inquest concluded that there was no evidence to suspect foul play, but everyone here believes differently. The general consensus is that your brother was murdered, probably somewhere here in the capital, and his body taken to Dorset and arranged to make it look like a cliff fall. Unfortunately, we haven't found a shred of evidence to back this theory and the London criminal fraternity have clammed up tight since his death – no-one's talking, we keep running into a brick wall.'

Paul hid his disappointment, he was hoping for more than this. 'There is no way I can accept the coroner's verdict, either. All his climbing equipment was still in the car. David would never undertake any climb without wearing and carrying the right gear, and the body damage he sustained was not in keeping with a climbing accident. Did David have any official reason to be over 100 miles from London?'

'No. He travelled the British Isles always searching for a new challenge, and his colleagues and his girlfriend were used to him going off on his own for a couple of days climbing: he maintained that it was the best way to get rid of his frustrations and clear his mind. Yours is boxing isn't it, Sergeant? I've done my homework. Natal light-heavyweight champion, the 2004 Olympics is a possibility I've been told.'

31

'That was my goal but now I'm not so sure. David's death has taken priority in my life and, until I know for certain how he died, the Olympics might have to wait another four years. What cases, other than the human trafficking, was my brother involved in?'

'That was your brother's main brief and he worked a lot in conjunction with the drug squad, but David was also involved in all our investigations: murder, terrorism, armed robbery, the usual assortment that is our daily life.'

'Do you think that there could be a link somewhere with any one of those cases?'

'No, not at all. I'm absolutely convinced that David's death was in some way linked to the drug smuggling. I'd bet my life on it. These are David's files, which will keep you occupied for the rest of the day. Tomorrow, DC Liam Jameson returns from sick leave and he'll be better able to answer any other questions you may have. Here we work as a team, but your brother worked a lot in partnership with Liam who will show you the ropes. He's a good copper who may bend the rules, but he never breaks them.'

David had often mentioned Liam in his letters, referring to him affectionately as 'the short-arsed scouser' who, when your back was up against the wall, was the one man you most wanted beside you: Paul felt he already knew him.

For the next half an hour the two policemen continued discussing David's death, their mutual respect growing by the minute; their belief that it was anything other than an accident becoming all consuming. For Paul it was reassuring to know that although there was no official police investigation, their enquiries continued. Where he went from here he wasn't quite certain. Still, the DCS had given him plenty of food for thought and when he called their meeting to a halt Paul was feeling a lot more positive about the future.

He took Paul down to the incident room, where he introduced him to Inspector Peter Watkinson, his new immediate superior officer. Paul felt that special tingle returning, the buzz which came with being a police officer once again as his new colleagues came and introduced themselves.

Refusing several offers to go out to lunch – he was too excited to eat – Paul sat down at his allotted desk and opened the top file. Flicking through, a name from the past suddenly jumped out at him, a name that brought back many painful memories: Abdul Karim.

Wanted in London four years ago on four counts of murder, it came to light that he was operating in Durban's slumland under their noses, offering the poor unfortunates a chance that they could not refuse. A free flight out of their living hell to London with enough money to tide them over when they arrived, plus the promise of work and a proper home – all they had to do was swallow this little package before take-off.

Since 'sniffer dogs' had become so successful this vile trade had blossomed, and Paul and his brother had spent most of their working days amongst these people with little result for their labours. Practically undetectable, this fast means of transportation ensured quick profits for the dealers and extreme danger to the carriers, but they were too wretched and frightened to listen.

Despite the efforts of the brothers and various social bodies, plus the news from London of another death, the relentless tide continued: such was their desperation to escape the poverty they seemed oblivious to the dangers involved.

Largely due to the fear that these people constantly lived under the brothers had had no success in tracing the supply route; among so many thousands of potential carriers their daily investigations had become 'mission impossible'.

Then one day a fourteen-year-old orphan prostitute that they had cultivated over many months was found barely alive amongst the rat-infested rubbish of one of the shanty towns.

Badly beaten and left for dead, it transpired that she had befriended an Arab who had promised her the world. This particular night he had sought her out on the streets and, in a drug-fuelled frenzy, had raped and beaten her senseless. To them it

33

was another needle in a haystack case, it happened all the time, and trying to trace one Arab among so many thousands was impossible.

However, their luck changed a week later when the girl was discharged into police care. As she was leaving the hospital a car mounted the pavement at great speed, heading straight for her, and only the quick reactions of her police minder saved them both. The car, nevertheless, kept on going and, jumping a red light at the cross roads, ploughed straight into a bus.

The driver was hospitalised with severe injuries and David identified him from pictures that he had received from Scotland Yard: Abdul Karim. When shown the pictures the girl's reaction had said it all but such was her fear she refused to commit herself further.

Nevertheless, London had issued an extradition warrant for him and when Karim was well enough to travel David was assigned the duty of escorting the prisoner to England. Having handed over Karim to the authorities, David was enjoying his first trip overseas when he was summoned to the Yard. Abdul Karim had been sprung from the prison van taking him from Pentonville to the Old Bailey and, three days later, his mutilated body had washed up in the low tide mud by Blackfriars Bridge: David had stayed in London.

6

Central Africa, March 1999

It was still raining. As Matthew edged towards the mine entrance he could hear it thundering down on the corrugated iron roof of the storehouse, confirming one thing in his mind: the hit would have to take place at the General's residence.

There was no way this egotistical monster would be going on one of his 'tours of the people' that was his trademark, which translated into him travelling up and down the country putting the fear of God into them all if they didn't support him. He had survived numerous attempts on his life and he now thought himself invincible. 'God was protecting him' he had told the world's press after the last failed coup, and the band of thugs under the guise of his loyal army which accompanied him everywhere were there more to intimidate the people than to protect their leader.

Matthew was gambling on this total lack of discipline for success: he had no idea of the internal layout of the building or the number of troops he would encounter, but the weather had left him no choice and he couldn't afford to hang around this country too long.

Suitably camouflaged, he exited the mine to be greeted by a sea of mud rushing past the entrance, carrying with it all kinds of wreckage. This put the main road to the palace out of the question so he sought the higher ground and tracked his way across the forest, while below him chaos erupted as the swollen river finally burst its banks, giving Matthew just the kind of diversion he needed. As the trees began to thin out he took to the ground, crawling his way over the thick sodden undergrowth until he was within 200 metres of the palace.

Sweeping the building with his binoculars, he wasn't surprised to find that there was no movement either inside or outside of the grounds – security, as he had expected, was non-existent. There was only one soldier outside the open gates and he was huddled up inside his sentry box, which the General had had built in the style of those outside Buckingham Palace. It seemed as if everyone else had deserted the place, even the half-starved Dobermanns that normally prowled the open ground around the palace had taken refuge somewhere.

Rising quickly, he ran down the exposed slope to the perimeter wall corner and, glancing round, saw the sentry was fast asleep. Crossing the road, he took cover in the ruins of an old house opposite the main gates, the rain-soaked stinking blankets covering his head and body weighing a ton, but he dared not remove them as he sat and contemplated his next move. Killing a soldier and taking his uniform was the easy part, it was how he could get through the gates and into the grounds without being seen that posed the problem.

A golden opportunity presented itself almost at once as the sentry left his post and, dashing across the road, entered the ruins, obviously to relieve himself. Deciding it was now or never the knife was out, in and out again in a flash, and Matthew stripped the body of its uniform. Then, under cover of the torrential rain, he accessed the grounds and, without being challenged, marched straight up the drive.

Where was everybody? He had expected minimal resistance but there was none. Mounting the steps, he went through the front door and, still without encountering a soul, found himself in a lavish marble hall with a giant mahogany staircase.

The palace was too quiet for Matthew's liking, nothing moved anywhere, but time was not on his side as the gate guard could be missed at any moment so, deciding that they must all be still in bed, Matthew mounted the stairs two at a time, still uncertain how he was going to locate the target.

Pausing at the top he glanced down a corridor and couldn't believe his luck. Outside a door to his left, leaning against the wall, was a soldier half-asleep: it had to be the General's suite. Matthew shot the soldier and went through the door like lightning, catching the General indulging in his other passion. Before the two women could scream he had shot them both and as the General begged for mercy Matthew put a bullet right between his eyes.

Throwing caution to the wind he ran back down the stairs, expecting a reception committee, but there was still no one around. Outside, there were two Land Rovers and an old seven-tonne truck that had seen better days and, in this flood water, he really had no choice other than to take the much slower truck and pray that his luck would hold out.

Through the gates without a shot being fired, Matthew turned towards the border, the truck's old gearbox uncooperative as he fought to control the vehicle against the rushing tide of water, knowing that if he made one mistake now he was finished.

The barrier was down but the post was still unmanned, and Matthew gunned the engine and crashed the truck through it. Glancing at the gauge he saw that he still had plenty of fuel and, although he would have liked more speed, retrieving the Land Rover was out of the question. He would have to leave it where he had hidden it and continue his escape in the truck.

Suddenly the rain stopped and the sun came out, and the deafening sound of torrential rain on steel was replaced by one that Matthew knew well as the noise of the old diesel engine filled the cab. The truck screamed in protest as it struggled up another hill and Matthew estimated that he was still an hour away from civilisation and safety. As the old truck reached the summit he was relieved to see, stretched below him in the sun-baked valley, the gateway to freedom.

*   *   *

It took two baths before Matthew started to feel human again. The body paint and the smell of that disgusting uniform seemed to fill the air as he scrubbed himself raw in an effort to remove every last trace. More than anything else he wanted to get home to his father but was disappointed to learn that there wasn't a direct flight to London for three days so, checking out of the hotel, he made his way to the British Embassy, where the Earl of Turnford was given a very warm reception by the Ambassador.

'A pleasure to meet you again, sir. The last time was about ten years ago at a garden party your mother organised.'

'She died three weeks ago which is why I'm in Africa. I've been visiting the places she worked so hard to raise money for as I try to come to terms with it all. Unfortunately, my father was too ill to accompany me.'

He felt a pang of guilt at using his mother's memory in this way but knew that she would understand and, as ever, forgive him.

'I'm so sorry; her charity work here in Africa was legendary. What can I do to help you?'

'There isn't a direct flight from here for three days and I was wondering if there was an alternative route that you could suggest.'

'There is a flight out of Mombawi tonight, but it is an eight-hour journey by road and you'll never make it in time. However, there may be a way. We have at our disposal a helicopter for emergency purposes and this is, after all, an emergency. I'll see if I can organise something for you: in the meantime make yourself at home, use the telephone if you want to.'

'Hello, Betty, how are you? Is Father there?'

'Oh, Mr Matthew, thank God you've phoned, I don't know what to do.'

She started sobbing heavily and was unable to continue.

'Betty, come on now, pull yourself together. What's happening? What's been going on?'

He could sense that she was trying very hard to get herself

under control and, as the fear mounted inside him, she suddenly blurted down the phone the worst news he could have expected.

'There has been a robbery and your father has been murdered: there are police everywhere, it's horrible, please come home quickly.'

Matthew sat there stunned, gripping the phone as if he was strangling it, his brain unable to immediately accept or to react to what she had said, He felt the colour drain from his face and the bile rise in his stomach and, as he tried hard to regain his self-control, he spoke in almost a whisper.

'Betty, I'm leaving Africa now. Just try and hang on till I can be with you.' With that he slammed down the phone and, as the horror of it all finally sank in, he began to weep.

7

London, October 2003

The news from London that Karim was dead had come as a hammer blow to Paul and his squad – although it meant that Karim would no longer be plying his evil trade, bringing death and misery to thousands of people, it also meant that any chance of his naming others had gone.

He had spent many wasted hours interrogating the man, to no avail, and he had hoped that once Karim got to London he would try and strike a deal with the authorities to lighten his sentence. The reports from his brother got worse, David often arriving too late to save someone's life and, despite the demise of Karim, the evil trade continued unabated.

Back in Durban, Paul and his men had continued their daily routine as before, travelling the shanty towns and questioning the inhabitants but, as always, the odds were stacked against them. They were fighting against an ever increasing tide of poverty and violence, the plane ticket out of there being many people's only chance of escape, so they had very limited success.

It seemed at times a futile struggle and despite constant surveillance of Durban airport, his men looking for the tell-tale signs of nervousness and fear that betrayed a carrier, they had little joy, getting it wrong more often than not, and he had found himself back to square one.

Occasionally, one of the carriers would panic and crack when stopped and questioned but, like the young prostitute, Martha, they clammed up tight even when threatened with the most severe jail sentence the law could enforce. With terrorism the most dominant of priorities at airports these days security was always at a maximum and, despite the most sophisticated electronic surveillance equipment available to them, somehow their prey continued to slip through the net.

Two months later, David had his first major success during the investigation into Karim's death when, after many hours of painstaking surveillance, he and Liam traced the warehouse where the packets from the human carriers were processed. The subsequent raid had produced heroin with a street value of ten million pounds, several small fry, but no big fish. As the reputation of the man they called 'The South African' grew in London, Paul at last got the breakthrough in Durban that they had waited so long for.

Martha had resumed her former existence. It was the only way of life she had ever known, but this time it was different for her in as much as she had a permanent roof over her head. Paul had found her lodgings and despite her protestations unofficially paid the meagre deposit. She was still very independent and proud but the incident with Karim had nevertheless left its mark and, although she had never admitted it to him, he had sensed that their friendship was very important to her.

As her confidence returned she began to wander the streets further and further from home and one day a shiny black limousine, the likes of which she had never seen before, slid silently to a halt beside her. The window came down and, after a brief exchange with the driver, she climbed into the back.

This was something Paul had warned her against doing many times, but something inside had told her that everything would be all right that day as the sumptuous leather seats enveloped her slim body. The car quickly left the city and wound its way up the twisting, turning road into the surrounding foothills that overlooked the Indian Ocean.

She had sat there breathless with the beauty of it all when

41

suddenly, as if by magic, a pair of giant iron gates opened up in front of them. The car sped up a tree-lined drive with lawns either side containing beautiful flower beds, and stopped in front of the biggest house she had ever seen. She was still totally at ease with the situation as the driver opened her door, gently took her by the arm, and led her around the side of the house. Inside, she was led up a winding wooden staircase and shown into a bedroom, told to shower and wait.

The size and splendour of the adjoining bathroom, like everything else that day, mesmerised her as she did as she had been told. After about half an hour a man of European appearance entered the room.

She was to make that journey several times before she told Paul anything about it, and he remembered her breathless excitement as she recounted every minute detail, her new-found happiness making it difficult for him to be cross with her. Whilst this whole new world had transformed Martha he knew it could only end in tears and had gently begun to interrogate her.

It transpired that the European was in fact Italian and came to the house every two to three weeks, staying three or four days. With him came an entourage of ten to twelve other men, including his own chef, and he would spend most of his days in his office, which was the only room in the house that was forbidden to Martha. She had the freedom of the rest of the estate and would pass the time wandering around the giant house, marvelling at the paintings and furniture, swimming in the pool or riding the horses that freely roamed the grounds.

The Italian was kind and generous to her as were his men, treating her like a human being rather than a piece of merchandise, something that Martha had never known before. The servants were quartered in an old stable block well away from the main building and didn't speak to her, but she didn't care – she was in paradise.

Back at the station he had arranged for a twenty-four-hour surveillance of the girl and contacted Immigration. They had informed him that a privately-owned Lear jet belonging to a Naples-based fruit processing company made regular flights from Naples via Sicily and Rwanda, and that the purpose of these visits was to purchase the abundance of fruit that was South Africa's wealth.

'Coffee, Sergeant?' A young woman detective interrupted Paul's thoughts, offering him one of two polystyrene cups she was carrying. 'They've got milk and sugar in if that's all right with you?'

'Fine for me, thanks. Tell me, do you get involved often in these cases of human trafficking?'

'All the time, Sergeant. As you know they arrive here full of hope and promise and heroin. If they are lucky enough to survive the journey, and the packets haven't split open and killed them, they are taken to an address where the packets are removed by laxative. From there they are taken to a safe house where they wait and wait: the money runs out, the job promised does not materialise, and then they are asked to return to South Africa to do it all over again.'

'And nobody talks for fear of death of another kind.' Paul remembered the early days and David telling him how impossible it was to penetrate this wall of silence.

'Exactly. Normally we arrive too late to save someone's life, but if we are in time they clam up and all we can do then is put them on the next plane home. Your brother was very successful at tracing reception houses, routes for the drugs, and so on, but as fast as we closed down one operation another would spring up.'

'I know the last time we spoke he was very confident of a major breakthrough. Two brothers had been arrested who were related to Abdul Karim, and David was certain that they would soon sing like canaries.'

'Yes, the Barolli twins. We've got them banged up in separate nicks at the moment awaiting trial on a GBH charge, but so far

43

they have not been too co-operative. Liam's planned a visit for this week so we may have better news when you two return.'

Again, Paul was amazed at how everyone here had just assumed that he would be joining the squad. Carlisle's man-management skills had welded together a formidable team into which Paul had immediately been accepted.

'I can't wait to meet Liam, my brother was very fond of him.'

'As we all were of your brother. Believe me, we will get the people responsible sooner or later, we all know that that was no accident.'

Paul returned to his thoughts, remembering the sequence of events as if it were yesterday. The surveillance of the girl had been an easy affair as her new-found wealth meant that she no longer needed to walk the streets and, instead, she spent her time shopping or sitting down by the harbour and gazing out to sea. She had not entertained anyone at her lodgings or ventured too far and then, after about a fortnight, she was collected once again by the limousine.

Having established the location of the house, he had installed round-the-clock observation, which had revealed plenty but, at the same time, nothing of significance. The comings and goings of small vans had been far too numerous for a private residence but he couldn't stop one and search it without giving the game away, and the photographs of the inhabitants he had sent to Interpol revealed that they were all small-time Naples scum, so he had bided his time.

Disappointed and with only his instincts as reason, which was not enough to obtain a search warrant, he had wanted to approach Martha to ask for her help but was frightened for her well-being. Then one day his patience paid off when on his computer screen appeared a picture of a middle-aged, good-looking Italian who had no previous but was wanted for questioning by the Italian authorities.

His name was Paolo Stromberti, and Paul remembered how he had felt the tingle down his spine and the quickening of his heartbeat as his whole being told him that this was the moment he and his brother had worked so hard for. Paolo Stromberti was a nephew of the Godfather, Illario Massimo.

The subsequent raid on the villa had been a bloody gun battle in which he had lost two of his men. Although from the outside all had appeared peace and calm, the minute the helicopters had landed all hell had broken loose as they were greeted by automatic gunfire.

They finally accessed the house to find Martha cowering in Stromberti's bed, but he had gone. Locating the office that had been out of bounds to her, they found hastily-lit fires of computer discs burning and, on moving the furniture, Stromberti's escape route. A flight of steps down opened into a long, well lit passageway where they had been met by more gunfire. Having secured this area they moved into a large underground canning factory where, after a brief skirmish, Stromberti and two of his surviving henchmen had surrendered.

Simultaneous raids on the warehouses of the van owners had revealed the ingenious system by which the drugs were distributed. They found boxes of oranges and grapefruits which had been cut in half, some of the fruit removed and a sachet of heroin inserted in its place. These were then distributed to street vendors, which was where the human traffickers would obtain their deadly cargo. The rest of the sachets were inserted into the cans, at the time of filling, for worldwide distribution.

Paul's delight at having finally closed down this highly sophisticated and organised operation was short-lived. Some weeks later David had phoned to say that life was continuing as before and the only explanation that he could think of was that there was a second factory somewhere – and so the nightmare had continued.

8

England, March 2000

The huge mansion looked a strange and unwelcoming place to Matthew as the taxi went up the drive; it was as if he had never lived here and all of his previous life had never happened. His despondency deepened as he got out of the cab and realised that not even Betty was there to welcome him home. Betty had been housekeeper at the hall for over thirty years but to Matthew she was more than that, she was his second mother, her two sons were his best friends and there had never been any class divide between them, they were all one big family.

Instead, he was met by a Detective Chief Inspector Gates, who offered his condolences as he led Matthew up the steps and into the large entrance hall, which Matthew found had been turned into a command centre, the house swarming with policemen. Entering the drawing room he found Betty being comforted by her two sons, the three of them just sitting there staring into space, their grief all-consuming as they rose to greet the son and heir. She threw herself at Matthew as she began crying again and, unable to speak, she just clung to him, sobbing, until the boys gently parted them.

'It was Mrs Anderson who found your father,' Gates broke the chilling silence that had descended on the room. 'I'm afraid she didn't hear or see anything from the cottage, and in fact has been too ill to talk that much to us.'

'What about the dogs? Nothing moves in the grounds without them knowing, surely someone must have heard them.'

'We're not dealing with local amateurs here, sir. This was the work of a highly professional gang that, for some reason, went wrong. The dogs were drugged with darts, the alarm by-passed, and all we can assume is that your father heard something and came down to investigate.'

Suddenly it hit Matthew why the house felt so strange and cold to him: it was half empty. Rushing angrily from the drawing room, he went from room to room discovering how much was missing: paintings, silver, and priceless pieces of furniture.

'They must have had inside information, Chief Inspector, as they've only taken the most valuable pieces. Also, they would have needed a very large lorry to have removed this much stuff and I cannot believe that they could have approached the house without waking my father.'

'As I have said, sir, this is the work of a specialised gang who, we suspect, have been responsible for three other similar robberies in the home counties over the past eighteen months. They avoided the gravel drive and used hand carts with big rubber wheels to transport everything to the lorry, which they had hidden behind that copse across the main road. Also, your father had been taking sleeping tablets prescribed by his doctor, which would explain why he took so long to hear anything.'

'Where did she find him?' Matthew had to see the place before he left the house for the last time. He had already decided that he was never going to return here again, but where his future home lay from now on he was uncertain of.

All he wanted to do was to get as far away as possible from this house and the veil of death that seemed to be consuming it. There was nothing left for him in this world now; he was all alone, confused, and very angry.

He said goodbye to his father at the chapel of rest where he lay looking so peaceful – at least for him the grieving was over. For Matthew it was something he would have to live with for the rest of his life and, as he boarded a plane at Heathrow for Ajaccio and the family holiday home, he knew that no matter where he went in this world the images of his dead parents would be forever at the forefront of his mind.

The local community would be in mourning for a long time but he would not attend the funeral, he had cut his ties with England forever. The disposal of the estate had been left in the hands of the family solicitors, and he had written to Betty and her sons explaining his decision and had made provision for them in the future. As the plane taxied to the end of the runway, turned, and began to gather speed, Matthew took his last look at England as the green fields raced by and quickly disappeared from his vision.

Corsica, April 2000

The days were long, the nights restless, the memories unending. He passed the time hunting and fishing up in the mountains alone with his thoughts, reliving a life that had been so cruelly snatched from him, and all the while the anger and need to avenge his father's murder was gnawing away at his insides. They had been a very close family and nothing had ever broken the bond. Not even when, on his fourteenth birthday, they had told him the truth about his birthplace, and why they had adopted him, had anything changed in their relationship and it never would.

They were his parents, and he would always be their son, and for such good people to die so young was inexplicable to him. The debt he owed to them could never be repaid, but the vow of vengeance he had made to his father was the one thing he could do something about.

His father's close friend and lawyer, Jonathon Rees-Jones, had been his crutch and confidant during his darker moments, but now he and his family had returned to England from their Easter holiday and Matthew made his next move.

There were too many people who knew where to find him so he reluctantly decided to sever his last links with his adoptive parents and sold the property. Anonymity was what he sought if he was to survive the world in which he now moved so he bought a smallholding high up in the mountains he loved so much, far away from prying eyes and curious neighbours.

The removal of the offending General and the subsequent installation of his successor had greatly benefited his anonymous employer, who had added a substantial bonus to the agreed fee. This had enabled Matthew to indulge in his other passion – the sea. He bought a small ocean-going yacht and when he was not hunting the abundant game that inhabited the mountains he would pass his days sailing to Sardinia or Italy, all the time trying to blot out the past and failing miserably.

As the Duke of Rushtington he had a passport which could open any door; as Mario Barolli, the name given to him when he was born, he was the young Italian recluse who, although pleasant enough, kept himself to himself.

He kept the boat at Ajaccio and once a week he would go into the city to replenish his provisions, but the real purpose of these excursions was to collect the week's editions of *The Times*. With the cruiser rocking gently at its moorings he would sit in the cabin and turn to the personal column of each newspaper, his sole reason for this weekly ritual. As the days turned into weeks the frustrations and anger became all-consuming, his daily existence a constant battle with his tormented soul.

Then one day it was there. His whole being came alive as he read the message he had waited so long for: My brother Mario in Corsica please come home there is a family crisis, Roberto. Release was only a phone call away.

9

London, October 2003

Paul was in the office by 8 am the next morning, Liam Jameson arriving shortly afterwards. After Inspector Watkinson had briefed the squad for the day the two of them left for what Liam described as an educational tour and, as they crossed Waterloo Bridge, Paul asked Liam if he could help him buy a car.

'No need to, Sergeant, we still have your brother's in the pound. We took it there after we found him and had it stripped looking for clues. Then, when I heard you were coming to join us, I had them put it back together for you. It should be ready tomorrow.'

'Thanks, Liam. Did they find anything that could give you an idea as to what happened to David?'

'No, nothing. His wasn't the cleanest car in the world and there were plenty of contrasting soil deposits, obviously from all the different places he went climbing, but nothing untoward and there were no foreign prints.'

His Liverpool accent was difficult for Paul to understand at first but as they cruised the city, with Liam describing the people and places they passed, he not only began to understand his every word but to feel an affinity with this very likeable character after only a couple of hours.

However, Paul's gentle introduction to his new patch suddenly came to an abrupt ending when, without warning, Liam pulled into the kerb opposite a small café and switched off the engine, Paul looking at him quizzically.

'The owner's one of my more reliable snouts and I want to find out if he has heard any whispers about your brother's murder while I've been away. Unfortunately, this town has clammed up tight since it happened and we are having a very hard time getting anybody to talk.'

Although there was no official police inquiry, Paul realised that Liam Jameson, like every other copper in the Met, was convinced that David's demise was anything but an accident and he was carrying out his own private investigation.

'Around the corner you'll find a newsvendor's stand run by one Brendan Cassidy, who was very fond of your brother and had become an invaluable source to him. I personally have never trusted the man, I don't know why, but your brother had a lot of results thanks to Brendan so I suggest you go round and introduce yourself.'

Paul found the dockland streets of London dirty and rundown much the same as Durban but, like those, they had their own distinct sort of vitality which made Paul feel immediately at home. Rounding a corner he saw the news-stand about fifty yards away and, taking refuge in a shop doorway, he stood observing the comings and goings of Brendan's clientele.

Awaiting the right moment, he was suddenly aware of a car coming down the road towards him at great speed. It screeched to a halt by the kiosk and shots rang out.

Paul drew his gun and began running towards the news-stand. The car sped towards him, swerving in his direction, and he hit the ground rolling out of its path just in time but, before he could fire a shot at the car, it had rounded a bend and disappeared. He found Brendan Cassidy lying across the stand, the newspapers soaking up his blood, as Liam arrived in the car.

'Jesus Christ! Sergeant, welcome to London. Is he still alive?'

Paul was feeling for a pulse and, as Liam called in for back-up, a crowd began to gather.

51

'He's still breathing, Liam, but his pulse is very weak. I don't think he's going to make it.'

They followed the ambulance to the hospital where, much to their surprise, Brendan was wheeled straight into surgery. Liam asked for, and immediately got, a twenty-four-hour surveillance put on Brendan and the hospital. On returning to the office he noticed that Paul was looking a bit shaken so he suggested a beer and a sandwich.

Just up the road from the Yard was a pub which Liam informed Paul was the watering hole for the Met, and Paul needed no introductions. His arrival, and the news of the morning's events, had already spread around the city, and immediately people came over to say hello and wish him luck or to offer their condolences. Paul felt a steely determination emanating from them all to discover the truth about David's death but, if they were no further forward, where did he go from here? David had been a very private person who always kept everything bottled up, as Michael Mamtoba had confirmed, so who, if anybody, would he have confided in?

When Liam returned with their lunch the two men sat in thoughtful silence for several minutes before the scouser finally spoke.

'That was no coincidence this morning, you know, Sergeant. Whoever was responsible knew you were here, and they knew you were on the job. I've just been talking to a couple of guys from the East End division whose snouts informed them, several days ago, that the brother of the "South African" was joining the force. My man in the café also knew of your arrival, which means that they have had time to get organised, and whatever Brendan has learnt meant he had to be extinguished before you saw him: that was a warning sign to everyone, a big warning.'

'Do you think it is linked to David's death, Liam?'

'Almost certainly. I just hope Brendan makes it because we need someone out there to talk and point us in the right direction, although this morning's episode won't have helped matters at all.'

The conversation drifted to Liam and his family, Paul discovering that he was married with a three-year-old daughter and lived up the river at Kew. Starting his career in Liverpool's Fazakerley district, he had applied for a transfer to the Met when his London-born wife found she could not settle in the north.

Although half listening, Paul's mind kept drifting back to the shooting. What had David found out that had led to his death? If Liam was right and his arrival was the signal to silence all possible connections, starting with this morning's attempt on Brendan's life, was he also now a target?

When they returned to the office Paul phoned the hospital and was put through to a very relieved Frances.

'Paul, are you all right? I heard what had happened when I got in.'

'I'm fine thanks, Frances, a bit shaken but the suit came off worse – you'll have to point me in the direction of a good tailor when I come home. What's the news on Brendan?'

'He's still in surgery but if there's any change I'll phone you immediately. Paul, is this connected in any way with David's death?'

'Liam is almost certain it is and my arrival seems to have panicked someone, that's for sure. Although there is a police presence at the hospital tell everyone to be extra vigilant and, if you have any suspicions phone me immediately, all right?'

'Paul, please be careful. I'll see you this evening.' Her voice trembling, Frances said goodbye and hung up.

'He's still in surgery so we may be lucky, Liam. Any news on the car or its occupants?'

'They've found the car in the river at Wapping, empty and with no prints. As for the vicinity of the shooting there are no eye witnesses – nobody saw anything or can remember anything, which doesn't come as a big surprise.'

The fear that was gripping the underworld became more and more apparent as officers from all over London phoned in to say that their sources had either gone to ground or were too frightened to say anything. Then, in mid-afternoon, Inspector Watkinson received a telephone call asking for a meet at Waterloo Station. He sent Detective Constables Jean Kent and Colin Baker, with strict instructions to be very vigilant.

While they were waiting for their return Liam brought Paul up to date on everything that had happened in the weeks leading up to David's death, and the arrest of the Barolli twins in Dorking. Paul recalled David's renewed enthusiasm when he had telephoned him with the news, convinced that the twins would point them in the right direction.

'David reckoned that with their records they are facing a long stretch and might be prepared to talk a trade, but they have never ever been convicted on any drug offences.'

'That's right, but their sister is Anna Karim, Abdul's wife, and, when not residing in one of Her Majesty's prisons, they have lived with her all their lives. Although their records show them to be a couple of psycho muscle men dealing in pornography, there is no way that they haven't been involved in the Karim business, and we have always suspected that she has protected them when the shit has hit the fan.'

'What were they pulled in for this time?'

'The usual psychotic violence. Three weeks ago the Dorking police were called to a night-club incident where these two little darlings, acting as bouncers, had lost it completely. They were beating the shit out of a group of lads out on a stag night and after being arrested and charged with ABH were refused bail despite the efforts of their sister. Unfortunately, one of the lads has taken a turn for the worse and the charge has been changed to one of GBH, which will keep them off the streets for many years to come.'

'The four counts of murder that Abdul was wanted for, was Anna implicated in any of them?'

'Eyewitnesses positively identified Abdul but not her, and there was no evidence to connect the two of them.'

'What did she have to say for herself when questioned about her husband's activities here and in South Africa?'

'David's resumé is in that blue file, as is her history. Basically, when she and Abdul came out after their last stretch they drifted apart and, although they were still husband and wife, she maintained that they had gone their separate ways. As you can see, this lady is category A without a doubt, and she and her lovely brothers are capable of anything including murder. David had them all in the frame for Abdul's death, but we couldn't find any evidence, and I personally am convinced that she was in some way responsible for David's demise.'

Paul opened Anna's file and quickly read through the facts.

Anna Maria Karim née Barolli. Born Naples 27.10.53. Parents deceased.

Arrived in England 02.04.65, with her twin bothers Joseph and Luigi and went to live with an aunt and uncle in the Fulham Road.

Arrested 10.05.70. Soliciting in the Euston Road – fined £20 and given a conditional discharge.

Arrested 14.07.70. Assault with a deadly weapon – 6 months in Holloway. She had slashed the face of a small-time pimp and whilst serving her time she badly beat up and maimed an over-amorous inmate. Her sentence was increased to eighteen months and, with no remission for good behaviour because of various other misdemeanours, she was released in February '72

Arrested 03.08.75. Blackmail and extortion – 4 years Holloway. Convicted with her brothers. She would compromise the clients, the brothers would take the photographs, and the clients would pay up or face the consequences at the hands of the Barolli twins. Released 11.05.79.

Whilst in Holloway she befriended an unfortunate Arab girl who had been arrested for shoplifting and was the subject of various racial and sexual harassments. Anna had dealt with the problem and on her release was met by the girl and her brother, who invited her to come and live with them. She married Abdul Karim in September '82.

Arrested 10.06.86. Possession of and dealing in narcotics – 8 years Holloway. Together with Abdul Karim, she had developed a highly sophisticated nationwide drug ring, which was finally broken following an international police investigation.

On their release in 1995 the couple moved to the respectable Surrey area of Dorking, where they bought a large, detached house. They were seen frequently in London and the home counties. Although raided on several occasions the premises yielded nothing.

Arrested 15.10.97 in connection with the deaths of four people from narcotic poisoning. Released 18.10.97 – no charges laid because of insufficient evidence. Since then she has resided at the Dorking address, where she was joined by her brothers on their release from a six-year stretch for armed robbery. Despite constant surveillance they all appear to have led a crime-free life until the night-club incident.

'What do you think, Liam?' Paul had formed a few ideas which the scouser confirmed for him.

'She's still dealing, but obviously not from the Surrey address. We've had her tailed on numerous occasions, but she is too streetwise for us and it has always turned out a big zero.'

Just then the phone rang; it was Frances for Paul.

'He's out of surgery, but the doctors still don't know one way or the other. The next forty-eight hours will be critical and I would say it will be at least another forty-eight hours after that before you could interview him.'

'Thanks, Frances. Stay alert and advise all the other staff to do the same – this is not over yet by a long way. I'll see you later,' and he hung up.

'Brendan's still breathing, Liam. I want to phone Durban to see if there is any news on Martha and whether there is a date yet for the Stromberti trial.'

He was becoming increasingly worried for the girl's safety. After the arrest of the Italian she had turned on him, refusing to be a witness at the trial or talk to him at all, and had in fact left her home and disappeared. Despite putting out all his resources to find her, Paul had drawn a blank.

10

Bosnia, October 2000

Commercial flights to the Balkan peninsula were still considered a risky affair, despite the various assurances by the local authorities, so Mario's anonymous employers had arranged a seat for him on a UN plane landing just outside Sarajevo. The former Yugoslavia was now a very divided country which would never be totally stable, the many religious and political factions making it an unattainable dream no matter how hard the rest of the world tried to broker a truce.

Mario now understood why it was an impossible task for any world body to bring an end to the wars as the plane dropped below the cloud cover revealing the mountainous terrain which stretched in either direction. This was the ideal territory for guerrilla warfare and, coupled with the inbred hatred that was fuelled by the tales of atrocities inflicted on them by their enemies down the family line, the presence of a United Nations peace-keeping force counted for nothing.

However, to Mario none of this was relevant. The whys and the wherefores did not matter to him. His only thoughts as the plane made its final approach were for his own personal safety, the thrill of the hunt and the kill to come.

Although he expected his immediate contacts would speak some English, once he was up in these mountains he would have to rely on sign language and basic instincts if he was to survive – these guerrilla fighters took no prisoners: a mass grave or the nearest tree was likely to be where you breathed your last with no questions asked!

He managed to secure a lift from the airport to his hotel, and he immediately sensed danger as he thought he felt a hundred pairs of eyes were watching him.

Checking in as instructed, he then changed into warmer clothing before he went for a stroll along the war-ravaged streets of this once beautiful city. To all intents and purposes he was just another foreign news reporter but first and foremost Mario was a soldier. He was back in the field, checking out places to hide and routes of escape as he casually made his way around the city, all the while trying to lose the tail he knew wouldn't be far behind him.

On his return to the hotel he found a note under his door telling him to check out in the morning and be outside for 9 am, when he would be collected.

The first snow of the winter was starting to fall as Mario casually leant against the wall of the hotel, fascinatedly watching the morning rush hour and admiring the fact that, despite the guerrilla war sweeping across the territories, the attitude of the citizens of Sarajevo seemed to be the same as in any city the world over under these conditions – life must go on. The pavements teemed with people going about their daily business, and buses and cars were navigating their way around the burned-out vehicles and piles of rubble that lay strewn everywhere.

So absorbed was he by the scene in front of him that he didn't notice the car pull up, or the two men who quickly got out of it. The first time he was aware of their presence was when a gruff voice in broken English penetrated his thoughts.

'You Mario?'

Either he had lost some of his sharpness during the weeks of inactivity or these people were very professional – whichever, he tried to move away and found his arms held in a bear-like grip. Looking them straight in the eyes he saw that these two were battle-hardened veterans who would kill him there and then if he tried to resist.

'Relax, Mario. Get in the back of that cream car and do not cause trouble, the streets are watching, we are all in danger.'

'All right, let go of my arms.' He casually approached the car and got in the rear, where there was already another person who seemed more interested in what was going on all around them than Mario himself. As the car pulled away his minders drew hand guns and Mario froze. How could he have been so stupid, he was trapped and there was no escape route! Sensing his fear, and reading his thoughts, the English speaker turned in the front seat.

'Do not worry, our friend. These are to protect us all, and this one is for you.'

They soon left the city and began what turned out to be the longest and most tortuous car journey of Mario's life. The roads were non-existent, just muddy tracks full of shell holes and rocks, and whenever they heard the sound of mortar or automatic fire they would stop while one of them went on ahead to scout the surrounding countryside. Then there was the mud. The old car was forever getting bogged down, and the tension would mount as they all got out to push, ever mindful that at any moment their lives could be terminated.

As they climbed higher and higher the snowfall became heavier, the road more treacherous and, with daylight fading fast, visibility was down to almost zero. Mario asked no questions and said nothing, although he expected at any moment that they would have to abandon the car and continue on foot. The journey came to a sudden end when they slid around yet another hairpin bend and Mario saw the road ahead was blocked by men armed with rifles and rocket launchers. He tensed, expecting the worst, but the atmosphere in the car immediately relaxed as the armed men swarmed all around them and, opening the doors, greeted their comrades in arms.

Mario was hugged and kissed, his back slapped raw, when the noisy welcome suddenly came to an abrupt end with the appearance of a big bull of a man pushing his way through the throng.

He said something to them which caused howls of laughter as he stood in front of Mario, eyeing him up and down. Mario looked at one of the men he had travelled with questioningly.

'This is General Josip Magarnac, our commanding officer. He says they have sent us a boy to do a man's job.'

Mario laughed and, still smiling, turned back to the General, offering his hand in welcome. As the big man reached forward he suddenly found himself flat on his back in the snow with a knife at his throat. More than thirty cocked rifles were pointing at Mario as he nicked the General's skin, drawing blood. 'Tell them he will die first,' Mario said to his minder and was surprised when the General spoke in English; 'My apologies, I will tell them.'

The atmosphere relaxed as Mario pulled the General to his feet, and as the big man embraced him he whispered in his ear, 'They told me you were good.'

They had prepared a feast for their guest, during which Josip Magarnac explained to Mario the history of the Balkans, his country's long struggle for independence, and their fight to regain the territories that had been stolen from them.

'Many of the women and children you see around you, Mario, were born up here high in the mountains and many will die here without ever knowing any other way of life than war.'

Mario was only half listening, his thoughts continually drifting back to his dead parents; the politics and religion were of no interest whatsoever, but he did begin to feel a growing bond with these people as the night went on.

Next morning at daybreak he ate what was to be his last hot meal for days and, afterwards, he was introduced to a man known simply as Lazio who, he was told, was the best tracker and guide in the mountains.

'He does not speak English,' the General told him, 'but that should not be a problem for you. Here is the rifle and sight that you have asked for, it cost us a lot of money so use it good, my friend.'

With that he embraced Mario once again and, with the cheering of the people ringing in his ears, Lazio led Mario off in the direction of the rising sun. Nothing was said all day as Lazio set a cracking pace, his agility and speed over the rocky terrain impressive, and their only stops were to drink the mountain water that tumbled copiously from the snow-capped peaks.

They spent their first night in a cave that Lazio had scouted for any signs of wild animals, the only moving creatures capable of surviving in this wilderness, as there was nothing up here to sustain mankind. Despite the intense cold, a fire was out of the question – its smoke would be spotted for miles around, so they ate their rations cold and, wrapping themselves tightly in their blankets, they fell into a deep, exhaustion-fed sleep.

It was Mario who woke first, the cold in his toes and fingers excruciatingly painful as he tried with some difficulty to extricate himself from his blankets. Gently massaging the chilblains that ravaged his feet and hands, he managed at last to get the circulation moving as his body began to respond to his movements.

He woke Lazio, which wasn't easy – the mountain man was in a deep sleep oblivious to the freezing temperature and he grinned from ear to ear when he saw Mario's toes and fingers. Taking from his pack a small tin of foul-smelling jelly, Lazio massaged it into his offending digits, Mario feeling the benefits almost immediately.

Smiling appreciatively, he slapped the guide on the back as Lazio pulled him to his feet, and Mario gingerly followed him to the entrance of the cave, his feet and hands now feeling as if they were on fire.

There, they discovered a blizzard raging which had already blocked the exit and obliterated the pathway beyond. Lazio however seemed unperturbed by this and they began digging their way out. This set the pattern for the day, as they climbed higher and higher, their progress painfully slow. The air became thinner and breathing more difficult as the guide led them up the treacherous mountain pass, and it was with great relief for Mario that finally they crossed over the summit.

Eventually, the sun managed to break through the low cloud base, its warmth cheering Mario as they continued their downward descent when, without warning, Lazio suddenly hit the deck, Mario almost tripping over his prone body as he followed suit. At first he could not see what had caught the guide's eye, and then he spotted the wisps of smoke rising from the valley floor.

Motioning for him to stay put, Lazio edged towards the side of the mountain path and then signalled for Mario to join him. Below them was a small town and, taking out the night sight, Mario spotted a large military contingent camped behind the church which dominated the area. Lazio gave him the thumbs up, they had arrived at their destination and it was now down to Mario as to what the next moves were.

There was no way they could continue their descent without being spotted, they would have to do that under the cover of darkness, so they made their way back up the path to a large, boulder-strewn ledge which would afford them some cover if they had any visitors. Although they were at a much lower altitude than the night before it would still be very cold, and Lazio made sure that Mario had the stinking jelly in place before they settled down for the night.

11

London, October 2003

The two detectives arrived back from the Waterloo Station meet with information that there had arrived in town an Italian hit man, who was staying at an address in Earls Court. DI Watkinson was alarmed but sceptical of this news and, undecided as to what action to take, immediately called a squad meeting to include DCI Tomlinson and DCS Carlisle.

'While it's a relief that finally someone out there has had the guts to talk, I find it highly suspicious that this particular snout should be the one to have come across such information as he's never been involved with the big boys before. I've known the man for many years and he's minor league, a small-time conman whose previous contributions have never been this significant, so what do we make of this information, ladies and gentlemen?' DI Watkinson looked intently at his squad for feedback.

'He was very frightened, sir, but he was very convincing.' DC Jean Kent recounted the meeting. 'He'd overheard a conversation in the toilets at the Duck and Orange and, although he wouldn't name names, said he knew the two parties involved. The men had talked about an Italian hit man who was staying at a hotel in Earls Court and, although they didn't name the target, they mentioned the arrival of Sergeant Mackenzie, and the fact that he had joined the force, and the shooting of Brendan Cassidy.'

'What intrigues me is why this toerag should suddenly appear out of the woodwork and what his reasons are. If whoever's behind all this finds out he's talked to us he will be the next one to be fished out of the river, surely he knows that.'

'Colin and I pushed him as far as we could but he just clammed up. He wanted a lot more money than we were prepared to pay – to name the other two – so maybe he saw this as his golden chance to make a few bob. We told him that we would have to go higher and he's phoning back at 5pm for an answer, sir.'

'I'm getting nasty feelings about all this,' DCS Carlisle intervened. 'An Italian hit man smacks of something straight out of the movies, and we don't have any high-ranking foreign politicians or royalty in the country at the moment which might explain such a presence. I cannot believe that someone has brought him in to remove Sergeant Mackenzie, we have enough nasties of our own who could fancy their chances, so I for one cannot accept this man's story.'

'I agree, sir. It has gone 5pm and matie has not phoned back. What should we do? Check it out or forget it?' Watkinson still had his reservations as he looked to his superior officers for guidance.

'We've got to check it out, Inspector.' The DCI looked at the DCS, who nodded his approval.

'OK, we'll keep it small and quiet, just four of you: I'll call the local nick and get some back-up in place, in case we need it. I want no heroics, just do what you have to do and if it turns nasty back off until I can get you some heavy support.

The address in Earls Court was a small corner hotel just up the road from the tube station. It was peak rush-hour time and Liam cursed the traffic as he fought his way in and out of one obstacle after another using just the flashing lights and no siren.

Colin and Jean were left outside to cover the rear exit and fire escape, while Paul and Liam went through the front entrance, where they were greeted by a terrified looking receptionist. She mumbled, 'Third floor, room 35' in answer to their question as if they were expected and Paul hesitated, wanting to question

65

her further, but Liam had already drawn his weapon and was climbing the stairs so he followed suit.

As he caught up with him, Liam called in for back-up and warned the other two to be on alert. Reaching the third floor, they located the direction of room 35 and were proceeding towards it cautiously when a tremendous explosion came from the room, blasting the door and surrounding brickwork into the path of the two men.

Paul lay there, his head throbbing and his body feeling as if it had been hit by a truck when, suddenly, through the dust cloud he was aware of movement and muffled voices filled his head. Everything was a fog to him and, unable to clearly hear a word that was being said, he shrugged aside the shapes around him and forced himself to sit up. Opening and closing his eyes, everything was swimming in his vision. Then, as his senses slowly returned, the events of the past few minutes came crashing back at him in a violent blend of sound and blinding light: that was when he remembered Liam.

He panicked and, looking around him, saw the little scouser lying inert ten feet away covered in brick dust and rubble, and Paul crawled across the corridor towards him, fearing the worst. Pushing aside his colleagues, he frantically began pulling the brickwork from the prone body and, taking him in his arms, he was relieved to see that Liam was still breathing. Refusing all offers of help, Paul held him tightly all the while calling out his name and gently shaking his body until, to his relief, Liam's eyes flickered open.

Somehow they had survived and although badly bruised and shaken they had suffered no broken bones, so they refused to be admitted to the hospital, preferring instead to be treated in the ambulance. When the two men had recovered sufficiently, they re-entered the hotel to find Jean Kent in the receptionist's office trying to calm down a very hysterical young lady.

Although still terrified, the girl started to respond to Paul's gentle manner as he began to question her. It turned out that when the two men had arrived, the bomber was under the counter holding a gun to her. There was no Italian registered, the room having been taken that morning by a man with a London accent who scene-of-crime officers later confirmed had detonated the bomb by remote control.

They had been set up and, for the second time in his first day on the job, Paul's life had been threatened. It was now obvious that this latest episode was meant to be more than a warning, that someone wanted him off the scene and alarm bells were ringing loud and clear – what did they think he knew? He was halfway through asking the girl another question when a thought crossed his mind and, grabbing hold of Liam's arm, he took him back outside.

'Frances, Liam! Could she be a target as they failed to get us? Could she and the flat be compromised?'

'I've also thought of another possibility, Paul. Could this have been set up to prevent us seeing the twins tomorrow? Whoever this is is playing for keeps and, as they failed to get to us, those two could have become expendable as well. We'd better phone in and get some advice.'

Having discussed their fears with DI Watkinson they went back inside to find that the receptionist had had to be sedated, and it would be several hours before she would be well enough to look at photographs – several hours that they didn't have. Not sure what was the next best move to take the decision was taken out of their hands when Liam's mobile rang. It was the DCS for Paul.

'You've had one hell of a first day, Sergeant. Are you sure you two shouldn't take yourselves off to the hospital for a check-up.'

'No, we're fine thank you, sir.'

'I've just spoken with the Home Secretary and he is arranging for the Barolli twins to be put in solitary immediately. As for Frances: I've spoken to the administrator at the hospital and he has agreed to her going on indefinite leave until this thing is over. Pick her up as soon as you can and get Jean to take you two to

67

some hotel outside the city where you can stay until we have checked the flat and installed twenty-four-hour surveillance. Good luck. I'll see you in the morning.'

Having explained to Liam what the DCS had suggested the two men decided that there was nothing further to be gained from staying there any longer, so they left immediately to collect Frances.

They found a very frightened but angry lady when they arrived, for not only had she been put on indefinite leave, the DCS had arranged for her to be placed under armed guard. This, combined with the shock of seeing the state of the two detectives, proved too much for her and she collapsed into hysterical crying, clinging to Paul unable to speak, and it was some time before he managed to calm her down.

'What's going on? They tell me I'm on leave until further notice. I can't leave my job just like that, Paul.'

'I'm sorry, Frances. We'll explain everything to you when we get to the hotel, there isn't time now.'

'What hotel? I want to go home to the flat, you know I feel safest there.'

'Please trust me. We'll stop en route to buy some toiletries and clothes, but we must leave now.'

The firmness in his voice momentarily silenced her, but she began to protest again as Jean drove them out of the hospital with a two-man back-up following them and, after stopping for shopping, she took them to a hotel at Twickenham which backed onto the river. By this time Frances had regained her composure and, although still badly shaken, she went inside to book the rooms while the detectives scouted the outside, establishing escape routes and possible weak security points.

Not only were his size and colour against him, they concluded jokingly, his war-torn appearance would make him totally unforgettable, so they decided that it would be better if Paul entered the hotel by the second-floor fire exit.

12

The thunder rolling through the valley woke them at around 4am and Mario decided that, rather than wait for the storm to subside, they should try to reach their objective before daybreak. It was a very risky decision as the torrential rain made it impossible to see the trail, and there was always the chance of running into a lookout patrol without warning, but the adrenalin was pumping and he felt no fear.

Then the lightning came, silhouetting the two men against the mountain backdrop, and they froze as it lit the entire valley. As fast as it came the storm subsided, the thunder rolling off into the distance and, with its parting, the peace and solitude of the night returned.

By this time the two men were well down the mountain, the risks increasing as they neared the town, the fear now kicking in, sharpening their senses. They took refuge in a burnt-out baker's shop, opposite the town square, and settled down to await the morning. Although cold and soaked through, Mario's spirits were in the ascendancy as he thought of the challenge ahead, the chase and the thrill of the kill to come.

As they sat in dawn's first light, the acrid smell of the burnt timbers overpowering, Mario began to make plans for their escape. From halfway up the mountain he had noticed that there was a fairly good road in and out of the town, and he had spotted some motorcycles with sidecars in the army compound so, being loath

69

to have to trek back over the mountains, he sketched his intentions on the dirt floor, looking to Lazio for confirmation.

'Good way.' Lazio's English took him by surprise.

Grinning all over his face, the mountain man nodded. 'Yes, little English talk.' He took the stick from Mario and drew an arrow pointing west. Writing Mostar he shook his head. 'No.' Then he drew an arrow in the opposite direction, Montenegro, 'Yes.'

The decision had been taken. All they had to do now was find and kill the target, and steal a motorbike or two, but Mario was beginning to have his doubts. The absence of foot patrols, in fact any movement whatsoever, seemed highly suspicious. This was obviously a garrison town living under war conditions and there had to be a curfew in place, so where were the soldiers to enforce it and where, more importantly, were all the people?

Suddenly, he grabbed Lazio and dragged him into an alleyway, throwing him to the floor. Before the guide could respond there was a knife at his throat, and he could see the hate in the young man's eyes as he applied the pressure.

'How much English do you speak, Lazio? Which side are you really on or do you take from both?'

Mario could see the comprehension in his frightened eyes but hesitated to finish him off; there was something telling him that he could be wrong. Relaxing his grip a little, allowing Lazio to breathe normally, he motioned with the knife for him to stay on the floor and, never taking his eyes off him, went back to the road and glanced up and down. There was still no change, the town seemed deserted, so what was going on?

Dawn was rising fast and he would be very exposed soon, he had to make a decision; kill the mountain man and try to get out of there on his own, or trust him and wait and see what happened. He signalled for Lazio to join him and pointing up and down the road shrugged his shoulders just as a faint rumbling sound came to them from the west.

Lazio turned and nodded knowingly in that direction as the noise became more discernible. Tanks. Now Mario understood the situation. These troops had received prior warning of this attack and were either waiting at the mouth of the valley in ambush or had taken refuge somewhere.

The villagers had probably fled their homes long ago, coming back only to go to the church, which appeared to be the only building not damaged in some way. If the two men stayed here they could find themselves caught in the middle of a bomb blitz, especially if the advancing troops were successful. Yet, on the other hand, his target could disappear up into the mountains and it could be months before they tracked him down. His instructions were to despatch with all speed so, turning to the guide, he offered his hand in apology.

It was a gesture that would signal the start of a long friendship, although neither man knew it at the time, as Lazio smiled and shook Mario's hand warmly.

'Tank you, English.'

The incident was closed and forgotten as the two men returned their concentration to the advancing problem and, gesturing to one another, formulated a plan.

There were a lot of risks involved in taking to the road by motorcycle, but they were countered by the need for speed of escape which, providing the road wasn't blown away, would be of prime importance. Lazio's other fear was for the bandits who roamed these parts and killed for the fun of it but, given the choice of road or back over the mountain, Mario was convinced that the former was worth a gamble.

They crossed the road under the shadow of the church and from there saw the compound, which was partly hidden by a small wood. At last they spotted some movement as the perimeter guards came into view, and although dispatching them would not be a problem, it was how many more remained inside the compound that bothered Mario. One thing was certain, these were battle-hardened guerrilla fighters and would not be taken easily. Mario drew his knife and hit the ground, heading for the compound, with Lazio following suit.

Cursing the overnight storm which had left the ground sodden, they reached the sanctuary of the wood, soaked through again, but without encountering any problems. Seeking Lazio's advice, he turned to the guide holding up four fingers and was met by a response he did not want. Six or eight, the guide indicated, shrugging his shoulders uncertainly, making this an impossible task without gunfire.

They had to kill all personnel if they were to escape back up the road unhindered, but how, without alerting those waiting in ambush? The solution came almost immediately as the dawn brought with it the sound of mortar and tank fire, and the ground beneath them began to shake. The attack had begun and the sentries, distracted by the commotion, momentarily lost their concentration. Mario seized the opportunity and he and Lazio pounced, killing the two men without a struggle.

They entered the compound on the run, going through the door of the quarters with their guns blazing and, although half awake, the men inside had no chance to react, Mario firing another burst into them to be sure.

It was then that Mario thanked his guardian angel that he had not killed Lazio earlier on a wild impulse as the guide began removing the side cars and starting the motorbikes – he was also a mechanic.

Leaving the bikes by the church, Lazio led them up the road to Mostar and the falling shells. At least the troops waiting in ambush would not be guarding their rear and as Mario swept the cliffs around them, looking for movement, he understood even more why the Balkans had been a war zone for so many centuries. Attacking and running, a small army could fight a war up here for ever without being defeated, provided someone kept supplying the arms.

As the mountains started to close in, Lazio began climbing a path that seemed to be taking them away from the fighting, but Mario trusted him implicitly now and his faith was rewarded several minutes later when he found himself on a ledge high above the battleground. Just how Lazio knew which side of the valley to be on would always remain a mystery to him, the mountain man just turning and smiling at him knowingly as Mario began surveying the valley below and the hidden gun emplacements.

Although they had sustained several casualties, the troops below had not as yet returned fire and as Mario lay there admiring the tactics of their commander and the discipline of his men, he felt a double tap on his legs. Sweeping to his right the target suddenly filled the sight, a tall man with long flowing grey hair whose picture was imprinted on Mario's brain.

He removed the cover from the rifle and lovingly fondled this weapon of destruction that he knew so well. Checking its every part, as he had done daily since they had left, he fitted the sight and began the long slow process of relaxing his body.

Breathing steadily and making himself comfortable, the tenseness flowed from him as the adrenalin heightened his senses. Fine-tuning the sight, his whole being now totally focused, he watched and waited as the rebel leader, a rocket launcher at his shoulder, timed the moment his men should open fire. As the first of the tanks appeared at the mouth of the gorge and his men came under increasing fire power, he turned to give the order and Mario gently stroked the trigger.

The head went back and the rocket launcher crashed to the ground followed by the man as all hell let loose, the troops around him turning their fire on their compatriots across the road, suspecting one of them had turned traitor and had killed their leader. This unexpected repercussion gave the two men an even better chance to escape back down the cliff without anyone noticing, and some extra time before the slaughter at the compound was discovered.

Setting fire to the remaining vehicles while Lazio started the bikes, Mario took one last look around him and, satisfied that he hadn't overlooked anything, the two men set off for the border with Montenegro and safety!

13

London, October 2003

They were sitting in Paul's room, the two men still running on adrenalin as they began to explain the day's events to Frances and why it had been necessary to take such drastic steps. Although she had calmed down considerably, and was almost back to her old self, she still held on to Paul's hands tightly as he and Liam analysed the day's events searching for a clue, trying hard to find some answers, and all the while suspecting that they had a leak.

Unthinkable as it was, a leak was the only explanation as to how Paul's impending arrival had reached the streets. However, they were too tired, both physically and mentally, to find any solutions as Liam, realising the time, stood up to go.

'Maybe tomorrow we will be able to think clearer, Paul. Although I've phoned her, my wife will start to worry soon so I'd better be leaving. If you don't want to be seen eating here there are a couple of pubs down the towpath which serve food, just don't forget to inform the other two, all right?'

'Thanks for everything, Liam. I can't wait to meet the twins tomorrow it should prove interesting, to say the least.'

Left on their own, Frances and Paul decided that they were too tired and shaken to eat so she said goodnight and went to her room. After a long, hot soak in the bath Paul was beginning to feel better and as he towelled himself down there was a knock at his door.

Frances was standing there, the tears welling up in her eyes.

'I'm sorry, Paul. I can't be alone tonight, can I share your room?'

Taking the bedding from her room he made himself comfortable on the floor alongside his bed, and they silently lay there holding hands as they fell into a welcome sleep.

She stirred first and, not wanting to venture far from the security she had now found in Paul, ran a bath in his bathroom, emerging to find him propped up on one elbow reading the hotel publicity.

'I hope you don't mind but I'm still a bit shaky, Paul.'

'That's understandable, I'm just sorry I have got you involved in this mess.'

'Do you really think that David was murdered and whoever was responsible now wants to kill you too?'

'It certainly looks that way, Frances. You will be safer here than at the hospital, and it will be easier for me to do my job knowing that you are not in any danger.'

'I do understand what you are saying, it's just that the hospital and my job are so important to me now David has gone and I don't want to let them down or lose my job.'

'You don't have to worry about that, DCS Carlisle has squared everything, your job is safe. Now go and get dressed, I think I've got my appetite back.'

When they arrived at the office Liam and Paul found it deserted except for DI Watkinson. As there had been no further contact from the snout the DI had given the order that he must be found and lifted without delay: not only did he know the people who were connected to yesterday's attempt on their lives, his own life was now in grave danger.

'When are you going to see the Barollis, Liam? I'm not sure whether I like the idea of you two running around London without an escort.'

'We're due at Pentonville at 10am and Wandsworth at midday.'

'Sergeant Mackenzie, how do you feel about things?'

'These visits are too important to cancel now, sir. After yesterday it's more than obvious that I, or the twins, know someone or something connected with David's death. Whatever, panic has set in and we must keep pushing. I'll take my chances if Liam's happy.'

Liam couldn't wait. 'Let's go and have a chat with the Barolli boys, Sergeant. I warn you now it won't be easy: like their sister, they are both very frustrating to interrogate. Luigi is the younger twin by fifteen minutes and the more vicious of the two. David and I had discussed the possibility of playing one against the other but they are both too intelligent to fall for that old trick so we need to touch a nerve somehow, find something that will open them up.'

As Luigi was led into the interview room handcuffed to two officers, he spotted Paul leaning against the opposite wall.

'So you're the brother of that other black bastard.' Instead of surprise, he clearly knew who Paul was and had been expecting him. Paul did not react and said nothing as the two officers sat him down at the table opposite Liam, handcuffing him to it, and as he was about to launch into another tirade Liam cut him short.

'Shut it, Barolli, and listen to me.' Liam nodded to the two screws, who reluctantly left. 'We haven't come here to listen to your sick mind at work but to make you an offer.'

'Stick your fucking charity, Jameson, I don't need it. Those tossers won't testify against me or my brother, we'll be free in no time at all, now get me back to the peace and quiet of my cell.'

'You like it in solitary do you, Luigi? You can thank us for that, we had you put there to save your life, tomorrow you are being transferred.'

For a moment Paul thought he saw fear in the man's eyes, then he started laughing.

'What game are you two playing at now? Nothing's going to happen to me in here.'

'It's no game, Luigi. It has nothing to do with the GBH charges, it's to do with your sister and the other business you're all webbed up in.'

Suddenly, he was out of the chair, taking the table with him as he tried to get to Liam. Paul reacted first, grabbing hold of his neck, his fingers applying pressure to the nerve as he forced him back down into the chair. The officers re-entered the room but Liam waved them away and, as he righted the table, he could see that doubt had replaced the cocky grin in the man's face despite the bravado still in his voice.

'You leave my sister alone, Jameson. What crap are you trying to pin on her now?'

Paul spoke for the first time. 'We're having the body of Abdul Karim exhumed tomorrow.'

'I had nothing to do with—' Luigi stopped too late in mid-sentence.

'Nothing to do with what, Barolli?' asked Paul. 'You were part of the team that sprung Karim from the prison van and put him or whoever six foot under.' Liam looked at Paul incredulously as he continued: 'Then there is the death of my brother; you're facing multiple sentences here and have no chance of seeing the outside world again unless you co-operate.'

'You know I couldn't have killed your brother, I was in here at the time.' Luigi was desperate now as Paul turned up the pressure.

'Yes, but you know who, and where, and how.'

Before he could say another word, Liam intervened: 'All we want is Anna's London address, Barolli. We can't make you any promises but, as the Sergeant has said, you're facing spending the rest of your days in the nick.'

'Stop wasting my time and get me back to my cell.'

'It's your life that is at stake here. Once we put the word out that you've been talking to us, it will be worthless. We can protect you and are prepared to offer you a trade.'

'You're bluffing, Jameson. You don't have any evidence to back up this crap.'

'You have twenty-four hours, Luigi. When we come back, we want Anna's London address or you and Joseph will face further charges.' Liam called in the warders to take him back to his cell and Luigi Barolli, a changed man from the one of half hour ago, left without saying another word.

Back in the car, Liam could contain himself no longer.

'That was inspired, Sergeant. He certainly bit when you mentioned Abdul Karim and he's very rattled but, as he says, we have no evidence. What made you think of Karim anyway and what did you mean by "whoever", are you saying that that wasn't him who Anna buried?'

'In the coroner's report there was no mention of any of the injuries he had sustained to the body from the accident, but when he arrived here he had come straight from the hospital in Durban. There was substantial bruising to the body still remaining and he had to wear a body brace for the spinal injuries, none of which is mentioned. And how was a headless torso with no fingerprints identified?'

'By a tattoo on his upper left arm. Apparently all the members of his tribe have it done at a certain point in their lives and each one is individual, his wife had no hesitation once she had seen it.'

'I remember it well from visiting him in the hospital. It was very ornate, a work of art. How difficult would it be to have the body exhumed?'

'Christ, Paul. You are talking deep religion here. It could take months, even years of legal wrangling, and I'm sure Anna would never give her approval anyway.'

'I bet the twins don't know that, and Luigi certainly got excited when I mentioned the idea. Let's go and see how Joseph reacts to the news.'

Joseph Barolli, slightly taller and stockier than his sibling, proved equally problematic and was even more vehement than his brother had been that the case against them would be dropped. However, when Paul mentioned the exhumation of Abdul Karim and the further charges that he was facing, including murder, he fell silent.

Although twins, they were totally different characters, and Paul could tell from his reactions that this one had all the brain cells;

he just sat there thinking without saying a word and when he finally spoke he chose his words carefully.

'You've obviously tried this one on my brother first and got nowhere with him so now it's my turn. You're desperate, Jameson, fishing in the dark and sinking fast, now piss off and leave me in peace before I press charges of harassment.'

'Joseph, this is no game we're playing here, we consider you too intelligent for that. You're right, we have spoken to Luigi and he's thinking it through, and we're offering you the same deal. Yesterday, there was an attempt on our lives to prevent us from talking to you and your brother today, and when that failed it was obvious who the next targets were, that's why we had you both put in solitary.'

'They wouldn't have us removed, we're family.'

'They, Joseph? Who are they, Anna and Abdul?' Liam once again shot Paul a shocked look, as Mackenzie continued.

'We want the London address of those two within the next twenty-four hours. In return we will arrange a deal on all further charges that you and your brother are facing.'

'Get me back to my cell.'

'Do you want to go back to the wing or solitary?' Liam asked the question, knowing full well the answer.

'Solitary, and I want my brief here immediately.'

As Joseph was led away, Liam turned to Paul. 'Correct me if I am wrong, Sergeant, but what you are saying is that Abdul Karim is alive and well and commuting between London and Durban, and the body that was fished out of the Thames was not his.'

'Exactly. He's got himself a new identity and I am the one person, outside of the family, who could positively identify him. It would explain why the human trafficking has continued unabated and, having had David removed, my arrival has put him under threat again.'

'But it's been four years since his supposed death, why did he take so long to act? Why didn't he have David killed straight away?'

'All I can think of is that up until recently David hadn't posed that big a threat, but he had uncovered something which Karim thinks he has passed on to me. My arrival here and the fact that I've joined the squad have confirmed his worse fears. He knows how weak the twins really are when backed up in to a corner and when he heard that I was going to interview them we all became expendable. You yourself said that Anna was completely ruthless and would stop at nothing, including the murder of her own brothers, to hold on to what she's got.'

'I'm impressed, Sergeant, but David hadn't mentioned he'd discovered any new evidence to do with the Karims, and although it all makes sense, those two well know, and you and I know, we haven't got a shred of evidence to prove any of it.'

'Liam, do you have anybody here in London who is an expert on Arabic culture? I would like to talk to someone about that tattoo.'

'There's an expert on North African civilisations working for the World Bank here in the city who we have used a couple of times. The bank has always been very cooperative in the past and I'll see if we can secure his services for a couple of hours tomorrow but Paul, as I've already told you, we can't exhume a body at the drop of a hat.'

'I know that but if I'm right and Karim is still alive, who the hell is that in the ground and who put him there?'

'Let's get back to the Yard and throw your theories around the place, maybe someone will come up with a bright idea.'

14

Bosnia, October 2000

It wasn't long after leaving the town that Mario realised he'd made a big mistake. The road turned out to be no different from any other in these parts and had quickly changed into a dirt track, the overnight rain turning it into the usual treacherous mudbath full of water-filled shell holes.

It became an arduous journey, their flight for the Montenegrin border not what Mario had intended it to be. Continually dismounting the bikes, they then had to circumnavigate these obstacles and remove the boulders and trees that lay strewn across the road.

Enough was enough; they were too vulnerable if there was a surprise attack and, looking to Lazio, he nodded agreement. It was time to abandon the bikes and take to the mountains again; their noise would have been audible for miles around anyway, and they had been lucky so far not to have encountered any bandits, plus the fact that all the time Lazio spent negotiating these obstacles he was not on the lookout for the signs of trouble which could hit them at any moment.

Lazio set his usual cracking pace, happy to be back where he felt the most comfortable, up in his beloved mountains.

All day and well into dusk, only stopping occasionally for Mario to sweep the terrain with the sight, Lazio headed east as the sun set behind them and twilight descended. Still Lazio pressed on and only when the black clouds had finally masked every shaft of moonlight did they acknowledge that that was enough for one day. Totally exhausted, they dropped to the ground and, too tired to talk or eat, or worry about the cold of night, they immediately fell asleep.

He tried to flick away the thing tickling his face and, as his subconscious became conscious, he realised the offending object was the barrel of a rifle and he was staring up into a sea of faces. Trying to sit up, feet painfully pinned him to the ground as he moved his head looking for Lazio. The mountain man was several feet away tied to a tree, and Mario looked into the faces of his captors, trying to discern whether they were of the same people or not, as he realised that his young life was hanging on a thread in Lazio's hands.

There were six of them and Lazio was talking animatedly, obviously trying to strike some sort of a deal and whatever had been said, and was being said, he didn't appear to have been too successful as the conversation got more heated.

Mario was suddenly aware of a hand being offered to him which he readily accepted and, not sure whether to try and take advantage or not, he erred on the side of caution as he was pulled to his feet. Whoever these men were they were comfortable with their situation as they had lit a welcoming fire, towards which Mario shuffled his frozen body, much to their amusement. He turned in Lazio's direction, looking at him quizzically and, with a barely perceptible movement of the head, Lazio indicated that all was far from well.

Mario casually began exercising his body, getting the blood circulating, all the time trying to gather his wits about him and assess the circumstances. So far they had made no move to tie him but three armed men's eyes never left his person, making it impossible for him to attempt anything.

Then the talking stopped, and while one of the inquisitors indicated for Mario to join them the other drew his knife and held it to Lazio's throat. Mario stalled, glancing from one to the other, and felt the barrel of a rifle in his back as he was propelled towards Lazio's interrogators.

Handing Mario his beautiful weapon, the man pointed to the horizon, where the dawn was just rising above the mountains, and Mario quickly realised what all the bargaining had been about. These people wanted to hire his services in return for their two lives but they wanted proof of his capabilities first. He nodded his understanding to them as he stripped and checked the rifle before loading it and fixing the sight. Going through the usual ritual before a kill, Mario settled himself down and swept the countryside below him, waiting for someone or something to move out there.

It was still far too early, and Mario got up, indicating so to the rebel leader, who angrily snatched the rifle from his hand and took up position. After what seemed an eternity he excitedly motioned for Mario to join him and, pointing down into the valley below, handed him back his weapon. Once again Mario settled himself as he searched the valley floor, uncertain as to what he was supposed to see down there.

Then a movement caught his eye and from behind a bush appeared a wild mountain goat. Mario waited until his body and the rifle were one. He brushed the trigger and, not waiting to see the result, stood up and threw the rifle at the rebel leader – the sound of the shot still echoing around the valley. There were gasps of astonishment as one by one his captors took it in turns to peer through the sight down to the dead animal, and this was followed by a lot of backslapping and delighted reverie as Mario was celebrated as their new hero.

Turning to their leader, Mario nodded in the direction of Lazio and, reluctantly, the order was given to untie the guide: at least for the moment he had bought them some time but Mario was under no illusions, he knew that they were still far from safe and that this band of ruffians would kill them at the slightest provocation.

Just then the heavens opened once more and they all took

shelter beneath an outcrop, where Lazio tried to explain everything to Mario under the wary gaze of the others. Sketching a map in the dried earth, the mountain man gesticulated and mimed as if his life depended on it until Mario finally smiled and nodded in comprehension.

It transpired that the men were Serbian guerrillas who were trying to recruit as many of their fellow countrymen as they could to go and fight the Albanian Muslims in Kosovo. Mario's target was one of the Muslim leaders whose removal would bring about a hasty collapse to the Muslim resistance in the area, but for Mario it was immaterial as to who, and where, and why, as long as it secured his and the guide's release.

Looking at the map, it appeared that they weren't too far from the Montenegrin border, where they would be met and then transported across the country; at least there might be a chance of a hot meal and some clean clothes, which appealed to Mario. He had no understanding of the Slavic mentality, nor could he read their faces, so he would have to rely on his instincts and Lazio if they were to get away with their lives.

Smiling broadly, he got up and went to shake his new employer's hand. This signalled an immediate change in the atmosphere, his captors' faces breaking into huge grins as one by one they shook Mario by the hand, and the party set off down the mountain as one big happy family. The difference from the day before though was that the pace was easier – Lazio wasn't leading.

15

They left the prison and were crossing the common when Paul noticed in the wing mirror a white Transit-type van pull in behind them two cars back.

'Liam, turn as soon as you can, I think we've got visitors.'

Liam glanced in his mirror. 'White Transit, got it, hold tight,' and without further warning turned right immediately, causing the two cars behind to brake violently. The van only just avoided them by pulling on to the wrong side of the road and took the corner clipping a stationary car. Gunning the Renault, Liam took the next left as Paul called in for assistance. Suddenly, gunshot peppered the rear window, taking it out completely as Paul turned and knelt on his seat, firing at the oncoming vehicle.

'Hold on Paul.' Liam, almost leaving it too late, swung the car right and the van passed their turning, its tyres burning rubber. Paul called in their latest position and direction as the van came back into view, but Liam had an open road and with siren and lights flashing put his foot to the floor.

The Transit was no more and Liam eased off the accelerator. Too late, he realised his mistake as the van reappeared from a left-hand turning in front of them, ramming the Renault and spinning it 180 degrees. Liam accelerated away and, as bullets tore into the bodywork, the engine spluttered and died.

Exiting the car, the two men returned fire as they ran up a nearby alleyway and, climbing a garden wall, entered a back yard. Going over another fence, they took cover behind a brick shed, which gave them a clear view back the way they had come as the air filled with the sound of sirens. Spotting some movement in the alleyway Paul opened fire, as Liam covered him, but instead of receiving return fire they were met by a police loudhailer.

'Hold it right there and throw out your guns, then come out with your hands behind your heads.'

'I'll go one better. I'll throw out our bloody warrant cards,' was Liam's angry response.

A neighbour, alerted by the shooting, had seen the two men enter the garden and directed the police there whilst their assailants had disappeared into the London streets. They were alive, but this latest incident dispelled any lingering doubts that anyone might have had: the removal of the brother of 'The South African' was top priority.

Paul phoned in to request that the surveillance on the Barollis be intensified, and for someone to come and collect them. He also demanded a squad meeting on their return.

'Our every movement is known, where we are going, who we are going to see – more than they could know by just putting a tail on us. Quite simply, there is a leak!' Paul let his words hang in the air, the room silent, as he continued, 'Everybody we have seen knew I was coming to London, even the twins in nick, and there have been two serious attempts on our lives; someone out there is determined to get rid of me, no matter what.'

Before he could continue, DI Watkinson interrupted. 'On the face of it you appear to be right, but that's a serious allegation, Sergeant.'

'I know. I'm a new boy here and I don't want to get off on the wrong foot, but how else do you explain what has happened? My arrival has triggered off two shootings and a bombing so it has got to be connected with David's death, and the human

86

traffickers and whoever is behind it all are two steps ahead of us every time.'

'OK, so if we accept what you are saying, do you have any idea as to who is pulling the strings?'

Paul went on to tell them about the interrogation of the twins, their reaction when he mentioned exhuming Abdul Karim, and his theories on Abdul Karim based on what he had read in the coroner's report. There followed a deathly silence, then suddenly the room came alive as Paul's words hit home.

'You're saying that Abdul Karim is out there somewhere and the body that his wife identified is not his?' An incredulous Jean Kent was the first to react.

'Yes, Jean. My brother had found out the truth, which was why he was murdered, and they think he has passed the information on to me. I'm certain that that is the reason for all this and it involves the twins and the Karims. They are responsible for whoever is lying six feet under and if we can get Anna's address I for one won't be surprised if we find Abdul there as well.'

'Your brother was a first-class copper who did everything by the book. This doesn't add up, Sergeant.' DI Watkinson was far from convinced. 'For what reason would he withhold evidence? He wasn't a glory seeker and, although a brave man, he would not take any unnecessary risks.'

As Paul started to reply the phone interrupted him. It was the hospital to say that an attempt had been made to get to Brendan Cassidy.

On their arrival they found one officer with severe head injuries, but Brendan was safe. Two men posing as hospital staff had managed to breach the outer security, but were confronted by the officer outside Brendan's room. The ensuing melee had aroused the others and the intruders had fled, dropping a syringe full of neat heroin which was obviously intended for Brendan.

Back at the Yard, Liam checked on both prisons and found that word had got around, the tension was mounting and the

Governors were not sure how long they could keep the lid on things; the sooner the Home Office issued the transfer papers the happier they would be.

Meanwhile, Paul had requested mugshots of the Karims. While those of Abdul were only four years old, Anna's went back to 1986. Still, it was better than nothing, and he had them distributed to all stations in London and the home counties with a warning that they were wanted for questioning on charges of attempted murder and were to be apprehended with all possible caution.

The fact still remained that they had no hard evidence to back up Paul's thinking. If they found Anna and no Abdul, her lawyer would have her released in no time. What they desperately needed was for the twins to talk, or to have the body of Abdul Karim exhumed.

Having discussed this with DI Watkinson and DCS Carlisle, it was decided that if all else failed they would apply for exhumation, but word should go out on the street that this was happening right away – to see what sort of reaction it provoked. It was also agreed that all known associates of the twins and the Karims be lifted for questioning in connection with the shootings. This operation would be very manpower intensive, and the DCS ordered that all leave be cancelled with immediate effect.

'We have to take the play to them, force their hand before someone gets killed,' was his reasoning. He was also adamant that Paul and Liam were to have a two-man backup twenty-four hours a day, until this was all over.

For Paul it was hard to believe that he had only been on the job for two days, so much had happened. As they left for the day he thought once again of his dead brother and of their last telephone conversation, trying hard to think of what David had said.

The journey back to the hotel passed in silence. Liam was still angry with himself for his earlier mistake that had nearly cost them their lives, and Paul was still thinking about that telephone call.

He was greeted by a very distressed Frances, who had spent the day watching the television, and had seen the footage covering the shooting. Having assured her that every step imaginable had been taken to protect him and Liam, he began to question her about David, and any conversations that they might have had with regard to his work. As with Michael Mamtoba, it was the same story. David kept everything bottled up, although Frances always knew when something bad had happened because he would take himself off for a long, solo walk, or go away climbing, and when he returned he was again the man that she knew and loved and that would be the end of it.

16

Montenegro, October 2000

Although the pace was slower it was another incredible day's march without interruption for meals, rest or calls of nature. Sure-footed over the dangerous terrain, the mountain fighters relentlessly pursued their objective, oblivious to the sounds of gun and mortar fire that continually reverberated around the mountains.

Even when nightfall overtook them the tempo never slackened. The moon remained hidden and the black was all-enveloping, and Mario stumbled blindly after the man in front of him, who was barely visible.

Hunger was beginning to gnaw at his insides: exhaustion was setting in and only his fierce pride was keeping him going when, unexpectedly, lights appeared on the horizon and the relentless pace thankfully came to a halt. Motioning for them to stay put, the leader and one of his men set off down into the valley as Mario sank to the ground in relief.

The two men returned half an hour later to collect them and they were not alone. They had reached their objective, a Serbian stronghold, and news of Mario's arrival had spread like wildfire, everyone wanting to come and greet the man with the magic rifle who would give them victory.

The fact that they first had to penetrate deep into enemy territory, and then had to find and eliminate the target was forgotten as, once again, Mario found himself being welcomed as a hero.

Lazio was a forgotten being who could have slipped away unnoticed into the night but, instead, he stayed close to Mario, watching and observing everything and everybody, guarding his friend with his life.

At last they ate a hot meal, Mario trying hard not to think of what was in the stew as the night became noisier, the party more boisterous, and the men more drunk. They could have escaped together at one point as the attention of their captors was totally focussed on the various fights that were breaking out, but Mario negated Lazio's signals. He was once again enjoying the company of soldiers at war, and the buzz that went with it.

Everything came to a sudden halt when one of the men staggered up to Mario and yelled something at him at the top of his voice, his comrades instantly seizing on his words and joining in the baiting. Looking to a worried Lazio for guidance, the mountain man indicated that he was being challenged to an arm wrestle. This was something that Mario excelled in, but he declined the challenge, indicating that he couldn't risk damaging his hand.

Although he could have taken the guy, no problem, he thought it politic not to upset anybody at this stage but, before things got out of hand, the incident was terminated by the leader of the rebels who said something that had an immediate and sobering effect on the entire gathering.

They were taken to a hut with a log fire burning in one corner and, together with about ten others, settled down for the night, Mario being allowed to keep hold of his beloved rifle and thankful for this respite from the cold.

He woke up feeling sick, not sure whether it was the stew or the stench in the hut, but desperate for some fresh air and quickly. He was heading for the door, trying hard to avoid the bodies around him and failing miserably, when he suddenly found himself confronted by the oaf from the night before, who he pushed to one side as he threw open the door.

Still half drunk, the man went for his knife and, before it had cleared his belt, Mario swivelled, putting his heel into the man's kneecap, shattering it. He fell to the ground screaming in agony, waking the entire camp, and men appeared from everywhere with rifles primed, fearing an attack. The clamour ceased as a smartly turned-out soldier, in full uniform, barked an order then turned to Mario.

'Will you follow me, please?'

Momentarily confused by the sound of English being spoken, Mario was rooted to the spot for several seconds before he followed the man into an underground bunker. Not only did it have electric lighting but some form of air conditioning, the unmistakable hum of a generator sounding in the background. This was no makeshift camp he was in, Mario realised, but the headquarters of the Serbian army in these parts.

'Good morning, soldier. You are a very long way from home.'

He turned towards the voice and saw a man of around fifty plus, who was without doubt the commanding officer, although Mario could not make out the rank. His natural reaction as a trained soldier was to salute this man, who had an aura about him that smacked of authority, but Mario resisted.

'Good morning, sir. You could say that.'

'My men tell me that you are the best that they have ever seen. Given a choice will you stay and help us, or do you want to leave?'

'I'd like to stay, thank you, sir.'

'Why, soldier? It's not your war, there is no money in it for you.'

'I like the hunt and the kill, that is all the reward I need.'

'No matter who or why?'

'Exactly, sir.' Mario liked this blunt-speaking man, and he instantly felt a sense of security knowing he was at the helm.

'Is there anything you need before we leave, soldier?'

'A shower and a change of clothes would be nice, thank you, sir.'

'We leave in twenty minutes. I will see to it. Good luck.' He shook an amazed Mario's hand and, having given the order, left him to be shown into a bedroom with a proper bathroom attached.

There was a change of atmosphere in the air, and in the attitude of the men, when Mario emerged from the bunker. Although they didn't salute him they now stood to attention as he passed them by, this motley crew of mountain fighters having been transformed into something resembling a disciplined army in the space of twenty minutes.

He heard orders being barked, and this ragged collection of men came together in four fairly straight rows as the commanding officer emerged from the bunker, Mario searching the ranks for Lazio. Fear started to set in as it became obvious to him that he was not amongst them: without the mountain man there would be no dead Muslim leader.

He started to approach the Commander in Chief and was intercepted by two of his subalterns, who led Mario to the line of trucks that stood waiting. At the rear of the second lorry they halted and pulled back the tarpaulin to reveal a smiling Lazio, fondly cradling the rifle. Mario made to join him in the back of the truck but was restrained by the soldiers who led him to the cab. He was to travel first class with blankets provided to keep him warm, and there were some sort of rations in dirty old tin cans strapped to the dashboard for the journey

The cab was freezing, the heater not working, and as they made their way down the mountain road every bump registered the length of his spine, the only relief coming when they stopped as one or another of the vehicles broke down. They would use the breakdown time to eat or answer calls of nature, but there seemed to be no urgency as the lorry in question was lovingly coaxed back to life and, without fear of attack, the atmosphere was relaxed as they crawled their way across Serbian territory. Mario was thankful for the blankets: with the temperature below zero the only other way to keep warm, and the circulation moving, was to clear the continually freezing windscreen as on and on they pressed well into the night.

At least the main roads were a little less demanding on the body, allowing Mario to snatch odd moments of sleep as the convoy of ancient vehicles finally reached the eastern town of Ivangrad.

Awaiting them were more troops and Mario realised that this was not a quick incursion he was involved in but a full-scale military offensive designed to defeat the enemy once and for all. He was escorted from the cab and taken to an impressive chateau-style residence, where he was shown into a beautifully furnished room, which seemed totally alien to him given the circumstances, and there he was greeted by the Commander in Chief.

'That was the easy part, soldier. Tomorrow we go on foot.'

'Excuse me for asking, sir. Where did you learn your excellent English?'

'Oxford and then Sandhurst which, if I'm not mistaken, has had the pleasure of your company at some time.'

'Exactly, sir.' Mario now knew why he was getting the red carpet treatment.

'I won't ask questions, soldier, but now I know for certain I'm even more sure of the success of this mission. It has been a long time since I shared an evening with a fellow officer from Sandhurst. Would you care to join me for dinner? It would make a pleasant change for me.'

17

Following overnight raids on homes in London and the home counties, a number of known criminal associates of the Karims and the Barolli brothers were now being held for questioning at the Yard, and in various police stations around the counties. It was still too early for anything positive to have come out of these arrests, so Paul decided to phone Durban while he was waiting and was surprised when he was put through to the Commissioner.

'Good morning, Sergeant. How is London treating you?'

'Rough, sir.' Paul then went on to describe the events of the past two days.

'Well, I have nothing but bad news, I'm afraid. The Italian authorities have requested extradition for Paolo Stromberti and you know what will happen if we agree, he will be out on the streets in no time at all and back in business.'

'You must try and stall them for as long as possible, sir. We lost two men, remember, and there is no way he must be allowed to walk.'

'I know, Sergeant. I'll do my very best but there is worse to come and I can't break this to you gently, Paul. We found Martha this morning, dead, pumped full of heroin.'

'She didn't do drugs, Commissioner,' Paul's angry voice reverberated down the line.

'I know, Sergeant. We are treating it as murder, but you know as well as I do what our chances are of finding her killer.'

'A big fat zero, sir.' Up to his departure Martha had refused to be a witness for the prosecution and Paul had thought of flying her to London so that she could see the misery her boyfriend was responsible for. 'Well, that's a possible key witness out of the way and, while we may never know her killer, we sure as hell know who was behind it. I'll be in touch, sir.'

'Martha's dead.' The Commissioner's words ringing in his ears Paul left the room, his anger rising. He went down the stairs, on the run, and was halfway out of the building when Liam caught up with him.

'What's going on, Paul? Where are you going?'

'I need to run, Liam, pound the streets, clear my head and get rid of my anger.' Then he told him about Martha.

'We'd better go back upstairs first and get clearance, Paul, then we'll go to the flat and pick up some gear.'

As they entered his office, the DI was just putting the phone down.

'Whatever you two want will have to wait. That was a call from Heathrow to say that the pilot of a South African Airways plane, due to land in half an hour, has radioed in that he has two dead on board. That means there must be others on that flight, so I want you over there as fast as you can, but I haven't requested that the airport be sealed off as it might frighten away the reception committee.'

The sight that greeted them, even for police officers hardened by the very worst that life could offer, was as distressing as it could get. A girl of about fourteen years old and her younger brother were huddled together in death, their hysterical parents being restrained by several officers and crew.

The appearance of Paul had an immediate effect on the couple and, speaking to them in their tribal tongue, he quickly calmed them down and persuaded them to go with the officers to the medical centre. Then they began interrogating the other passengers and such was their fear now, the guilty ones soon came forward begging for help.

As the terrified carriers awaited their fate, Liam and Paul began to cross-examine them but without much success. Facing the possibility of death and the certainty of a jail sentence after they had been deported, all of their experience counted for nothing when faced with these odds.

The only new information the two men managed to learn was that the removal of the packages by laxative no longer waited until the carriers reached a safe house. Instead, the human carriers were given a capsule when they received their fruit containing the drugs with instructions to take it just before landing and use the facilities in the main concourse before they were collected.

Their disappointment was further added to moments later when the airport police reported that they had drawn a blank in their search for the reception vehicles; the collectors, obviously alerted by the time delay between the plane's arrival and the appearance of their payload, had panicked and were long gone. Liam and Paul had thought of offering the carriers a chance, carry on as if nothing had happened and then follow them, but that idea now appeared to be hopeless.

This was a very valuable cargo, however, and even though the transport was gone the collectors of the packets could still be hanging around. Discounting the parents of the dead children, there were still eighteen people carrying sacs of heroin worth tens of thousands of pounds.

Paul spoke to DI Watkinson, who obtained permission for them to offer the carriers immunity, and a safe passage home, in return for their cooperation. They were becoming more and more agitated as they waited to rid themselves of their deadly cargo and, with their dreams of a new and better life laying in tatters, Paul and Liam had little difficulty in gaining their co-operation.

Putting camera surveillance on the toilets in the main concourse the two men released the passengers and waited. They watched them enter the toilets displaying 'out of order' signs, as they had been instructed, and after they had all left and the minutes ticked by the two men began to doubt their plan and the information they had gleaned. No one had followed them into the lavatories and the only outsider to enter was an airport cleaner who emerged, removed the signs, and carried on sweeping and cleaning the main concourse.

'At least the heroin's down the loo now,' a disappointed Liam broke the silence. 'Let's get back and interview them some more, it's obviously too late.'

'Is it, Liam?' Paul had continued monitoring the screen and was watching the cleaner. 'I'd like to keep an eye on him and see what happens next – better still, move Jean and Colin into closer proximity.'

The cleaner continued with his routine and then headed for a door, which was obviously a store cupboard. He emerged almost immediately without the trolley.

'Let him clear the concourse, Liam, then have him picked up. Hang on, someone else has entered the cupboard. Jean, Colin, to your left, grab that man leaving in cleaner's overalls.'

Back in Immigration the distraught parents had been sedated and Paul and Liam decided that that was enough of an ordeal for everyone for one day. Having made arrangements for all of them to go to a safe house, pending deportation, the two men were preparing to leave when Jean cut in on the radio.

'Got them both, Sergeant, and the goods, what do you want us to do?'

'Let's get them back to the Yard and see what we can learn, there is nothing more for us here.'

18

His host turned out to be the Supreme Commander of the Serbian forces, a charming and interesting man but a soldier's soldier above all else, with a deep and burning passion for his country and its heritage. He wasn't a desk man, and never would be, his place was in the front line with his troops. Mario very quickly learned the next day that to the people and soldiers of Serbia he was a god. They would stand and fight to the bitter end alongside this man, and Mario found himself tempted to join them. At dinner the previous night he had felt privileged to share the man's company. Not once had he probed into Mario's life, respecting his 'raison d'etre', as they discussed a wide range of topics, of which sport was his other passion.

As they approached the Kosovon border they came under fire from a Muslim border patrol, this skirmish the first of many that day as they pressed deeper into Kosovo.

Encounter, engage and destroy. He was among some of the fiercest fighting men he had ever known but Mario, with his trusted friend alongside him, was never in any danger. They had thrown a protective wall of men around the two of them, and kept them well away from the front line, Mario now regarded as second only to their leader and given all due respect.

It soon became obvious to Mario that everything was not going according to plan and as they lost more and more men the order

99

went out to dig in. Summoned to the Commander's bivouac, he found a very concerned CIC surrounded by his officers.

'Come on in, soldier, we have a problem concerning your mission. As you have probably realised, we are facing much bigger resistance than our intelligence led us to believe was in the area, and this has slowed us down considerably. Our fear is that your objective will have moved on by the time we eventually reach his current position, or someone has talked and they know of your presence.'

'How far do you estimate, sir, are we away from the target?'

'What's your thinking, soldier?'

'I take off with half a dozen men, it will be a lot quicker and we will be less conspicuous.'

The General smiled and nodded his approval then turned and spoke to his officers, and there followed a lively discussion amongst them which the General translated for Mario.

'It appears there are three ways one can go from here to reach your objective. You can go over the mountain, which is the safest but longest route, the opinion being that there will be little or no resistance up there. Continue on this road which is the most direct way, but as you have seen is full of enemy troops; or go straight down the side of the mountain on ropes and then follow the river which leads to the town. No one knows the distances or times involved, but whichever you choose will make no difference if the rabbit is already up and running. If you reach the town and find that to be the case, then wait for us and we will have to decide whether to continue or abandon the chase.'

'I'm going to need someone to identify the target and at least five other top soldiers. If you can spare your English-speaking officer it would help with the other men, and do you have anyone who speaks the local tongue?'

There followed a period of time where Mario sat with the chosen men and Lazio, discussing the pros and cons of the various routes. The majority, including the mountain man, were in favour of the most direct – straight down.

100

'Well, soldier, it's your call – what do you want to do? No one here is sure what you might encounter down there, or if there is even a trail, and there will be no back-up if you run into trouble.'

'Are you going to continue to try and reach the town on this road, sir?'

'We have no other option. It's the most direct route and we must take that town and establish a stronghold, that's our first priority.'

'Very well, sir. I'll see you in the town. We will leave immediately, going straight down into the valley, which looks the best bet to me also.'

Mario shook his hand and then saluted as a British Officer, the Commander returning the gesture with pride in his eyes.

The first part of the journey, abseiling down to the tree line, was easy but, as the forest and undergrowth closed in around them, Mario began to have reservations about their choice. They could easily have been spotted as they descended and, as a result, were proceeding cautiously expecting to be ambushed at any moment.

It was taking far too long for his liking, so he decided to throw caution to the wind and signalled his thinking to Lazio. The mountain man quickened the pace, leading them down in as straight a line as possible, and soon after they heard the welcome sound of running water. Lazio suddenly stopped and fell to the ground indicating for Mario to join him and, crawling up to his friend, Mario couldn't believe his luck. They had arrived at the bridge which took the mountain road across the river and straight into town.

His joy, however, was quickly tempered as he realised that the bridge was heavily fortified and, scanning the surrounding cliffs, spotted several gun emplacements. This was where it would all end for the General and his army because even if he managed to overcome the enemy troops, it was odds-on that the bridge would be ready to blow. Not knowing the territory but seeing the size of the force here, it was obvious to Mario that the General and his army were expected, and that this was the only way in and out for miles.

Glancing at his men he saw that they too had also realised the implications of this bridge, and the consequences for their comrades in arms coming behind. It was not his battle, not his war, he had enough problems trying to find his way around this huge obstacle, yet something was gnawing away at his subconscious. It was something only a soldier would feel as he gave the order to fall back into the forest.

Looking from one to the other their eyes confirmed his thinking, and he could tell that he had no other choice. They regarded him as they did their Commander, trusting his decisions implicitly, and the feelings he had had when dining with the General came flooding back: is this where I truly belong, is this my destiny?

They were only eight in total and as Mario sketched the bridge and surrounding area in the dirt another thought came to him. The soldiers guarding the bridge head were expecting a full-scale attack from the west, not a commando-style raid, and as such would be fairly lax at the moment. Thankful to have the English speaker with him, he began to outline his plan.

19

Benim al Takeda, 'call me Beni', was the second son of one of Tunisia's largest manufacturers of clothing. His elder brother would inherit the reins one day so, not wishing to be number two for the rest of his life, Beni had sought out a new career in banking. Very quickly his paymasters had recognised his business acumen and he was transferred to London, where he had spent five very successful years.

His first passion, though, was North African culture and as the two men from opposite ends of this giant continent exchanged pleasantries, Liam was struck by the pride and love that they showed for their respective countries.

'The reason we've asked you over, Beni, is to see if you can tell us anything about this tattoo.' Liam passed him the photographs and immediately Beni's face lit up.

'This is a work of art which I haven't seen for a long time. It's Algerian in origin and belongs to a nomadic desert tribe called the Atakaras. On their eighteenth birthday each male member must make the giant trek between Atakar and Ain Sefra and are then given this tattoo to mark their coming of age.'

'Do the tattoos vary from male to male?'

'Only slightly. They follow a very strict and ancient rite, the difference being this writing here, which is the date of birth.'

'How many people are there who can carry out this work?'

'Half a dozen at the most, at any one time. The inks used are from plants which are only found in the country and their source is a closely guarded secret, as is the design, which is handed down from father to son.'

'Would there be anyone in this country who could do this sort of work?'

'A good tattooist might be able to reproduce it, but the dyes wouldn't be right and an expert could easily spot the differences.'

'Well, thanks for coming over, Beni. How strong a stomach have you?'

'Depends what for, Sergeant.'

'We may need you to look at a body that I'm trying to have exhumed.'

'I should be all right, providing that you keep the face covered up.' His nervous laughter concealed the fear that he felt.

'You'll be OK with this one, Beni. It hasn't got a head.'

Beni looked from one to the other, a puzzled expression on his face, sensing that the Sergeant wasn't joking.

'He's serious,' said Liam. 'The only means of ID is that tattoo.'

'Call me if you need me. I think I'll get back to the normality of banking now, I've had enough excitement for one day.'

After he left, Paul went through the Coroner's report on David once again and, skipping over the technical jargon, he arrived at the Coroner's conclusions. Cause of death, multiple wounds to the chest and stomach as a result of a fall. Verdict – accidental death. Simple and to the point, almost dismissive. Paul knew where he had to visit next.

'Liam. I want to see the cliffs where my brother was found and have a nose around. David was a professional-standard climber who never took any risks, this just doesn't add up at all.'

'The gear was still in the boot of the car when I went to collect it; every rope was neatly coiled and all his tools were in place as were his boots.'

'Exactly, Liam, and if David wasn't using his equipment, how did he get the rope burns on his wrists? Also, no matter how anybody falls, there are always breakages to the legs or arms, but

David had none. No, Liam, the whole thing stinks. I'll go and get clearance from the DI.'

The DI greeted him with the news that the parents of the dead children were refusing to be interviewed by anyone other than Paul, so he and Liam set off back towards Heathrow and the safe house.

It was a vastly changed group of carriers that confronted them when they arrived. Relieved of their deadly cargo and awaiting deportation back to Africa, their only thoughts now were to try and avoid being repatriated. Everyone began talking at once, offering their cooperation in exchange for asylum, and it was several minutes before they could quieten the room.

Paul had noticed the children's parents sitting apart from the others, their faces twisted with grief, their guilt weighing heavily on their shoulders and, leaving the rest to Liam, he took them upstairs. Putting an arm around each one he held them tightly, saying nothing, and as they felt his calming influence over them the father began to tell their tale   a tale Paul knew so well.

They lived in the ghetto and no matter how hard he tried he couldn't get a permanent job so when this offer of a chance to escape to a new life came along they grabbed it, basically for the children's sake.

Here they broke down again but Paul, still holding on to them, waited patiently and when their composure returned the mother spoke for the first time. She'd been approached in the market by an Arab who had organised everything, including their passports, and had promised to be at Heathrow to meet them. He had convinced them that there was no danger involved, and told them that hundreds of people had successfully escaped from their living hell in this way: that they were now living happily in Britain and their children were being educated.

Paul was rooted to the spot for several seconds before gently letting them go. He took the photographs from his pocket, hardly daring to breathe, not sure what his reaction would be if he had got it all wrong.

There was no hesitancy, no doubt: Abdul Karim was alive and still plying his evil trade, commuting between the two countries under Paul's nose. How he had managed to enter and leave Durban without being spotted was something that would have to be investigated later. More importantly, here were two more people who could positively identify him and what about those downstairs?

Where was he now, which country? Had he left London today when the operation failed, or was he with Anna? Paul's mind was racing as he rushed downstairs to find Liam, who was still having trouble controlling the others, but the room silenced the minute he entered and Liam stood back and admired the way people respected this man – it had been the same with his brother.

Nodding to the little scouser, a smile on his face, he showed the mug shots to the people, who once again became an animated mass. No one recognised Anna but of Abdul Karim there was now no shadow of a doubt.

Paul's elation, however, was tempered by the realisation that this was probably what David had uncovered and why he had been murdered, but why he had kept it to himself would always stay a mystery. The fact remained that they still had no hard evidence as to who had killed him or how he had died, and only supposition as to why.

Nevertheless, it was enough for DCS Carlisle to open an official police inquiry into the death of Detective Sergeant David Johans Mackenzie, and to have drawn up a warrant for the arrest of Abdul Karim on two charges of murder.

Paul phoned Commissioner Van den Hootzen in Durban to tell him the bad news, and to ask him to start an investigation into how Abdul could come and go without anyone in Immigration recognising him. Four years ago his mug shot had been distributed to all points of entry into the state, and for trained people such as that his was a face that you don't forget in a hurry. In addition, a round-the-clock surveillance was put on Heathrow, although Paul doubted whether this merited the manpower; either

Abdul had gone to ground in London or he had left the country hours ago. The twins had to be visited again, and soon – more than ever they needed to know where Anna Karim was.

Paul and Liam decided to call it a day. Emotionally drained, they headed out of London for the hotel at Twickenham unable to erase from their minds the faces of those two dead children.

Frances was at breaking point, completely unable to control herself, and once more she burst into tears the minute Paul entered the room. For the past two days she had been cooped up there, unable even to call her friends, and the strain was proving too much. She sobbed uncontrollably, clinging to Paul and not saying a word until he finally managed to calm her down and, picking her up, he laid her on the bed and sat down beside her.

'I'm sorry, Paul. You look like you have had an awful day and I'm being very selfish, but with so much time on my hands I've been thinking about everything. David had opened up a whole new world to me, and at the same time I had a feeling of safeness and security, and now I feel so alone and vulnerable. If I could just be among my friends at the hospital, bury myself in my work, I might feel better; I'm even thinking that I might quit England and go back to live in Jamaica as soon as this is all over.'

'You must hang on a bit longer, Frances. It's going to turn even nastier out there in the next few days, and there is no way I or any other policeman would want you in London. I won't go into details, the least you know the better, but suffice to say that we are now more than convinced that David was murdered.'

Frances fell silent as Paul's words sank in. As a staff nurse in the Accident and Emergency unit she had witnessed many horrific sights in her career and as a professional had become immune to the suffering. But this was David they were talking about, and she was unable to control her emotions as horrific images filled her mind as to what his murder might have entailed

'Look, Frances. We're going down to Dorset tomorrow, to have a look at where they found David; it won't be a pleasant trip but

107

if you come with us it will at least get you out of here for a few hours.'

She studied his face intently while she considered her answer. So like his brother in nature, she began to feel the wall of security being rebuilt.

'Yes, I would like to come with you, it might help me to lay some demons at the same time.'

'OK. Now I'm going to order us some dinner. If you don't mind I'd rather eat up here; I couldn't face a restaurant full of people and the less we are seen the better.'

20

The heavy storms had turned the river into a raging, frenzied torrent fed by hundreds of waterfalls that cascaded down the mountainside and to have any chance of reaching his objective Mario had firstly to find a way across this terrifying maelstrom and then a route around the bridgehead.

He could not take the chance of any of them getting wet as there was no way that they could risk lighting a fire and, coupled with the freezing temperatures, a man soaked to the skin would die very quickly out here. Working their way back from the bridge it seemed an impossible task, the angry waters now rising so fast that they had started to breach the banks, forcing them back deep into the forest.

His opportunity came when the woodland suddenly ended and they found themselves on the edge of a vast man-made clearing, high above the water level. It was very dangerous to be this exposed but they had no other choice, there might not be another chance and time was running out. Dusk was falling and Mario had no idea if it was possible to approach the bridge from the other side, a journey they must make within the hour.

Explaining his intentions, he was surprised when one of the smaller men volunteered to take on the job, but was assured by the English-speaking officer that the task was in good hands. Tying a small log to a rope, he began swinging it above his head and, as the momentum grew, he launched it across the river and into a tree.

Mario, not believing what he had witnessed, just stood there in amazement, but his joy was short lived as the log began to fall through the branches. Grabbing the rope to pull it back, he was relieved to see it catch once more, this time resisting all their efforts to dislodge it. Tying the other end to a nearby tree, the little man stood there smiling, and then, before Mario could react, had climbed the rope and was working his way effortlessly across to the other side.

As Mario had feared, it was virgin territory. The wild undergrowth was a tangled mass that tore skin from legs and arms as they hacked their way through, with the raging river, only inches away, threatening to wash them all to a watery grave. Time soon ran out, night returned rapidly and Mario once again found himself confronted by the seemingly impenetrable wall of black. Although he had no idea of how far they had to go they had to continue, they couldn't camp here, there was no knowing what the river might do!

He was on the point of surrender, he knew his men couldn't take much more and they had to stop, when he felt a tug on his tunic. Looking up, he blinked the exhaustion from his eyes and shook his head and then he saw it. Silhouetted not 100 metres around the corner of the mountain was a part of the bridge.

There was no way that they could take it. All they could do was to remove the explosives and leave the fighting to the others; in that way they would at least have a chance of reaching the town. For once Mario was thankful for the rain, the giant clouds hiding the moon as he, Lazio, and two others inched their way closer to the target. It was an old bridge of steel construction upon which the passage of time had taken its toll, the rusting girders were eaten away, its days numbered. After cutting the connecting wires and removing the dynamite they retreated back to their camp, where Mario decided that, despite their exhaustion, they should try and reach the town under the cover of darkness.

The ever present sound of gunfire seemed to be getting closer and closer, and he wanted to be well out of the area before the impending battle for the bridge began, but he couldn't let the General walk into this ambush – he had to warn him first.

Mario's understanding of the opposition was that they were not highly trained soldiers but a people's army led by a handful of military personnel, so he decided to rattle their cage and see what the response was. His thinking was that not only might it panic some of them into flight, the noise would certainly alert the army fighting their way down the mountain, and it would also give Mario and his men a diversion to help them pass the bridgehead.

Hugging the side of the mountain, they inched their way forward again until they reached a large overhang on which, he had noticed from the other side of the river, were several troops with mortars. Mario prayed that the moon didn't reappear from behind the clouds, knowing that if that happened they would be sitting targets, as they placed the dynamite they had taken from the bridge into the rocky crevices.

They retreated back to the others and Lazio lovingly removed the rifle from its cover. He was now in charge of the weapon and had already prepared it for firing, Mario trusting him implicitly as he took the gun from him.

Through the night sight Mario sought out the dynamite, then turned the weapon towards the bridge. There were two men there on patrol and Mario despatched them to a watery grave, the sound of the shots galvanising their comrades into action.

A generator kicked into life and, as the bridge lit up like a Christmas tree, the soldiers above began firing wildly at nothing. Before anyone could gain control of them, Mario fired the dynamite, bringing down the overhang and, as the lights on the bridge went out, the chaos he had hoped for erupted.

There was the sound of heavy engines starting up as the terrified troops tried to flee, the headlights of their vehicles illuminating the scene and making them a sitting target for Mario and his men as they broke cover.

111

As they clambered over the boulder-strewn terrain that now surrounded the bridgehead a lorry up ahead exploded, confirming Mario's worst fears. The road had been mined. But there was no going back now, they were committed and, as they neared the burning truck, they came under automatic gunfire.

Hitting the ground, they returned fire and, rather than risk being trapped here, Mario was up almost immediately, pulling the pin on a grenade as the others followed suit. Launching the grenades in the direction of the gunfire they kept running as behind them there was a huge rumbling and part of the mountain began to break up and fall. If it hit the bridge then it would bring it down but it was too late now to worry about that as the road ahead filled with troops and Mario once again opened fire.

The rain dripping on his face brought him back to reality, although it was several seconds before the events of the previous night clicked into place. He sat bolt upright and was relieved to see Lazio alongside him, cradling the rifle in his sleep. Glancing around, he counted four others.

They all appeared to be sleeping and uninjured. Mario recalled the chaos, the running gun battle, the headlong flight into oblivion; it was all like some giant nightmare from which he had just awoken – only it had been real! It was inevitable that there had been casualties, fortunately only two. He roused the guide, who shook his hand and embraced him warmly. The others awoke then and did the same, relieved that somehow they were alive to fight another day.

Impatient to be on the move, Mario glanced around the door of the old shepherd's hut and saw that they were on the edge of a fairly flat plain with the mountains behind them and smoke rising far off in the distance. He reasoned that that must be the town and, rather than risk all their lives, he decided to send a man on ahead to do a recce. News of their survival must have filtered through by now and they were hunted men; he needed information.

Once again he began to doubt the allegiance of these soldiers as the hours went by and the man had not returned. Had he been captured or defected? Either way, Mario couldn't risk waiting any longer: if the man had talked they were all dead. Looking from one to the other he gave the order to move out and crawled from the hut, the long grass the only cover available.

They were totally exposed out here but there was no going back now, he had committed his men because he wanted more. More of the fighting, more of the killing: Mario was alive again and relishing the challenge, pushing himself to the limit as they finally reached the safety of another crumbling building.

This was a more substantial affair with a steel framework, enabling him to climb into the roof space and sweep the terrain ahead. Locating the position of the town, he then swept east and froze. Heading their way was an armoured division complete with tanks, obviously to intercept the General, but more of an immediate problem was the advance guard who were searching every building as they crossed the plain – his worst fears were realised.

As he had suspected the previous night, the troops guarding the bridge were expendable volunteers and, far from being a defeated force, there was a sizeable army waiting in reserve. The battle ahead would be long and hard, but Mario's immediate problem was where to go from here and how long could his luck hold out? With no idea of what lay ahead they broke cover, this time on the run as he led them towards the west of the town.

21

England, October 2003

The silence in the car was heavy as they made their way down the M3 to Dorset and Frances, although glad to be out of her hotel prison, was starting to wish she had never said yes to this journey. She fought the nausea which had been ever present since David's death as she stared aimlessly at the passing countryside, the two men in front ignoring her totally, their attention focussed on everything happening around them. Visions of David lying in the mortuary vividly appeared once more as she closed her eyes and the tears began forming, her anguish being broken by the car radio bursting into life. It was Jean and Colin, in the back-up car.

'Not too sure about two motorcycles we picked up ten minutes ago. They've tucked in behind you two cars back.'

Paul adjusted his mirrors. 'Got them. We'll take the next exit, nice and gently, see what happens. Frances, I want you to lie down in the back until we've checked this out.'

As they climbed the slip road off the motorway they saw the two bikes continue south below them, so Liam immediately rejoined the road behind them and everyone breathed a sigh of relief. The rest of the journey passed without further incident, Frances more than thankful when they pulled into the police station at Lyme Regis to ask directions.

'You'll have difficulty finding it on your own but I have a spare constable and a car who can lead you there, it will save you a lot of time.'

Paul reflected on the desk sergeant's words when they suddenly left the narrow lane they were on for an almost hidden track which disappeared into the forest, coming to an abrupt ending in a clearing surrounded by cliffs.

'How did my brother know of this place, Liam? Even the locals would have difficulty finding it!'

'I've been thinking the same thing. David always talked about his climbing, where he had been, where he was going, but he had never mentioned this place.'

'Who found him?'

'A young couple who live in the village down the lane. They come here regularly to exercise their dogs.'

The constable led them to a narrow opening in the cliffs, a tiny passage formed by millions of years of erosion, which brought them out on to a boulder-strewn beach. Luckily the tide was out as he led them to a huge rock way down the shore from where, looking up at the cliffs and the surrounding terrain, it was obvious even to the uninitiated that it would be impossible to climb any of the cliff face without the proper equipment.

Frances and Paul held one another tightly as they said a prayer for David, while Liam just stood there, looking around him, silently thinking about everything. Then he spoke:

'We've all been barking up the wrong tree! Because David was found here we have all assumed that his demise was meant to look like a climbing accident. I don't think whoever is responsible even knew about the climbing. What I'm now certain of is that David was killed elsewhere, probably London, and his car and body brought here.' Liam had everyone's attention as he continued. 'Whoever was responsible had to live locally or have relations who knew of this place. They placed David on that rock knowing that the tide would wash him out to sea and, when his body came back ashore, it would look like an accident, but he was found before the tide could take him. What we have to do now is look at the history of those we pulled in yesterday, those villains who are known locally and see if there is a connection.'

115

Although it still didn't explain how David had died, they all agreed that it was the most logical reason for his being found here, and that in itself was a big step forward. As there was nothing further to be gained by staying there any longer they thanked the constable for his help and set off back to London, the gloom once again descending upon them. Paul phoned DI Watkinson, explaining what conclusions they had come to and what information they required, and he in turn related the morning's news.

London was still clammed up tight with nobody talking, so they were no further forward in finding the Karims. The Barolli twins were due to be moved later in the day, after they had made their statements, and Brendan Cassidy was alive but still in a coma. It was the two airport cleaners who provided the best news, and raids were being carried out on addresses in Southall, Ealing and Hounslow.

After dropping Frances off at Twickenham they decided to stop for lunch before returning to the office, although neither of them felt much like eating. It had been another harrowing morning, and although it had produced a probable explanation as to the circumstances surrounding David's death, they were still no closer to the truth. Frustrated, they drank up and were just leaving when Paul's mobile rang. It was the DI.

'This could be game, set, and match, Sergeant, but I don't want to raise anybody's hopes, yet. One of those we lifted yesterday, and are still questioning, is a William Geoffrey Legg, born February 1966 at Bridport in Dorset. His history is very heavy duty: armed robbery, GBH, narcotic dealing, and he has a brother doing a five stretch at Portland for drug-related offences whose last given address is a village not two miles from where David was found. The icing on the cake though is that William Legg's last stretch was a six in "the scrubs" in the company of, Luigi Barolli and Andrew James Mackinley. We are still looking for Mackinley, he wasn't at his known address when we raided it last night.'

'That's good news, sir. How much longer can you hold Legg before you have to let him go?'

'I've already applied for an extension on the grounds that new evidence has become available. How long before you get back?'

'We'll be with you within the hour, sir.'

'Mad Mack, I should have guessed that one, Paul. They don't come any more evil than that bastard – we're in for a rough ride before this is finished.' Liam was now more than convinced that David was murdered in London, and that Mackinley and Legg were involved somewhere along the line.

When they arrived back they were greeted by the bad news that the twins were stalling. Detectives Mark Burley and John Lindsey were seasoned officers who had each received two commendations for bravery in the line of duty. On both occasions Andrew Mackinley had been involved and, in Liam's opinion, they were the only other members of the squad who could 'squeeze' anything out of the Barollis.

'As you said, Liam, we found Joseph to be more cooperative than Luigi, but all we've got is small-time stuff. I get the feeling that they know something is in the air and that their circumstances are going to change.'

'Like the GBH charges being dropped, which means they will be out of nick like a shot and we will have a devil's own job finding them again or, there is a move afoot to spring them. Someone's got word to them, that's for sure. They now believe they're safe, which means we're wasting our time.'

'You're going to have to give them another fright, Mark.' Paul told them about their visit to Dorset, the conclusions they had drawn, and how the three villains had all been in Wormwood Scrubs at the same time.

'That bastard Mackinley, again. We've still got the scars from the last time we met.'

'So, let the twins know that we've got Legg and Mackinley banged up and see what reaction that provokes. I don't want them transferred tonight, we'd better talk to the DCS and get it stopped.' Liam was taking no chances. The fact that many of the villains they would have liked to interview were nowhere to be found meant something was going on: someone was putting together a big operation, possibly to free the twins or terminate their lives, or to remove Paul from the scene.

Back at his desk, Paul returned to the file on Anna Karim. Born Naples, parents deceased, lived with an aunt and uncle in Fulham.

'Jean, can you get me some names to go with these? Parents, mother's maiden name, aunt and uncle's names, aunt's maiden name, and try and find out how the parents died.'

What else had David learnt? Was there something other than the fact that Abdul Karim was still alive? As he returned to the file the phone rang. Ignore it and go home, he told himself, he had had enough for one day, but something deep down was telling him differently so he lifted the receiver.

'Sergeant Mackenzie. There are some very pissed-off people in and around London who want you out of the game. I suggest that you pay a visit to the old water treatment station at Wapping in one hour. Liam knows where it is.'

The man hung up before Paul could reply and Liam immediately realised the importance of the call when Paul described the accented voice and the meeting place.

'This could be the breakthrough we've been waiting for. Your caller was Marco Santini, who owns a pizzaria restaurant where you can get anything but drugs. Three years ago he was raided and charged with various firearms offences but your brother got him a deal which kept him out of prison and in business. If he wants to see us then he knows something. His clientele reads like the Criminal Records Office and, if they are not inside, they all meet there when they want something or someone.'

'If that's the case why wasn't surveillance put on the premises when all this started?'

'It was part of the deal your brother struck but when Marco calls it's never anything trivial. We have to trust him and he has always come up trumps: if we had him watched word would get out very quickly and his life would be over. I'll tell the DI the good news before we leave.'

Marco seemed genuinely pleased to see the two men and, after shaking Liam's hand, he turned and greeted Paul like a long-lost brother.

'I'm glad you two are still alive, but you are going to have to be very very careful from now on. The lady is determined to get rid of you, no matter what and no matter the cost.'

Paul hid his surprise at this news. 'There are a lot of others, Marco, who know what we know, so killing us is not going to stop her from going down.'

'To say you've stirred things up, Sergeant, is an understatement. There's a lot of money being mentioned for your removal, and a lot of people who fancy their chances, it's gone too far now to stop.'

'What about Mackinley? Do you have any ideas where we might find him?'

'That's the main reason you're here but be warned, he's well tooled up and surrounded by a very heavy bunch. There's an old warehouse in Bermondsey, on the river, that used to belong to the Thames River Trading Co., part of the name is still visible. It looks like it's falling down but that is only the front part. At the rear Messrs Mackinley and Legg have their "office" so to speak.'

'We're holding Legg at the moment but haven't got anything out of him so far. Does Mackinley live at the warehouse all the time or does he have another address?'

Marco looked from one to the other in surprise. 'I thought you knew, Liam. He and the lady have been an item for years now, although she's very much the boss still and he the hired muscle. From what I can make out he has never moved in full-time but if he's not at the warehouse then he will be with her, somewhere. I know what your next question is going to be and the answer is no. Rumour has it it's somewhere on the river, but it is a closely guarded secret, that one.'

'One other thing before you go, Marco. Nearly every move we make seems to be known; have we got a leak that you know of?'

'The Karim network is extensive and the hold she has between the drugs and the muscle she controls puts her at number one here in London. Her network of informants is such that I do not trust anybody anymore, but I'll keep my ear to the ground and call you as soon as I hear anything.'

The men shook hands and Marco left the two officers standing in the old pumping station, digesting what they had just learnt. They had an address: it wasn't Anna's but it was a good starting point, except if they charged in it could turn into a bloodbath. It was Anna, and not Abdul, who was pulling the strings and was responsible for everything that had happened since his arrival, and probably David's death. Mackinley was putting together a team, possibly to spring the twins, probably to eradicate Paul.

'The twins have to be our priority, Liam. We must break them and quickly. Phone the DI and let him know what we've learnt and get him to arrange another visit to those two first thing tomorrow.'

22

Kosovo, October 2000

Cutting a zigzag path in close formation they found themselves leaving the protection of the long grass and once again came upon the river, or a tributary of it, as its turbulence was nothing like the day before. Here they rested while Mario once again swept the horizon and then the mountains behind them and, satisfied that there appeared to be no movement anywhere, he decided to follow the river's course, hoping that it either flowed through the town or, at the very least, its outskirts.

Lazio was never a yard away from Mario's shoulder, his determination to protect this young lion all-consuming as he anxiously scanned the surrounding countryside. He had been fighting a war all his life and he had never met a soldier like this one, even placing him above their leader, seeing in Mario the possibility that peace may at last be more than a dream: that this one man could be just the person to bring an end to the fighting and stop the madness that ravaged the Balkans. Mario's inspirational leadership and military acumen could drive his countrymen to victory and finally force their enemies into submission, possibly to the point where they would at long last all sit around a table and negotiate a truce.

However, he sensed that this was a troubled young man who was driven by demons, not a cause, that once this was over he could vanish into thin air, but Lazio nurtured the dream.

As they rounded a bend in the river they came across another

121

fortified bridge, which obviously carried the top road from the mountains into the town, but at least they didn't have to cross it, just avoid being spotted. To their right were some houses and, deciding to use them as cover, Mario signalled his intentions to the mountain man.

All the time in the back of Mario's mind was the fact that everything could have been compromised, that they were expected, so as the guide led them out on a long, slow belly crawl, he once again reminded his men to be extra vigilant.

Reaching the shelter of the buildings Mario realised that they wouldn't afford much cover for long, they were mostly bombed-out ruins, and they would be very exposed soon if they continued on this route, yet there seemed no alternative.

Looking from one to the other he sensed that the men were getting impatient for action: he couldn't fail them now, not after what they had all endured to get this far, he had to find an answer and find it quick. An audacious plan began forming in his mind that might just work and although it was a highly dangerous move that could result in the deaths of them all, the more he thought about it the more feasible it became. Except for the English-speaking officer, who looked more northern European than the others, the rest could pass as being part of the local community. If they made out that they had captured a Serbian officer they might be able to commandeer a vehicle to get them into town.

It worked like a dream, the patrolling militia only too happy to hand over their jeep when they saw that one of the enemy from last night's incursion had been captured. The journey into town was one long procession of waving, cheering locals and Mario, a rifle under the soldier's throat, waved back enthusiastically as they passed.

So far so good, but what now? They had reached the outskirts of the town and were likely to encounter a lot more soldiers at any moment so Mario decided that their first priority was to hide the jeep ready for their escape. Next, they had to find a change of clothing for the officer and, having left some poor unfortunate passer-by bound and gagged, they began mingling with the local population, listening to the conversations and trying to get their bearings, Mario all the time on the lookout for signs of trouble, feeling the tension in the air.

All was not lost, they soon discovered. Following last night's successful defeat of the Serbian forces the local population felt more secure, their leader telling them that they could withstand a siege if need be. He was still here then, still inciting the population with his lies, still leading these people to a certain death, all Mario had to do now was to find him.

This proved easier than hoped for as more and more people began to take to the streets, all heading in the same direction, and Mario and his men joined the frenzied throng. There was to be another rallying of the troops, another brainwashing of the people, and Mario fought his way through the swirling mass of obsessed humanity with Lazio beside him, the rifle safely hidden beneath his coat.

After all he had endured the ending was an anti-climax for Mario; it was all so easy. Using the last of the dynamite, they set up simultaneous explosions at the time of the hit, which left the town in total chaos, the five survivors making an easy escape amidst the panic. The troops guarding the bridge had deserted their post, fleeing at the first sign of trouble, and they crossed the river without a shot being fired.

As the old jeep effortlessly took them back up the mountain road towards the Montenegrin border and safety, Mario started to relax, Lazio and the others assuring him that border patrols on this route were very unlikely.

Although the extreme cold and wet had at times demoralised him, his intense will to succeed and his fierce pride had carried him through once again. Now all he wanted to do was to return quickly to his beloved Corsica and the warmth and the solitude that was waiting for him there.

To this end, Mario had decided that the simplest way home

for him was across the Adriatic Sea, landing somewhere in Italy, although Lazio was sceptical of this plan. The Adriatic itself was a war zone as far as the Italian authorities were concerned, and they raged a daily running battle trying to intercept boat-loads of Albanians seeking asylum, drug smugglers from south-west Asia, and prostitutes heading for the Italian mainland and easy pickings.

Mario, however, was adamant. After what they had been through he wanted the shortest, quickest route home possible so, after they had said their emotional farewells to the other four, Lazio and Mario turned south for the coast and a fishing port where Lazio knew someone who might be able to help.

Although the roads were better, the journey south was tortuous in the old jeep, Mario looking daggers at Lazio every time he hit an obstacle. After an hour the mountain man turned west and then stopped on the edge of a village, indicating for Mario to get out. Not quite sure what the guide was up to he hesitated, but Lazio smiled and nodded, so Mario obliged. With that Lazio drove off, leaving him sitting by the roadside, bemused but not worried, at least he was in a friendly country now.

All was revealed half an hour later when the guide returned driving a white Mercedes saloon and, grinning from ear to ear, he opened the boot to reveal a veritable feast of hot meats and vegetables. After the feast and feeling much better than he had in weeks, Mario nodded off as Lazio turned south once again, the Mercedes purring along over the uneven surfaces. It was dusk when they reached a small fishing port that looked like its best days were behind it; beached rotting boats lay everywhere, their torn nets hanging over the sides, the place seemingly deserted.

Lazio eventually found the man he was looking for, an elderly fisherman who, it transpired, hardly put to sea these days because of the troubles in the Adriatic.

There followed the usual long and heated discussion which, Mario realised now, was the way business was conducted in these parts. Whether it was over the price or the dangers involved he wasn't sure but, suddenly, the talking stopped and the old fisher-man smiled and came over and embraced Mario, Lazio smiling and nodding at him in the background.

Lazio gave him the rifle as they said their goodbyes. 'Take, English come back,' was all he could say, but Mario understood his body language and signs. The rifle was a gift from a grateful people which Mario proudly accepted, but he was unsure of how he was going to travel through mainland Europe with it!

23

London, October 2003

Liam and Paul entered the office next morning to find that, following their meeting with Marco, the DI had requested the help of the river division with the surveillance of the warehouse at Bermondsey. He had also sent them mugshots of the Karims and Andrew Mackinley with strict instructions to observe only and in no circumstances were they to try to apprehend any of them.

Although nothing of significance had occurred on the water, there had been considerable road traffic to and from the warehouse during the night. To this end DI Watkinson had applied for armed twenty-four-hour surveillance on all roads leading to and from the premises.

On Paul's desk were two pieces of paper, one of which was a fax from Inspector Preetzius, his immediate superior in Durban:

> I think we may have found a way in to the new distribution network. We suspect that they are now using second-hand vehicles and private drivers, not big firms with new company vans as before, which makes them less conspicuous but more vulnerable to breakdown. As you well know, we waste a lot of police time sorting out traffic jams caused by old cars and vans breaking down, and this morning we received a call to say that a vehicle was causing congestion in the city centre.

When our men arrived they found the driver frantically trying to push his motor into a side street and, although empty, we traced his movements for the morning to find that he had delivered boxes of fruit to street markets around the city. He was employed by, and the van registered to, a firm called 'Citruso Inc.', a farm company out in the valley which has its headquaters in Messina, Sicily. Needless to say he had no licence so, in return for his information, we have not pressed charges. I have started surveillance on the street vendors and will contact you later.

This was the good news he had been hoping for, for months now they had been targeting the wrong vehicles. But it was the second note that set Paul's mind racing;

Anna Francesca Karim – née Barolli.
Parents: Paolo Luigi and Donna Barolli – née Massimo.
Killed 5th April 1965 in a police raid on their canning premises in Milan.
Donna Barolli was the sister of Illario Massimo – The Godfather.

Aunt and Uncle.
Frederic Antonio and Theresa Stromberti née Massimo, sister of Donna Barolli.
Run a fruit and vegetable business from their residence in the Fulham Road.

'Liam. How certain are you that the Karims don't visit or stay with Anna's aunt and uncle from time to time?'

'Sorry to dash your hopes, Paul, but we've had the premises under surveillance on more than one occasion to no avail. Your brother and I have interviewed them both a number of times, and we've searched the place from top to bottom – all we have ever got is a load of abuse from Aunty.'

127

'Still, I think it is worth another shot, given the circumstances. Let's get a warrant and pay them a visit, we've got nothing to lose and they are family of the guy we caught in Durban.'

'OK, but I think you are going to be disappointed, Paul. At least it will fill in time till we get to see the Barollis.

Liam's phone rang. It was the DI, requesting their presence at a meeting in DCI Tomlinson's office. 'What have we done wrong now? He generally only gets involved when someone's toes have been stepped on.'

Liam didn't see eye to eye with the DCI and caught Paul's gaze. 'It's old history. I'll tell you about it sometime.'

Liam's suspicions were confirmed the minute they entered the room; as well as the DI, DCS Carlisle was also sitting there.

'Good morning, gentlemen. Sit yourselves down. We have been discussing the events of the past few days and your arrival, Sergeant, has triggered off a chain of unbelievable events which have given us the breakthrough we needed, and confirmed our worst suspicions. However, we feel that we cannot continue to use you as live bait, especially after what you have learnt yesterday evening, so we have concluded that, for your own safety, you should return to South Africa immediately.'

'I'm not running away now, we're too close, sir. The Barollis are going to talk soon, of this I'm certain, and we know where to find Mackinley.'

'It's not running away, Sergeant,' the DCS interrupted. 'Now that we know Abdul Karim is still alive, wouldn't it be better if you returned home and pushed from that end?'

'My brother died at the hands of these people, of that I'm certain and although I will have to go home in two weeks' time, for the Stromberti trial, I will return to continue this investigation here in London, officially or unofficially, until this is finished.'

'What do you think, Liam?' As soon as he had asked it he realised it was a stupid question, Tomlinson already knew the answer.

'I want David's killers as much as his brother does, and I want him with me when we end this. After last night with Marco, I think once we get Mackinley the twins will talk.'

'Can you trust Marco? I know he's always been reliable in the past but this case is about as heavy as it gets and maybe they've got to him also.'

'He's the one person who has had the guts to come forward and, knowing of his respect for David, I would say, yes. If he'd been sussed out he'd have disappeared off the face of the earth long ago. No, Marco's all right, but we must be extremely careful in our dealings with him and not over-expose him; he is of the opinion that almost everybody is in the pay of Anna Karim so his name must be used very discreetly.'

'Which brings us to another major problem that has arisen this morning.' DCS Carlisle looked reluctantly at Paul and Liam. 'I've had the twins' brief on the phone. I'm afraid you're going to have to lay off those two for the time being or they will lay police harassment charges against us.'

'They're webbed up in all this and you know it, sir. Why don't you try and get them out of solitary? I know what their reaction would be; they're shit scared, no matter what they've heard to the contrary, and their lives aren't worth a damn to anyone but us.'

'I know what you're saying, Liam, but our hands are tied for the moment. I'll speak to the brief at lunchtime, and maybe in a couple of days they will have calmed down.'

Liam exploded. 'We don't have a couple of days. All the time we're sitting here talking they're getting further away from us!' He rose to leave but Paul restrained him.

'Liam's right. We need to keep the pressure on – who else have we got? William Legg. He hasn't exactly been cooperative and unless we charge him soon we will have to let him go. Then there is Mackinley: I suggest, and I know Liam agrees with me, that we let him sweat, it isn't worth a bloodbath until we have hard evidence. So where does that leave us? The twins and maybe Uncle and Aunty in Fulham who appear to have been kept out of it but now I'm not so sure.' Paul went on to tell them about the Stromberti connection.

The DCS conceded. 'All right, gentlemen, you pay Uncle and Aunty a visit and, if nothing comes of it, we will go after the twins, somehow.'

'Thank you, sir. Will that be all?'

'No, Sergeant. We didn't think for one moment that you would agree to our proposal that you return home and, quite frankly, we don't want to lose you yet. Although keeping you two alive is our top priority we have to look at all angles and be realistic here. Liam, Sandra and the baby could also become targets if they fail to get to you two directly, and it's obvious that the Karims are prepared to go to any lengths to protect their empire, so we can't rule out anything.'

'If she finds out she's under surveillance my life won't be worth living.'

'That's not what we're proposing to do, it isn't secure enough. She knows Frances very well and we want to put them all into a safe house, well away from London, until this is over. There they can be free and secure, which will take the pressure off you two.'

Liam looked at Paul, who nodded his agreement.

'Very well, sir, set it up, but I'll have to go home now and explain things to her first.' Liam knew that this was going to be the hard part.

24

Montenegro, November 2000

From the Montenegrin coast the old fisherman set a south westerly course for the Italian mainland and, as the last of the harbour lights disappeared over the horizon, the dark of night quickly engulfed them. Mario was sitting in the bow with the night-sight in his hand, contemplating how and where he was going to land, when the old man beckoned for him to join him. Cutting the engine they then proceeded to cast the nets, a highly dangerous manoeuvre as they were showing no lights and might have to take quick evasive action.

What was the old boy playing at? In response to Mario's worried look he gave a knowing smile as he relit his pipe and settled down on the bridge and, once more, Mario found his young life entrusted to a complete stranger. Scanning all around him he could see nothing and as the minutes turned into hours the first of the dawn's rays started to appear on the horizon.

All this time the old man hadn't moved and just when Mario thought his nerves could take no more the sound of a heavy engine came to him on the breeze. Mario looked anxiously towards the fisherman, who simply smiled and nodded in reply as he started the engine and began hauling in the nets. Pointing the boat in the direction of the oncoming vessel he switched on and off some powerful spotlights, which brought a response of two short flashes, and a huge grin spread across the old man's face as he slapped Mario on the back and proceeded towards the mystery craft.

She was beautiful. A huge, white private yacht that even in the half light of dawn set Mario's pulse racing, and his earlier fears disappeared as a ladder was thrown over the side and Mario bade the old man goodbye.

Flying the Greek flag and crewed by a mixture of English-speaking Europeans, it transpired that the vessel was owned by an Arab sheik who spent most of his time tending his oil wells – leaving the crew to kick their heels sailing the seven seas. They assured him that there would be no problems as they entered the notorious waters of the straits of Otranto and, true to their words, they sailed on south unimpeded, passing several Italian naval vessels with a wave and a sounding of the horn.

Mario had immediately felt an empathy with this motley crew who had the best of both worlds, well-paid jobs and the chance to live life on the edge, a way of life that he could equate with. They asked no questions, and when he enquired as to how he was to pay them and what was their destination he was told that they were returning a favour and all would be revealed.

He was more than happy to go along with this, enjoying the sheer luxury that was this beautiful craft after the deprivations of the past few weeks. Journey's end, however, came as a complete surprise to him when they sailed into the harbour at Ajaccio, where the port authorities welcomed them as old friends, the skipper winking at Mario as they came alongside a berth that was obviously reserved for them.

They'd brought him all the way home! There were a dozen questions he couldn't ask, all he could do was to show his grat-itude, so he invited them all ashore for a drink. With the warmth of the Corsican sun once again on his back, Mario sat on the veranda of the bar enjoying the company of this loveable band of rogues, wondering if they would ever meet again. His thoughts were interrupted by the Greek captain, Alexis, who, although not much older than him, was definitely the skipper when at sea.

'What you do now, Mario? Would you like to join us, we have a lot of sport to do before our boss come back?'

132

Mario didn't dare think what his interpretation of the word 'sport' entailed but was sorely tempted to accept the offer, and then he thought of his father and the promise that he had made him.

'Not this time, I'm afraid, Alexis. There are things I have to finish elsewhere first but give me a number where I can contact you.'

He said his goodbyes certain in the knowledge that they would meet again and, happy to be alone once more, he wandered the quay, soaking up the atmosphere as he watched the cruise liners discharge their passengers for another day of shopping and sight-seeing and unaware that he had been joined by two men.

As he turned to board his cruiser they approached him.

'Excuse me, sir. Are you Matthew Simon Richardson, the fifth Duke of Rushtington?'

He was taken aback for a moment, it seemed another world away since anybody had addressed him so. How could they have found him? He looked nothing like a member of the English gentry, he was dishevelled and unshaven. Then it dawned on him: the cruiser. He had registered it in London in his titled name and everybody from his home village knew he had come to Corsica. Matthew was undecided as to whether he should try and bluff it out or not as his visitors continued:

'We represent someone in England who would like to talk to you urgently.' This voice was Australian and the man looked useful but, like his partner, he was flabby. Matthew decided that if things turned nasty he would have no problem dealing with these two so, indicating that he wanted to search them, they lifted their arms obligingly and, when satisfied, he invited them aboard.

'I assume that you are the person we have come to see so I won't waste any more time.' The Australian was obviously in charge, Matthew starting to dislike him as he spoke for the first time.

'One question. How did you know it was me?'

133

'How many people are there around here who are six foot two? Although when you turned around I did think we had made a mistake.'

That made him feel better; he could do nothing about his height but at least he could pass for a local. 'Fair comment. What do you want?'

'You were recommended to our employer as someone who could solve a problem. Everything you need to know is in this envelope.'

That was it: they got up and without another word they left, leaving Matthew holding a buff-coloured A4 envelope, his plans for the next few days up in smoke. More important though was the fact that his safe haven had been breached and his cover blown: what could be the repercussions of that he dared not contemplate at this moment, but one thing was for certain, Ajaccio was finished for him now.

Fighting his curiosity, Matthew decided to take a much needed shower and fix himself something to eat first before he opened the envelope. He was tempted to put to sea but decided that his life wasn't in any immediate danger and he would achieve nothing by running away.

Feeling more human he settled down in one of the leather armchairs and broke the seal on the envelope. As the contents spilt onto the table a flood of painful memories came rushing back and reawoke the anger that was always simmering just below the surface. There were newspaper clippings covering the robbery and murder of his father, together with those concerning similar robberies, a note, and a photograph.

She was sensational, with a smile that took your trousers off, although he couldn't quite place the nationality. The instructions were short and to the point: 'If you would like to learn more, I will be at the Hotel Crillon, Place de la Concorde, Paris, between 16th and 20th November.'

He had two days before she would arrive, leaving him time enough, tomorrow, to go up to the mountains and check out the house.

The next morning he collected his battered four-wheel-drive from the garage which the young apprentice, Joseph, had once again lovingly cleaned and polished, and then his mountain of *Times* newspapers that had accumulated during his absence. With everybody so pleased to see him back again it all took much longer than he had anticipated so, as it was almost lunch time, he decided to stay in town and eat before going home.

His favourite restaurant was well away from the main streets and he used it whenever he could, not sure whether it was the superb food or the owner's daughter that was the main attraction. He was still too early for lunch, which gave him a rare chance to sit and chat to the lovely Claudia behind the bar while he waited, under the wary eye of her parents in the kitchen behind.

Remembering that his wallet was still in the four-wheel-drive, Matthew excused himself and, on exiting from the alleyway, saw his visitors from the day before leaning against his vehicle. They appeared totally relaxed as they leant on the car, chatting and observing all around them, then the Australian suddenly bent down and placed something under the rear wheel arch. Still standing by the car, they continued talking a while longer before casually walking away. Matthew concluded that it must be some sort of tracking device and not an explosive, so he decided to make them wait and, after retrieving his wallet, returned to the restaurant.

Should he just kill them both or try and find out more about who had sent these two, and then kill them? The usual wonderful meal was taking second place in his thoughts as he tried to think who would know so much about his previous life and what they might want. It would be simple to remove them but their boss would only send someone else so, with his mind in turmoil, Matthew finished his meal, thanked his hosts, and wandered back to the car, once more the soldier on alert.

Obviously the two men had spent the night observing his cruiser and followed his movements this morning, but why bug the four track now? And why did they need to know his every move — they'd supposedly carried out their instructions? If their orders were to remove him then maybe the boat was now primed and ready to blow as a back-up if they failed to get him elsewhere.

No matter what, he had to retrieve the rifle if he was to stand any chance with these two, so he returned to the harbour. The boat seemed as secure as when he had left it, and the doors and hatchways did not appear to have been tampered with, so if there were any explosives aboard they would be under the vessel and detonated by remote control.

He was certain that they would be watching him now, but that was a chance he had to take as he unlocked the door of the saloon. His nerve-ends jangling, he removed the rifle from its hiding place and, expecting to be blown to smithereens at any second, went up the companionway two steps at a time and dived off the stern. Unsure as to what depth he had, or what awaited him when he surfaced, Matthew's first concern was to put as much distance as he could between him and the boat.

25

London, October 2003

Frederic Antonio Stromberti was as big as his wife was little but, as Liam had said earlier, it was obvious who wore the trousers. The moment the two officers entered the premises she flew into a vitriolic rage, her still heavily-accented English ringing around the shop. The two men just stood there as she blamed the authorities for all of her family's misfortunes, the police for driving her family into a life of crime and violence. Liam had heard it all before and he cut her off in mid-sentence.

'We didn't make Anna a prostitute, or her brothers psychopaths; it's in the family blood, Theresa, as you well know. So stop wasting our time and tell us where they are living in London?'

'I don't know where she is living, we haven't seen or spoken to her or her husband in months.'

'Whoops, big mistake, Theresa, or have you forgotten that her husband has been dead for four years? I think you two had better join us at the Yard for a little talk while we search this place.'

She fell silent and turned to her husband for help but he was already putting his coat on and, after saying something to her in Italian, she hurriedly did the same. During all this time the big man had said nothing to the two detectives and as they awaited a car to take them to the Yard he crossed the shop floor, his head bowed, and took his wife in his arms. Then, looking up at Paul, he spoke for the first time.

'Please be gentle with her, that's all I ask of you.'

Liam was about to say something, but Paul placed a restraining hand on his arm and just nodded at Uncle Freddie.

Had he and David got it wrong all this time? Liam asked himself the question as they began a systematic search of the accommodation, which was on three floors above the shop.

Each room was immaculately furnished, the bedroom wardrobes full of men's and women's clothing which were certainly not of the sizes of Frederic and Theresa Stromberti, but they found nothing which was incriminating. Parked around the back of the premises was a fairly new Mercedes and a sign-written Transit, which Freddie obviously used for collecting and delivering fruit and vegetables, but again they contained nothing of significance.

'What else do you think he uses the van for, Liam? Collecting and delivering the Karims, or perhaps delivering their cargo, human or otherwise? Let's get it printed and circulate a picture of the van around the airports, someone might recognise it.'

'I still don't think the Karims stay here, Paul. There has got to be another house somewhere closer to the river with a mooring for a small cruiser which gives them their mobility. Let's get back and interrogate those two. At least Aunty has admitted to knowing that Abdul is still alive and Uncle Freddie seemed resigned to his fate!'

They were exiting the alleyway when a car window shattered in front of them and, as the two men hit the pavement, bullets ricocheted off the ground from all angles.

'They're using silencers, Liam, I can't pinpoint the direction. Get hold of Colin and Jean!'

From a front bedroom window Colin acknowledged their call as he spotted the two trapped men lying on the pavement.

'Try and draw their fire, Liam, I have a good view from here. Jean will be coming out of the front door as soon as I give the word, but we have to be careful as there are a lot of people around.'

Liam rolled away from the refuge of the car, back towards the safety of the alley, and was met by another volley of bullets.

'Got them, Liam. Grey Ford Granada Estate on the other side of the road, three occupants including the driver. I'm going for the tyres first. Jean, the target is to your right one hundred yards up the road but be careful there are a lot of public in the vicinity.'

As Colin began firing, the car leapt forward, burning rubber as it screeched towards the downed officers. Jean ran out of the shop in to the middle of the road, shooting at the oncoming vehicle and shattering its windscreen.

The car careered towards her, its driver struggling to control the stricken vehicle as it smashed into various stationary cars, and she hit the road, rolling out of its path just in time. All four officers began firing at the rear end, breaking the lights and window, but the Granada somehow kept going.

People were running and screaming everywhere which forced them to cease firing, and the car disappeared up the road, scattering pedestrians and forcing other motorists to pull over. Liam called in for help while Paul ran to Jean, who was still lying on the ground. She'd taken a bullet to the thigh but luckily it had gone straight through and, although she was bleeding quite badly, she was more shocked than injured.

Once again they had been set up, their lives threatened, and unearthing the source of the leak was now as much a priority as finding Anna Karim. One or both had to be discovered quickly before their luck ran out, and all the while growing in Liam's mind was the belief that maybe the Strombertis had been the missing link all along. As the local police sealed off the area, DI Watkinson arrived, and he brought with him Mark Burley and John Lindsey as replacement back-up.

He also brought them the bad news that, as expected, the DI's snout from the Waterloo Station meet had been found floating in the river that morning, which ended any chance that they might have had of quickly tracing the leak. They decided to strip-search the property this time, not quite sure of what they were looking for, but hoping for something. Emptying drawers, lifting carpets, and moving furniture, they went from room to room until Liam found that something.

In one of the bedrooms he had removed a fire screen and, reaching up the chimney, discovered a brick shelf with a polythene bag on it. Inside were four passports, two for each of the Karims; Aunty and Uncle were up to their necks in it now and Paul and Liam couldn't wait to return to question them.

The pictures of Abdul were undoubtedly him, despite the beard and change of hairstyle, although Anna was completely unrecognisable. Gone was the long black hair, replaced by a short auburn crop, and she had aged considerably. What this find also meant was that, where witnesses had failed to identify Anna previously, perhaps now they could.

On their return to the Yard they were surprised to find that Uncle Freddie was already waiting for them in the interview room. The big man said nothing as they entered and just sat there staring into space as Paul sat down opposite him and switched on the tape machine.

'I have to inform you, Mr Stromberti, that our conversation will be recorded and may be used in evidence against you, so I need your approval before we continue.'

Freddie looked at Paul with heavy sad eyes.

'I beg of you once again, Sergeant. Will you try and keep my beautiful Theresa out of prison? She has suffered all her life and has not been deeply involved in any of what I'm about to tell you.'

'But she has been involved, so I can't make promises here and now but, providing you don't waste our time, I will personally look into it, is that fair enough?'

Freddie nodded and, as if he had rehearsed his story for years in readiness for this inevitable moment, he began:

'Theresa and I came to England almost fifty years ago to try and start a new life, away from Italy, away from the family. When she was thirteen she had been shot in the stomach, during a police raid, which was why we couldn't have children. This affected her badly so, after we had got married, her brother Illario gave us his blessing to leave, together with some money from the family funds.

With this we bought the shop and everything was going well for us until 1965 when he phoned to say that my brother and sister-in-law had been killed, orphaning their three children.

He felt it would be better if the children too left Italy and Theresa jumped at the chance of a ready-made family, especially her sister's children. Immediately there were problems with them at school, the language barrier being broken by sheer violence and, although only ten years old, the twins were already bitter and twisted against all authority.

My wife and I were forever visiting the school or the local police station, where the boys would end up after beating up some poor innocent who wouldn't give up his pocket money, or his lunch box. After a year they were all taken from us and placed in a preventive care home, but this did not change them. It only hardened their resolve that the world was against them, that they would take what they wanted, when they wanted it, and by any means possible.

Anna was released back into our custody on her sixteenth birthday, and started serving in the shop and helping around the house, but she never had enough money. She began walking the streets and soon got herself arrested for the first time. Then the twins returned and, with no intention of working, began roaming the streets, forming a gang with other local delinquents, robbing and terrifying the neighbourhood.

They went down for their first stretch, along with Anna, in 1975 and on her release we were introduced to Abdul Karim.

My Anna was not the marrying type, no man could control her, but she wouldn't listen to us and went ahead and married that damned Arab – I still don't know why, he was evil.'

Freddie disappeared into the past, a silence descending over the interview room as he became lost in his memories. Liam quickly lost patience with the man.

141

'Stromberti, stop stalling and get on with it.'

He turned with a start towards Liam then did as he was told.

'Shortly afterwards, Abdul and Anna went back to Italy for a couple of weeks and when they returned they, and the twins, all moved into a house they had bought in Islington. In the meantime Illario had phoned to say that they were going to start a canned fruit importing business and would I help them with the distribution until they got established. The property in Islington had a small warehouse attached and we would collect the boxes from another warehouse on the river at Bermondsey.'

'The Thames River Trading Co.?' Paul interrupted.

'Yes, that's the one. From there we would take the boxes back to Islington for distribution to various shops in and around London.'

'Did you ever take any back to your own shop, for sale?'

'Come on, Sergeant. You know as well as I do what the family is all about and I didn't want to get that involved. I drew the line when it came to drugs and my own business.'

Paul hid his pleasure at this confession as he caught Liam's eye.

'But you were involved, Freddie. You were willingly ferrying boxes of drugs around London and the home counties, knowing the misery that they would cause families everywhere.'

At this he broke down, and the big proud Italian became a shadow of his former self as he laid his head on his arms on the desk and fought back the tears. The betrayal of his family was hurting him badly and the guilt he had lived with for so many years had finally caught up with him.

'Freddie, do you want a break?'

As if he hadn't heard Paul he sat up, back in control of himself, and continued from where he had left off, the only important thing to him now was the purging of his soul.

'Blood is thicker than water, Sergeant. We are family no matter what, and we look after each other. That is our way. Theresa and

142

I had what we had because of the family and we were obliged to help Anna and her brothers.'

Liam interrupted. 'Where was Abdul Karim during this time?'

'Abdul would come and go regularly. I never asked questions, although I did see him from time to time at one of the shops I delivered to.'

'Do you remember any of the addresses?'

'No. We would deliver to the same three or four shops for about four months, then there would be new ones. The old ones we passed were closed down, and we never went back to old addresses. Gradually they used me less and less and our lives returned to normal until 1986, when Abdul and Anna were arrested following a raid on the Islington address.

Although we were questioned, and our premises searched, no charges were laid against us or the twins. Illario contacted me and once again I agreed to help with distribution from a warehouse down by the old KGV docks. There was a relative of Abdul's who was running the show, with the twins around as muscle and debt collectors.'

Paul and Liam glanced at each other, the same thought running through their minds. Was he the poor unfortunate who was lying six feet under?

'The twins moved back to live with us above the shop and, as before, my involvement became less and less. Anna and Abdul had protected us all, by not naming names, and once again the family closed ranks.'

At this point, Liam, sensing that Freddie was tiring, suggested a break.

'Thank you, Freddie. I think you need to have a rest and something to eat, we'll continue this in an hour's time.' Freddie said nothing in reply as two officers led him from the room, his head bowed, Paul looking at the man dispassionately.

The two men's disappointment at the results of their interrogation was further compounded by the news that, as Uncle Freddie had said, Theresa Stromberti knew very little and had been very uncooperative, spending most of the time mouthing the same old vitriol. Although they could charge Uncle Freddie, they were no nearer to the Karims or to who had murdered David, so they decided to persevere as he obviously had a lot more to say and maybe something would come out of it. He was their only hope apart from William Legg, who still was refusing to cooperate, and the twins, who were temporarily out of reach.

26

As the air in his lungs ran out, Matthew tried hard not to swallow the foul water as he made his way to the surface. Where were they? Treading water, he desperately looked around him, trying to spot some movement somewhere, then he saw a jetty with a ladder about 100 metres from his vehicle and struck out in its direction.

With the rifle still in his hand he gingerly raised his head above the jetty level and, convinced that it was safe, he hauled himself out of the water and made a dash for the four-wheel-drive. If they had witnessed the whole scene they would now know he was armed, but Matthew was certain that he had panicked unduly and that they were just sitting somewhere watching the tracking monitor. Not knowing what their intentions were, he decided that his first priority was to clean and assemble the rifle, and then get out of the foul-smelling clothes so, starting the motor, he set off for the old family home.

He had sold the property to a French couple who, like his parents, only wanted it for a holiday home, and he was gambling on their not being in residence as he made his way up the steep winding drive. Where it entered the property there was a track off to the left which led into the surrounding woodland, and Matthew drove deep into the trees.

They would be on his territory now; from here he could change, clean and assemble the rifle, and control the play. When

145

he got out he thought he heard the distant sound of a car engine, which stopped almost immediately, so he quickly made his way around the side of the house to where the swimming pool was situated. As luck would have it they had changed nothing. The shower and changing room were unlocked; his father had never seen the need to secure these areas and neither, it seems, had the new owners.

He'd only just got himself comfortable when two armed men came into view, the same two as earlier. This was good news because it meant that they were working as a duo without back-up, which would make his task simpler. As they cautiously moved from tree to tree he took aim and fired, removing one man's ear lobe and, as he fell to the ground, the Australian froze on the spot.

'Now throw both guns as far as you possibly can, Aussie.'

With his partner writhing in agony beside him he did as he was told, and Matthew could see that he was trying to pinpoint his position so he fired another round into the ground beside him, which brought him up short.

Realising that his task was hopeless he put his hands together behind his neck, a movement which confirmed to Matthew that these two were trained professionals and, as such, would have to be watched very carefully.

'Let's have the truth, now. You know I can despatch the pair of you anytime I want.'

'Let me help my mate first, damn you. You could have blown his fucking head off.'

'I will with the next bullet unless you stop stalling.' Matthew could see the confusion on the man's face as his voice rang around the trees.

'If you kill us, there will be others.'

'They will end up the same way. The choice is yours and the clock is ticking.'

'You are a wealthy young man now, surely you want to live to a ripe old age and enjoy that money.'

146

Matthew ignored him, patiently waiting. It was his partner who spoke next as he realised that the Australian's attempt to talk their way out of this wasn't going to work.

'Let him get me to a hospital, for Christ's sake. We'll meet you on the boat tonight.'

'What's this all about? You're going to bleed a lot more until I know.'

'Your father's death. Our employer has a mutual interest in that and sent us to find you.'

'I know, I've opened the envelope. So tell me something I don't know, for example, why this fiasco? '

'We were told to test you out, see if you were as good as our boss had heard. That's her picture and it's her you'll be meeting.'

'Don't go to the hospital in town. Go along the coast a bit further south, there's a retreat on the main road that asks no questions – The Sisters of Mercy – you can't miss it. I'll see you at the boat tonight.'

When they had gone, Matthew sat down by the pool, wondering just what this beautiful women was up to, and what did she expect of him. To have been able to learn of his other world meant that she must have powerful connections, and that she wanted somebody removed, but he would not risk returning to England. Of one thing he was certain, they didn't have orders to kill him. Although, after today, there were now two more people in this world who he would have to look out for.

Removing the bug from the four track, he set off for the house in the mountains; he would let them sweat for a day or two then, when he was ready, he'd go back to Ajaccio. After unpacking the car his first task was to dismantle the rifle, clean and oil it, and then stash it in the hiding place he'd thought of the night before. Although nobody ever seemed to appear within the vicinity of the house, he was taking no chances, the boat was compromised now so he would have to keep the rifle here.

Lighting the gas lamps he began the usual routine with the newspapers that had accumulated, glancing at the headlines and

147

searching for the personal column. As the pile diminished, his thoughts drifted back to the day's events and what effect they would have on his future security. Would he have to leave the island totally, or just sell the boat? His reverie was broken as the headline leapt from the paper he was holding:

Duke and Duchess of Braeside
robbed at gunpoint

Early yesterday morning, the Duke and Duchess of Braeside were discovered in their stables, bound and gagged.

Although they were unharmed they have been detained in hospital, for observation, and are unable to make a statement at present. They were found by their gardener who has, however, confirmed that the house had been selectively stripped of priceless paintings, furniture and silver. This is the fourth such robbery of the nobility in the past two years, a police spokesman confirming that they were almost certain that they were all the work of the same gang. However, their investigations, including the hunt for the killer of the Duke of Rushtington during a robbery at his home, were still no further forward despite a concerted police effort.

Balling the newspaper he tossed it angrily into the fire, he had to finish this but how? And where were today's events leading him? His curiosity got the better of him, so he reopened the envelope and sat staring at the photograph of this irresistible women, the alarm bells ringing clearly in his head. She had hold of him and, like a dog with a new bone, she wasn't going to let go, that was for certain. It was no good, he couldn't wait any longer, he had to get to Paris and quickly.

France, November 2000

Although he had been tempted by the thought of being waited on hand and foot, he decided not to stay at the Hotel Crillon as it would not have been practical. For a start the staff knew him well and he needed anonymity and, secondly, the place was far too busy, which would make it difficult to observe his client. So, after leaving her a message, he booked in to a small hotel on the Boulevard Raspail, deciding to bring the game to him.

For over an hour the next morning Matthew stood in the doorway of his hotel observing the Café de la Paix just down the street, and although there appeared to be nothing untoward happening in its vicinity, his instincts were telling him differently.

Leaving it to the last possible moment before the rendezvous time, he left the safety of the hotel and proceeded warily along the Boulevard, uncertain as to where the trouble would come from but knowing that it wasn't far away As he had hoped, she arrived in a taxi and, before she could get out, he got in alongside her, telling the driver in perfect French the destination. As the cab pulled away Matthew turned in the seat and spotted the trouble: the Australian and his bandaged partner had just left an adjacent store and were running up the street after them, frantically trying to hail a passing taxi to no avail.

'How do I address you?' She appeared totally unfazed by the events of the past two minutes.

'Matthew will do.'

'Well, good morning, Matthew. I'm Consuela del Cabellorenti. You are as good as I've heard, but please don't shoot any more of my people.'

'Pull over.' This time in English, Matthew gave the instruction and the taxi driver did as he was ordered before he realised his mistake.

Matthew hauled her out of the taxi before he could drive off

149

again and, as the driver tried to leave the cab, Matthew kicked the door in his face.

'Now tell him to disappear, preferably in English as he seems to understand that as well.'

'You are a vicious bastard.'

'And you are a scheming cow, now get rid of him.'

As the taxi drove off Matthew hailed another, and on reaching its destination he half dragged her across the street and into a nearby café where he found a corner booth.

'Empty your bag on the table.'

During all this time she had not said a word and she looked at him defiantly, then relented as she felt the pressure on her wrist, sensing he could snap it in two if he wanted to. She wasn't armed and what he was looking for wasn't in the bag, but in the lining. It was the same type of bug that the Australian had put on the four track. Matthew crushed it under his heel before releasing her wrist.

A concerned-looking proprietor approached the table and Matthew returned to his charming self as he ordered coffee and ham baguettes, then he fell silent. He had hurt her, and more than anything else in this world he hated violence towards women, but he consoled himself with the fact that she had left him no alternative.

'Are you all right? Why couldn't you have trusted me instead of bringing along that bunch of morons?'

'I'm sorry, it isn't you that I don't trust. There is too much at stake to take any chances so they were here for both of us, although I realise now you don't need anyone else.'

'You're a good actress, I'll say that for you. What's your real name?'

'That is my real married name. My husband is the Count Cabellorenti of Turin, although now we live in England.'

As the waiter arrived with their order, Consuela began her tale. Matthew, only half listening, was totally captivated by her charm and beauty, soon realising that she was capable of manipulating any man. Never had he felt such excitement coursing through his body as he fought to regain the upper hand, a battle he was in danger of losing unless he walked away now.

'How can I trust you? How do I know that you are telling me the truth?' Matthew just wanted to throw all caution to the wind in the hope that he could somehow spend more time with this wonderful woman, but he had to be certain.

Those dark, soulful eyes penetrated his entire being as she finished her coffee and stood up to leave.

'Whatever else I am, or might have been in the past, I have never reneged on a deal. You know where to find me.'

He took hold of her wrist again, but this time with a gentleness of touch as he indicated for her to sit down – Consuela smiled and nodded agreement.

Alone again in his hotel room, Matthew paced the floor, his mind and body reeling from the after-effects of an afternoon spent in the arms of Consuela Cabellorenti. Women, and the emotional strings that come with the package, had never before plundered the depths of his emotions but, in a few short hours, this women had stripped his being bare.

For twenty-six years his whole world had revolved around self-discipline and, if he didn't regain control of himself, he knew this women would be his downfall. He'd known from that first moment, when he had opened the envelope, that he was trapped, and what the consequences would be. It wasn't just sex that was her attraction, it was her whole being, her smile, the smell of her perfume, her gaiety: all thoughts that could cross his mind at the wrong moment and cost him his life.

Now, if he was to survive in the future, there must not be any more distractions of the Consuela kind. Exactly what path his life would take from now on he did not know but of one thing he was certain, he had to leave Paris immediately and return to the solitude of his mountain retreat before he totally lost all reasoning.

His biggest concern now was that she could expose him when-ever she wanted to and if she had been able to discover his double life, how easy would it be for others to do the same? As he packed his bag his mind was in turmoil, knowing that his entire world had been irrevocably turned upside down.

27

As soon as Freddie was led back in he continued from where he had left off.

'The twins moved out again, around 1991, to an address in Dorking which their sister had bought. Shortly afterwards they went back to prison and Illario phoned once again to ask for my help. This time, I refused: I had had enough and, after an almighty row with Illario, I cut my ties with the family and even Anna and Abdul didn't contact us when they were discharged from prison. We were traitors in their eyes but I didn't care, as far as I was concerned we had repaid our debt and owed them nothing.

Then, out of the blue, she phoned to say that Abdul had had a bad car crash in South Africa and was not expected to live. She asked if she could borrow the van as theirs was at the airport and they didn't have time to collect it. I refused at first but, as ever, Anna twisted me around her little finger – that was something that hadn't changed.

They didn't come to the shop – her instructions were to leave it somewhere along the river and collect it from there two days later. This happened several times over the next few months and it was always at a different place.'

'Tell me, Freddie, where is Anna's riverside home?' Liam could not wait any longer.

'On my wife's life, they have never told us.'

'But she does have a riverside address?'

153

'I honestly don't know if it is on the river or not, we don't even have a phone number, but she does use a small cruiser to get around the city.'

'Freddie, I don't believe any of this crap!' Liam looked at him hard and long as he continued. 'They stay with you when they are not in Dorking, your wardrobes are full of their clothes, and we found these up one of your chimneys.' He threw the passports on the table and Freddie looked at them in utter astonishment.

'Believe me, I have never seen these before. As for the clothes: I collected them from Dorking a couple of days ago after Anna had phoned to say that she was selling the house and asked if I would clear the place for her. She wanted us to store the stuff until she found a new home.'

'OK, Freddie, carry on.' Liam's disappointment was evident in his voice, but at least his theory about a river boat had been confirmed.

'The next time I heard from Anna was when she called to say that Abdul had made a miraculous recovery and would be returning to England shortly. He needed special hospital treatment, which he could only get in London, and would we put him up for a few days along with the twins and two of their friends?

Joseph and Luigi duly arrived, along with two other men, and three days later they came home with Abdul. The television was full of a daring daylight raid on a police van and Abdul's picture was everywhere.'

Paul slid the photographs of Mackinley and Legg across the table but Freddie barely glanced at them.

'That's them. When they got back, I took them all in the van to a riverside meeting place where the cruiser was waiting.'

'You know, Freddie, that you are in a lot of deep water here and it's going to be very difficult to keep you out of prison unless you give us a lot more.'

'Please, Sergeant, I beg of you. I am seventy-four years old and I have had enough, which is why I'm telling you all this. I am not proud of what I have done, or what I am doing now, all I ask is to spend my last years with Theresa somewhere warm and away from all this. Even if I have to go to prison for a while, I ask you once again to keep Theresa out of everything. Her only crime was being born a Massimo.'

'Tell me, Freddie, when did you last see my brother?'

The abrupt change of questioning caught him off-guard, and he suddenly looked frightened and began sweating profusely as Paul repeated the question.

'About a month ago. He came to the shop and started asking questions about Anna and Abdul – where had I last seen them and where did they live?'

Liam's shocked expression said it all, Paul had been proved right. Somehow, David had discovered the truth and, for whatever reason, had gone solo, conducting his own investigation without telling anybody.

'What did my brother tell you?'

Freddie just sat there staring at the wall as the realisation of the enormity of his involvement sank in. 'The South African' had called twice and he had told Anna about the conversations the next time she had phoned. Now he was dead.

'Come on, Freddie, what did my brother tell you?' Paul was standing in front of him now, his eyes penetrating this crumbling man.

'He told me that he knew of my involvement in the freeing of Abdul and that I was facing a prison sentence. He said he knew that Abdul was still alive and that the body Anna had identified as Abdul's, was in fact a relative of his. All he wanted was their address and, in return, he would keep me out of it. Despite my protesting that I didn't have any idea where they were he said he would give me a couple of days to think about things.'

'What happened next?'

'Your brother returned as threatened. At first he still did not believe me. Then, when he realised that I was telling him the truth, he told me all about the human trafficking. How Abdul would recruit the carriers in Africa, how they obtained the drugs, and what sometimes happened to them on the journey here.'

Paul took out the photograph of Paolo Stromberti. 'Do you know who this is, Freddie?'

'No, but I would say he's family. Probably one of my brother's sons at a guess.'

'You're right. Paolo Stromberti. We arrested him some time ago and he is in prison in Durban awaiting trial. He ran the operation in South Africa and was Anna's and Abdul's contact there, canning the fruit that you distributed and processing the packets for the human carriers.'

This proved the final straw for Freddie and, as he slumped in his chair, the tears poured from his guilt-wracked body. They patiently waited until he had calmed down, Paul then deciding that that was enough for one day.

As he was led from the room, Freddie turned to Paul and whispered: 'Anything, Sergeant, anything else I can remember I will send for you. It's personal now, it's time to put an end to this madness.'

28

France, November 2000

He flew in to Nice and took a taxi to Antibes, where he had moored the cruiser, intending to leave it there for sale, but now he was not so sure as he sat in the saloon once again thinking about Consuela.

Of one thing he had been right. She was an actress who had left her native Venezuela to further her career in Europe, joining a touring company in Spain which one day arrived in Turin. The Count, who was patron of the arts in the city, never missed a performance the whole time that they were there, his personal generosity to the whole troupe overwhelming. From Turin they had toured all the major Italian towns and cities before returning there, where once again the Count was present for their first night.

Although he was in his mid-sixties he had loved the after-show partying, dancing and drinking the night away, always the life and soul of the party. When he proposed to her, Consuela had not hesitated, she loved him more than life itself and still did today despite his failing health. When she spoke of her husband Matthew had sensed that here she was not acting, that for her he was the most important thing in her life.

As for the rest of her story, Matthew was undecided. The carrot was that she thought she knew who was behind the stately home robberies and, therefore, who was indirectly responsible for his father's murder. In return she wanted the removal of someone who was 'a major obstacle in my life' without going in to any great detail, just handing him a photo and an address.

His strict code of non-involvement with a client had been broken and he couldn't wait to see her again. So instead of sailing for Corsica, Matthew set a course for Genoa, his heart ruling his head, not even thinking of what could be the consequences of his actions.

Italy, December 2000

He had stalked his prey for four days now, the pattern as regular as clockwork, his choices of place to make the hit multiple. In a bustling, noisy city like Turin it was easier to blend in to the surroundings despite his height, which up to the incident in Ajaccio had never bothered him before.

Choosing a hotel, not for its rating but because it had three exits and rooms that were not overlooked, he settled down and began the long wait, passing the hours trying hard not to think of Consuela and failing miserably. Then he thought of his father, which was the main reason that he was here, and this restored some of his former self but, as the target came into sight, he felt no rising excitement and he knew then that it would never be the same again.

France, December 2000

She had agreed to meet him in Paris in the first week of December and Matthew was alarmed and very disappointed to find a note waiting for him at the hotel: 'My husband has had a stroke and I have returned to be with him. I will contact you soon, Consuela.'

A whole range of contradictory feelings set in and, with his anger mounting, he hastily left the city and booked himself on the first flight to Ajaccio, all the while fighting a deep temptation to fly to England to try and find her.

She never left his mind on the journey down and once more he felt all those dormant emotions rising to the fore again, but common sense prevailed as he realised that any hasty action now could prove his undoing

Corsica, January 2001

Despite the harsh winter weather he passed the days walking the multitude of mountain tracks, the solitude and the challenge for survival slowly restoring his equilibrium, although he was still convinced that he had been duped. Once a week he went down to Ajaccio to collect the papers and have lunch and although the food was as good as ever, and Claudia as lovely, he began to get restless, the longing for some action returning once again.

He had thought about sailing south to escape the winter damp, but he knew deep down that that would not fulfil the need that was gnawing away at his soul.

Release came at the end of the month when, in reply to a message in *The Times*, Matthew found himself in the Middle East, and he was thankful to have the warmth on his back once again but, more importantly, the chance once more to walk the thin line between life and death. The constant danger and fear of exposure were still food and drink to him and always would be. Nevertheless, he hated the desert and the dust, the flies and the stinking camels, and he was pleased when it was all over, even more pleased to return to his beloved Corsica.

He loved Ajaccio too much to leave it; nowhere else on the island held the same fascination for him, so he decided to take his chances and stay, although he made one change to his arrangements. He found a private jetty just outside the city where he could berth the cruiser in relative secrecy, and had various security arrangements installed for back-up.

Matthew wandered down to the harbour, his only thoughts these days being for his father and how he could finally lay him to rest in peace. Perhaps when that happened he would reassess his life but, for the moment, his world still revolved around the personal column of *The Times*. Although the thrill had been extinguished, he was still a trained killer, that was something which could never be removed from his soul, the money being immaterial to him as he travelled the globe, plying his trade, not caring about who or where or why.

Corsica, September 2001

It had been eighteen months since the death of his father and, although there had been further robberies, the news reports stated that the police were still no nearer to finding the gang, or his killer. Up to now Matthew had resisted the urge to return to England: what was the point if the police were no further forward? Then his thoughts returned to Consuela.

He had dismissed as total fabrication all that she had told him that day in Paris, his hurt pride dictating his actions since. He had not even contacted the hotel again to see if there was indeed another message for him, but for some inexplicable reason he felt her presence growing daily and, no matter how hard he tried to forget her, she was always there in his thoughts.

Deciding that a couple of hours in the company of Claudia would be therapeutic, Matthew locked the house and drove down to the harbour at Ajaccio. The mountains and the solitude of his life there would always be his first choice, but there was something about the hustle and bustle of the busy port that he found irresistible as he wandered along the quay, oblivious to the storm that raged all about him.

He heard his name being called first then everything became a blur as he found himself standing in the pouring rain with Consuela in his arms, clinging tightly to him, the pair of them not wanting to let go.

Matthew had been wrong, something she would not let him

forget as she playfully teased him over the next few days. She had sent a further message and, when he had not contacted her, she had sent another, but until now she had been unable to come and find him herself, not trusting to send her bodyguards, who had vowed revenge on Matthew.

The Count had died, not as a result of the stroke but of complications that had set in afterwards. It had been a long, slow death during which time Consuela had never left his side, and even now she was struggling to come to terms with her loss. He could tell that she was flat, her sparkle dimmed, but he didn't care, she was with him now and, for whatever reason, she had sought him out.

They stayed on the cruiser, going out most days around the island or across to Sardinia, Matthew resisting the temptation to take her up to his mountain retreat, deciding that the house should remain his own private haven. She had told him that everybody thought that she had gone home to Venezuela, which Matthew accepted but not without reservations, and on her return she would decide on whether to sell up or stay.

It all seemed so plausible and then she told him the part of the deal he had been waiting for, who she thought was responsible for the series of robberies of country estates, and why she had come to these conclusions.

'The Count was one of the leading experts on eighteenth-century French furniture and we have a priceless collection at our home in Wokingham, as well as several pieces on exhibition in Turin. There are others who would lay claim to this collection but he assured me that he was the legitimate owner and, when he died, they would be my inheritance. That is why he hired a private security firm, not to guard the furniture but to protect me from the family who knew of his intentions.

About two years ago we were introduced to a gentleman at one of those many boring garden parties which I am sure you remember well, the Earl of Thatcham. He was supposedly an expert himself on French period furniture and very quickly became a good friend of my husband's, visiting us on several occasions at Wokingham.'

Matthew couldn't place the name, but he remembered his father telling him once that he had met someone very knowledgeable in antiques, and that he was advising him on the values of the various family heirlooms for insurance purposes.

'We had heard rumours that he was a fairly undesirable character so my husband had him investigated. It turned out that he was unmarried and lived not too far from us in a run-down mansion with several acres of arable farmland, which he rents out. He also owns a large antique gallery in Chelsea which has among its clientele several cabinet ministers and members of the royal household, and his grandfather made the family fortune mostly from land deals in the Caribbean.

He left him a sizeable trust fund to live on but this, plus the other various forms of income, appear not to be sufficient enough to fund his lifestyle which revolves around young men and cocaine. He is reportedly always only one step away from bankruptcy.'

Matthew thought back to those days, the never-ending merry-go-round of garden parties and charity events, the procession of people trying to fit in where they didn't belong. He imagined the Earl fitted in to this category, his own kind gentle parents being part of the social circle obliged to entertain him. They were happiest when mixing with the local community at the village pub, or out hunting with the farmers and estate workers, as was Matthew himself.

'Where are you, Matthew? I don't think you have heard a word I've said.'

'Sorry. I was thinking of my parents and how easy it would have been for the Earl to gain their confidence and trust.'

'That's what I was saying. Despite the negative report, my husband continued to invite him to the house, and we have both visited the gallery on several occasions. He is a very charming and likeable person who appears to be very knowledgeable not only about the furniture but antiques in general. He even phoned

162

up last week to offer his condolences and to say that, should I need to dispose of anything, he would be only to happy to advise and help.'

'I'm sure he would,' replied Matthew. 'Obviously he doesn't partake in the actual robbery but I go along with your suspicions. He would have gained an intimate knowledge of the property, the value of the contents, security systems, etc., and he has in the gallery the perfect front to dispose of the goods. In fact, I would think that he has sold most of the stuff before it's stolen.'

'Exactly, and now that my husband has died our house will probably be his next target.'

'Why don't you just tell the police of your suspicions? They could stake out the property and catch the gang red-handed, and I'm sure they would find something at one of the Earl's properties to incriminate him or someone would talk.'

'What about your father? We struck a deal, Matthew, and, as I said in Paris, I am a person of my word. Don't you want the people responsible for his death?'

He'd spent endless hours thinking about nothing else, planning for this moment, but had always ended up confronted by the same obstacle. Even if he came face to face with the gang, how could he identify the guilty person? What was the point of knowing all this if he couldn't take it any further? He'd been blinded by anger but in the cold light of day it seemed an impossible task.

Then there was Consuela herself. Matthew had rebuilt the wall and this time she hadn't breached it completely, so how much of this was truth and how much was fiction? Did she have an ulterior motive? He was leaving for Africa in two days and it would be interesting to see how she reacted to this news.

29

London, October 2003

'William Geoffrey Legg, you are charged that on Wednesday 15th September 1999 you did, in cooperation with others, unlawfully remove from police custody one Abdul Karim, and that you did conspire to the murder of a person as yet unidentified. Do you have anything to say to these charges? I must warn you that anything you do say will be taken down and may be used in evidence against you.'

Legg remained silent, staring at the floor.

'The accused said nothing,' DI Watkinson continued. 'Take him to his cell.'

At last they could lay other charges on the Barollis and issue a warrant for the arrest of Andrew Mackinley, something that Liam couldn't wait to do, but the DCS tempered their enthusiasm by telling them it would not be possible that night and they would have to wait till the morning.

On their way back to the squad room Paul was handed a fax from Durban which confirmed his suspicions; the Lear jet had made three trips within the preceding ten days, the last landing three days ago. On board were nine people, eight of Italian nationality and one Arab, and as yet the captain had not filed a return flight plan.

'That's it, Liam. We've been targeting the wrong airport. Abdul Karim comes and goes not from Heathrow, but Gatwick. That was why they bought the house at Dorking, it's only twenty minutes from the airport. He catches a schedule to any one of the national airports in Italy, then the Lear takes him on to Africa.'

'Do you think they would use that route sometimes for the human trafficking?'

'No. It's too long, and therefore too much of a gamble, although Anna could come and go as she pleases, which would explain why she hasn't been seen much around town.'

'I still think she has a house somewhere along the river, and Freddie has confirmed that she uses a cruiser. Let's call it a day now, tomorrow could be very interesting.'

When they entered Pentonville the next morning the two men immediately felt the friction in the air, that feeling of tension that something big was about to happen that was peculiar to prisons. The word was out, nothing ever seemed to stay secret inside, and as they entered the interview room the intimidating rumbling sounds of voices began to reverberate around the walls and the slow, scary tapping of the metal heating pipes and radiators filled their ears. The place was a powder keg ready to explode.

Luigi was led in grinning from ear to ear, the cocky bravado was back, and Liam couldn't wait to wipe the smile from his face.

'You two are in trouble now. Don't you understand English? We're off-limits.'

'You have two choices, Barolli. You can either sit down and shut it, or you can go down for the rest of your life.'

'Not another one of your games, Jameson. I want my brief informed of this intrusion, in fact I want my brief here now.'

'He's on his way as we speak, so are you going to listen to us or not?'

Luigi looked from one to the other, the smug smile slowly disappearing from his face as he realised that this was serious: he sat down.

'That's better. Now, what we've come to tell you is that we have had a long chat with your Uncle Freddie and, as a result, your friend Billy Legg has been charged with the freeing of Abdul Karim and the murder of a person as yet unidentified. The same charges will be laid to you, your brother and your other friend, Andrew Mackinley, plus various charges connected with the trafficking of narcotic substances. You are going down big time, Luigi, unless we get that address and we get it now.'

He sat there silently, there were no denials, the bluffing was over and when he spoke the words were, in their own way, a confession of guilt.

'What's in it for me?'

'We can't make promises, you know that, but you certainly won't spend the rest of your life in here. It's for the lawyers to sort out and we'll get your brother the same deal.'

'Get my brief in here before I decide anything.'

'He should be waiting outside by now. Remember, no more games or you will never see the outside world again.'

Half an hour later Luigi's solicitor emerged and, after handing Paul a slip of paper, left without saying a word. Just then Liam's mobile rang, it was DI Watkinson.

'Where are you, Liam?'

'We are just about to leave Pentonville. We've got it, sir.'

'That's great news but I'm afraid you can't leave the prison yet. You had better give me Anna's address now so I can get things set up this end, we don't want to leave it till you get back, time isn't on our side. Your back-up has called in to say that some sort of reception committee is forming in the surrounding streets, waiting for you to appear so, until I can get you some more support, you're not to go anywhere. There are at least three vehicles cruising the area, two four tracks and a white transit van that they are certain of and, on their second pass, they managed to get the number of one of the four tracks which was stolen from Esher only this morning.

I've asked for three fully armed units, which should be with you in twenty minutes, and the roads to be cleared. Mark and John are under strict instructions not to break cover until I tell them to. When I give you the word you are to exit left from the prison, down the Caledonian Road with lights and siren on. I

166

want no heroics from you two, this sounds as heavy as it is likely to get. I have other units going in to place so your backs will be covered all the way home. You will have an open line the whole time. Good luck.'

The nerve-wracking noise within the prison was reaching fever pitch as the two men sat waiting in the car behind the outer doors, Paul having drawn his gun and removed the safety catch. The wait seemed an eternity, the two men tense and silent, knowing that their lives now were in the hands of others.

'Go.' The DI's voice broke the tension. As Liam switched on the lights and siren the giant doors swung open and he put his foot to the floor. Through the doors and turning left, as instructed, Paul glanced in the wing mirror to see a white van pull out behind them. Its path was immediately blocked by an unmarked van, armed officers spilling from it, as the traffic seemed to part in front of them. Paul called out their position as Liam turned left down the Grays Inn Road where they were suddenly confronted by a four track, which he just managed to avoid by turning across it in to Theobalds Road, then left down Red Lion Street.

'There's a four track on our back, we're coming down Red Lion Street heading for High Holborn but no sight yet of the other one.'

'It's already taken care of. Turn right and left down Kingsway and I'll have the one on your back intercepted before you get to the Aldwych where there is an escort waiting to bring you in.'

As they passed Portugal Street, an unmarked car pulled across the road behind them, but Liam didn't look to see what happened, he just kept going until he saw the flashing lights of the escort car ahead. As they went around the Aldwych, another car fell in behind, and without further incident they arrived back at the Yard to find a very relieved but angry DI. He had been hauled over the coals, as in fact had all his superiors up the line; the politicians were getting involved.

'This is now beyond a joke, gentlemen. Too many lives are

being threatened and questions are being asked, we have to end this and end this soon – that's an order from way on high.

The media coverage is crucifying us and unless we get a result by the end of the week we're to back off. The Commissioner is at No.10 as we speak, explaining our position to the PM, and after this afternoon's episode I hate to think what the tabloids will print tomorrow.'

He threw the morning editions on the desk in disgust, the banner headlines screaming for explanations 'Our lawless capital' 'Have the police lost control' 'Is it safe to walk our streets, Mr Prime Minister?' 'How long before someone dies?'

'It's obvious from reading these that someone has fabricated a story, blowing the whole situation out of proportion, and fed it to the press. Let's go and lift that bitch of a woman and maybe, then, we can all sleep a little easier tonight.'

South Africa, July 2003

It was almost morning and the cold breeze coming off the Indian Ocean blew across the plain. Jomo Banzuto pulled the blanket up around his neck as he sat guarding the cattle that were his village's wealth, awaiting the dawn, whose beauty had mesmerised him for over thirty years.

Whilst he wanted for nothing, and had been blissfully content living his life, the seeds of restlessness had been sown these past few weeks. Sitting there pondering his future he thought he saw movement up in the tree line and, as the cattle started to become agitated, he woke his two friends and the three of them began talking to and calming the animals as they made their way up to the copse.

There, around a campfire they had just lit, stood four men known to them all, one-time friends who had quit the village and gone to the big city, where they had been promised wealth beyond their wildest dreams. Certainly they looked and were dressed like the rich white folk with shoes on their feet, which always amused Jomo. He'd been there only twice in his life, when he was a young boy, and on both occasions he had been intimidated by the size of the buildings, the speed of the cars, and the general pace of life. A month ago they had returned to offer him a chance to join them, and he had dismissed the idea completely, but a subsequent visit had begun to change his thinking and now they were here for an answer.

How could he leave his parents, his brothers and sisters? As the eldest he was responsible for them all but, if he had a chance to earn a lot of money, he could improve their lives as well. It was a big decision. Then there was his wife and small son – he had not mentioned it for fear of frightening her. She had never left the village in her life and, if he went, he would have to leave them behind at first until he got himself settled.

The seven men embraced one another then sat down around the fire, as they had done all their lives, talking small talk about the village and its inhabitants. Then the conversation changed and, wide-eyed with wonderment, Jomo and his two friends sat there transfixed by the tales of all-night parties, drives up into the Drakensburg mountains for picnics, swimming in the sea, and eating in restaurants – things that he had heard about but, up till now, had never really given much thought to. He had everything he had ever wanted right here in this beautiful valley, yet something was telling him differently, something was enticing him away and he couldn't fight it any longer – Jomo was converted.

'OK. I'll join you here and now. I won't say a word to anybody, it will be easier all round, but I would like to leave them some money.'

'That's no problem, Jomo. Here's a hundred rand, will that be enough?' His oldest friend, Willy, handed him the money.

To Jomo, it was a fortune. 'I can't take this, I'll never be able to pay you back, Willy, it's far too much.'

'Believe me, you'll be able to pay it back soon enough and,

when we get to the city, we'll buy you some clothes and shoes: now what about you two?'

They declined and were quite shocked by Jomo's quick decision so, taking the money to give to his family, they said their farewells and left. As the party began the trek back down the hill to find their truck, Jomo looked back as the golden ball began its majestic climb into the morning sky. For a moment he faltered.

Despite the tiredness he lay awake, as he had done for the past fortnight, thinking of his wife and son, wondering when he would see them again and hoping it would be soon. The days were long and hard, but he enjoyed waking as each day brought something new for him to see or somewhere new to visit.

They lived in the giant barn of a grand manor house owned by an Arab, who he saw fleetingly but never spoke to. Apparently he came and went frequently, stopping for just a few days at a time, and although Jomo asked questions it soon became obvious that one didn't talk about him or his business.

Jomo would go out every day in a lorry or van, driven by Willy, collecting boxes of fruit from the various farms in the valley, which they would bring back to the house. They would sometimes deliver boxes to shops and market stalls in the city, Jomo very quickly adapting to the different pace of life, and he would stand in wonderment staring at this new world that had been opened up to him, the excitement of it all even erasing the thoughts of his family at times.

Then one day Willy told Jomo that it was about time he learnt to drive, that he could earn more money this way, and so it was a month later that Jomo found himself with his own van and his independence. He was in paradise, the excitement that came with this new-found freedom tempered only when he thought of the village, and the longing inside him to see his family surfaced.

When the Arab was away they had some time off, which the others used to get drunk or find a woman, while Jomo would drive down to the harbour and sit and dream. The news he had longed for came soon after, when Willy told him that, the next time the Arab left, he could go home for a few days. His joy knew no bounds, and he set about his daily tasks with a new vigour, looking forward to that day when he could at last explain his actions to his family.

30

London, October 2003

The winter was drawing in, the days shortening, and although she loved it here on the river, Anna always longed for the warmth of Italy when the winter came. After almost thirty years of living on the wrong side of the law she had amassed more than enough money to quit England for some sunnier clime, and to live her life out in luxury. Her marriage to Abdul Karim was a sham, a means to an end, and these last few years had taken their toll, but she could not let go.

Although her body was mentally and physically exhausted, she would think of the power she had, the lives she controlled, and something within would kick-start the adrenalin and she would crave for more. However, she felt the events of the past few weeks were telling her something, and last night's television coverage of the bungled shooting in the Fulham Road had confirmed it: it was time to call it a day.

Added to this, there had been no response when she had telephoned Aunty and Uncle yesterday evening and again this morning, which could only mean one thing: they had been taken in for questioning. Were Uncle Freddie's loyalties still to the family, despite the rift with his brother-in-law, or would he betray them all?

Her answer came almost immediately as the ringing of her mobile broke the melancholy. 'Get out now!' Short and to the point, it was the moment she had dreaded for years but had planned for to the finest degree. No clothes to pack, a rucksack with everything she would need always ready, she grabbed it and the crash helmet, ran down the stairs and out of the back door.

Climbing over the fence she entered her neighbour's garage where she kept the bike, and from there the road led straight to the Chiswick flyover, where she could easily lose anyone in the traffic in minutes.

There was a police car stationed at the end of the road. Anna tensed as she passed it, but it appeared to take no notice and, as she turned right onto the Great Chertsey Road, she started to relax again.

'Bravo Tango Delta 437 X-ray, just exited Hartington Road heading for the Hogarth Roundabout, one person aboard proceeding normally.'

'Roger car three, we'll run that.'

By the time Liam, Paul and the DI arrived everything was in place. The river police had two craft in position, three hundred yards apart, to cover any escape in that direction and armed officers had cordoned off all exit roads and surrounded the house.

DI Watkinson was about to give the order to move in when his radio crackled the bad news. The plates on the motorbike were false, she'd flown the nest and, although an all-points was circulated, everyone knew she would have an elaborate escape route and it was a waste of time.

Paul and Liam vented their anger on the car roof. Liam was unapproachable. So very close, they had been betrayed by Luigi Barolli, who had somehow managed to get a message out. A bent screw, his brief, whoever – a lot of police officers had had their lives put on the line today and for it to end like this was totally unacceptable – someone had to pay.

'Let's get back to Pentonville, I want words with that little shit, he's not getting away with this.'

'Not a good idea, Liam,' replied Watkinson. 'I couldn't fix it up for a start and you've both had enough for one day. Go home, cool off, and we will reassess in the morning. We're going to turn her drum over anyway, although I doubt that we will find anything, and I'll get the river boys to see if they can find the cruiser.'

So Luigi had shopped her. For over thirty years she had covered his backside and, when push came to shove, he'd chickened out to save himself. She wasn't in a hurry for retribution – the bastard could sit and sweat for months, even years, she would know his every move and could pick the time and place. More important was how much had Uncle Freddie told them, that they could have pushed him that far?

She dialled a number and let it ring three times, rang off then dialled it again.

'Mack, I've had visitors, heavy duty visitors but, luckily, I got the tip in time. It looks like Luigi has opened us up and, as I can't get hold of Aunty and Uncle, I can only assume that they've got to Freddie. It's the brother who's doing all the damage and I told you to get rid of him, but your bunch of morons have failed again.'

'The local boys aren't good enough, Anna. You're going to have to pay for a pro if you want the job finished.'

'I don't care what it costs, Mack, just get him out of the way, and get him out of the way quick. Also, I want someone competent to sniff round the shop and find out what's been going on. Until I know exactly how deep we've been penetrated I'm taking no chances and you'd better get the warehouse emptied today.'

'I've got a problem with manpower, Anna. I lost four more regulars this afternoon and Billy Legg is still being held, you know I don't like using unknowns.'

'Mack, I don't care who we use, just get it shifted today, right now. For all I know you could have visitors at any minute and I pay you good money to take care of things, so take care of things, all right? Now, you and I had better quit these shores and quickly, so pack a few things. We can't use the river so I'll change the plates on the bike and pick you up at Tower Bridge, usual place at midnight and don't forget, they are everywhere so watch your back the whole time.' Anna cut the phone before he could answer, her female emotions starting to take over the cold logic.

Whilst she tried very hard not to submit to her feelings, she was very fond of Mackinley. They'd started sleeping together four years ago, but he was not demanding of her, very obedient and loyal and, in her lighter moments, she did wonder what it might be like to live as a normal couple, although she doubted very much if Mackinley could ever settle down anywhere. Then the excitement of the chase kicked back in, and Anna became her cold, calculating self, as she set about changing the plates.

She had bought this lock-up, which was just around the corner from the Chiswick house, some years ago, and here she kept a spare motorbike, some clothes, passports, money and guns. While the police had sealed every port and airport, and put road blocks on every strategic route, Anna Karim, the most wanted women in Great Britain, was calmly preparing to pick up her lover not ten minutes from where they were tearing her house apart.

31

Instead of going home as ordered, Liam and Paul decided to grab a burger before visiting one or two of Liam's 'debtors' as he liked to call them; they were both still pumped up and very angry, and sleep was the furthest thing from their minds as they began cruising the streets of London.

First stop was the Nightingale Club in Soho, which was owned by a couple of Jamaican brothers who had both done time for firearms offences. Liam was never made welcome on the outside, the bouncers and henchmen always gave him a hard time, but this charade was just for the customers' benefit; once inside the inner sanctum he was treated royally.

They were villains and would always be villains but they respected Liam's 'no beating around the bush' type of policing and had forged an unusual bond with the little scouser. Their knowledge of firearms and where you can find them, anything from handguns to missiles, was invaluable and Liam always liked visiting these two very hospitable characters. Wesley and Vincent Young ran a very smart establishment, which surprised Paul as much as the mixed race clientele and, after more harassment as they crossed the dance floor, they were led into the brothers' office.

'Welcome, brother. You've certainly spiced up the town since your arrival. What would you like to drink?' Wesley rose from behind his desk and went to shake Paul's hand, his brother, Vincent, following suit.

Paul looked at Liam, who nodded agreement. They were off

duty and Paul had already sensed that these two wouldn't take no for an answer.

'Thanks, I'd like a white rum and coke please, Wesley. I must say I'm very impressed with your establishment.'

'No drugs, Sergeant. Liam will tell you, we don't even allow users in here. The usual for you, Liam?'

'Thanks, Wesley. You know why we've come calling, what's going on out there?'

'Yes, you two have taken some heavy flak in the past few days and you want to know where the next bullet is coming from. Well, Mad Mack is getting short on numbers and temper, and he's been phoning around all afternoon trying to hire some muscle. The lady it seems is determined to rid herself of you, Sergeant, no matter the cost, and Mackinley's talking about using a sniper either from here or across the water.'

'Any ideas, Wesley?' Liam looked him long and hard in the eye.

Wesley broke the eye contact and took a long swallow from his glass before answering. He knew what Liam meant.

'This is not our scene, Liam, you know that, we are not in the hired killer market.'

'No, but you'd probably be approached for the weaponry, which amounts to the same thing, so you would know who, when and where if Mackinley was successful. I repeat, this can't be allowed to happen.'

The initial ambience was fast disappearing, Liam's words hitting deep and hard, the brothers' smiles now gone from their faces. It was Vincent who spoke next.

'Liam. Out there, as you well know, are a thousand and one ex-SAS, secret service agents, etc, etc. All trained killers, a lot of whom are jobless and whose pensions are insufficient. Any one of them could do the job, and the price is such that very soon Mackinley will have a taker. Many of them are already armed so, unless there's a careless whisper, we wouldn't know until after the event.'

Liam looked to Paul and back to the brothers it had been a long shot but he knew there was only truth in what Vincent had said.

'What about overseas?'

'French and Italian mafia are always possible sources. I'm surprised the lady hasn't arranged something direct.'

'What's the word on her?'

'She's not holed up with Mackinley, that's for certain. The rumour is she's gone north, got family in the Manchester region somewhere.'

'Where's Mackinley?'

'He's mobile, no fixed abode at the moment, probably a hotel somewhere close.'

'I'd appreciate a call as soon as you hear anything.'

They chatted on for a few more minutes, finished their drinks and, as they left the brothers' office, a silence descended over the club. Liam, recognising a couple of faces, stopped, turned and pointing at the brothers, said:

'You two are on sticky ground. Don't fuck with me ever again.' Then, brushing aside the heavies, the two men left.

'That should be all over London in half an hour. Let's go and see if we can find old Charlie.'

'Tell me about Charlie.'

'You'll like him as well, Paul. Charlie is a dosser – not a wino, just an eccentric man who has chosen this way of life and is one of the most contented people you will ever meet. I don't know his history, he has never talked about the past, but he knows of so many people in London and so many people know of him that he is an invaluable source of information. The problem is he roams all over the city and is often impossible to find.'

This proved the case as they drove around the almost deserted backstreets, Liam stopping frequently to question the down and outs and the prostitutes, but to no avail; Charlie was nowhere to be found. The events of the day were starting to catch up with

178

them, they were both tired and scratchy now, their nerve ends frayed, and Paul decided enough was enough.

'Let's call it a day, Liam. We're not going to achieve much at this time of night and tomorrow we go for Mackinley, so we need a good night's sleep.'

Just as they were crossing the river at Tower Bridge, Anna was turning into the hotel car park and, from the shadows, Andrew Mackinley emerged, put on the spare helmet and, without a word being spoken, they disappeared into the night.

Liam's mobile gave him a rude awakening. Glancing at his watch he saw that it was only 4 am; they had only been in bed four hours and he wanted to ignore it, then he thought it could be Sandra and that something was wrong.

'Liam. I want you and the Sergeant to get down to Bermondsey now.' It was DCI Tomlinson. 'There has been a lot of movement during the night and we're going in in twenty minutes.'

When they arrived, Tooley Street and Jamaica Road had been sealed off, as had Wapping High Street across the river. Proceeding on foot, they found DI Watkinson 100 yards from the Thames River Trading Co. warehouse, which was surrounded by police marksmen. Donning the bullet-proof vests he offered them, Paul and Liam made their way up the road, taking cover behind a burnt-out car lying on the pavement.

All that remained of the front portion of the warehouse was the steel framework but the rear section was still intact and in the doorway, sticking front out, was a box Transit van.

'There are at least four men inside the warehouse and the van hasn't moved for about two hours; before that it had already made four trips, which was why we were alerted.'

'So, whatever they are moving isn't going too far away and, after last night's fiasco, they can't use the river.' Liam's mind was racing. 'How long was the van away for each trip, and what direction did it take?'

'Approximately forty to forty-five minutes heading east. What's your thinking, Liam?'

'Allowing fifteen minutes for unloading and a breather they are only fifteen minutes away from here, and I would guess still somewhere on the river. We can't follow them at this time of the morning, we'd be spotted, but I would think somewhere in Rotherhithe Street is a good bet, sir. I suggest we block all exits now before we move in.'

Paul had remained silent. He wanted it to end here and now but he knew that Anna would not be hanging around, and he very much doubted if Mackinley was here either.

'What do you think, Sergeant?'

'Liam's right but I don't think we are going to find either of those two here, just some more low life and possibly more heroin.'

'I do tend to agree with your thinking, Sergeant, but if that is the case we will at least remove some more players and prevent that shit from reaching the streets.'

Just then his radio cut in – it was the river division. 'Two persons are moving in the vicinity of the rear of the building. What do you want us to do?'

'If they go for the river pick them up, we've got the other three sides covered. Everybody move in.'

Shadows converged on the warehouse from all angles and as Paul and Liam reached the van they heard the sound of a helicopter coming up the river, its powerful spotlights illuminating the area.

'Gone! Everything gone! Not a box, not a person, sod all. They've made complete fools of us and once this gets around we'll be the laughing stock of London. We have had under surveillance for the best part of two hours an empty van and warehouse and where's Mackinley and Anna Karim? How could they all walk away without being noticed?' DI Watkinson voiced everyone's feelings as he fought to control his anger.

A closer inspection of what had once been offices revealed that

180

at least one person had lived here permanently. There were calor gas fires, a chemical toilet, beds and cupboards full of food and drink, with a view from the rear that had total command of the river in either direction as well as the surrounding streets.

'David was murdered here!' Paul's voice echoed around the building catching everyone's attention. 'I suggest we get forensics to check the steelwork for rope marks, Inspector.' He went on to explain about the burns he'd seen on David's wrists. 'Also, the body that Anna identified as her husband's was probably butchered in this place, then taken upriver in the cruiser and pushed overboard, and God knows how many other poor souls have perished here.'

How did David die? Paul shuddered as the vibrations in his body told him that this was the place, and he fought the emotions rising within him as he began to examine the whole area.

'Liam, Inspector, down here.' Paul nodded to the corner where stood a rusting old digger, the type that swung a huge steel ball which was used to demolish buildings.

'No, Paul.' Liam realised what he was thinking, then the coroner's report leapt out at him. *Severe burns to the wrists and extensive injuries to the upper body due to a fall.* 'You're saying those sick bastards hung him by his wrists from the steelwork then used the ball on David, and afterwards they took him to Dorset.' No longer the hard little scouser, Liam's voice choked back his angry feelings as the grim reality of it all hit him.

Inspector Watkinson immediately had the entire area sealed off, instructing forensics as to what he was looking for, then he went outside to find the two men comforting one another.

He sat down beside them, sharing this very intimate moment and saying nothing, just feeling as they did. He was hoping that Paul was wrong, that no one could commit such a barbaric act, but deep down he knew he would be proved right.

'Do you two want to call it a day or do you have any ideas where we go from here?'

It was some time before Liam spoke.

'I don't think we should go and see Luigi right now, we'd prob-ably end up killing him, but his brief needs serious investigation that's for sure. What I'd like to do is talk to Marco again but it will have to be done under the guise of a raid, if you can set it up, sir. What do you want to do, Paul?'

'What would we do all day, Liam? Get drunk and mope about which would get us nowhere; no, Marco seems the best bet, let's set it up.'

32

The raid on Marco's Pizzeria was low-key but enough to convince anyone watching that it was for real. There were only two customers in the restaurant who, after questioning, were released, leaving just Marco and a young part-time assistant – Marco's wife having taken the children to her sister's for the day. The young girl was terrified, and it took several minutes before a female officer could calm her down and then escort her home, finally leaving the three men alone.

'We're sorry for the pantomime, Marco, but we needed to talk to you urgently: I just hope we haven't scared the staff away.'

'She's the daughter of a good friend who knows my history, it will be sorted, don't worry. I was waiting for the wife to return then I was going to call you anyway.'

'Well, we think we know now how and where my brother was murdered and, without going into details, it wasn't very nice. We've lost Anna and Mackinley and we need pointing in the right direction.'

'The last forty-eight hours haven't exactly been the finest in the history of the Met, that's for certain, the best news being that you two have somehow managed to survive. The reason I was going to contact you is that I think I have found a possible answer to your suspected mole problem. It's very dangerous ground I'm on here, if this ever gets back, so you must handle this discreetly. Jonathon Rees-Jones QC, the family brief.'

'We have him in the frame but what makes you so certain it's him.'

'He's retained by Anna and has been in her pocket for nearly thirty years, the word being that he has a habit. Not drugs, children. As you know, the twins are heavily into pornography and they have been keeping him happy all this time. He has access to some very high places and the confidence of many prominent people and, apparently, can charm the words out of a stone statue: I don't think you need look any further.'

'This habit of his, Marco, is it visual or physical?'

'I've only heard of the internet being used and, of course, the magazines supplied by the twins.'

'Good. If he's downloading we can get it traced. What about Mackinley and Anna, any ideas where they could be at all?'

'No, only that they are together.'

Paul interrupted before he could continue. 'Are you sure of this, Marco? We were told not twelve hours ago that the lady is in Manchester and he's still in London, so what's happened to make you think otherwise?'

'That was last night's news. The word this morning is that Paddy is now running the show and those two are going to lie low together somewhere until things calm down. They're waiting for passports so obviously they intend to cross the water but where to I haven't heard.'

'Who's Paddy, Liam?'

'Mackinley's right-hand man, Brian "Paddy" Dennison. No one knows where the "Paddy" comes from, he's neither Irish nor of Irish stock. Unfortunately, he's another one we missed out on when we did the big round-up. An absolute psycho, I'd be very surprised if he wasn't involved in yesterday's Pentonville attempt on our lives.

He likes a drink and normally you can find him in one of the pubs in Wapping, but even he has gone to ground somewhere, probably at the warehouse until last night. Who's doing the passports, Marco – "Fingers"?'

'No. There's someone moving up the ladder fast from the Ealing/Southall area, specialises mainly in Asians. "Fingers" has retired, says he couldn't do another stretch, he's too old.'

'What have you heard about Mackinley looking for a sniper?'

'You should take that one very seriously. The Sergeant here is public enemy No1 as far as the lady is concerned and money is no object. There are plenty of types who pass through here who could do it, ex-military looking for an earner, he shouldn't have any difficulty finding someone.'

'OK, Marco. As usual we owe you big time, call us if you need anything. Do you want to go out in cuffs or will you be all right?'

'I'll be all right thanks, Liam. I'll just throw some verbal after you as you leave.'

West Africa, October 2001

The stinking fishing boat buffeted by an angry Atlantic Ocean had been his home now for the past four days, giving him time to reflect on the previous two weeks in the arms of Consuela Cabellorenti, two weeks that once again had torn him in every direction.

He had resisted asking her outright who the Turin target had been, but was now more than certain it was a member of the Count's family, as she had stated on more than one occasion that she was the sole beneficiary of the Count's estates in England and Italy.

Despite her pleadings he had refused to join her in England, although he would have to return there one day if he was ever to lay his father's memory to rest. The anger and hatred were ever present and he still could not trust himself to act rationally if confronted with his past and, anyway, his restless spirit meant that he would never stay in one place for long. He still felt an ominous presence surrounding Consuela and he certainly didn't want to spend the rest of his life as someone's plaything, which is what he would be.

She had turned very nasty when he had told her that he was leaving for Africa without her and, after another heated argument, had stormed off the boat, leaving him no choice but to dump her belongings on the quay and put to sea.

Ajaccio was definitely finished for him now, the port no longer a safe haven, although he doubted whether she could trace the house – at least Corsica could remain his home base.

What he had to do now was definitely sell the cruiser and, to this end, he had left it in the South of France in the hands of a boat dealer, offering him a vast commission for his silence.

His day-dreaming was broken as the old rust bucket shipped another giant wave and, losing his footing, he was thrown across the galley. The Portuguese skipper appeared, grinning at Mario's predicament, and as he helped him to his feet the vessel creaked and groaned and shipped another big one.

Each wave seemed to flush out more of the stinking rotted fish and Mario decided to take his chances on deck, his stomach unable to cope any longer. Visibility was poor as the boat rose and sank into trough after trough but as it rose once more Mario thought he saw land through the heavy spray.

Signalling for the captain to join him on deck, Mario strained to see through the curtain of mist, beginning to doubt his eyes when, suddenly, it parted to reveal a long sandy beach.

The skipper checked his charts and changed course, heading towards the shore then, slowing the engines, he turned once again and, running parallel with the deserted beach, found what he was looking for. It was a large river estuary which obviously had enough draught for the boat as he then turned inland, while his crew, now armed and very alert, nervously scanned the banks with binoculars.

The jungle began to close in and the engines were shut down as they drifted silently upstream, the captain ordering the crew to lower the dinghy. A small clearing with two grass huts appeared on the port side and the captain nodded at Mario: they had reached their destination.

Grabbing his only baggage, the rifle, Mario climbed over the side as his stomach once again began to rebel at the stench and, fighting the nausea, he paddled ashore. No sooner had his feet touched the riverbank than, to his dismay, the dinghy was immediately hauled back to the boat and the skipper restarted the engines and turned back towards the ocean.

The fear and sickness were forgotten as his survival instincts kicked in and he scouted the perimeter of the clearing, checking for footprints. Satisfied that there were none, he looked for a suitable tree to climb, reckoning that it would be the safest place to wait and observe. Anyone for miles would have heard the boat's engines start up so he didn't expect it would be long before he had visitors, friend or foe, but when they arrived he was pleasantly surprised.

British mercenaries. There were five of them. Soldiers for hire, they were some of the toughest fighting men in the world who, when they had done their time, couldn't let go. Like himself, once a soldier always a soldier, and he didn't have to wait too long to see how good they were.

They had dispersed into the trees as quickly as they had appeared, Mario unable to spot any one of them, but he knew if he waited long enough they would tire of the game.

'OK, Corsican, we know you're here, what do we call you?'

The voice was hard Cockney.

'Mario.'

'Do you speak English, Mario? '

'As good as you do, cockney.'

'Bleeding hell, Mickey, they've sent us a toff.' This one was a Taffy, somewhere to Mario's right.

'I suggest you five get yourselves out into that clearing and we can introduce ourselves better.'

Mickey the Cockney, who was obviously the leader, gave the order, and the five men warily emerged from the shadows as Mario climbed out of the tree. As had always been the case, there was something about his bearing that commanded respect and, despite his youth, the five men sensed immediately that this was someone special as they introduced themselves.

187

'The first thing we have to do when we get back, Mario, is to get you out of those clothes. Even if the enemy can't see you they'll be able to smell you a mile off.'

This wasn't said as a joke, and no one laughed; it was the words of a professional soldier fighting a war covering every contingency. He put the Cockney at around forty years old, the others much older, all seasoned veterans who Mario knew would spend the rest of their days fighting a war somewhere. 'We've brought along a spare weapon for you. I've a nasty feeling you're going to need it soon.'

It was a Kalashnikov, the most universal and preferred weapon of fighting men throughout the world, which Mario stripped, checked and rebuilt at incredible speed in front of their astonished eyes, dispelling any lingering doubts about his capabilities. As Mickey described the next stage of the journey to Mario, the others turned to cover the forest.

'Are you expecting visitors soon, Mickey?'

'Whoever's out there will know something is going on and come looking. Not only is there a civil war going on here, there are several other tribal factions trying to muscle in on the action, so someone will turn up soon, that's for certain. We've been here too long as it is, let's move out: Taffy, you take the point and Jon, you cover his arse, everybody stay alert – it's been far too quiet lately.'

They followed a narrow pathway which had been hacked through the jungle, their progress painfully slow as they continually scanned the canopy above and the path behind them, but at least they didn't have to worry about an attack from either side, the dense undergrowth providing a natural defence.

Taffy pushed on ahead, checking the ground in front with his minder not far behind, and Mario was impressed with the fitness of these not so young men as they pressed onward hour after hour without a break – it was reassuring to know that he was in the company of such professional soldiers.

The jungle began to thin out, the sunlight now fully penetrating the green ceiling, and with this the atmosphere relaxed, they had reached the safety of base camp. Up ahead Taffy and Jon were sitting on the ground surrounded by several tribesmen, laughing and joking, and when Mario arrived he could see that he was the butt of their humour as the locals danced around him holding their noses.

They led him down to the river, where they were joined by several women armed with soap and towels, and he had no choice other than to strip off. The whole town arrived then as the women began soaping him down and washing the offending garments, and as was always the case his arrival was the signal for great rejoicing and the singing started and the whole place began to party.

Despite this euphoria the fear remained heavy in the air and Mickey, with Mario accompanying him, toured the perimeters of the town, checking that the men assigned to night-guard duty were in place and not half drunk, and once again Mario was impressed by the standards that he set.

He had been assigned two of the local handmaidens to feed him and tend to his every need, even to join him under the animal skins during the harsh, cold African night but, as ever, he soon became bored and restless.

As each day passed the tension in the town mounted, the fear became more palpable, and Mickey's relentless discipline more intense. Mario could sense that everybody was close to breaking point as he patrolled the streets, checking the security, and was very relieved when the news filtered through that the President had arrived back in the capital and was waiting to meet him.

This galvanised the whole town into action, and within the hour, they were ready to move out, but this time by jeep and lorry. The capital was thirty miles away on a fairly good dirt road and, surprisingly, they reached there without any incident, further confirming Mickey's gut feeling that something big was brewing.

The President greeted Mario warmly but did not regale him with the politics of war, respecting his neutrality, preferring instead to talk about Britain and how much he would like to return there one day. He was a witty, entertaining host, the evening relaxed and full of laughter but, as dinner came to an end, Mickey's worst fears were realised.

Without warning the unmistakeable sound of shells whistling through the air reached them and they dived for cover under the tables. Luckily, the first salvo missed the palace, which gave them a chance to get the President to the safety of his bunker just before the second salvo, which was a direct hit.

They were outnumbered and, despite Mickey's discipline and tactical awareness, were incurring huge losses as they repelled wave after wave of enemy forces. Mario was certain that they would not be able to survive as the battle continued well into the night but, finally, they managed to force their attackers to retreat and a welcome silence descended over the palace.

It was decided that this would be the best time for Mario to leave so, with two of the mercenaries and four of the President's most trusted soldiers, he set off into the night. Visibility was almost zero but the pace was fast, all caution thrown to the wind as they made their way through the undergrowth with the sounds of the jungle at night for accompaniment.

This risky strategy came to an abrupt and tragic end when the ground disappeared from under the feet of the two lead men, their screams piercing the night as they became impaled on the spiked timbers below, the others just managing to stop in time before they too fell into the animal trap.

As they skirted the pit they could see that there was nothing that they could do for their comrades, but those screams would have been heard for miles so any chance that they had had of surprise was surely gone. The dangers had doubled now that their presence was known, but they had no choice other than to continue and hope that fortune might smile on them. The fatigue in their bodies was no more as the tension mounted and, at a more cautious pace, they pressed on as the dawn began to filter through the vegetation.

33

London, October 2003

Jonathon Rees-Jones QC, age fifty-four. A brilliant legal mind, his speciality is corporate law although he still practises criminal law, as in the case of the Barollis and one or two others. He has an office in the city and branches in the home counties, a large estate in Egham and another home in the Corsican hills near Ajaccio. His two teenage sons go to Eton and his wife, Carolyne, is the only daughter of Sir Angus Philpott, chairman of Granthams, one of the oldest firms of merchant bankers in the city.

Considered by many to be destined for a government position, he is a pillar of society and includes amongst his friends several cabinet ministers, members of the royal family, and is a member of the same club and a very close friend of DCS Carlisle.

'Oh shit,' were the first words from DI Watkinson after he had read the page, already his mind working overtime as to how to handle this potential time bomb and its repercussions, while Liam and Paul sat there saying nothing. They had realised the minute they had put this together that this was a political minefield of the highest order.

'First of all, I have to say that I'm impressed, Liam. Where did you get all this from, and in such a short time?'

'It may surprise you to know, Inspector, that I do mix with

191

people outside of the criminal fraternity. A couple of drinks here, a phone call there, and a rummage through some old *Country Lifes* – it was quite easy really.'

'Have you shown this to anybody else?'

'We're not complete idiots, sir, but if the underworld knows of his preference then that might cause a problem, although I would think Anna keeps that under control. It's obviously his connection with the DCS that's going to be the biggest factor in deciding our next move.'

'Exactly, Liam. As if we haven't got enough egg on our faces you two have to come up with this. I know it's my decision but I would appreciate your views on what we do next.'

'Inspector, you and I have worked together for over ten years, during which time we have seen the Met's name dragged through the mud on several occasions, but if this gets out it would be the worst by far. On the other hand, we have got the biggest intro into the Karim empire if it's handled properly. What we can't afford to do is sit around and talk, we've lost out too many times this week, so I suggest you get on the phone now and get the DCS in here right away.'

'Sergeant, what do you think?'

'I'm the new boy here, but I know of the pride that is this force and the damage that could come if we don't act quickly. I agree with Liam, get the man in here now before it's too late.'

DCS Carlisle arrived within the hour, still dressed in his gardening clothes. He was above all a 24/7 copper, who realised when he got the call that time was of the essence, and having read the piece of paper handed it back to the DI without saying a word. Watkinson then took the lead.

'Nothing you have read there, sir, will come as news to you, but we have learnt today from Marco that your friend is probably the Karim mole. He's been in the pay of Anna Karim for nearly thirty years, but there is worse to come. He is also heavily into child pornography, the Barolli twins fuelling his vile habit during this time, and he downloads from the internet.'

192

The DI had known DSC Carlisle for all of his police career, but he had never seen him look like this. All the colour had drained from his face as he sat rooted to his chair, the shocking revelation almost too much to digest, trying hard to reassert his authority and make an instant decision. When he spoke his voice was no more than a whisper:

'Does he have any idea of what we know, Peter?'

'As far as we know, no sir.'

'Good, that gives us some breathing space. You've obviously talked this through, all of you, what do you want to do next?'

'As we see it, if he has been in her pay for so long then he is party to everything that's gone on and, because of his vulnerability, that makes him more important to us than the twins. To this end, we need him alive and talking as soon as possible.'

'Do you think she would have him killed if she finds out that we know all this?'

'He is susceptible to every low-life who knows the score so she wouldn't have to do anything other than let his secret be known in certain circles.'

'So what do you want me to do. Talk to him and offer him anonymity in return for Anna?'

'We can't do that, sir,' Liam countered. 'What he has been doing should not go unpunished. He will have to resign from the bar and face charges.' Liam was not happy with the way this was going.

'I agree, Liam, but he will know that for the rest of his life we will be watching him. Also, his loss of status both in society and the legal world would I think be punishment enough, and I'm not letting personal feelings into this. I will phone him first thing in the morning and try to get a meeting as soon as possible. Now what other bad news have you for me?'

Peter Watkinson told him about the raid on the warehouse and ended by telling him what conclusions Liam and Paul had come to with regard to David's death. Again Carlisle seemed momentarily to crumble as the enormity of the horror hit him.

193

'I think we should all call it a day, gentlemen, and hope we can get something positive in the morning.'

He rose as Liam and Paul got up to leave and silently shook their hands, the emotion in them all simmering just below the surface.

Although he slept well Paul woke up still feeling lousy, the need to go and run for a couple of hours to clear his head and relax his body gnawing away at him. Liam was snoring soundly in the next room so, rather than wake him, he put on his trainers and was half-way out of the door when common sense prevailed. Damn that bloody Karim woman, his resentment rising he went back inside – he was almost as much a prisoner as the twins.

The two men arrived at the office to find that there had been a call from the hospital to say that Brendan Cassidy had regained consciousness in the night and, although still very weak, he might be all right for a five-minute interview. Going to see the DI before they left they found him sitting behind his desk, looking as if he had been there all night, which wasn't far from the truth.

'After you two left last night we called in the DCI and, between us, have agreed that we get the brief in before we decide our next move. Now, what are your plans for the day bearing in mind that, although Anna is looking across the water for someone, there are still a lot of locals who fancy their chances of a good payday?'

'We're not going to back off now and leave it to the others, that's for certain.' Liam was adamant. 'Firstly, we are going to talk to Brendan Cassidy then we're going to see "Fingers", by which time the DCS might have something. Have the river boys come up with anything?'

'They have drawn a blank on all fronts. Anna's boat is nowhere to be found, the two people at the back of the warehouse were ours, and all traffic on the river has been checked and cleared.'

'What about the goods from the warehouse? Has anybody got a clue where they might be, or seen any unusual movement?'

194

'Sorry, Liam. Whilst I agree with your analysis, a sweep over the whole area has revealed nothing.'

They were interrupted by a knock at the door and an officer entered the room and, without saying anything, handed the DI a piece of paper and left.

'Sit down, you two, this is the forensic report on the warehouse; I won't read it all, just the salient points. The fingerprints lifted read like a who's who of the criminal world. There are plenty we know of and a few new ones, but gloves were worn in the van which had been stolen two weeks ago. Inspection of the steel girders has revealed rope fibres and friction marks comparable to the suspension of a heavy load. The mechanical digger has several prints on it, but the only known ones are those of Mackinley.'

Paul tensed, knowing what was coming next as the DI hesitated, looked up and nodded.

'I'm sorry, Paul. The steel ball had traces of human hair, blood, skin and bone, which match.'

Any lingering hopes that Paul would be proved wrong were gone and only raw emotion coursed their veins as the three men took it all in. They thought they had heard and seen it all, that they were immune to the horrors of life, but nothing could prepare one for something as barbaric and personal as this.

Without a word Paul got up and left the room and Liam went to follow, but the DI called him back.

'No, Liam. Leave him for a bit. We've all got to get ourselves back under control before we continue.'

Liam found Paul in the toilets and, as the two men embraced, other officers came and went, silently placing a hand on Paul's shoulder. The news had spread like wildfire and this was a very angry police force: retribution was the only thing on their minds and it would need all the skill and expertise of its senior officers to keep the lid on things. Paul splashed himself with cold water, dried his face, and turned to Liam.

'I'll be OK, Liam, thank you. Now let's go and finish this.'

195

DCS Carlisle sat at his desk staring at the phone. He'd just received confirmation of how 'The South African' had died and never in his career had he doubted his ability to handle a situation until now.

Reflecting on the past ten days, he had seen Jonathon Rees-Jones three times and, up until yesterday, had not given the fact any thought. Normally they would see one another just once a week, at the club, and dine together once a month unless Jonathon had something urgent to discuss, then it would be a pub somewhere.

But three times in ten days! What had they talked about? What were the reasons for these meetings? What did I say to this silver-tongued man who could hold a jury spellbound for days? Inadvertently, am I the mole, am I responsible in some way for the death of this fine young man and all that has happened since?

The isolation that goes with a position of command enveloping him, he reached for the phone. He was still not quite sure of exactly what he was going to say to this man, a man he had thought of as a friend and who had betrayed his trust, as he dialled the number.

34

South Africa, October 2003

Jomo was becoming more and more discontented, the longing to see his family tearing him apart. All the wonder of his new-found world had quickly evaporated and each day he found himself working longer hours, often well into the night, as the Arab became more and more demanding of them. Even the sack of money he had hidden in the hollow of a dead tree no longer excited him and only the fear of Willy kept him from walking away.

Another thing that bothered Jomo was that everything was surrounded in secrecy here, no one ever talked about their day's work, in fact they hardly ever talked at all, even his friends from the village never wanted to sit around a fire and chat like they used to.

So it was that, as he made his way out of the city that night, tired, confused and as ever thinking of his son, Jomo momentarily lost concentration and, narrowly avoiding an oncoming lorry, left the road, went through a fence, and ended up in a ditch.

He sat there not feeling any pain, then fear and panic set in as the realisation of the consequences of all this hit him. He had to run away but he couldn't open the door, he was trapped, and then he felt the blood trickling down his face as he slipped into unconsciousness.

London, October 2003

At the hospital the doctor in charge emphasised once again that Brendan was still very weak and that five minutes was the absolute maximum. Entering the room they found Brendan dozing but as they neared the bed his eyes flickered opened, then shut again.

If he hadn't known better, Brendan thought he had died and gone to heaven, such was the resemblance, as he reopened his eyes staring at Paul. 'You're the brother I've been expecting.' He tried to raise his hand in welcome, but the effort was too much for him so Paul took hold of his hand.

'Glad you're still with us, Brendan.' Paul leant over the man as his breathing became broken.

'Bermondsey, Thames River Trading Co,' he gasped, as the effort became too much for him and he closed his eyes in pain.

The two officers thanked him and, realising that it was far too soon, said goodbye, promising to come and visit him when he was stronger.

'I was told that you two would be calling.' 'Fingers' looked up from the paper he was reading as the two men entered the property.

Wilfred 'Fingers' Lewis ran a legitimate little hardware store with his wife, Pauline, who appeared the minute she had heard his voice. She said nothing, and just shot her husband a worried glance, as he led the two men out the back through the store-room into the living accommodation.

Thirty years ago Lewis was the best 'peter man' in Britain. If you wanted a safe cracked he was the one you got in touch with but, when he regained his freedom after his second stretch, the march of time had caught up with him. He found a whole new world of electronic safes and laser security waiting to greet him, so he decided to diversify.

He'd shared a cell with a notorious forger, who had taught

him the tricks of the trade and, as with safecracking, his natural ability for this new sideline quickly established him as the man you went to for passports, visas, in fact any legal document. He'd done two further stretches for forgery and, as he took them into the living room, Paul was struck by how ordinary this man was, not your average criminal type at all.

'I know what you want, Mr. Jameson. No names, except this time I'm innocent. I've gone in to retirement.'

'So we've heard, "Fingers". What do you know about this new man in Southall?'

'He's Asian and he's good. I've seen some of his work.'

Paul took out the passports they had found at Uncle Freddie's. 'We know that this is your work but what we need to know is are there any others using these photographs?'

'Fingers' stared long and hard at the two officers, his face asking the question.

'No charges, we'll keep you out of it.'

'I told them I couldn't take another stretch but I didn't have much choice in the matter, you don't say no to the lady and live. These and two others each all had the same photographs, with different names.'

'What names, "Fingers"? Can you remember any of them?'

'His were all Arabic like these. I couldn't begin to think of one of them but the lady wanted to use simple names, like Smith, Brown was another, Wright, if I remember correctly, was another.'

'Were you approached for this latest one?'

'Of course. It got a bit nasty when I refused, nothing physical just verbal, but they calmed down when I told them about the Asian.'

'Who called?'

'New boys to me. London accents, but that's all I can remember about them.'

'OK, "Fingers", you keep your nose clean now. We'll be in touch.'

*   *   *

It had been another frustrating morning and they were still no nearer to Anna Karim or Andrew Mackinley. If she was waiting for a new passport it was obvious that she would have changed her identity once again and those they had found at the Strombertis served no purpose. Undecided where to turn to next, they returned to the office to find a call awaiting Paul from Inspector Preetzius in Durban.

'Good morning, Sergeant. It seems we are on the right track as we've now traced the broken-down van back to its origins. About six months ago the Electricity Company changed its fleet, and a Mr Makem al Fahid purchased ten vehicles as a job lot on behalf of Citruso Inc. This same name was on the passenger listing of the Lear jet.'

'That's brilliant. I'm sending a new photo down the wire of Abdul Karim, so if you can get a positive ID we're in business. Is the Lear still on the tarmac?'

'It hasn't moved since it landed four days ago, Immigration are going to phone me when the pilot files a flight plan.'

'Knowing Abdul he probably has an alternative escape route and the jet is standing there as a dummy; nevertheless, we'll have to wait and see. In the meantime I have more bad news for you.'

Paul then brought him up to date on everything that had happened, ending by telling him how David had died and at whose hands.

'We won't let Karim escape this time, Sergeant,' was all the Inspector could manage to say, as Paul heard him breaking down on the line, then he mumbled a goodbye and hung up.

Paul knew that he would take the news badly. Before he had left Durban, David had shared a flat with Kiefer Preetzius for five years: climbing together most weekends, they had also shared many dangerous experiences as police officers and Kiefer Preetzius would be another very angry policeman tonight.

DCS Carlisle continued to wrestle with his conscience, going over in his mind the last three meetings with Rees-Jones, trying hard to think of what they had talked about. Of one thing he was certain, the QC had phoned him each time to ask for a meeting and he had not thought it unusual, he had had no need to. Now, looking at it from a different perspective, the reasons for the meets were pretty insignificant, but the urgency with which Rees-Jones had arranged them was not. Had he been a complete fool and sold his men down the river without realising it? He tried the number again.

Either he smelt a rat, or he was genuinely otherwise engaged, but Rees-Jones's secretary apologised again, saying that she had been unable to make contact with him.

'It's very unusual, sir. I do have a list of his appointments for the day, and I will leave a message with them for him.'

'Do you know if he has a lunch appointment, or if he is going to the club today?'

'No, I'm sorry, there is no mention of either in his diary.'

He thanked her and hung up. Which way to go was now the big decision: with time running out and his men dependent on this meeting, what alternatives were there? Where the hell was Rees-Jones?

As the DCS searched for a way forward, Anna's puppet was completing the first part of his instructions. She had called the previous evening and told him to drop everything and be on the fifth floor of the multi-storey car park in Windsor Street at 10 am.

He was to leave the car with the boot ajar and come back at 11am, when he was to proceed to the car park at Canterbury Cathedral. Not wanting to arouse any suspicions in the office he had cancelled his day's appointments himself and, having parked the car, found a café just around the corner.

He returned an hour later to find the boot shut, so he slid behind the wheel and headed for the M2. He had played messenger boy before but had never let his curiosity get the better of him, working on the principle that the less he knew the better so, resisting the temptation to pull over and open the boot, he put his mind to other things.

He made good time to Canterbury and, pulling into a space in front of the Cathedral, put on a CD and settled down expecting a long wait. Before he knew it the boot was up and down again, and all he saw were two leather-clad bikers in the wing mirror.

Sorely tempted to take the rest of the day off, maybe even visit the Cathedral, Jonathon Rees-Jones decided that it was not a good idea. He would only end up spending the time reflecting on this mess that was his life, his family and his future. He switched the mobile back on. It was better to bury himself in his work, he told himself, and not think too deeply about everything because that frightened him.

There were three messages, all from his secretary, so he searched the number. 'Angela, I'm just leaving Eton, what's the problem?'

'It's DCS Carlisle. He has been trying to get hold of you all morning.'

'OK, I'll phone him now. Anything else come up?'

'No. It's been very quiet here this morning. Will you be coming back into the office today?'

'It depends on what Carlisle wants. I'll let you know later.'

'Hello Martin, it's Jonathon. Sorry, I had to rush off to Eton this morning, usual problem with the boys, lack of funds. What can I do for you?'

'It's a bit delicate, Jonathon. Could you possibly call in today, I'd rather not talk about it on the phone if you don't mind.'

'I'm just leaving Eton now. Allowing for the traffic, I could be with you in about an hour's time.'

'Thank you, I'll tell security to expect you.'

35

They had made this journey many times in the van and knew the route by heart. Every bend, every crossroads, a route that steered clear of all the little villages that were scattered in this flat unfriendly countryside, a route that avoided the gaze of prying eyes. However, Anna was not relaxed, she knew the coast-guard services would have been alerted and that a helicopter could appear from nowhere at any second as they swept the coastline.

They were too exposed out here for her liking but it was a chance they had to take if they were to make the rendez-vous. High tide was at 2 pm so they hadn't much time – if they weren't there when the boat docked the skipper would put to sea immediately. The crossing had to be made in daytime if they were to stand a chance, any fishing boat moving around here at night would arouse suspicion and would easily be spotted on the radar. It was the way they brought the cigarettes and alcohol in and now, ironically, it was the only way out for Anna and Mackinley.

The tiny inlet appeared below them and, glancing out to sea, Anna saw a small craft alone on the horizon; they'd made it in time. Then, as she took the track down the cliff towards the jetty, she felt a slap on her back and, looking up, saw a speck in the sky. It could only be the coastguards.

Braking hard, she dropped the bike, Mackinley on the back throwing himself clear as Anna and machine slid into an incontrollable skid hurtling down the path. Somehow they did not go over the edge but continued on down until they hit a sandy plateau which brought their death-defying plunge to a sudden halt.

She lay there breathless but not feeling any pain and then looked up. The dust cloud she had created hung like a waving flag above her but fortunately for her the now visible helicopter had already turned towards the horizon, attracted by the small vessel, and Anna slowly moved her head, looking for Mackinley. Thinking he'd gone over the cliff, Anna rolled over and belly-crawled towards the brink.

Looking down she could see nothing and then she felt something touching her leg. Startled, she looked round and saw Mackinley beside her and, without any thought for their safety, sat up and threw her arms around his neck.

Within seconds the precariousness of their situation hit home and she let go of Mackinley and they both fell to the ground looking out to sea. The boat had hove to and the helicopter was hovering above the vessel. The two of them lay there transfixed as the scene evolved in front of their eyes. Had the coastguards radioed in their spot and were awaiting confirmation or were they taking pictures for future reference? Either way it should pose no problems. The boat was legally registered and had every right to be in these waters, so Anna was not unduly worried; the problem would be if the chopper turned inland – there was no cover anywhere.

She had stumbled across the illegal trafficking of cigarettes and alcohol quite by chance several years ago and had muscled in on it very easily. The boat was owned and crewed by two brothers who, along with their sons, had long ago become disillusioned with the income from fishing and had sought alternative revenue. Anna had invested heavily in equipping the boat with the finest electronic surveillance systems and, after modifying the holds to include false compartments, they now made two runs a week from the northern French coast, her intended destination today.

For what seemed an eternity they lay there, watching the scene unfold out to sea, frightened to move, certain that the helicopter would swing inland once it was satisfied with the vessel's identity.

Then what would the brothers do? Would they abort the docking or would they take the chance? They'd just have to sweat it out and see. The weather was worsening, the sea starting to swell – unless the trawler docked within the next twenty minutes they would have to abandon this attempt and hole up for twenty-four hours until the next day-tide, something Anna didn't fancy doing.

Then, without realising it for several seconds, the chopper was gone, heading south and away from them and they rose quickly and sought out the stricken bike. Fortunately, the damage was only superficial and the bike started immediately. They continued their descent, arriving just as the trawler tied up alongside the jetty.

Although choppy, the crossing was relatively easy and they reached their destination without further incident just as dusk descended. Within twenty minutes they had reached the motorway south; they were free, home and dry and Anna, realising that they hadn't eaten in twenty-four hours, pulled into the first services.

Instead of feeling relief, Anna sat there on edge, picking at her food with all kinds of negative thoughts flittering through her mind. She could see that Mackinley was getting twitchy and knew that he wouldn't feel secure until they got under way again. He didn't like not being in control of a situation like this, and she feared the worst if anybody stopped and questioned them.

Try as hard as she could to shut them out, the doubts kept returning: could she really let go, just up and walk away and leave the firm to others to run, even though she knew the only other option was prison? That thought strengthened her resolve: there was no way she was going back to another stretch so what alternative did she have? She tried hard to put these thoughts to the back of her mind but they would not go away, and neither would the nagging doubts that everything they were leaving behind was in safe hands. It was no good, she couldn't just up and run from her past, it was food and drink to her: those bastard Mackenzie brothers had forced her hand, turned her family against her, she had to have her revenge – she had to return one day soon.

Then there was the man across the table from her. He was the first man in her life she felt she could trust, a man who made her laugh, a man who made her feel like a woman, but were they really going to be able to live together normally as a couple? That was only a pipe dream. They both had known only one way of life, it was in their blood and could never be washed away: there was no escaping from it, you were in till you breathed your last.

'I want to phone Paddy, Anna. I'm not happy leaving him with that lorry-load of goods.'

Mackinley had confirmed her doubts and Anna, angrily pushing her plate away, got up and stormed out of the restaurant. Mackinley followed her, his mobile in his hand searching for the number.

'Do you really think he might try and go solo? Personally, Mack, I doubt it, he hasn't got the brains or the bottle, and who would deal with him?'

'It's not that that bothers me, it's his love of the whiskey that's the problem. Paddy, it's Mack, can you hear me?' The background noise was deafening. 'You're in a sodding pub again! What did I tell you?'

'I'll go outside, Mack, hang on. That's better. I've only had a couple of pints, honest.'

'Look, Paddy. I can't have you driving that lorry around the streets of London, half pissed. I told you not to drink, you've got to move that stuff tonight.'

'I'm fine, honest, but things here are not. The streets are crawling with "bill" looking for you two, when are you thinking of coming back?'

'When it's quietened down a bit. Just don't let me down, Paddy, you know I'm not a nice person when I get upset.'

Mackinley hung up before he could say another word and looked at Anna, knowing what was coming next.

'Damn it, Mack, why did you put that drunk in charge? He could lose us everything.'

'There was no one else. Despite the drink he's the best we've got left.'

They were both quiet now, with Anna thinking what to do for the best, when Mackinley interrupted her thoughts.

'How about "fancy pants" Jones? Can't you get him to help us?'

Mackinley didn't like him at all but accepted the reasons why he was on the payroll, and had grudgingly admitted when he went down for his last stretch that without Jones as his brief he would probably still be in nick.

Anna burst out laughing. 'For a start he doesn't have an HGV licence and, secondly, can you see him driving an artic around London in the middle of the night?' Her attempt at humour was lost on Mackinley but she knew what he was getting at, the man had a lot of contacts in and around London on the wrong side of the fence. She put her arm through Mackinley's and looked up at him. 'If all else fails, that's a good option, Mack.'

'Come in, Jonathon, and sit down.' DCS Carlisle did not get up to greet him, or shake his proffered hand. Immediately, Rees-Jones felt uncomfortable, as if the man opposite him was a complete stranger, and his stomach started to turn.

'Its all over, Jonathon. I know exactly what's been going on, who your paymaster is, and all about your vile habit.'

Before he could say a word, Carlisle continued. 'I also know that you haven't been to Eton today, Jonathon, so where did you go to meet Anna and Mackinley?'

The suave, smooth lawyer exterior remained, as he looked the DCS straight in the eyes but, inside, his mind was in turmoil searching for the right words.

'Martin, you are playing a game of bluff. You don't have a shred of evidence and, if you don't want to see your golden career flushed down the toilet, I suggest you back off now.'

'You surf the internet, Jonathon, pursuing your perverted pleasure, and you've downloaded from a site which has just been closed down, plus you and the Barolli twins have had a business arrangement for the past thirty years. I'm not bluffing here, you know me better than that, and what would happen to Carolyne and the boys if this ever became public?'

'You wouldn't dare say a word. What if our association became public, how would the shining star look then?'

Carlisle ignored him. 'Where are they, Jonathon? I want those two locked up and the keys thrown away. In return, you will resign from the Bar and go into retirement for whatever reason you think best. There will be no charges and I promise I will keep you out of it.'

He knew it would come to this one day. He was tired of the lies, the secrecy, the sickness, all he really wanted was for it all to end, but could he trust this stranger opposite him?

'Complete immunity?'

'You have my word on that, providing I get what I want. Where are they?'

'Would you believe me if I told you I don't know?'

'Where did you meet them today? What was said?'

'Canterbury Cathedral. We never talk on meets like this, they just take what they want from the boot of the car and leave.'

'What was in the boot, Jonathon? Money? Passports? Tickets? Come on, you're not helping yourself here.'

'I never look to see what is in the boot, it's always delivered by a third party who puts it straight in.'

'Did you see the car, what model was it?'

'Anna doesn't drive a car, she and Mackinley are fanatical bikers.'

Martin Carlisle's eyes had never left the lawyer's face and, as they penetrated his soul, he began to feel a kind of pity for this man, who he had genuinely thought of as his friend. Then when he thought of his own children the loathing and hatred returned, and he remembered Liam Jameson's disgust yesterday when he learnt that he would not be prosecuted.

No, he could not go back on his word, although many people, including a large proportion of the police force, considered this the most heinous of crimes.

Carlisle picked up his phone. 'Sergeant Mackenzie. It looks like those two have flown the nest. I have a visitor in my office who delivered something, probably Mackinley's passport and maybe a new one for Anna, to Canterbury Cathedral this morning. If this is so it means she has a new ID and the photos we have count for nothing. However, I don't believe even she would have the balls to risk taking a regular ferry out of one of the ports so I think it's safe to assume that they have alternative arrangements somewhere along the east coast. It's a long shot but you had better contact the coastguard service and put them on alert.'

'Where do we go from here, Martin?' asked Jonathon after a long silence.

'We sit and wait.'

'You don't expect me to sit here all afternoon, do you?'

'All afternoon, all night and even all day tomorrow if need be. However long this takes, you and I stay together until those two are banged up in this nick.'

'How do I explain that to Carolyne and to the office? Also I'm due in court tomorrow morning at 10 am.' He shuddered internally as the double meaning of what he had just said hit home.

'I'm sure you will think of something.'

Rees-Jones's mobile started to ring and Carlisle motioned for him to pass over the phone, but it was a withheld number and he handed it back.

'No funny business; if it's them; try and act normal.'

Jonathon answered, knowing already who it was.

'Got a problem, I need £10,000 tonight. Be outside the Tower Bridge Hotel at midnight.'

Short and to the point, the caller hung up but Carlisle had instantly recognised the woman's voice. He'd been present at the interrogation when Abdul had escaped and would never forget it; cold and heartless, slightly accented, it was Anna Karim.

'It looks like the puppet is back on the string, Jonathon, only this time we'll be working you.' He reached for his phone. 'Sergeant Mackenzie. I don't know quite what's going on but Madam has just phoned arranging a meet for tonight. Either they are still holed up here on the mainland or are returning, probably by scheduled ferry. Whichever, I suggest you alert the ports: they are not to try and apprehend, just inform us if they arrive.'

36

South Africa, October 2003

Willy and the boys were getting worried. Jomo was long overdue and Willy feared the worst, that Jomo couldn't wait any longer and had returned to the village. In itself it was a natural thing to want to do, but if the Arab found out that one of his vans was missing and he was short of a driver, then there would be hell to pay in the morning.

They had witnessed the Arab in a temper and some of them bore the scars of his viciousness; he wouldn't miss it tonight, he was too interested in the women in his bed, so they had a few hours to think of something.

There was no way any one of them would attempt to go and find Jomo on a night as black as this, as navigating without the moon and stars was impossible, and then there were the lions! Willy shuddered at the thought, then he heard the sound of an engine way down in the valley and breathed a sigh of relief.

Willy detested the Arab. He hated the way he abused the women and treated everyone like dirt, but then there was the money. Willy earned double the amount of the others because he was the man the Arab left in charge when he went away, and he also knew about everything that went on here. There would never be another chance like this one again, which was why he was so hard on the others, and why he was so angry with Jomo. The Arab would blame him and, although the beating would hurt,

211

that didn't worry him, it was the thought of losing this job that mattered most to Willy.

As the sound of the approaching vehicle got louder, Willy realised that it was a bigger engine noise than the van and he rushed up into the roof of the barn. Looking down the hill, he made out the headlights of what appeared to be an old Ford truck, the sort used for interstate transportation.

What should he do now? Willy was undecided. There had never been a delivery this late and the Arab would be out of his brains by now, as would his men. It was probably a special delivery and he would have to handle it, there was no other choice.

Willy gave the orders to open the main gates and the giant barn doors, and as the truck rumbled round the final bend with its old engine labouring, Jomo slipped unnoticed out of the side. Taking refuge behind a giant baobab tree, he watched as the truck crawled up the drive and into the barn and, as it came to a halt, he saw the back doors fly open and armed police poured out of the back so fast that Willy and the boys didn't have a chance to run away.

After everybody had been rounded up the officer in charge spoke for the first time, words that shook Willy rigid.

'Which one of you is Willy?'

He must have looked guilty because the officer marched straight up to him before he could answer and, taking him by the arm, led him round to the back of the truck. Willy had never been so frightened in his life.

'If you tell the truth you will be free to go but, if you lie, you will go to prison for a long time, OK?'

Still trembling with fear, he nodded agreement.

'I want to know how many men are in the house. Are they all armed, and which room is the Arab's?' Inspector Preetzius could not believe how different this was from the last time, so far not a shot had been fired.

As Willy led the officers through a connecting door into the main house they became suspicious, no gunfire greeted them, in fact no one greeted them. Willy nodded upstairs but no one moved, fearing they were being led into a trap.

'Where is everyone, Willy? You told us that there were eight armed men in here, plus the Arab, so what game are you playing at?'

'It's no game, boss. Every night it is the same here, whoring and drinking and the other stuff, they are always smashed by this time, including the women.'

Still not convinced, Kiefer Preetzius led his men cautiously up the staircase as Willy pointed to a pair of double doors at the end of a corridor.

'The Arab's in there and the others are spread around this floor.' Willy's whispered words had barely left his mouth as all hell broke out around him.

It was so easy Preetzius couldn't believe it. Three men tried for their weapons, but were either too drunk or otherwise engaged to do much, and they found Abdul Karim in another universe. Inspector Preetzius read him his rights but he was wasting his breath and, as they half carried and half dragged Abdul Karim down the stairway, he dedicated this night to the memory of his best friend, David Mackenzie.

Willy was devastated. In the space of twenty minutes his whole life had been turned upside down, and he did not know which way to turn now. After showing the police where everything was, the underground canning plant and the big steel walk-in safe with the stuff in it, they had told him he could go, but go where? He could not return to the village with the others in the morning, he had lost face and would have to live the rest of his life in shame and, in any case, there was no way he wanted to return to being a cattle-herder.

He had discovered an exciting new world and he wanted more and, although money wasn't a problem for now, he knew that what he had wouldn't last for ever. However, he had learned how and where there was big money to be gained, and he did know the right connections in the city, it was the only place to head for.

Damn Jomo, I'll skin his whinging hide if I ever catch up with him, Willy thought as he went round the back of the house and down to the thicket of thorn trees that grew in a small hollow. Using a large stick he pushed back a vicious overhanging branch and retrieved the tin box that was his passport to the future.

All this time Jomo had remained rooted to the spot, shaking from head to foot as he witnessed firstly his terrified friends being rounded up like cattle, then the Arab and his men being dragged and carried to the lorry, protesting vehemently as they were thrown into the back.

He saw Willy disappear around the side of the house the minute the lorry was gone and, pulling himself together, he ran up the drive. Retrieving the sack from the dead tree he stuffed the bank notes into his pockets, shivering not from the fast-descending night cold but fear of the retribution he would face in the morning!

37

West Africa, October 2001

The sun rose in the sky as the five men crawled to the edge of the clearing, unsure of exactly what awaited them but certain that their presence here must surely be known of.

Through the sight Mario could see the town on the other side of the river, and, although bigger than its neighbour, it looked poorer and seemed to lack the military discipline of a cockney Mickey.

What was obvious was that something was definitely wrong, all of them could sense it, but no one could put their finger on it. The town appeared to have been evacuated, or was lying in wait for something or someone, for there were no sounds or movement anywhere, not even a child or an animal could be seen or heard.

They retreated back into the forest to decide on their next move, Mario casting the sight over the umbrella of trees certain that he would spot something. Nothing! Had they fallen into a giant trap or was the town expecting other visitors? Their nerve ends were raw now, the fear knotting their stomachs, but of one thing Mario was decided, he would have to make the kill from this side of the water. The river was much wider here and there was no way of crossing it without being spotted, even at night, although he estimated that the firing distance would be at the absolute maximum of the rifle's capacity, increasing the difficulty of the kill.

All their questions were answered some five minutes later when the town came under mortar fire from the surrounding hills and, immediately, hidden gun emplacements around the outskirts of the town began returning fire, the war within a civil war was erupting once again.

This was the good fortune that they had been hoping for. The soldiers here had been too occupied preparing for this attack to take notice of any screams in the night, all Mario needed now was a sighting of the target. He was hoping that if things got too sticky the General would withdraw his troops across the river and lay a trap here in the jungle, which would make the hit much simpler.

If this didn't happen, what alternatives did he have? They couldn't stay here much longer without being discovered, and they couldn't risk crossing the water. He was on the point of changing the plan for the kill when the bombardment stopped, the ground no longer shaking beneath them, and an eerie silence once more descended on the area.

Not sure of what to expect next, Mario signalled for them to stay hidden as he climbed a tree and from there he saw that the town centre was burning fiercely. Then, to his amazement, dozens of women and children appeared as if from nowhere, and were being herded into lorries as if the order had gone out to abandon it.

Where were all the soldiers? Yes, there were those who had returned fire earlier, but that was only a handful of men. According to Mickey's intelligence, there was a force of several hundred troops here who seemed to have disappeared off the face of the earth.

As the trucks began to leave, the bombardment of the town recommenced, and the attacking faction came down the hill in a classic pincer movement, cutting off any chance of escape in that direction, as the mortars from the town opened fire in defence once more. Too late, the invading force realised their folly. From out of the ground hundreds of soldiers appeared, catching them in a wicked crossfire which massacred many of their troops and drove the rest back up the hill to where the mortars were landing.

Mario could only sit and admire his target's strategy, although he detested the idea of using women and children as bait, as he finally pinpointed the victorious leader being driven back to town. Unsure of the man's destination, Mario hurriedly left the tree and, returning to the edge of the clearing, he took up a position which gave him a clear shot straight up the main street – this would be his one and only chance.

France, October 2003

It had all been so simple two hours ago and now they were returning to who knows what, even the lawyer seemed to be acting funny on the phone. Although she was tempted to open the throttle and just keep going, Anna knew Mackinley's doubts were justified. Paddy was a loose cannon, so they had phoned around until they found someone with an HGV licence. Ten grand was an exorbitant price for a couple of hours' work, but the guy would know what he would be moving once he knew who he was working for and, considering the value of the load, it was peanuts.

They were taking a tremendous risk by using a scheduled ferry service but Anna was counting on the fact that the authorities would be on the lookout for them leaving and not entering the country. Her other problem was Mackinley, who was getting more and more wound up, and she just hoped that there wouldn't be any complications before they arrived back in London.

38

London, October 2003

Paul and Liam had spent a frustrating afternoon trying to trace the destination of the van that had emptied the Thames River Trading Co. premises. Within a twenty-minute radius, every building had been searched on both sides of the river, as had everything on the water, to no avail, and the arrival of DCS Carlisle and DCI Tomlinson came as a welcome relief.

'Ladies and gentlemen. You'll be pleased to hear that my guest has just received a phone call arranging a meet for midnight tonight at the Tower Bridge Hotel. Those two have need of £10,000 urgently but I don't know what for, and I can't guarantee that one or both of them will show up to make the collection, so the decision we have to take now is which way to play this. Almost certainly they will be on a motorbike, which means that it will be impossible to follow them as they will spot and lose a tail very easily.'

'Also, they will be wearing leathers and helmets, making identification impossible.' Paul intervened, liking this less and less. 'They might even send one of their minions and we'll be no closer to her than we are now.'

'So what do you suggest, Sergeant? Let them take the ten grand and hope we get another chance?' The sarcasm was heavy in the voice of the DCI.

'She's got us by the balls again, sir.' Liam leapt to Paul's defence. 'The Sergeant's right, identity will be impossible and we know that the lady is far too canny to risk anything. Yes, she doesn't know there will be a trap, and yes, the odds are in our favour, but I doubt very much whether she would take a chance with herself or Mackinley. The best we can hope for is that we nab someone who can point a finger.'

'There is the question of ten grand in all this – would they trust a third party to handle that?' DI Watkinson made a valid point.

'If they send someone else the chances are that that person won't have a clue as to what they are collecting and, anyway, they all live in fear of those two and nobody would take the risk of incurring their wrath for just ten grand.' Liam, like Paul, knew that this was going to be another wasted night.

'So that's it, is it?' DCS Carlisle was disappointed in his team but, looking at it logically, they were right. 'We grab whoever turns up and hope it is them or someone who might sing. Set it up, Inspector, it's the only choice we've got.'

It was an awful night for this type of police work, the rain pouring down incessantly, with an icy wind coming off the river and visibility greatly reduced. With his officers strategically placed, DI Watkinson, Liam and Paul sat in the unmarked van monitoring the movements in the car park. As midnight came and went the tension mounted and the doubts began to form in their minds when, suddenly, a motorbike roared into the car park without a pillion, the rider obviously looking for something.

'All units stand by.'

'That's not Anna, that's for certain,' Liam said. 'The rider's too big, but it could well be Mackinley.'

'Everybody be very careful, this could be Mackinley.' The DI's worst fears were about to be realised as whoever it was spotted Rees-Jones' car and in a flash had the boot up and down.

'Move in.'

From cars and shadows armed police converged on the biker, who opened the throttle and roared for the exit. Pulling a gun from the leathers, the biker began firing as Liam drove the van across the road, blocking its path, and DI Watkinson gave the order. 'Fire at the bike.'

A volley of shots rang out, and sparks flew from the bike as the bullets hit it and its rider, causing the person to lose control. It crashed to the ground, throwing the rider clear. The bike slid into the van as the driver staggered to stand, firing wildly, until the smashed legs could take no more and he fell to the ground in a crumpled heap. Liam and Paul were there like a shot, their guns pointing to the head as they tried to remove the helmet.

'Lower your guns now, you two.' DI Watkinson's voice rose above everything else as he sensed what might happen, and for a moment they hesitated until the red mist started to recede. Under the helmet they found Paddy Dennison, his face contorted in agony but still able to mouth obscenities at them as the DI read him his rights.

Rees-Jones was still sitting in his car, quivering like a jelly and unable to move, when they went to collect him. Totally traumatised, he realised that his life was worth nothing now, as Anna and Mackinley would have worked out who was responsible for this. Even if they didn't do the job themselves they could easily find someone else to do it – or they'd put a word out here and there, exposing him, and Carolyne and the boys would have to live with his shame for the rest of their lives, as would he.

He began sobbing hysterically and, as they got him out of his vehicle and half carried him to a waiting police car, he started to beg for protection.

Meanwhile, Anna had been sitting in the lorry's cab, staring aimlessly out on the river, her patience fast running out while Mackinley, as usual, was outside pacing up and down in the rain, cursing everyone and everything. The driver they had hired was certainly not used to this type of work and, as he sat there sweating profusely and continually glancing at his watch, Anna began to worry about how he would react if things started to go wrong.

What a mess! Today had confirmed her earlier thinking: it was time to call it a day and get out before her luck ran out, the writing was on the wall and she certainly didn't fancy doing another stretch. She had managed to keep Mackinley reasonably calm on the journey back, although he did keep threatening to rip Paddy's head from his shoulders when they caught up with him. Thankfully, Paddy was sober and, although there was a lot of verbal, she had managed to keep them apart, which was why she had sent Paddy to collect the money instead of going herself.

When they had arrived back at Dover there was a considerable police presence but they were not stopped, even at customs. It had all been so easy, too easy, as if they were saying 'we know who you are and we've got you tagged'. Her imagination was running wild now, or was it? She wound down the window.

'Something's wrong, Mack. Get in the cab, we're getting out of here.'

As Mackinley opened the door the sound of gunfire came across the water and the night sky was lit by flashing blue lights.

'Go!' Anna yelled at the driver. 'Head for the tunnel.'

'I'm going nowhere, lady, without my money.'

Mackinley exploded and, grabbing him by the throat, was half throttling him when Anna intervened.

'He's no good to us dead, Mack. Back off.'

The driver was red in the face, gasping for breath, as Mackinley slowly released his grip.

'You heard the lady, head for the tunnel.'

In the back of the police van a relieved Peter Watkinson was counting the cost of another abortive attempt to catch Anna Karim. All his officers had escaped injury, the only thing damaged was the van and the morale of his troops. They stood around outside, oblivious to the weather, the adrenalin still pumping and not accepting that all was lost this night.

The unanswered questions were, why did they come back, and what did they need ten grand for so urgently? It was Paul who inadvertently came up with the solution.

'What if, when they emptied the warehouse, they didn't transfer the goods to another building or a barge but into a trailer? All this time it has been sitting in a car park or lay-by, in full view under our noses, while we've been searching all around it. We have removed from the play a lot of their henchmen and, having forced those two into hiding, they were obliged to leave everything in Dennison's hands. For one reason or another they panicked and, no longer trusting Dennison to do the job, had to return to find a driver with an HGV, hence the money. If they are using a trailer it must be in the area we've searched and is probably now hooked up to a unit waiting for the cash to pay the driver. Madam and Mackinley, I would guess, are probably in the cab as well.'

'If you are right, Sergeant, the sound of shooting would have frightened them off by now. However, it all sounds very feasible so I suggest we cruise the area and take a look, we've nothing more to lose and how many artics are there moving around at this time of night?'

Everyone was still keyed up and willing to try anything, so they dissected the area both sides of the river and set off, Paul, Liam and the Inspector going over the bridge and turning left along the river. Although it was the last place that any one of them wanted to revisit, they pulled into the Thames River Trading Co. warehouse. It was an old trick that Mackinley might have tried but, as before, it was empty.

They continued down Jamaica Road and round Rotherhithe Street, checking all the stationary lorries en route, but to no avail. There was no movement of any sort, either people or vehicles and, having checked with the other units and found the same result, the DI decided to call it a night.

Once again Anna Karim was sending them home angry and frustrated and tomorrow morning Jonathon Rees-Jones QC was going to be cross-examined like he had never cross-examined anyone before, of that Liam Jameson was certain.

*   *   *

As they sped through the Blackwall Tunnel, Anna's mind was a racing jumble of anger and hatred, the events of the past few weeks all challenging for a place in her thoughts, as she pieced together when and why it all had started to unravel.

She was angry because she had been double-crossed by her own family. For over thirty years she had protected them all, putting a roof over their heads and keeping them out of nick, and this was how they had repaid her.

She was full of hatred when she thought again of the man who had started all this and then his damn brother, who wouldn't stay at home, and had pushed her family this far.

Even if she had to do the job herself she vowed that, before this was over, the Mackenzie brothers would be reunited in hell. She had wanted to get rid of the 'South African' years ago but Abdul had persuaded her differently, and this was the result. And where was he now? Probably safe back in South Africa, leaving her to carry the can and clear up the mess. He hadn't even bothered to warn her after the airport fiasco.

Then there was the call to the brief. He'd never reacted to her calls like that before, saying next to nothing, mumbling down the phone, so she took out her mobile and searched for the number.

It was switched off. That was rule number one, the mobile must never be turned off; what was Jones playing at? Had they finally got to him through the twins or a whisper, and was he responsible for tonight's disaster? Or had Paddy opened his big mouth in some pub somewhere?

Anna's mind was working overtime now. If they have got to the brief, how much has he told them, and what happens to it all if he goes down? Everything was channelled through an off-shore account in the Isle of Man including the ownership of the properties, the various bank accounts, the shares, indeed all her wealth, and although she had access to a couple of mainland accounts the amounts deposited wouldn't get her very far.

She had no right of entry to any of it. On Jones's advice she had given him total control and then it dawned on her, the bile rising within as the earth-shattering truth hit home. Who was the real puppet on a string? All these years she had thought that she had him in her pocket and he'd been milking her rotten.

'Pull over, stop the lorry, I'm going to be sick!'

She leapt out before it had stopped moving, Mackinley quickly following her, then everything happened so fast. Before they knew it the driver had put the vehicle in gear and, with the momentum he already had, began to pull away.

Mackinley pulled his gun and aimed at the rear tyres of the disappearing lorry but Anna knocked his gun off aim and started to run after the truck, but it was too late, it had sufficient speed and was gone.

They sat by the roadside, the rain still pouring down, not believing what had just happened. How could they have been so stupid? She had never seen Mackinley this angry and, for the first time ever, she was frightened of him. In the cab of the lorry was her handbag, with money, passports, cheque book and mobile phone in it, and she was God knows where in the middle of the night.

'What the bloody hell was all that about?' Mackinley finally spoke. 'You've just lost us everything we had.'

So she told him her thoughts about Rees-Jones, and the conclusions she'd come to, which started him ranting again. Anna had never seen this side of him before, totally maniacal and, if they were to get out of this mess, she would have to get him back under control and quickly. The first thing they had to do was to get off the road: anyone seeing them might report it or, worse still, there could be a passing patrol car and they were both armed.

'Give me your phone, Mack, we've got to get out of here fast. Do you have any idea of what road we are on, or where we are?'

Before he could reply his mobile rang, and Anna snatched it from him.

'I want fifty grand to tell you where the trailer is.'

'My bag's in the cab. If you want that kind of money you're going to have to come and collect us.'

Anna was quickly back in control of the situation. Wherever he was he was stationary as there was no engine noise and, looking at her watch, she calculated he couldn't be more than five miles away.

'I'll come back and pick you up, lady, but Mackinley stays put. I don't want him in the cab with me.'

'We can't leave him out here, it's too risky. If you want the money it's the both of us or nothing.'

There was a long silence which was broken just as Anna's patience was about to run out.

'OK, here's what we'll do, lady. I'm going to pick up another trailer and, when I pull up, he goes inside it and tell him there is to be no funny business.'

'Come and get us.' Anna had no other choice, and neither had Mackinley. The problem now was how to raise the money. She didn't have enough in the local accounts, and if Rees-Jones was banged up and his mobile confiscated then she was finished. The load was worth millions, and maybe the driver would do a deal, but then she couldn't sell any of it and get the money that quickly. No, her only hope was to somehow contact the brief and act as if it was business as usual, but how?

Although he had calmed down by the time they got him back to the Yard, Rees-Jones was still a very frightened and depressed man. Everything he possessed in the world counted for nothing at this moment in time, as he sat in his cell contemplating the future. They had removed his tie, belt, and shoelaces, and put him under twenty-four-hour suicide surveillance, but he knew he didn't have the guts for that, although it did seem the only alternative.

What would he do once they released him? Where would he go and how could he evade Anna Karim's revenge once she realised the truth? There were many influential friends in his social circle who he could turn to, but how could he explain why? No, he had dug himself a big hole and there seemed no way out, it was filling in fast around him. In the morning he would face interrogation, which didn't bother him, he just had to decide what, and how much, he was going to tell them: as long as it got him released that was the most important thing at this moment.

As he lay there thinking about everything a thought came to him through the doom. Anna would need money in the morning and, after last night's debacle, he needed to keep Anna and Mackinley at arm's length. He controlled the purse strings so they needed to keep him alive and the lid on the other business. It was a simple solution which might work and in this way he could protect Carolyne and the boys. As the puppeteer he could control the show, Carlisle as well, and at the same time secure his freedom.

39

France, November 2001

His flight from Africa had been less eventful than his arrival, a grateful President giving him the use of his private plane to the destination of his choice. He decided that he was in need of solitude and a chance to recharge the batteries so he had chosen Ajaccio and immediately headed straight for the mountains. He slept long and heavy for several days, only venturing from the house to hunt for food, and when he felt ready he drove back to Ajaccio and booked a flight to Nice.

He had left the cruiser in the hands of a local dealer with instructions to sell but not complete on the transaction until he returned. Feeling safer walking the streets of Nice, he sought out the man, a colourful French/Italian known all along the waterfront as Christophe le Grand.

True to form, he found him in a bar chatting to the local girls and appearing not to have a care in the world, until he saw Matthew. This had an instant sobering effect on Christophe as he left his company without saying a word and, grabbing hold of his arm, hurried Matthew back outside.

'You've got a lot of explaining to do, mon ami, and my fee has certainly doubled if not tripled. What makes you the most popular man on the Riviera? As well as the police I've had visits from some unsavoury characters, which is not good for my business or my reputation.'

'Do you think that you are being followed or has the boat been found and they are watching that?'

'I don't think I've a tail, but I can't be certain about the boat. I've denied all knowledge of you, and it's been general inquiries up to now, but whether I've succeeded in convincing them or not is another matter.'

'Thank you for that. I can assure you that it has nothing to do with drugs or firearms, if that is what you are worried about; it's to do with something much closer to your heart, if I'm not mistaken. A married woman.'

The relief on Christophe's face was evident in the huge grin that appeared as he put his arm around Matthew's shoulder and led him to the car.

'That's all right then, let's get back to business. I've sold her for you and I've found a replacement.'

Matthew nervously glanced all around him as they drove along the Promenade des Anglais towards Cannes, at the same time wondering how they could possibly have found the boat here in Nice. Then it dawned on him.

'Stop the car as soon as you can, Christophe, and pull over.'

First he tried the wheel arches, then he lay on his back and pulled himself under the car. He found nothing and, as Christophe continued to question him, he lifted the bonnet. There it was, the same type of little chip as before, which meant Consuela must have bugged the cruiser at some time and, if he was not mistaken, they were being followed now.

'Christophe. I want another favour from you. This thing is a tracking device, which means whoever is following me is probably not far away. I want you to drive off slowly around the block and pick me up in about ten minutes.'

The traffic was very light, which made his task that much easier as he took up a position behind a small scrub fence close to the road. His worst fears were confirmed almost immediately when an airport hire car, driven by the Australian with his partner next to him, cruised by.

Christophe's timing was perfect and, as he pulled up, Matthew signalled for him to open the bonnet.

'Right, my friend, let's get rid of them first then go and see this new beauty you've found for me.'

They stopped at some traffic lights and Matthew got out of the car and approached the bus in front of them, leaving a bemused Christophe unsure as to what to expect next.

'What was all that about? Life with you is certainly not boring.'

'Let's just say our friends are about to take a scenic tour.'

Matthew smiled and gave him a wink and, although he didn't quite understand what was going on, Christophe sensed that there would be no further problems as they arrived at the harbour at Cannes.

He didn't need anyone to tell him. The beautiful craft just stood out proud and elegant as she bobbed gently at her mooring, Matthew already the owner before he had stepped on board.

'You're a genius, Christophe. You've definitely earned your bonus this time. When can I take possession?'

'I knew the minute you saw her what your reaction would be so I've had the notaire's office draw up all the paperwork and all it needs is your signature.'

He couldn't wait to leave Cannes so he hurriedly put to sea heading for his beloved Corsica. It was good to be alone and back in control of his life but he knew it couldn't last, as long as Consuela was around his life would never be his own.

For the moment, though, he had a new love in his life, who responded to his slightest touch and, as the harbour at Ajaccio came into view, he was sorely tempted to turn around not wanting this new affair to end.

Up until now he had resisted the temptation to look at his mound of newspapers, but curiosity got the better of him. Headlines and personal column, the usual depressing stories from around the world greeted him, but there did not appear to have been another robbery.

What there was, though, shook him rigid as he turned to the

personal column of the edition dated five days ago. *My Corsican, I forgive you and need you urgently. Please come home by the nineteenth, before it is too late.* Damn it! Why had he told her how to contact him? But it did explain why those two were tracking him – Consuela was still pulling his strings. The nightmare would not go away, he had to finish this thing now before it destroyed him, but what was she up to? Today was the sixteenth, which left him precious little time to plan anything; he had no one in England who could help him and, more importantly, was this a trap and had she informed the police of his identity?

The old saying that 'hell has no fury like a women scorned' kept going around in his head, and he reflected on these words as he tried to work out his options.

For a start he wasn't going to walk into the lion's den without being armed, but where could he find a gun in England at such short notice? If the police knew of his identity, would he have some sort of reception committee waiting for him, and how could he check that out without anyone to contact? She had him cold, there just wasn't enough time to get organised, but he knew it had to be now or spend the rest of his life looking over his shoulder, so he decided to take the risk and return to England.

London, October 2003

Luigi Barolli sat in solitary, wondering what the hell was going on. He had been told that his lifeline to the outside world was unobtainable for a second time and he was facing spending the rest of his life in this or some other stinking nick. Where was that pervert Jones when he needed him, and had Anna been caught? Was the deal still on or had Anna escaped, which meant that he was a dead man out of solitary, certainly in this nick? His sister could get any one of half a dozen in here to do the job, the sooner he was transferred the better.

The cell door opened and two screws he had never seen before

230

entered. Luigi tensed as they handcuffed him, fear spreading through his body, not sure whether he was being led to his death or not.

'Come on, Barolli, you've got visitors.'

More than one, that ruled out Jones, and he was quite relieved when he entered the room to see who it was, although their faces told him that this was more bad news.

'You are going to have to find yourself another brief, Barolli. We've got yours banged up.'

Mark Burley let him have it before he could say a word.

'Your sister's on the run, thanks to him, and you don't need us to tell you that your lifespan has now reached zero. We can still protect you and offer you a deal, what we need to know is everything: addresses, names, where your sister might be holed up, who would help her, we want the works and we want it now or you perish!'

40

He had been a far from happy man with the arrangements, but Anna was back in control and he was once again the obedient employee as the lorry sped back towards London. It was a calculated risk to go to the Chiswick lock-up but they had no other choice, they needed the spare bike above everything else if they were to have any chance of getting out of this mess.

It was still very early morning, the traffic was light, and she was gambling that the police would not have begun to question Rees-Jones as they entered the Cromwell Road. Anna had decided that it would be less conspicuous if the lorry was to back up to a building site around the corner from the lock-up, where she could let Mackinley out of the trailer unnoticed. Also, it meant that the driver didn't have a clue as to where the lock-up was situated and they could walk there in relative safety, although two people dressed in leathers strolling the streets at that time of the morning was an unusual sight.

They stood watching the lock-up and observing the stationary cars and the people who appeared to be going nowhere in particular. Anna decided to take the chance. It was too risky to hang around here for too long so she crossed the road and approached the doors while Mackinley kept his eyes on everything around them. She was in and out before he knew it, and they set off to find a hotel from where she could once again control the play.

It was a real 'morning after the night before' in the squad room when Liam and Paul arrived the next morning. Everyone had a hangover, caused by a very late night and too much disappointment, the gloom hanging suspended in the air. The only light on the horizon was the QC but as the two men entered the interview room, they found a different man from the night before.

He appeared to be very much back under control, his normal smooth, assured, superior self had returned and they sensed that this wasn't going to be easy. It had been decided that Paul would lead the interview as Liam was still seething at the deal that had been done, even though it now meant that they could use this creature as live bait to catch Anna and Mackinley. So Liam sat there fighting his emotions, trying to keep himself under control, all the while hating the "old pals act" which would see this man walk free.

'When did you first meet the Barollis?'

'In 1973.'

'How?'

Jones looked at the floor as he sought the right words.

'Look, the sooner you cooperate the sooner you are out of here.' Paul was in no mood either for lawyer-type games.

'Now I want answers and I want the truth, or all deals are off and you're going down. How did you meet the Barollis?'

'I got picked up one night in a bar by Anna and we ended up in a small hotel off the Bayswater Road. You know the rest, they all went down for it in 1975.'

'We don't know the rest, we are waiting for you to tell us.'

He hesitated, this was not how he had planned it, but maybe it was for the best. Maybe it was time for the truth.

'I was in my final year at Law School and engaged to be married to the daughter of a partner in an old established firm of solicitors. I'd been promised a junior partnership when I qualified and everything in the garden was rosy. The night I met Anna changed my life forever. Not because of the other business but because I was smitten, hopelessly and forever. She was the woman of my dreams and, even after I had learnt the truth, we still saw one another.

233

I would dance to her tune and pay the money. I didn't care about the other men, I just hoped and prayed that I could change her ways. We would spend fantastic nights and days together, when she wasn't otherwise engaged, then she just disappeared. I tried searching for her but the twins warned me off and, luckily for me, we were not together when she got arrested.'

Liam looked at Paul as the lawyer momentarily faltered. This was the last thing that they had expected and it was obvious that he still worshipped her today, which could cause problems later. Before Paul could say anything, Rees-Jones carried on.

'The extortion didn't end there. Although they were in prison Anna and the twins controlled other people on the outside and I kept paying. By the time they came out, in 1979, I had married Juliette Bamforth and was established as a junior partner in the firm of Bamforth, Bamforth and Jones, which is still the trading name today.

'Anna came to see me soon after her discharge, saying that she wanted to buy a property in Islington and would I handle the conveyancing? She said that I would not have to pay any more providing I managed all her business affairs from then on.'

'How many properties does she own at the moment?'

'The ones you know about at Dorking and Chiswick, plus a small lock-up not far from the Chiswick house. Then there are a couple of old warehouses on the river and various leasehold properties, shops mostly, but they change so often I can't remember the addresses.'

'But you have a record of them at the office?'

'Of course, everything is legal and above board.'

'Does she own any properties in Italy or South Africa?'

'Yes. Again all the details are on file.'

'What about the lock-up in Chiswick, where is it?' Liam broke his silence as he thought about the night of the raid on Anna's house.

'In the Goldhawk Road, just up the road from the tube station.'

'And where does she keep the boat moored?'

'I haven't any idea. I don't think she has a permanent berth because I'd know about it for legal reasons.'

Liam hid his delight at confirmation of his theory and continued. 'What's the name of the boat?'

'Napoli.'

Paul called in the constable from outside the door and gave him the information on the lock-up and the boat to convey to the DI, although he realised that by this time one would be empty and the other would have had a facelift.

'Where is she at the moment? Who would be sheltering her?'

'Sadly, Anna has no friends and only that animal Mackinley that she can trust, so they will be staying in a hotel somewhere for the time being.'

'You said you had married Juliette Bamforth, what happened?

'A riding accident. She got thrown and never regained consciousness, was never likely to, so we had to make the decision to turn off the life-support system.'

'Were you aware of the business Anna and Abdul were in at that time?'

'Not at first. Then they bought more properties and it became obvious that the sort of money they were generating didn't come from gainful employment.' He was starting to relax now, but his attempt at humour was ignored.

'What happened to Abdul's share? We know he is alive so don't try and deny it.'

Rees-Jones looked at the two men, totally shocked. This was news to him, but it did explain a lot of things.

'You really didn't know?' Paul could tell from his expression and the way he just sat there that this was something he had not been a party to.

'No. There is an automatic monthly transfer of funds to South Africa, but I always assumed that it was to pay for the drugs.'

'You handle all her affairs, how are the finances managed?'

'Everything is channelled through an off-shore company I set up in the Isle of Man called The Thames Valley Investment Company.'

Paul suddenly realised just how clever this man was and that Anna Karim needed to keep him alive and out of jail to get to the money, if he hadn't salted it all away.

'What have you done with all the money, where is it?'

'In the same place it's always been.'

'But only you can access it directly,' Paul cut him off.

They called in the constable and headed for the third floor. They had to talk to the DCS – Rees-Jones was his baby.

Once again this case had taken another bizarre turn and Martin Carlisle sat there, momentarily speechless, as the two men related the details of the interrogation: Rees-Jones and Anna Karim had been lovers, this world never failed to amaze him.

'This puts a totally different light on things. You say he is still besotted by her, so do you think that that could have an influence on how he behaves from now on?'

'Without a doubt, sir. However, he holds the trump card, the key to the money. This will keep him alive and his secret safe all the time Anna's at large, but what happens to him afterwards?'

'That's a good point, Liam, and I'm sure he has thought of that as well. So, what do you want to do now, bearing in mind that he is our one chance of ending this?'

'We need to let him run and give him back his mobile.' This was the last thing that Liam really wanted to do but he knew they had no other choice. 'Anna is desperate for money and Rees-Jones is her only source so, even if she has worked out what has happened, she will still take the chance on contacting him.'

'Can we trust him to play by the rules?'

'I wouldn't trust him at all, he is too shrewd a character, but he has got that big cloud hanging over his head so he can't afford not to.'

'OK, gentlemen. Give him back his mobile and let him contact her before we let him go. It's a big gamble but, you're right, we have no other choice.'

DCS Carlisle sat looking at the man across the desk from him, still unable to come to grips with the truth. He too had noticed a change in him from the day before, a change that made his policeman's instincts sit up, as Rees-Jones dialled the number and, instantly, that unforgettable voice answered.

'Where the bloody hell have you been? What's happened?'

'It's all over, Anna. I'm at the Yard, have been all night.'

'And Carlisle is with you now, that's why you're still using the mobile?'

'Exactly, sitting opposite me.'

'What have you told them?'

'Everything.'

'And I'm the bait that keeps you out.'

'Of course.'

'I need £75,000 today, and time to think.'

'Where and how?'

'I'll call you back.'

During this time Carlisle had sat there biting his tongue and saying nothing. He knew that he was placing his career on the line here but he had no other alternative and, although he hated not being in total control, he would have to play along with the game for now. There was no chance of him talking her into giving herself and Mackinley up, that would never happen, this whole affair was only going to end one way – in bloodshed. He was about to embark on a dangerous journey which would go all the way down to the wire, but it was the only way that they could finish this nightmare.

'Can you organise that amount of money in such a short space of time?' He was already trying to look for any possible snags that might occur.

'It won't be a problem, but first I must phone the office to rearrange my workload and then Carolyne. She will be beside herself by now.'

Martin Carlisle was in a quandary. Do I let him go and trust him or do I tail him? If he is still carrying a torch for Anna Karim, will he make one last gesture to help her, knowing that his is a hopeless situation? Rees-Jones' mobile rang again, breaking his thinking.

'Thank God, Jonathon, where are you? What's going on?' Carlisle could hear Carolyne's frantic tones. 'I've been trying to get hold of you all night. Your mother's had a stroke and been taken to the Surrey County at Guildford. You never switch your mobile off, what are you playing at?'

'I'm with Martin discussing a very confidential police matter, but I will leave for the hospital immediately.'

'I'll see you there in about an hour. Do you want a change of clothes or anything?'

'Yes please, that would be nice. See you soon.'

The lies continued, and the remorse returned, as he once again felt that big shadow enveloping him. The mother who was his rock, who had always supported him, how would she take all this? He hadn't even given her a thought in the last twenty-four hours and when she needed him most he had not been available. He just sat there letting everything sink in. All the money in the world could not compensate for this feeling of helplessness and, one thing was for sure, the truth would kill his beloved mother, the shame too much for her to bear.

'Jonathon.' Carlisle was talking but he was oblivious. 'Jonathon, you've got to get a grip. You had better go and see your mother now and you will have to stall Anna when she calls back. Don't cross me on this otherwise I will have you behind bars and charged before you know it.'

The hare was up and running, all Carlisle could do now was hope and pray that his men were ready for the feast.

41

'Hello, Mark, this is Consuela. I'm back in Wokingham and wondered if you might like to come to dinner one evening?'

'That would be nice, but are you sure it's not too soon?' As ever, he sounded his usual charming, caring self but Consuela was not fooled.

'Not at all. I'm quite uncertain as to the future and feeling very lost, but that is to be expected. I'm in need of some entertaining company and immediately thought of you. Also, I have a little business proposition that might be of interest to you.'

'It wouldn't be the furniture, would it?'

She could feel his excitement coming down the phone. She had him dangling – the fool.

'How about next Wednesday at 8 pm, we can talk about it then? See you, bye for now.'

He sat there staring at the phone in his hand, his excitement clouding his thinking, as he recalled all the priceless furniture that made up this collection. He had repeatedly told Consuela and her husband that without the pieces in Turin the value of the collection was diminished, but now the Count was dead she must have had them shipped to Wokingham.

She had forced his hand, and there really wasn't enough time to get organised, but if she was considering selling the whole collection he would have to act quickly. Finding buyers at such short notice wasn't a problem, he had been planning this day for

239

a long time and had several takers in the pipeline, the biggest obstacle was the armed bodyguards. His team could handle the security systems but they were not into firearms or unarmed combat so, somehow, he would have to draw her, and them, away from the place. He picked up the phone.

'Consuela, this is Mark. I'm sorry, I had forgotten that I have a sale on here next Wednesday and I won't be closing till late. How about you coming up here and I'll treat you to your favourite restaurant?'

'I'm not sure how safe it is for me to leave the estate again. The Count has a very large family and, until all the legalities are finalised, my life continues to be in danger.'

'Surely if you bring your men with you, you'll be all right. They look a very competent bunch, and I'm sure you would be much safer in the hustle and bustle of London than Wokingham.'

Her mind was in overdrive. Did she have enough time to fit all the other pieces of the jigsaw together? Her burning desire to finish this had overtaken all reason and it had to be sooner rather than later.

'OK, Mark. You are right. I cannot stay cooped up here indefinitely, and a trip to London might make me feel better. I'll be at the gallery some time after seven.'

It was a depressingly cold and damp Heathrow that greeted Matthew on his return to England, doubling his resolve to get this over with quickly. He felt uncomfortable as he passed through Immigration: it was as if they were expecting him and he feared that at any moment he would be arrested. He had taken a huge gamble in coming back, and although he had committed no crime on the British mainland, there could well be an extradition warrant on him issued by another country.

Matthew had no illusions about the world that he moved in. He was a means to an end, a tool used by faceless oligarchs that could be sacrificed at any time and used as a piece of bargaining merchandise if it served some political end.

He knew nothing about his contact here in London, and the stark truth was that he was all alone in this and had no one to turn to for help. Still not convinced that all was well, he left Arrivals and searched for a car hire desk, all the time observing every movement around him.

'Hello, Consuela Cabellorenti.'

'It's Matthew. What game are you playing at now?'

'My darling Matthew, why are you always so suspicious of me? I think the Earl is going to make his move tonight and I'd given up all hope that you would come. Where are you now? I've never been so frightened.'

'I'm in London but I won't come down to Wokingham. Sorry Consuela, you are going to have to use that bunch of amateurs to do your dirty work, I'm not getting involved in any more of your games.'

'Don't you want the man who killed your father?' She knew the instant she had said it what his reaction would be.

'You really are a scheming bitch, do you know that?'

'So, why are you phoning me? Why have you come to England? Come on, Matthew, don't act the hurt little boy with me; you want his killer more than anything in life. I'm handing him to you on a plate just as I promised that day in Paris.'

She really was some actress and Matthew could feel the walls he had rebuilt starting to crumble again but, if he was honest with himself, he would forgive her for everything just to spend another few hours in her company.

'No bugs, no tail, just you and me, Consuela. This time I will kill first and ask questions afterwards, OK?'

'It will have to be today. Have you got a car?'

'I will meet you at Reading station at three o'clock. You will come alone and by train, otherwise you are on your own in this.' Matthew hung up before she could answer. He needed to get back to observing the house, maybe she would play by the rules but he very much doubted it.

Unless she had moved very quickly after his call, Consuela was still in the house, and with seemingly no armed guards patrolling the grounds everything appeared very calm, only the light hum of the distant motorway traffic carrying on the breeze.

Having parked his car back up the road he'd taken cover behind a huge old oak, opposite the electronically-controlled front gates, and was just getting settled when a British Telecom van pulled up and three men got out. Two of them began mounting ladders against a pole just up the road, while the third nonchalantly lit a cigarette and strolled up and down in front of the gates. Consuela's intuition had been right.

To any passing motorist it was a familiar sight in Britain, but Matthew knew differently: as DCI Gates had said, this was a very professional gang. They were fitting electronically-controlled devices to open the gates and switch off the alarms, leaving only the armed bodyguards to contend with, who obviously would not be around when it happened, that was for certain.

In less than ten minutes they drove off, just as the flashing warning light came on and the gates started to open. Matthew was unsure whether to run back and get the car or wait and see what happened. He decided on the latter as a silver blue Mercedes coupe came down the drive: it had to be Consuela, it was her sort of car. She turned left in the direction of the town but it was far too early to catch the train to Reading so, instead of following her, he waited to see what might develop here.

What happened next came as a complete shock although, on second thoughts, it was nothing more than he would have expected of this lady. The gates had remained open and a removal lorry, complete with trailer, turned into the drive. Either she had already sold the furniture or she was removing it with the intention of hiding the contents and claiming against the insurance. And Matthew would be there tonight waiting to confront the gang, and the police, following a tip-off, would arrive to find them all together, although what she had in mind for the Earl he wasn't quite certain.

However, Matthew was not bitter, he'd realised a long time ago what Consuela was all about and could only admire the lady's thinking, but his problem still was how to keep the promise he had made to his father.

Logically it was impossible, and he knew it, and although he was still angry inside maybe he should let common sense prevail and time heal the wound. If he was honest with himself, one of the main reasons for his being here was to see her again, and this time it had almost landed him in prison, but how was he going to get her off his back?

Despite everything she had planned for his demise, Matthew decided to keep their rendezvous, the chance to spend one last afternoon with her was something he couldn't resist.

42

Paul sat at his desk, still not quite able to digest the telephone conversation he had just had with Inspector Preetzius. Was this nightmare finally drawing to a close, and had the supply line once and for all been terminated? He found it difficult to accept that the success he and his brother had worked so long for could be within his grasp.

All they had to do now was shut down the distribution, a task easier said than done, as his thoughts turned to Rees-Jones and Anna Karim and the dangerous game he and the squad were about to play. The pitfalls were countless, careers were being put on the line, and the lives of a lot of police officers endangered in one last desperate attempt to bring this case to an end.

Mark Burley and John Lindsey had been assigned the task of tailing Rees-Jones, leaving Paul and Liam to go and visit Paddy Dennison. Paddy had been in surgery most of the night and although they had inserted steel plates to rebuild his shattered left leg, they were still not certain that they could save it. The surgeon advised them that he had not yet regained consciousness and they should give it another twenty-four hours by which time he should be fit enough to be interrogated.

Frustrated, the two men were undecided as to where to turn to next: they had hoped that Dennison could have pointed them in the right direction and tomorrow would be too late.

'Let's go to Chiswick, Paul, see if we can find anything out about that boat of hers, it's got to be there somewhere.'

Rees-Jones was met at the hospital by a very tearful but distant Carolyne, who could not believe how awful he looked. She had never seen her husband like this, and her female intuition began to put all kinds of ideas into her head, ideas that she wanted to, but could not, dismiss.

They greeted one another like two strangers then disappeared into the hospital, Mark and John waiting outside, the situation for the moment out of their hands. Twenty minutes later Rees-Jones re-emerged alone and set off back in the direction of London, the two cars behind keeping a good distance back. This was the easy part, the problems would come when they hit traffic and had to move in much closer.

Anna lay on the bed thinking the whole thing through for the hundredth time, the restless Mackinley beside her a human bomb ready to explode. At least the boat had not been compromised, and as far as they could tell no one had been near it, so they had loaded the bike on board and taken it across the water to the opposite bank. They had then cruised up and down the river looking for alternative docking places, Anna as usual leaving nothing to chance. The hotel was only two minutes away from where the boat was now moored and, satisfied that everything was in place, she re-dialled the number, her doubts resurfacing as the answer phone cut in once again. What was he up to now? She hung up without leaving a message.

She spent the next hour trying to convince Mackinley that it would work, and keeping him calm, but as the minutes ticked slowly by she began to think that Mackinley's reasoning was right. Everything depended on Rees-Jones and that was what was worrying him and now her. Carlisle was risking everything to try and catch her, using the brief as a pawn in what had become a personal game of chess between them, and what had Carlisle promised the man? Would he deliver or chicken out? That was the big question as she called the number once again and this time it started ringing.

'Where are you, I keep getting the answer-phone? What are you up to?'

'I had to make a detour, Anna. My mother's had a stroke and I went to visit her at Guildford. I've arranged for the transfer of the money and am on my way now to collect it.'

'I'll phone you again in thirty minutes, Jonathon. No fancy games, and try and lose your tail.'

'I haven't got one, Anna, I've been checking. Carlisle is trusting me to play by the rules.'

'Carlisle wouldn't trust his own mother, Jonathon. Don't be so stupid, find it and lose it.'

Anna and Mackinley got up, showered and got dressed, the time had come to reel in the paymaster, recover the load and retire. They had decided that, although it would be a difficult thing to do, they were getting out and Abdul could have whatever was left. After they had sold the load Rees-Jones would become expendable, and once Abdul found out the truth his life wouldn't be worth living. He could keep the money and the properties, but she doubted if he could keep out of Abdul's clutches and, surprisingly, she found herself feeling sorry for the man.

'John. I'm going to move in closer and sit on his tail. I suggest you move up behind me now before we hit the heavy traffic.'

'If he's heading for the bank around the corner from his office, then he will park in the underground car park in Park Lane. We could have communication difficulties down there and he could easily give us the slip by jumping into a cab.'

'He's indicating left. Either he's sussed us or she has rung telling him to make sure. I'm going straight on and you follow him.'

For whatever reasons Rees-Jones was starting to play games

and Mark Burley, concerned that they could easily lose him, phoned the DCS.

'I don't like it, sir. We are coming up to the Hammersmith flyover and he's starting to mess around. We don't think he's on to us, just making sure, but we could easily lose him in this traffic.' Mark then went on to explain his fears about the bank.

'Well, he hasn't phoned me yet to say that she has made contact, and I don't think he'd cross us because there is no other way out for him.' Then Carlisle thought about Anna and Rees-Jones. Would he really sacrifice his freedom for her? 'Stay in there as best you can, I'm going to call him and see what is going on.'

'Martin, you said you were going to trust me on this, so why have I got a tail? Anna won't make a move if I'm being followed.'

'How could I ever trust you again? You just dance to her tune and I want to know each step you take, before you take it. Now, has she contacted you yet?'

'Yes, but only a check-up call. She's due to call again in about ten minutes, after I have picked the money up.'

'I want to know the minute she's phoned. Remember, Jonathon, no silly games or I'll have you lifted all right.'

'Sergeant Mackenzie, where are you?'

'South of the river, sir. We're checking out the riverbank a mile in either direction from the house in the hope that we might spot the cruiser, but going on Stromberti's description it could be any one of a dozen that are moving about out here.'

'OK. I want you to stay where you are. He hasn't received instructions yet or collected the money but I'm sure the river is favourite. I'm also going to get the river division to provide some back-up and a rapid response team to Hammersmith Bridge and Kew.'

DCS Carlisle was also worried about another factor which, because of Rees-Jones's deviation to Guildford, had entered the equation – time. It was an overcast day and at best they had little under an hour before it would be dark, after which it would be impossible to spot or tail anybody.

The phone rang, its echoing tone causing him to start.

'I've got the money and she has told me to proceed to the house in Chiswick.'

'And do what?'

'Nothing. She's phoning me back in twenty minutes.'

Damn the woman, she's going to play the runaround game: Carlisle was starting to get twitchy as he thought out all the possibilities.

'All units. He's proceeding to the house at Chiswick and awaiting instructions. I want all units to be within the vicinity of Chiswick Bridge as it now seems certain that they are going to use the river in some way; Hammersmith and Kew are covered.'

The traffic was heavy and slow-moving and Rees-Jones couldn't wait for this nightmare to end quickly. Once again the sight of his critically ill mother flashed through his mind, and although she was expected to live they had no idea as yet of the long-term damage. If only she had died it would have been one less complication in my life, he told himself, instantly regretting the thought.

Then there was Carolyne. No matter how plausible it had all sounded to him, he knew she wasn't convinced. This had been the first real serious test of their marriage and, without a doubt, things would never be the same again. He glanced in the rear-view mirror as he turned into Hartington Road but there did not appear to be a car following him. Doubting that Martin had seen reason and called off the hounds, he pulled over, got out of the car and walked back up the road, checking the various parked vehicles. Satisfied that he was alone, he dialled her number.

Liam and Paul decided to take one final cruise back the way they had come, convinced that the river was the simplest and quickest route out. They were heading for Mortlake High Street and Chiswick Bridge when they noticed a medium-sized cruiser heading in the same direction, its speed normal, its appearance ordinary, but something was telling them differently.

'Let's check it out, Liam, it's a possibility, we can stop on the bridge.'

'I'm getting bad feelings about this, you'd better call it in, Sergeant.'

As he picked up the phone, the radio cut in.

'All units. Rees-Jones is at the Chiswick address awaiting instructions. Do not make a move without calling in first. The lady must be somewhere in the vicinity, probably checking things out before her next move.'

'Mackenzie here, sir. There is a boat that fits just approaching Chiswick Bridge, direction Kew. We can't see how many persons are on board but are tailing it.'

'Jonathon, there are police everywhere. I thought you said you had lost them.'

'I've checked the area on foot and, honestly Anna, there are none around the house.'

'I'm on the river and have just passed the house heading for Kew and, believe me, they are still with you. I will turn around at the islands just past there and I want you on Chiswick Bridge as I come back, not before. You will drop the bag after we have passed under, OK?'

'What about the river division, you'll be cut off before you can get very far?'

'That's taken care of, you just concentrate on your part.'

'I won't let you down, Anna. Goodbye and good luck.'

Rees-Jones was at breaking point, his mind in turmoil. He had just said goodbye to the only woman he had truly loved in his life, and he could not betray her at this final moment. He would always be her puppet no matter what the circumstances.

He looked upriver and, seeing the boat coming slowly back downstream, took the sack from the car and proceeded towards the bridge. Anna was right, I can feel eyes watching me, he thought as he suddenly stopped and turned. There was no one there, but still not convinced he decided to leave it until the final second.

In the control room, DCS Carlisle appeared very much the Commanding Officer on the outside, but the doubts were nibbling away at his conscience as the minutes ticked by.

'DI Watkinson, where are you now?'

'Heading for Mortlake, sir.'

'What river strength are we getting as support?'

'At the moment none, sir. They have phoned to say that they have a big incident at the old KGV docks and will release a craft as soon as possible.'

'Damn it, she's definitely going for the river, Inspector. Close Hammersmith and Kew bridges now, and await further instructions.'

What was she playing at? Carlisle feared the worst as he dialled the brief's number and, when he got no reply, he pushed the button.

'All units, Rees-Jones has crossed us, lift him now. Sergeant Mackenzie, what's happening your end, can you see him?

'No, sir, but that same boat is coming back upriver, still going slowly.'

'Stay in position, but try and keep that boat in your sights as far as you can. There will be no river back-up, the lady has seen to that.'

As Anna approached the bridge, Rees-Jones's last words came back to her.

'Goodbye and good luck.' Had he sold her out? She didn't think so, then her mind went back thirty years. No, surely not after all this time. Poor Jonathon, if only you knew the truth!

'This is Burley, he's up and running towards the bridge. I'm in pursuit.'

'Sergeant Mackenzie, can you see him?'

'Not yet, but the boat is picking up speed.'

Just then Rees-Jones appeared on the far end of the bridge and, miraculously avoiding getting killed by the traffic, crossed the road and leant over the parapet.

'He's made the drop, sir, but she's got some kind of engine in that thing, we won't be able to keep contact for long.'

Liam put his foot to the floor as they momentarily lost sight of the river, then, as it reappeared, they saw the cruiser heading for their bank.

'Mackenzie here, sir. We don't know what they are playing at but it looks like they are coming in to our bank. Request urgent back-up.'

'Take no chances, Sergeant, shoot to kill if you have to, that's an order. Where are you now?'

'Lonsdale Road, we're pulling over.'

'Inspector Watkinson, cover the other end of Lonsdale Road.'

Rees-Jones had remained transfixed to the spot, watching the fast-disappearing cruiser, when he was suddenly aware of Mark Burley trying to cross the road to get to him. Burley was having difficulty negotiating the intense traffic and Rees-Jones grabbed the chance to escape. Waiting until Burley was halfway across, he ran back in the direction of the car then re-crossed the road, not sure of what he was going to do next or where he was going to go.

He reached the car and started the engine just as Burley caught up with him and, as the officer tried to open the car door, Jones pulled away, leaving him in the gutter as dusk set in and the weather worsened.

'He's mobile, sir, but I haven't got a clue as to which direction he's going to take.'

'I've got him,' John Lindsey's voice cut in. 'He's heading for the flyover and I'm going after him.'

The traffic was heavy and slow because of the wet, gloomy conditions but Rees-Jones was driving like a man possessed, overtaking cars and seemingly oblivious to everything and everybody around him.

'Sir. He's going to kill a lot of people driving like this, I can't keep up.'

The DCS picked up his phone and dialled the number. Whatever was possessing the man he had to try and bring him under control, for the sake of others. The phone just kept ringing.

'Jesus Christ!' John Lindsey's voice broke over the airways. 'There's a giant fireball ahead.'

All around him cars came to a screeching halt, some of them not making it in time, and the sickening sound of crunching metal filled the air. Without a thought for his own safety he left his car and ran towards the flames, but there was nothing he could do. Almost unrecognisable, Rees-Jones's car had driven straight into the back of an articulated lorry and burst into flames, the heat so intense that the trailer had started to ignite.

Paul and Liam had taken position behind their car doors just up the road from the landing jetty when Paul noticed a motorbike they had passed earlier and not taken any notice of.

'Liam, that bike in the hedge, I bet that's hers!'

'Sir. They've got a motorbike waiting for them on this side, that's why they're docking. Hang on, here they come now, where is the back-up?'

Even at a hundred yards and wearing leathers and helmets, there was no doubt it was Anna and Mackinley and, as Liam and Paul rose from behind the doors, their guns levelled at them, they continued to stroll casually towards the motorbike.

'Hold it right there, you two.' As Liam's voice penetrated their helmets, they froze for an instant then, spotting the two men, Mackinley pulled a gun and started firing as Anna pulled him over the hedge.

The two men returned fire just as Inspector Watkinson and Colin Baker arrived from the other end and, signalling their intentions, Liam and Paul began running towards the water's edge as the powerful sound of the boat's engine cut in.

As they neared the bike they were met by a hail of gunfire as Mackinley, standing in the rear of the cruiser, opened fire once again, a gun in each hand. Liam went down and, as Watkinson and Baker shot at the boat, Anna opened the throttle and took off.

'Officer down.' Peter Watkinson called for the emergency services. 'All units at Hammersmith Bridge, stand by. Blue and cream cruiser approaching at great speed, shoot on sight.'

'Inspector, who's been shot?'

'It's Liam, sir. He's still breathing but we don't know where he has been hit.'

Mackinley was lying on the floor of the cruiser badly injured as Anna took the Hammersmith bend at high speed, her mind working overtime. If she could make it to Wandsworth there was an inlet there that she could hole up in while she reassessed the situation, but where could she get help for Mackinley from?

'Mack!' she screamed, 'can you move?'

They were fast approaching the bridge and as Mackinley managed to raise himself up on one elbow they were met by a volley of gunfire. He tried to return fire as Anna weaved from side to side, going under the bridge and, on exiting, they were met by a further barrage of bullets. She swung to the right trying to avoid an oncoming barge and now, broadside on, the shells tore in to the hull, finding the fuel tank, and the boat exploded.

43

In the back of the ambulance that was rushing Liam to the hospital, Paul received the news that they had recovered Mackinley's badly burnt body from the river almost immediately but had had to abandon the search for Anna Karim as night set in and the weather worsened. Liam had taken two bullets which, thanks to his jacket, had not penetrated the upper body, but he was unconscious and the ambulance crew were very concerned about his breathing.

All the while Martin Carlisle had sat at his desk as the reports came in. Luckily, despite the carnage, there had been no other deaths in the pile-up on the M4. and for that he was more than thankful, but could he have played things any differently?

One thing was for certain, he would have many a sleepless night going over the events of the past few days and the repercussions to come. This was not how he had envisaged it would all end, and there were still a lot of loose ends that needed tidying up, but his immediate concern was for Liam Jameson, the non-conformist but best copper he had ever had under his command.

He was a Londoner born and bred and proud of the fact, an ex-docker, one of the old breed of British working men whose life had followed the maxim – work hard and play hard. There had been times when the money had been plentiful, especially during the golden era of British shipping when the docks were working twenty-four hours a day, seven days a week, but since their decline the jobs had been various, the money at times minimal, but somehow he had always provided for his family. However he had no complaints, he had his wife of forty years, two sons who had toed the line and were in good jobs, and three grandchildren who were his pride and joy.

The two boys had bought his council house, giving him and his wife a roof over their heads for the rest of their lives, which meant each day he awoke a contented and thankful man wanting for nothing. An occasional night out with the missus or a pint or two and a chat with his mates, a game of dominoes or darts, watching 'The Hammers' at the weekend, he was more than satisfied with his daily lot.

The river was his blood, his oxygen, and had provided for him and his family all his working days until his retirement, and never a day passed without him spending at least a couple of hours with the love of his life. Every inlet, every reach, all the bridges, the tides, Harry Townsend could write volumes on his favourite subject and its inhabitants, human or otherwise.

His one luxury in life was a tiny clinker-built cabin cruiser that he kept in pristine condition, and every day Harry would proudly cruise the waterway, stopping to visit various friends along the banks or simply reminiscing. Today he had lingered longer, the fascination as if it was the first time he had passed this way, remembering the wharves, the warehouses, and the giant cranes that used to dominate the skyline, replaced now by concrete monstrosities that housed this new electronic modern world. He was rudely shaken from his reverie by the noise of gunfire, which was quickly followed by the sound of an explosion and then he saw a giant fireball rise high above the water just up the river.

Whatever had caused it would be reduced to wreckage and therefore there would be nothing left to see, but Harry's curiosity overcame his common sense and he headed upriver. Approaching the Albert Bridge he was aware of three police launches coming up behind, who overtook him as he went under, their wash catching the tiny craft. Nearing Chelsea Reach, burnt timbers floated by on the tide but what caught his eye was a blue polythene sack that had snagged on one of these pieces of wood.

Harry had pulled several sacks like this from the water, usually too late, the puppies and kittens inside already dead. Grabbing the boathook, he turned towards the flotsam and managed to pull it inward. Lifting it from the water, he realised that there was no movement or noise inside, another one to throw back, but something stopped him. It was the weight and feel that was wrong and Harry tried to open the sack but it was sealed with plastic ties and he didn't have a knife, so he turned for home, his curiosity mounting. Berthing the boat he hurried back to the house, sack in hand, not even stopping for his ritual evening pint.

Thankfully his wife was out babysitting, at least he wouldn't get the usual 'not more bloody cats and dogs' as he hurried through the house out to the back yard and the other sanctuary in his life – his garden shed. Taking out his Stanley knife he cut the plastic ties, not quite sure whether he was doing the right thing or not, but if it was in the river it could only be something that was rubbish. He stood staring at the sack for several seconds, almost not daring to touch what he saw, then he reached inside. Money, bundles of money, a King's ransom but who did it belong to and what should he do with it?

'Harry, are you out there?' His wife's voice caused him to start and, before he could answer, she appeared in the doorway. Momentarily dumbstruck, she stood there open-mouthed at the sight that greeted her.

'Where the hell did you get that lot from?'

'Would you believe me if I told you I've just pulled it from the river?'

'I'll phone the police, Harry, they'll know what to do with it.'

'Hang on, Mavis, it was in the water with all the other rubbish that floats around out there, finders keepers, I say. Anyway, nobody could accidentally lose something like this, if it's in the water it's there for no good reason and I say we hang on to it.'

Mavis looked long and hard at her husband: he was a good

man who over the years had always made the correct decisions and she knew he would be proved right again. Then she thought of her twin brother in New Zealand who she hadn't seen in twenty-five years.

'You're right as usual, Harry. Let's give it a couple of weeks to see if there is any news then we'll split it with the boys.'

When he arrived at the hospital DCS Carlisle found Paul and DI Watkinson pacing up and down outside the operating theatre and, without ceremony, he embraced the two men as he shook their hands and congratulated them. A nurse appeared then from the theatre, the smile on her face instantly erasing their fears as she gave them the news they so wanted.

'He's going to be all right, gentlemen. The jacket did its job, but the impact had interfered with one of his lungs which we are repairing at the moment, and he should be back on his feet in a couple of days.'

'That's the best report of the day, Sister,' a very relieved DCS expressed their feelings and thanked the lady. 'How about we all go and have a pint somewhere and I'll fill you two in on the rest of the evening's events?'

Paul didn't want to leave Liam's side, but the nursing staff assured him that everything was fine and that it would be several hours before he regained consciousness, so he reluctantly left the little man in their more than capable hands.

Almost every night without fail for over forty years Sister Ruth Bartok had taken the same walk in the same direction, despite all weathers, and tonight was no exception. Away from the retreat, and the responsibilities of being Mother Superior, she could find more peace and sanctuary here by the river than she could within those walls.

As they had been every day during this time, her thoughts were for her dead parents, remembering how they had sacrificed their lives so that she could escape the Russian invasion of her

257

beloved Budapest. She had returned there on several occasions but, such was her love for her adopted city and its people, she had remained here and would do so till her mentor called.

It was God's doing, a night like this, but he had a reason for everything she thought as she bent into the wind. Just then the rain eased a little and the moon appeared from behind a cloud, its light transforming the whole scene and, as ever, the twinkling lights mesmerised her as she gazed out over the water towards the far bank deep in thought.

The magic was broken by a movement in the mire and she stared at the spot for several moments, convinced her failing eyesight was playing tricks. There it was again and, as Ruth focused intently, she realised that it was a human body trapped by the sludge and filth that was the Thames at low tide.

She was unable to reach it without sinking into the mud herself so she hurried back to the retreat for help. Quickly organising the sisters into two teams, one to prepare the surgery and the other to assist with the rescue, they returned to the river's edge to find the tide rising fast as they started to inch the planks onto the stinking sludge. They needed some stronger hands but time wasn't on their side, there was no one around on a night like this, so they had to make do themselves.

It was taking too long, the rising water beginning to lap the planks, as Sister Ruth edged her way towards the now buoyant body. Even in this light it was a terrible sight to behold, and she offered up a quick prayer for guidance as she managed to grab hold of a leg, just as the corpse drifted away from her. Tying a rope around the ankles, the sisters began to pull, the rising tide now a blessing as the floating figure came ashore.

As soon as they reached the treatment room of the hospice they realised that there was still life in this burnt mess as the body started to spasm, and so Sister Ruth phoned Father Alistair.

She had sat in her husband's study since she had received the news, staring at his law books that adorned three walls and the photographs that covered his desk, clinging to this last link with the man she had worshipped. The tears had dried up but Carolyne Rees-Jones was still numb, trying to fathom out everything that had happened in the past forty-eight hours, trying to accept that during that short space of time her calm orderly life had been totally and utterly destroyed for ever.

Financially she had no problems, but the boys were at an age where they needed the guidance of a father and she herself had never had to pay a bill, mend anything, do anything – all her life everything had been done for her.

What had caused her husband to change so dramatically that she had hardly recognised him as the man she loved at the hospital? Seeking some answers she reached for the phone, then put it down again. Martin Carlisle had phoned earlier conveying his condolences but had said nothing else and she wanted desperately to phone him back, certain there was a connection, but frightened to learn the truth.

Instead, she picked up the phone and dialled her brother's number, it was time that she faced the children and gave them the tragic news.

England, November 2001

As the train from Wokingham pulled into the station Matthew lowered his newspaper to observe the alighting passengers and, seeing the unmistakeable figure of Consuela descend from a carriage, he dashed up the platform, pulling her back on to the train just as it was leaving. Running up the platform, desperately trying to open a door, were the Australian and his partner but they were too late, Matthew was waving goodbye as the train gathered speed and passed them by.

'You sure know how to make friends, Matthew. If it wasn't for me he would have killed you long ago.'

He ignored her comments and, pushing her into a corner,

frisked her top to bottom, front and back, then took her bag and emptied it on the table. Luckily there were no other passengers in the compartment as Consuela just stood there smiling at him, Matthew already fighting his feelings and hating himself for being so weak. There appeared to be no bugs this time, and he motioned for her to sit down, but he was still very wary of this irresistible women as she sat there silently, still smiling mockingly at him.

The hotel overlooked the Thames, but the beautiful setting was lost on them as the hostilities ceased and once again the physical attraction took over, Matthew throwing all caution to the wind. In a few hours she was proposing to throw him to the lions but that didn't matter, at this moment in time nothing mattered except to be in the arms of Consuela del Cabellorenti once again.

He said goodbye to her on the platform at Reading knowing that that would be the last time he would see her, she heading for her meeting with the Earl, and he uncertain as to how and where this day would end.

His thoughts turned to his kind, gentle father once more wondering what he would think of Matthew's intentions and, knowing instantly the answer, he changed his plans and headed for Heathrow. Of one thing he was now certain, there was nothing to keep him in England and his decision to leave had been the right one, but what about the future? As the fifth Duke of Rushtington, and with his qualifications, he could walk into almost any job in the world he chose to but, unless it involved danger and excitement, he knew he could never settle very long anywhere.

Although the thrill of the kill was gone it was what he did best, the fortune amassing in his Jersey bank account of no importance to him, he had inherited more than enough from his father to live a life of luxury.

Once again an afternoon with that women had stirred his every emotion and maybe one day he would find someone, somewhere, who would permanently remove his inner demons, but in the meantime he had a ghost to lay.

The rising exhilaration coursing his body, assisted by the cocaine he was snorting, was causing a stirring in his loins, he wanted sex but there wasn't time. It was always the same on the night of a robbery. The excitement of the planning, the controlling of his impulses not to rush in until he was absolutely certain of every minute detail always aroused him, but it paled into insignificance when the time finally came.

However, tonight was different. He had to entertain the victim, a woman he had had reservations about from the first time he had met her and nothing she had said or done since had altered his opinion of her.

She was a gold-digger, the type of woman that had caused empires to crumble, wars to break out, and he had not been deceived by the accented voice that had bewitched her husband or the filthy female body that caused men everywhere to fall at her feet. She was a whore with a brain, a deadly combination and, as the minutes ticked by to her arrival, he felt the cravings of his body being replaced by fear as the uncertainty rose within him. Twice earlier he had reached for the phone wanting to call the whole thing off but knew he was too committed. The money was sitting in the bank account, the donors people you did not renege on, there was no going back now.

The melodic sound of the wind chimes drifting across the showroom signalled her arrival and, glancing through his office window, he saw her standing there surveying the gallery, her two 'pet monkeys' in tow. Pulling himself together he rose to greet her and surprisingly felt his legs buckle. Steadying himself with his desk, he switched on the charm and opened the door.

'My dearest Consuela, you look even more exotic than ever.' He took her outstretched hand and kissed it.

'Mark, it is always a pleasure to be in your company especially here in your beautiful gallery. How did the sale go?'

261

'Beyond all my expectations, I'll tell you all about it over dinner.'

'You can cancel the reservation, Mark, we will do all our talking here.'

She signalled to the Australian and his partner, who promptly slipped the door catches. 'Now turn off the outside lights, Mark, and the ones in the gallery.'

He felt his bowels slacken as he clung to the door jamb, desperately trying to clear his furred mind and, without uttering a sound, reached for the switches.

'Good, now sit down, Mark, I have a story to tell you, but do correct me if I have any of the facts wrong.'

Standing dominantly over him she took out a mobile phone which she placed on the desk in front of him. 'Are you sitting comfortably? Then I'll begin.'

'You are Mark Dominic Westerby, Lord Thatcham, educated at Winchester and Oxford, residing at Easterby Hall, Bagshot when not at 22 Holbury Gardens WC1 with your cortege of coke-filled young rent boys. You have a half brother, Philip Morgan Davidson, who has a record as long as your arm, everything from extortion to burglary – do you want me to continue, there's a lot more?'

'How much?' Through all this time he'd fought the rising bile: his insatiable lust had dictated his life and dominated his common sense and this was the result. He should have listened to his inner voices and not let the greed dominate.

'Fifty per cent of the gross.'

'Impossible, there isn't much left after expenses.'

'See that phone on your desk. The first number stored in the memory is that of a Detective Chief Inspector Gates; two clicks and I will have his undivided attention, of that I am certain – need I say more?'

'You have no evidence, you've put two and two together and got five.'

'Two clicks and that nice policeman will be waiting tonight for your brother and his men who, I'm sure, will keep him riveted for several hours afterwards with their tales, including the one that makes you accessory to murder.'

His fine clothes clung to his body, he could smell himself and it sickened him as he sought desperately for a way out. He'd always hated women but his feelings for this one went beyond hatred, way beyond as the anger burst from within him.

'You fucking bitch, I had you marked from day one.' He leapt from his chair and pulled a small pistol from the drawer of the desk. Before the two minders could react he had hold of Consuela, his arm around her neck, half throttling her, as he placed her between them with the gun to her head.

'What are you going to do now, Mark, kill me?' You really are a pathetic creature, you haven't the guts.' Totally unperturbed by what was happening to her, Consuela spat out the words as she continued her acerbic assault. 'Your young men are not going to save you, nobody's going to save you, you're going to die if you don't let me go.'

Totally overcome with rage he tightened the grip around her neck, lifting her off the floor and she began to kick out as the air supply to her lungs was cut.

Sensing an opportunity, the Aussie dropped to the floor pulling his gun and went for a knee shot. The scream that followed filled the gallery as the stricken Westerby collapsed to the floor on top of Consuela and there followed a muffled gunshot. He was still screaming as the two men dragged him off her prostrate body but it was too late, the dark red patch told them the bad news.

'You bastard.' He put the gun to the Earl's head but, before he could pull the trigger, the Aussie knocked his hand away.

'Let him rot, mate, we've got to get out of here and quick.'

'He'll talk, we can't take the chance.'

'You're right, sport' and, turning, the Aussie put a bullet between the man's eyes.

44

London, October 2003

Liam awoke. Slowly opening his eyes, he tried to focus on the sights and sounds around him, his brain struggling to tell him things. Then he saw Paul sitting there, felt his hand in his, and everything came rushing back so quickly that he tried to sit up, but Paul gently restrained him.

'Welcome back, Liam. They reckon if you had been normal height, we wouldn't be having this conversation – there is something to be said for being a short-arsed Scouser after all.'

Liam grinned as Paul started to tell him about the previous afternoon's events, but he was still too groggy to take it all in and soon drifted back to sleep.

The weather had lifted slightly, even the sun was making an effort, as Paul left the hospital and made his way to the Yard, his body still numb with shock, crying out for sleep.

The atmosphere was electric when he arrived, but deep down he could sense the feeling of dissatisfaction at the way things had turned out. This feeling went right to the top as he found out when summoned to the office of the DCS.

'You look wonderful, Sergeant. Sit down before you fall down.' Carlisle came to sit on his desk in front of Paul.

'You don't need me to tell you that this case is far from over. We were lucky yesterday in that no more innocent parties were killed, but the way things turned out has left us all with a bad taste in our mouths and still with a lot of problems. Somewhere out there is a lot of heroin and we do not know whose hands it's in. Anna Karim's body has still not been found and, although I cannot see how she could have survived, her shadow still hangs over all of us. Then there is the question of who takes over the empire with those two out of the way.'

'We have to talk to Dennison right away,' Paul interrupted. 'He was Mackinley's right hand and, now he's out of the equation, might point us in the right direction.'

'What about the twins? Do you think there could be any mileage in seeing them again?'

'Let's try Paddy first, sir. Then if that fails we'll try the twins again, although personally I don't think they know a lot.'

Paddy Dennison launched into a violent tirade the minute Paul and Colin entered the room, so they just stood there and waited until a combination of pain and exhaustion overcame Paddy and he subsided into calm.

'Right, now you've had your say, we'll have ours.' Paul approached the bed cautiously, but Paddy was too weak to move and just lay there staring.

'Mackinley and Anna are dead, which leaves you as number one guilty person, and we have statements from the twins as to your involvement in everything, including the death of my brother.'

'Mackinley killed him, you can't hang that one on me!'

'No, but you stood there and watched as he let that ball slam into his defenceless body.' The red mist came back and, as Paul advanced on Dennison, Colin restrained him.

For what seemed an eternity, the two men were eyeball to eyeball, then Paul saw the hate rescind in Dennison's eyes as he realised that cooperation was the only answer if he was not to spend the rest of his life in a prison.

'Where's the lorry with the stuff on board, Paddy?' Paul decided to put his theory to the test straight away.

'It was waiting for me down the Jamaica Road until you lot showed up.'

265

'Where were you taking it to?'

'She has a new warehouse at Hatton Cross close to Heathrow.'

'What went wrong with the arrangements? Why were you sent to collect the money?'

'That's what was in the boot of the brief's car, I didn't know. She sent me to collect it instead of going herself, to keep me and that bastard Mackinley apart.'

'Why did they come back, they'd made it to France?'

'I was supposed to be moving the goods but Mackinley panicked. He thought I was getting pissed up, so he arranged for this other guy to do the job. Serve him right, I hope he rots in hell!'

'Name, Paddy?'

'Haven't a clue. Someone recommended him, I don't know who, honest.'

'What about the trailer? Any marks, any old sign-writing that shows through? You haven't exactly helped your cause so far.'

'Nothing. It was a plain white job, which had never been written, the sort you see everywhere.'

'What's this new address of hers at Hatton Cross?'

'I don't know, I was supposed to get a call from the brief nearer the time with all the details.'

Paul was getting frustrated and nowhere fast. Dennison, like all the others, was just a psycho muscle man who did as he was told. Then he had an idea.

'Who's going to take over now, Paddy? You're banged up and those two are dead, but there's still the drugs, the protection racket, the cigarette smuggling, the prostitution, etc. What's going to happen to it all? Someone's going to try and take control, and then there is that lorry-load of heroin.'

Dennison just lay there saying nothing. Paul realised that he was probably too thick to have thought of all this and now his mind was working overtime.

'Come on, Paddy. I want a name, or you are going to rot in prison for a long time?'

'The book-keeper, Mackinley's cousin. Runs a respectable

firm of chartered accountants in Charlton, near the football ground.'

'Come off it, Paddy. What would they want an accountant for? It's not the sort of business where you need to show accounts, or make a yearly tax return on.'

'No, but someone had to keep control of every movement, who had what, who owed what. There were too many people skimming the pot, so they recruited the cousin, who was a whiz-kid with computers. Every movement here, in Africa, and all over the world is monitored by him.'

'So he would know about the lorry and what it is worth?'

'That's why he'd be the obvious choice.'

'Name, Paddy.'

'Thompson, Gerald Thompson.'

'Would he be able to hold it all together?'

'He's got the brains, all he needs to do is recruit the right staff, so to speak.'

Alistair David Sullivan had taken the cloth late in life after quitting his post as a hospital doctor, which had become a daily struggle with bureaucracy. The lack of staff and the right equipment meant each day was governed by a thin line between life and death, until one day he had lost a battle.

As he had admitted to the Mother Superior, the first time they had met, the patient was sixty-eight years old and very ill but he shouldn't have died. His allegiance to the Hippocratic Oath would never wane, but the pressures of the job had already cost him his marriage and this had been the final straw for him.

Then one morning he had awoken to the now familiar sight that greeted him in the mirror, and decided enough was enough. An excess of Guinness and Ramji Bhutar's wonderful curries were taking their toll on his body, he was on a dangerous downward spiral and, no matter how hard he tried, there was no other employment that could fill the void.

He was not a religious man but believed strongly in Christian principles, and he had started to spend his days helping the Jesuit Brethren tending the down and outs. Instantly, his life took on a new meaning and, although he spent many long hours with some of the worst that society had to offer, the rewards were far more gratifying spiritually.

The drug addicts who managed to stay clean and rejoin the real world were perhaps the most satisfying, as were the reformed alcoholics. Then there were those from broken homes, young kids with all their lives in front of them who needed guidance before it was too late. The prostitutes both male and female, with all the dangers that that entailed. It was a full-time job of some immensity so, after a long chat with the Father Abbot, he applied to join the Brethren.

As a bonus there was Sister Ruth Bartok and her nuns who administered to these same people with such dignity and grace that you felt humble in their presence. Her wonderful accent came across as if she were the fiercest woman in the world, which was the furthest you could get from the truth, and if ever there was such a being as a living saint it was her.

'This is a fine night for you ladies to be playing by the river. What poor soul have we got here then?'

As they led him into the room the smell was all-pervading and one that sent a shiver down his spine – burnt flesh. His immediate thoughts were that they should send for an ambulance, it was very specialised treating a case as bad as this, but something deep within told him to wait. Thanks to a beneficiary the retreat had a facility that any hospital would be envious of, although he doubted whether they would be able to provide the necessary on this occasion.

'I've got to phone someone on this, Sister. It's too big a task for one man, and I'm not sure my friend will approve of us working here. Time is of the essence: that skin is starting to rot and, once that sets in, we won't have a chance. Cut the leathers on the right arm but be careful of that hand.'

He went to the medical cupboard, as Sister Ruth called it

although it was more like a pharmacist's shop and, filling a syringe with morphine, returned to inject the now twitching figure being restrained by the sisters.

Even through mud-encrusted eyes the lights were blinding, the pain indescribable as Anna felt the hands on her body. Indiscernible voices filled her head and she wanted to scream out in protest but nothing came from a mouth filled with sludge. Then she felt something sharp in her arm and she felt herself floating into some sort of pain-free nirvana.

'That should deaden the pain and I had better inject something to ward off the threat of streptococcus infection. Be very careful and try to wash off some of that mud while I'm gone; there are probably more germs in that than anything else.'

Removing the remains of the helmet they began washing the mud from the face, which luckily was hardly burnt when, suddenly, there were gasps of astonishment from the senior sisters as they slowly realised who they had just pulled from the jaws of death.

Although the hair was now short and dyed blond instead of long and black, there was no mistaking this lady. Known to them all simply as Donna, she had never forgotten how the sisters had helped her when she was just twenty and pregnant with no one else to turn to. Over the following years Donna had made several visits to the retreat, not to enquire as to the welfare of her son but to donate vast sums of money for its upkeep.

The sisters had continually prayed for her, knowing that she was a tormented and lost soul, but had never asked questions. Her instructions at the time of birth for her son's future had been explicit. Mario was to be offered for adoption and never put in a council-run home, and his new parents must be able to give him every opportunity in life to succeed, a tall order but one the Sisters had managed to attain without any difficulty.

The Duchess of Rushtington was one of the retreat's biggest providers of funds, her tireless efforts raising tens of thousands of pounds each year, and she knew of Mario but not of his history. She was nearly thirty years old and had had several miscarriages when the doctors told her the bad news, she would never be able to have children. She jumped at the opportunity to adopt him and her husband, who was as desperate as she was to have a child, agreed the moment she mentioned it. Their joy was worth more than everything that they possessed in the world and little Mario entered the privileged world of the British aristocracy, his mother assured by the sisters that he would never ever want for anything.

'The effect of the morphine is wearing off, Mother Superior. Should we administer another shot or put her on a drip?' The woman's body was beginning to move again, as the pain returned.

'If the Father does not return in ten minutes, start a morphine drip, in the meantime let's try and cut away some of this clothing.'

It was easier said than done, the tough motorbike leathers difficult to cut, but they had obviously saved her life and limited the extent of her burns. As they peeled off the last pieces, a relieved Ruth Bartok was pleased to see the Father return, together with a very aged and stooped man.

'Ladies, may I introduce you to Doctor Gordon Ferguson, the best burns man in the country.'

'Come now, Alistair, there's no need for flattery. What I think we need here is more of a miracle.' His gentle Scottish burr was a reassuring influence on them all as he began to examine the red raw flesh.

'Tell me, are we acting within the law or is this one of those cases you keep telling me about, Alistair? Whatever, we will need a sterile room and gowns, as well as specialised drugs, which can only be found in a hospital.'

'We don't know the circumstances as yet but come with me, Fergy, and then you can tell me what you think our chances are.'

He led the surgeon into the next room, and Doctor Gordon Ferguson just stood there shaking his head. He felt like a child who had been given the keys to the toy shop as he surveyed the operating theatre and equipment which were available to him.

'Until I know the extent of the damage it's difficult to say but I would think maybe, just maybe for now, we could save this poor soul without having to move her.'

45

Corsica, December 2001

Matthew was back where he felt happiest, high up in the mountains and all alone with only the birds of prey and other wildlife for company. The memories of the afternoon spent with Consuela were still too fresh in his mind to forget and he knew that she would be forever simmering in some corner of his soul, no matter what, but he did not regret his actions.

Before he had left England he had made two phone calls. One to his London contact, informing him that he would be unavailable for some time to come, and the other to Detective Chief Inspector Gates.

Gates was the investigating officer into his father's murder and the only person Matthew could think of turning to. However, what he had thought would be a routine call turned out to be far from that as Gates confirmed Matthew's worst fears, his activities were known of by the British authorities.

He had informed Gates of the impending robbery, fabricating the story slightly as to his involvement, when the policeman had cut him short.

'You'll forgive me, sir, but we both know why you have returned to this country, so let's be honest with one another. I find you a very likeable young man, however, it goes against my principles and I detest strongly the world that you move in. I'm being frank with you because I feel you would prefer it that way. As a policeman I cannot condone any taking of life for whatever reason and, to that end, anything that happens tonight had better not involve you. If it does, I will pull you faster than you can imagine and take my chances with my career – do you understand?'

Matthew reflected on this conversation, and its implications, as he stalked his lunch. How many countries had he visited in the past few years who would give anything to live as a democracy policed by men such as Gates. Instead they needed mercenaries like himself and Mickey to help control things and whether right or wrong, the bullet was the only law they understood.

Deciding on a change of scenery for a while, Matthew shut up the house and drove down to Ajaccio to make a phone call. If the offer was still open, a few months at sea in the company of Alexis the Greek skipper and his motley crew would make a welcome change.

London, October 2003

The colours were cold now, the atmosphere alien and, as Frances wandered aimlessly around a flat that was almost unrecognisable as her home, she knew for certain that her life was changed forever and that it was time to move on.

A week had gone by since she had returned and, while her life was no longer in danger, she still felt threatened. Although David's murderer was dead his evil cloud would be ever present if she stayed in London, and the painful memories of the past two months would never be assuaged.

The hospital, and her friends there, were no longer a comfort, the job that she lived for now laid bare for what it was: a daily excursion into the world of violence. Every time a victim of aggression had been wheeled into the A and E unit she had only seen David lying there, and had struggled to handle each case.

When she had come home Paul had picked up the pieces, and the following day, with her resolve strengthened, she would return to face her demons. But it was no good: her dedicated world had been invaded, she needed a new start. Although in some ways it was a backward step there was only one place where she could find the solace she sought: she was going home to Jamaica.

She had written to her parents, telling them of her intentions, knowing what the reaction would be. Her father, a paediatric surgeon at the hospital in Kingston, would have already secured her a job which, with her qualifications, wouldn't be difficult.

However, Jamaica was one of the poorer West Indian islands and Frances felt her future life may be better spent in trying to alleviate the poverty, rather than nursing the poor people when it was too late to save them. To this end she had applied to The Foundation, a charity organisation set up to deal with the country's shanty towns.

Her father would be very disappointed but she knew he would understand and, although it would be a thankless task with very little money, it was the right direction for her to take.

Detective Chief Superintendent Martin Carlisle knew the minute he had taken the call that this was going to be more bad news, and he was not mistaken. As Sergeant Mackenzie and DI Watkinson entered his office, it was written all over their faces. The Sergeant filled him in on the interrogation of Paddy Dennison and then told him about Gerald Thompson and Dennison's appraisal of the situation

'What do we know about him, Inspector?'

'Not a lot, sir. He has no previous, despite being Mackinley's cousin, and he runs a very large and successful practice. However, what enquiries we have been able to make at this time have revealed a lifestyle that isn't in keeping with your average accountant. He owns a huge house at Epping, has another in the south of France close to Jones', keeps a yacht on the Hamble and, I'm afraid, he is also a member of your club, sir.'

Carlisle knew what was coming before he had said it. As it was, the repercussions from the death of Rees-Jones hadn't had time to surface yet, and now there was another possible scandal looming which would shake the establishment rigid.

The club had as its members some of the most prominent people in British society who, if inadvertently connected to the lawyer, could be ruined and, indeed, if the truth ever got out, even he would be placed in a very difficult situation. Jones must have sponsored the membership of Thompson, but how many others were there in this can of worms?

'I can't place the name, or put a face to it, but it seems the nightmare continues, gentlemen! At least we now know that the drugs are definitely on a lorry, but where is it, and who's got it? That's got to be our first priority, gentlemen, find and secure that load before the situation gets out of hand, because once news gets around of its existence every drug baron in the country will be after it and the consequences could be frightening. Open gang warfare could return to the streets of London and if the load is in the hands of an amateur, his life won't be worth a damn.'

'What do you want us to do about Thompson? If he's going to try and run the show, he's going to need some heavy support from somewhere.'

'Leave him to me for the time being, Inspector. I'll make some enquiries at the club and come back to you.'

46

Martin Carlisle climbed the steps of the club and was greeted by a very sombre Bunny Johnson, who was suitably dressed in black tie and armband. Bunny, nobody knew where he got the name from, was the club's major-domo. He could remember every member's name and when they had last visited the club, but no one could remember the last time he had taken a holiday or had been off sick – it always seemed that Bunny was ever present.

'Good morning, Chief Superintendent, and my condolences. Mr Rees-Jones will be missed by us all, such a gentleman.'

'Thank you, Bunny. Tell me, is Mr Gerald Thompson in the club today?'

'Yes, sir. He's in the billiard room with Sir Neville Denton – shall I have him paged?'

'No thanks, Bunny. I'll just wander up there after I've had a drink or two.'

The alarm bells were ringing in his head, the weight on his shoulders seeming to get heavier with each step, as he climbed the stairs to the billiard room. Sir Neville Denton was a philanthropist whose generosity had benefited many of the club's members. Was Thompson now desperately trying to raise funds to establish his credentials within the underworld? With the death of Rees-Jones the key to the Karim money box had gone and, if he wasn't the vicious thug type, his success would depend on who he employed as muscle and getting hold of that lorry and its cargo very quickly. As the book-keeper, he knew what the business was worth and, more importantly, where everything was, but without the right reinforcements all that knowledge was worthless and the empire would soon crumble around him.

'Good morning, Chief Superintendent. What a great shock this has been for all of us. Do you know Jonathon's business associate, Gerald Thompson?'

'Good morning, Sir Neville. No, we've never met. How do you do? Martin Carlisle.'

He had decided to declare his intentions from the outset, let Thompson know that he was around and, at the same time, hopefully put some pressure on him.

'Good morning, Chief Superintendent. This is a terrible tragedy for everybody, he was such a wonderfully generous man who always spoke very highly of you, it's a pleasure to meet you at last. Would you care to join us for a game?'

'Thank you, no. I've never been able to master this game but, if you don't mind, I'd like to sit and watch for a while. You two carry on, pretend I'm not here.'

He put Gerald Thompson at around forty years of age, slim, smooth and charming – it was as if Rees-Jones had returned from the dead. This one would have to be watched very carefully.

The two doctors had toiled through the night and, with the team of highly trained nuns by their sides, had managed to stabilise the woman, although she was far from out of danger. The battle had only just begun and the fear of infection occurring was ever present but, luckily, there had been no broken bones to complicate matters.

Her hands and feet had suffered the worst, the heavy leathers greatly reducing the burns to her body, but the big question was, how did she receive these injuries?

'Let's clean up and have some breakfast, Fergy.' Despite the tiredness and stress of the past seven hours, Alistair Sullivan could eat a horse and always relished the thought of eating at the retreat. As well as all their other attributes the sisters were amazing cooks, and he often thought that if they ever wanted a change of direction they could run the most successful restaurant in London.

'I'm going to the hospital to talk to a few old friends.' Fergy, despite the success of the night's work, was always trying to find something he might have missed.

'Until we know what has happened here, we don't want too many people to know about this, Gordon, so be very careful as to what you say, my friend.'

'Hey laddie, I'm a canny Scotsman don't forget! They won't even remember what they've told me, but I think it's a good idea. There may be some new wonder drug that even this place hasn't got, although I doubt it.'

'After you two have finished your breakfast, you're going to go and lie down first before anyone goes anywhere.' The Mother Superior was back in charge, her Hungarian accent adding authority to her orders. 'I don't want either of you falling by the wayside and we'll wake you if there is any change. After that we can decide the best way forward.'

Alistair knew better than to question this formidable lady, so he and Gordon retired to their rooms, leaving the good sisters to watch and pray for the life of Donna.

It was Doctor Gordon Ferguson who returned to the retreat with the bad news. Having slept well, he had visited the hospital as planned, and on his way back saw the banner headlines screaming at him from the newsagent's billboard. Buying a newspaper was something he'd given up doing years ago when he became tired of the filth and violence that seemed to dominate the daily news, but today was an exception. Finding a bench by the river, he sat there in total disbelief as he discovered the awful truth about the woman whose life he had spent all night saving.

'You don't need me to quote you the good book and what our Lord says with regard to sinners. We have done the Lord's work, and as such we cannot reproach ourselves.'

They were sitting in Sister Ruth's office discussing the moral and lawful implications of their actions, with Fergy far from happy with the situation.

'Surely, we must inform the authorities, Sister? You're harbouring a wanted criminal who's caused suffering to thousands of people, and her crimes should not go unpunished.' Fergy had always been a black and white person, to him there was never any grey.

'What do you think, Father Alistair, you're normally the one who has the answer for most of the problems that arise around here?'

'I agree with both of your arguments but maybe this is the Lord's doing. To have died instantly would have been the easy way out for her, but to live and suffer as she is suffering, and will be for the rest of her life, is perhaps the punishment that he has decided upon. She will never be able to walk again unaided, so she is as much a prisoner behind these walls as she would be in Holloway. I say we continue to concentrate on saving her life; our first obligation, Fergy, is to the oath we have both taken and hold so dearly, and Sister Ruth will, I'm sure, make the right decision when the time comes.'

'Aye you're right, laddie, let's go and see how our patient is getting along. I learnt nothing from my visit to the hospital and we have everything we need here. As you have said, it's in the hands of our maker now.'

'Sergeant Mackenzie? The usual place in one hour.' The accented voice now familiar in his ear, Paul informed the DI of the meet and set off for the disused waterworks at Wapping. A call from Marco was always good news and good for the morale.

'I've heard Liam is going to be all right, but you have left one hell of mess out there, Sergeant. Has the lady's body come to light yet?'

'No, but I hope it does soon, then we can be sure it's all over.' Paul was amazed at how Marco always seemed to have his finger on the button.

'You don't know this river, Sergeant, it could take months before she surfaces, but as far as everybody is concerned around here she's history anyway. However, her demise has meant that every villain around fancies their chances of taking over, and I've also heard that there is a lorry-load of her stuff holed up somewhere and the driver is looking for a buyer.'

'We know about the lorry, Marco, but not who's in the bidding.'

'There are a lot of people interested, obviously, but at the end of the day it comes down to big money and there are very few who have the means. Your problem is that it could all turn very nasty as those interested also want to take control of the other parts of the business as well.'

'Our first priority, Marco, is that lorry. It's in the hands of a complete amateur, who won't last five minutes on his own, so what names do you have?'

'As far as I've heard there are three genuine contenders, you can forget the rest. There's the Karim book-keeper, Thompson, who obviously has the finances. Then there's the Asian, Moushtak, who controls the west end and the suburbs, and some real heavies from Manchester have moved down. I don't know much about them, yet, except they are brothers and are well connected.'

'We've heard about Thompson from Dennison, but he doesn't seem the type. Moushtak is the squad's favourite and certainly has the funds but I had better find out about these brothers. What else do you know about the book-keeper?'

'Probably as much as you do, but don't underestimate him. He's the one who had control of everything and, if he gets the right support, could be the dark horse.'

'We've got to find this lorry first, Marco. Forgetting its street value, there could be a lot of killing in this one and I don't just mean the bad guys.'

'As soon as I hear anything I'll be in touch. Give me five minutes before you leave, just to be sure.'

Richard Anthony Wilding, together with his brother Peter James, seemed to control all crime in the north of England, their history on a par with that of the Krays in London thirty years ago and, as he read the report from Manchester, DI Watkinson realised the implications of their involvement.

'We'd be better off helping Thompson take over, at least we could keep the lid on things; if these guys get control around here it will put the clock back to those bad old days.'

'Surely they would be too stretched if they did succeed? My guess, sir, is that all they're interested in is that lorry.'

'I hope you're right, Sergeant, but we are still no nearer finding it.'

'How about we do a concentrated sweep both sides of the river? There are a lot of unemployed lowlife now who, I am sure, will not have put anything aside for a rainy day and will need a payday soon. One of them was contacted and went to Thompson, that's who we need to find.'

47

Gerald Thompson was starting to feel the pressure of his inheritance as he sat in his office smoking yet another cigarette. He realised now that what he thought would be an easy transition into the seat of total control was going to be far from that.

He didn't have the £150,000 in readies needed to retrieve the lorry but that could be easily remedied. His problem was how he could keep hold of everything and keep the predators at bay. With the Barolli twins and Dennison off the scene he needed to find a right-hand man quickly, not only someone he could trust but someone who could keep everyone else under control. It had to be somebody who didn't need to prove himself, and was a known and feared name throughout the underworld.

The alternative was to sit back and let the money come in every month from the off-shore account, wash his hands totally of the business and let the others fight for control. Then the greed kicked back in, and although the monthly transfer was a lot of money, it paled into insignificance when he thought of the revenue that was and could be generated from the business. His other problem was Carlisle. Did he know of his involvement in all this, or was yesterday a chance encounter? It seemed rather strange that he should introduce himself after all this time. There was a knock on his door and his secretary came in, her appearance always a welcome distraction.

'What's wrong, Gerry? You're smoking again and you know how ill it makes you. I'm not nagging, it's just that I hate to see you killing yourself!'

Jane Clark was not just his secretary, she was his confidante, his crutch and his mistress, although he hated to think of her like that. Five years older, with three teenage children, she had lost her husband to cancer and would always be indebted to him, although she never asked for or expected anything. The odd night out and occasional sex was how it was and how it would always be, she was not a marriage breaker.

'I'm sorry, honey. You know I'm always honest with you and I'll tell you all about it soon, promise.'

'Well, whatever's going on, you've changed these past few days and I don't like the vibes I'm getting or the people who are calling, either. There's another one outside in reception saying it's urgent.'

'Give me five minutes to cancel lunch then show him in. What's his name?'

'Who said it's a man? She wouldn't give her name, just said you would want to talk to her.'

As Jane showed her in Thomson sat up. Dyed blond hair, the make-up liberally applied but, nevertheless, very attractive, he could understand his secretary's attitude. Not only was she being protective, she could sense competition when she saw it.

'How do you do? I'm Gerald Thompson and how may I help you?' The old charm was switched back on but he somehow felt it was wasted on this one.

'It's more a case of how I can help you, I think. You're going to be in a lot of trouble soon unless you act quickly. I'm Sharon Dennison, Paddy's wife, or is it ex-wife now? I don't think I'm going to have a husband for a long, long time and with the breadwinner gone I need to secure my future.'

'Is this blackmail or will you settle for a lump sum, Sharon?'

'Boy, you do need help, Mr Thompson. You really haven't got a clue, have you? I haven't been able to talk to Paddy without the "bill" listening to everything, so I've come straight to you. The word is out on the street that you intend to run the business yourself and, quite frankly, you haven't got a chance in hell of survival.'

'Muscle, is that what you are talking about?'

'Maybe there is some hope for you after all, that's exactly what I'm talking about. You need it, and I have plenty to offer you.'

'What are you proposing here, a deal of some kind?'

'We'll talk about that when you've heard what I'm offering you.'

'Not here, let's find a pub somewhere where neither of us are known: these walls have ears!'

He was going to have difficulty explaining this to Jane, but he couldn't afford to miss the chance of perhaps solving his problem – he pushed the intercom button.

'Jane, I'm going out for a couple of hours. If Mrs Soper arrives before I get back will you keep her sweet for me? Thanks.'

He found Sharon Dennison intimidating, although his first impressions were that he could trust her, unlike her husband, he had always been wary of him. They found a pub that was unknown to the pair of them and, thankfully, there was no one in there that either of them knew. Settling down with a drink and a sandwich, Sharon, who he put at around forty, immediately outlined her plan.

'You've still got four of the old team left but no one is going to take any orders from any of them and, quite frankly, they are pretty lightweight. Now, I have three brothers, who are well known along the river, and no one messes with them. They would be ideal for you.'

'How could I trust them and, more importantly, how could I control them?'

'That's where I come in. Our mother died when they were teenagers and I have run the family ever since, believe me, I'm the boss.'

Thompson could believe that, he had already decided that this was a lady you don't cross.

'If they are any good why weren't they working with Paddy for the Karims?'

'I've always hated drugs and kept the boys away from them. They can be evil little buggers when they have to be, but they won't get involved with that stuff.'

'They're no good to me then, I'm expecting a shipment very soon.'

'Mr Thompson, you're not expecting anything. You're running around in circles trying to find the lorry that Paddy was supposed to be moving. They can find that lorry for you and the deal is this – distribute the stuff and that's it, no more drugs. We will then run the rest of the business for you, plus we will throw in our territory as well. Call it a sort of merger if you like.'

'How come Paddy didn't work with you then?'

'Call it a clash of personalities, he and the boys were forever at each other's throats, it was better without him.'

'What are you into, Sharon?'

'Much the same as you, but we need to expand.'

'Why don't you just muscle in and take over?' Thompson couldn't understand why she was being so civilised.

'Respectability, Mr Thompson. Moving in with you will give us that, plus we need your connections. I've done my homework: the club and all that goes with it, you know the right people.'

So that was it. He felt a rush of excitement as he realised he could keep it all, plus more. 'Sharon, let's talk business.'

'She's starting to have nightmares, keeps calling out for someone called Mack to help her, and her temperature's rising.' After the Mother Superior, Sister Mika was the longest resident of the retreat and had been present at the birth of baby Mario.

'Increase the morphine and monitor that temperature closely over the next hour. I'll get the doctors back, but it could just be the body adjusting to the drugs.'

'This is a terrible mess, Mother Superior, and it is the first time that I have felt that I've really failed in life. She came to us for help, and yes, we saved the baby, but we didn't save her from herself. Instead we let her go without any guidance to cause so much suffering to others.'

'I have known you for over forty years, Sister Mika, and I have never heard you talk like this before. Do not reproach yourself, my dear friend, she is not the first that we have failed and she won't be the last. Now go and try to keep her alive, at least we can help her now.'

It was Anna's feet that were causing the gravest concern and Fergy was convinced that they would have to be amputated, but Alistair wasn't so sure.

'Let's give it twenty-four hours to see if the infection comes under control. If we amputate, then what do we do for artificial limbs? She would have to leave the hospice then and that's impossible.'

'We're playing God here, laddie, and I don't like it. If she dies, then we have failed our oath.'

'Come now, you two, you've done all you can for this poor soul.' Sister Bartok intervened. 'If she were to die now it would not be your fault, but amputation, Doctor Gordon, is something we must try and avoid at all costs.'

'If that's the case then there isn't a lot more I can do for her. If you need me, Alistair, you know where to find me: I'll leave her in yours and the Lord's more than capable hands.'

Despite an intensive sweep all along the river, there had been no success in tracing the intermediary connected with the selling of the lorry's cargo, as once again a wall of silence descended on the underworld. Nevertheless, the officers had felt a nervousness among the criminal fraternity, almost fear, as if they were expecting something big to happen very soon.

'Let's pull Thompson and see what he has to say about life.' Jean Kent voiced her opinion after they had listened to the DCS reporting on his encounter with the book-keeper.

Liam, who had returned to a hero's welcome and despite the DCS's reservations had insisted on returning to duty, wasn't so sure. He felt angry and cheated at the way things had turned out and wanted someone's head on a platter to answer for all that had happened.

'I don't know if we will achieve much by doing that; it will only put him on his guard and I would prefer that we tag him a bit longer – see where it leads us.'

The DCS, more than anybody, was pleased to have Liam back. He liked his no-frills logical thinking and respected the fact that he had no time for the diplomatic softly softly approach that was Carlisle's world.

'Quiet frankly, sir, we cocked up before and we can't afford to frighten off Thompson now. I don't think we could have played Rees-Jones any other way, but we should have tried to take one of those two alive. This is still one hell of a mess we are in and Thompson's the only one who knows it all.'

'What about these Wilding brothers and the Asian? Has anyone any ideas as to their whereabouts?'

'Both active along the river, according to Marco, but we don't think they are any closer to the goods than us.'

'OK, Sergeant. We will give it twenty-four hours. You and Liam get over to Charlton and have a ferret around Thompson's yard and I'll keep pushing from this end.' He saw the look on Liam's face then. 'I know, Liam, the old pals act that you so detest, but believe me it does have its uses from time to time.'

They were preparing to leave when Liam took a phone call that seemed to transform the little man.

'Come on, chauffeur, we've got to go calling, someone wants to see us urgently.'

They drove south across the river, and Liam filled Paul in on the mysterious caller who had revitalised the scouser.

'She's a lady called Michelle who comes from my part of the world, and many moons ago had problems with her alcoholic husband. They lived up the road from me and the missus and one night she took refuge in our house, bruised and battered once again. I tried to get her to lay charges but she refused and, unfortunately for him, he traced her to our door that night – suffice to say he never bothered her again.

She came south to start afresh, and kept in touch with me and Sandra, finally finding herself a new partner and seemed very happy. Then she found out that his source of income was from protection: smuggling, prostitution, you name it, he was into it. Unfortunately, she loved this guy more than anything else in the world, he was kind and generous and gave her the security she had longed for, so she stuck with him.

It turned out he had a sister and three brothers, and between them were public enemy number one in Essex and parts of Kent, vicious little thugs who the sister ruled with a rod of iron. Michelle got fed up with the sister always interfering, trying to lead their lives, so she walked out one day never to return, although he still calls to see her without his sister knowing.'

Liam was enjoying this, Paul could tell, and he just wanted the little man to get to the punchline. 'Are you going to take all day, or are you going to tell me soon what's got you so worked up?'

'Patience, Sergeant, I've nearly finished. I suggest you pull over before we have an accident.'

Paul found a place to stop, switched off, and turned towards the scouser. 'Right, Liam, you have my full attention, this better be worth it.'

'The family name is Phillips. There is Kevin, Michelle's "partner", for want of a better word, there are his brothers, Stuart and Eric, and there is Sharon the sister: or, to give her her full married name, Sharon Elizabeth Dennison.'

'Sorry, Liam, I don't understand. So she is Paddy's wife, so what?'

'Young Kevin paid Michelle a visit last night. It seems sister Sharon has decided that they have got to expand, get respectable, so she is joining forces with some fancy accountant who's running London.'

'OK, so Thompson gets his muscle and Mrs Dennison controls everything, but we're still no nearer finding that lorry, Liam.'

'Michelle said that there was more, but was scared that Kevin might walk in at any moment, which is why we're meeting her in Chatham.'

They parked on the top floor of a multi-storey car park and, as Liam got out, a tall, leggy brunette, very pretty, came running towards him from out of the shadows. Paul could see that she was extremely nervous and frightened to be seen with him, as they hurriedly embraced and Liam opened the back door of the car for her.

'Sorry about the dramatics, Liam, but you two don't exactly look like a couple of friends that one would bump into in a car park.'

'I'm learning to live with my problem, Michelle. This is Sergeant Paul Mackenzie, Durban Police Department.'

She smiled as she shook his hand and Paul was pleasantly surprised to find that she was a warm, gentle lady and not the hard woman bearing the scars of her past and present life that he had expected.

'Ignore him, Sergeant, he's only jealous of us normal people.' Michelle started to relax as the banter continued between these two friends, and Paul was happy to sit back and listen to their infectious scouse humour as Liam steered the conversation around to the purpose of their meeting.

'So what has Kevin got himself into now, Michelle?'

'It's that pushy sister of his that's done it. Her old man's going down for a long time and she hasn't hesitated to sort out her future. You know most of it, I'm sure, but she has filled Kevin's head with all kinds of nonsense, and the whole deal hinges on them finding some lorry full of goods which Kevin says he's confident of doing.'

'Why are you telling us all this? Surely you will be in danger if she ever finds out.' Paul couldn't understand why she was risking her skin if she was that terrified of Sharon Dennison.

'Believe me, it's not revenge for her splitting me and Kevin up, if I'm honest that would have happened without her interference. It's just that I don't want to see Kevin get into deeper trouble than he is in already. I have never condoned his activities but you'll never change him, he'll always be a villain. However, this sounds like he's moving well out of his league and I don't want to see him get hurt, no matter what has happened between us.'

'Did he say anything about the lorry, where it might be, or who might have it?'

'What's on the lorry, Liam? Are they getting involved in drugs now, because that is something the family has never touched before, and something that would make me move away from here?'

'Michelle, we need to find that lorry above everything else. Yes, you're right, the lorry is full of heroin, but whether Sharon intends to keep dealing or it's a one-off remains to be seen. You say that they've never dealt before, so I would think that this is a chance for the Phillips boys to prove themselves and that would be the end of it.'

'Even so, it involves drugs, Liam. If they get caught they will go down for a long time.'

'Michelle,' Paul intervened, he was worried she would clam up and that was the last thing they wanted to happen. 'We don't want to use you, and we don't want to endanger your life, but the repercussions of this load falling into the wrong hands are enormous. You are our one chance of preventing gang warfare breaking out on the streets of London so we need you to stay where you are for the time being, and we want you to tell us where and when.'

'How am I going to know? He only turns up when he feels like it, I don't phone him ever.'

'Where do they hang out most days?'

She looked from one to the other as she opened the car door. 'The snooker club in town. I'll be in touch, promise. Bye, you two.'

48

Now that she knew the whole truth, Michelle was even more determined to save Kevin from going to prison for a long time. Uncertain as to what more she could say to him, or how she could persuade him differently, she wandered the streets of Chatham with her mind in turmoil as she reflected on what might have been. She couldn't give a damn about Sharon and the brothers, they could rot in hell, there wasn't a single nice thing that could be said for any of them, but Kevin was somehow different.

'Hello, Michelle, what are you doing in these parts?'

She jumped as Kevin's brother Eric came up alongside her and then realised that she was just around the corner from the snooker club.

'Christ, Eric, you frightened the life out of me!'

'Sorry, Michelle. It's good to see you again, how's life?'

'It goes on. How's that brother of yours, still up to no good?'

'Do you want to talk to him? He's in the club up to his usual tricks.'

Michelle knew what he meant. Kevin's usual trick was convincing some poor mug that he couldn't play snooker, then taking him for a lot of money. If he had knuckled down he could have been a great champion alongside Steve Davis and Jimmy White, but after his mother died there was only one way he was going, despite Sharon's iron fist.

'At least it keeps him off the street. I won't disturb him, it might cost him money.'

With that Eric said goodbye as they reached the club and he disappeared inside, Michelle counting the seconds, knowing exactly what was going to happen next.

'Hey, Michelle, hang on – it's me.' She had reached the corner when the familiar voice rose above the sound of the traffic. He caught her up effortlessly. Kevin was neither a smoker or a drinker and, despite the life he led, was very fit.

'If I didn't know better, I'd think you were looking for me.'

His boyish grin always had the same effect on her, and Michelle fought her feelings, determined not to give in.

'Still stiffing the punters are we, Kevin? You'll never change.'

'Still giving me a hard time, Mich? Come on, let me buy you a coffee.'

'Your Sharon won't like it if we are seen together, you'll get a real hard time if she finds out.'

'Sod Sharon. She's going to have to change a bit when we get up west. I'm glad I've bumped into you, though: we're going to be away for a few days and I wouldn't have had time to tell you.'

Steering her into a nearby café, they found a table out of hearing and away from the window – despite all the verbal Kevin was still frightened of Sharon and always would be.

'So where are you off to then, Blackpool for the weekend?'

'Don't be daft, Mich. It's that business I told you about. I'll have some real money soon and then maybe things might change between us.'

'I don't want your money, Kevin, and nothing will be the same between us ever again, you know that. Sharon will be the only woman in your life from now on, believe me.'

He looked sad as Michelle's words hit home. She hated hurting him like this, but he was intelligent enough to know that she was right.

'I hope all this money brings you happiness, Kevin, I really do. Just try and stay out of prison, will you?'

She was losing it and, as her feelings for this loveable villain rose once again to the fore, all she wanted to do was to disappear with him somewhere out of the clutches of Sharon, but she knew that that was an impossible dream.

'I'll be fine, honestly. Tomorrow we've got a meet in Chigwell, then Sharon's taking us to stay in some posh hotel in London and to meet our new partner.'

The thought of the Phillips clan in a posh hotel didn't bear thinking about. Sharon was moving them too fast and into a world that was beyond them and it could only end in disaster. Michelle's spirits plummeted as she became resigned to the inevitable.

'So you've found what you were looking for and that's your reward, is it? She's getting generous in her old age!'

'Come on, Michelle, she's not that bad. She kept the shirts on our backs and put food in our stomachs when times were hard and, without her, we wouldn't have got this far.

'I'm sorry, Kevin, this really is goodbye time. I can't stay around here and watch you get sucked into something that's beyond you, you've never listened to me, and you never will.'

She stood up and kissed him on the cheek as the tears streamed down her face. It was time to move on. Maybe for her it would be third time lucky but, of one thing she was certain, Kevin Phillips would always have a very special place in her heart.

As he drank his umpteenth cup of tea that morning, Tommy Hughes sat reflecting on how his calm, simple life had been irreversibly turned upside down. Always a good employee, he had spent his entire working life driving – buses, lorries, trains, diggers amongst other things – until the day the postman delivered a letter that was to change his life.

It was from a firm of solicitors in Canada saying that an uncle of his had died leaving him a sum of money and, although it wasn't enough to retire on, it was enough for him to realise a dream. He could buy his own articulated unit and work for himself, hiring his services to whoever he pleased without always having to say yes. So why, when he got the call from Andrew Mackinley, did he agree to help him?

He knew of Mackinley and what he was all about, the drugs, the organised crime, etc. and the money being offered wasn't a King's ransom, but to move a trailer from A to B for £10,000 was too good to turn down.

Whatever had possessed him that morning when he had left those two on the side of the road he still did not know but, having seen the television reports on the demise of Mackinley and Anna Karim, he had thought it would be a simple thing to offload the goods and secure his future. The sums being offered had been beyond his wildest dreams but with them had come the down side: his contact repeatedly warning him what would happen to him and his family if he didn't play straight.

He had never broken the law before and this whole business was a world of which he knew very little, except that people died and people suffered because of it. There were twenty-four hours left before the buyers would arrive, twenty-four hours in which to change his mind: then once again the thought of the £150,000 he had agreed on for the goods overtook the common sense and his see-saw mind was in turmoil once more. It was more than enough for him and Maureen to buy that house in Spain and retire comfortably, much more than he could expect to earn from driving until he retired, and then he thought again of his children and grandchildren. He reached for the phone.

'There's a phone call for you, Liam, on line one. A lady who wouldn't give her name.'

That immediately set the squad room going, as the banter started, and the Liverpudlian made various gestures with his fingers.

'Liam Jameson.'

'It's Michelle, Liam. They are leaving tomorrow for a meet at Chigwell, but I don't know where exactly, although it seems that they have found the lorry or who the driver is. Afterwards, Sharon is taking them up to London, to stay in a fancy hotel and meet their new partner, were his words.'

'You are a diamond, Michelle. What are you going to do now?'

'I don't quite know where to turn, Liam. I've cut my ties with Kevin completely so there is no point in staying around here.'

'Come and stay with us for a while until you get sorted. Give Sandra a ring and talk it through.'

'Thanks, Liam, that would be nice. Good luck, I might see you shortly.'

DCS Carlisle entered the room feeling more like his old self and immediately sensed the change in atmosphere. Everyone had been lifted by the news, and the buzz was back, although Carlisle knew that there were still many pitfalls ahead, the first being to try and find exactly where in Chigwell the meet was taking place.

To this end it was decided that the only way to solve the problem was to put a tail on Sharon Dennison and her brothers and, having organised that, the DI then told Liam and Paul to get over to Charlton and keep an eye on Thompson. However, the DCS was still far from being convinced that they had the situation in hand: there were far too many imponderables for his liking and they could not afford any mistakes this time.

'What worries me, Inspector, are these Phillips brothers. Their records show them to be vicious bastards, but they have never been convicted for anything in the big league so we don't know how they will react when the going gets tough.'

'Our information tells us that they would run through a brick wall if Sharon Dennison told them to, sir; apparently she rules them with a rod of iron. Personally, I think our biggest concern in all this is what the driver of that lorry will do when things turn nasty?'

49

Tommy was at breaking point and as the hours ticked away the pressure was becoming unbearable; his contact had not phoned back to confirm the meet, and his wife would be home soon and the third degree would start again. After thirty-two years of marriage he was in danger of losing his Maureen, which was unthinkable. He hated himself for lying to her and tried to convince himself that she would understand, but he knew that he was only fooling himself.

Then there was the contact: how could he trust him not to lead him into a trap? Tommy had never played on the other side before and he couldn't think of how to secure his payday and come out alive: he'd got in too deep and, although there was still time to walk away, what would be the repercussions for him and his family? He froze as his mobile started ringing and he sat there staring at it for several seconds, before forcing himself to answer it.

'Chigwell M11 junction 5, direction Waltham Abbey. There's a café on the left. Wait there at 11 am and take your mobile for further instructions.'

'What's the destination?' He was too late, the caller had hung up, but he wouldn't forget that female voice in a hurry.

He scribbled a quick note for his wife and, checking that he had everything, went out of the door. Rather than face another stressful night in the company of Maureen, he'd decided to spend the night in the cab: maybe when it was all over things might improve, but he doubted it very much.

*   *   *

'Good afternoon, is Mr Thompson available please? I haven't got an appointment, just called in on the off-chance.'

'What is your name, sir?'

'Wilson. Charles Wilson.'

The receptionist spoke to someone on the intercom who appeared almost immediately; an attractive woman, definitely his PA thought Liam.

'Mr Wilson, how may we help you?'

'I'm starting my own business and someone recommended Mr Thompson as a good person to talk to with regards to all the financial aspects.'

Jane was getting those bad vibes again. She'd tried to talk to Gerald only this morning but he had been incommunicable.

'I'm sorry, he's tied up all afternoon. Can I make you an appointment for next week?'

'Thank you. I can be here on Tuesday if that's possible?'

'Yes. Tuesday's fine, say 10.30 am.'

'See you Tuesday then. Goodbye.'

'Goodbye, Mr Wilson.' Jane didn't bother to write it in the diary.

'He's still here, according to his PA, but I think she either knows what's going on or smells a rat.'

'Well, I've been having a nose round and it's just been confirmed that that Jaguar parked in the corner is his. I've also found a place where we can sit, almost unnoticed, and keep an eye on everything, so I presume we stay here and wait to see what, if anything, happens.'

'Let's phone in and see if there is any news. I personally would like some form of back-up in the vicinity as this is where it could all happen, and Sharon Dennison is nobody's fool, she'll suss out a tail in no time.'

Liam's worst fears were confirmed shortly afterwards, but were nothing like he had expected. Firstly, the unmistakeable figure of Sharon Dennison pulled into the car park alongside the Jaguar and, without turning off the engine, got out and removed a holdall from its boot. She was gone in a flash then, just as Paul was calling in for instructions, all hell broke out.

A car and a van screeched in to the car park and from the back of the van came six armed Asians, who entered the premises at a run and emerged soon afterwards, dragging Thompson with them.

'Inspector. Thompson's just been lifted by some Asians. I'd say they were Moushtak's men and Sharon has called and taken something from the boot of his car, what do you want us to do?'

'Sharon's covered, so see if you can follow Thompson.'

'What about the office staff – I don't know how heavy they got?'

'Leave it to the back-up, they're not far away, you just try and keep Thompson in your sights.'

Although the van was keeping within the speed limits, the build-up of traffic was hindering them, and they soon lost the vehicle when it went through a changing light.

'Inspector, they're gone.'

'OK, Liam. The odds are that they are Moushtak's men so I'll inform the Southall police to keep an eye out for them. We must assume that they've lifted Thompson to use him as a pawn in an exchange tomorrow, which puts another fly in the ointment. What do you want to do now?'

'Go back and talk to that PA. She may be party to everything that goes on but I doubt it. Still, she is Thompson's right hand and as such could inadvertently give us a clue or point us in the right direction.'

'Very well, Liam. The back-up team have had a quick word with everyone in the office and sent them home. I'll get you her details. Her name is Jane Clark and she lives at 49 Deep Dale Close, Charlton. She's 45 years old and a widow. We've run her through the system and nothing has showed up.'

Deep Dale Close was a typical 1930s-built cul-de-sac of semi-detached houses but number 49 stood out from the rest, it had had every conceivable addition and alteration done to it. The woman who answered the door, though, was barely recognisable from the one Liam had met only an hour ago, and the tears were still running down her face as she reluctantly let them in.

'I'm sorry we have to trouble you so soon, Mrs Clark, but this is a matter of utmost priority.' As she led them in to the lounge she stumbled, and Paul caught hold of her as she almost collapsed on the floor.

'Liam, send for a policewoman and a doctor, I think Mrs Clark had better have some attention before we continue.'

'I don't need anybody else, I'll be all right. All I need is for someone to tell me the truth, please.'

So, Paul sat her down on the settee and, still holding her hand, he told her everything. The human trafficking, his brother, who her boss had been working for, the lorry and the search for it. They could tell from her reactions that she didn't have a clue about any of it as the shock and horror registered on her face, and she just sat there shaking her head.

'What happens next?'

'Do you have children due home at any time now, Mrs Clark?'

'No, they've gone to stay with my brother for the night, Gerald was taking me up west to celebrate some deal and explain things, he said. Why did he get involved? He had a very successful business, none of this makes sense.'

Before Paul could reply the penny dropped as Jane Clark suddenly realised the source of all her belongings and, leaping from the settee, she swept everything off the mantelpiece and sideboard. Then she started smashing all her possessions, the two men struggling to control her as this betrayed women lashed out with arms and legs, until the anger finally subsided and the tears returned. Refusing once again any outside help she just sat there staring into space, the two men waiting patiently as she gradually regained her self control.

'Where do we go from here?'

'Mrs Clark, we need your help today. I'm afraid tomorrow will be too late, even your boyfriend could be dead.'

'Don't call him that, he was a good friend to me and I don't want any cheap remarks.'

'We need to go through the office, and we need you there. Do you think you are up to it?'

'Let me go and straighten myself out, put some make-up on.'

'We'll have to come with you, I'm afraid. It's more than our jobs are worth to let you out of our sight, Mrs Clark.'

'Call me Jane, please. Surely you're not coming to the loo as well?' She turned to the two men as they followed her upstairs, a smile back on her face. At least her humour was returning.

Saudi Arabia, July 2003

As Mario expected, life on the Sheik's yacht had been one big round of parties in every port, with an endless procession of beautiful women passing through his bed, attracted more by the craft than Mario himself – and still the emptiness continued to eat away at his soul. The Sheik was a generous man, who treated his crew well, but Mario quickly tired of this way of life and was wondering what to do next, when the Sheik took him aside one day and offered him alternative employment.

There had been an instant rapport between the two men the first time they had met and, although Mario hated the desert and the intense heat, he readily accepted the offer as head of security at the Sheik's refineries. He hadn't expected for one moment that the Sheik would employ him without having vetted him first but, when the Sheik revealed his total knowledge of Mario's past life, Mario knew then that his rescue from the Adriatic Sea wasn't a chance encounter: the Sheik was part of the faceless web that manipulated people's lives across the globe.

The sheer luxury of his new life more than compensated for the inconveniences that go with living in the desert, and he had grown to like and respect the man immensely, but Corsica and his former existence were slowly hauling him in.

He had always known that this was just a stop-over in his journey through life, and that the Sheik wasn't expecting him to stay long; so it was with a mixture of feelings that he informed the Sheik one day that he needed to contact London.

50

Jane Clark was definitely back under control as she led the two
men around the offices, explaining the totally computerised world
that was modern business. Gone were the days, Liam reflected,
when a lot of police time was spent going through endless files
and thousands of bits of paper. Opening the fire-proof safe in
her office she showed them the hard discs which held all their
client accounts and information, her pride in her job still intact
despite all that had happened.

'Is there anything in here, Jane, that you are not party to, any
discs or paperwork?' Liam was getting worried, the clock was
running down and everything here seemed in order.

'No, Mr Thompson told me everything.' Then she stopped
short as she realised how untrue that statement was.

'Not everything it seems, Jane. We had better go through his
desk first. I presume you have the keys?'

They found nothing. No keys stuck underneath desks or behind
cupboards, no secret hiding place, the two men were running out
of options and time.

'Jane, I'm sorry to press you like this, but is there anywhere
you can think of that might be a hiding place; what about the
car?'

'I have the spare keys, but I can't see that being a possibility,
he always keeps it so immaculate.'

She was right, the vehicle was typical of his ilk. Not a scrap

302

of dust anywhere, the bodywork immaculately polished, and it was also empty! No maps, no CDs, no sweet wrappers, even the boot had nothing in it and, when Paul lifted the boot carpet, no spare wheel either, but in its place was a locked metal container made to fit the space exactly. There were no odd keys on the ring, so they returned to the office, where Thompson's jacket was still hanging behind the door.

Inside the jacket they found the usual male possessions but no keys and Paul was about to suggest that they get the motor back to the Yard when he felt something hard in the lining. It wasn't a key as such but a slim piece of plastic, obviously computerised, because when they entered it in the lock nothing happened for several seconds and then they heard a double click.

Bingo! Inside the box was a laptop computer and hard discs – surely this was the pot of gold, all they had to do now was find someone who could gain access.

'Will you be all right, Jane? We have to get this back to the Yard now if we are to have any chance of finding him alive.'

'To me he's dead already. You do what you have to do, I'll be fine. There are always vacancies for experienced PAs, only next time I won't get so involved.'

Somewhere there was a phone ringing. Why doesn't someone answer it? Paul was confused as he awoke to find that it was still dark outside, and then he realised that the ringing was his mobile.

'Sergeant. You'd better go and collect Liam and come in straight away. This is pure dynamite that you two have unearthed and I've called in everybody from the DCS down.'

The Duty Inspector hung up and Paul looked at the clock: 5am. This was going to be another long day.

Despite the early start, there was an excited buzz around the place when the two men arrived. The realisation that finally they had the information to finish this had motivated everyone and a silence descended over the room as DCS Carlisle entered and, after a curt good morning, he signalled for the Inspector to begin.

'It is obvious from the discs that we have recovered that our Mr Thompson is nobody's fool, that these are not only a complete record of all transactions over the past five years, but his insurance policy and pension fund for the future. We don't know exactly how long he has been webbed up with the Karims, but I would think it is safe to say that he would have set this up very soon after they recruited him. Our computer boys have not as yet put a total value on what is involved here, but I'm sure it won't come as a shock to say that we are talking tens of millions of pounds worldwide. I have to warn you now that there are some things in there which are going to leave a bad taste in our mouths, but first to today's problem, the whereabouts of Thompson and that lorry.

The night we took out Paddy Dennison they were, according to him, moving the stuff to a new warehouse near Heathrow. The address is a small industrial estate on the Great South West road, near Hatton Cross, on which Jonathon Rees-Jones had just secured a 21-year lease. That, ladies and gentlemen, if I'm not mistaken is where all today's business will be carried out, and where hopefully we will finally end this nightmare.'

The room erupted, with Liam and Paul the centre of attention, as the Inspector waited patiently for calm to return before continuing.

'Sergeant Mackenzie. You will be pleased to learn that every contact and every movement throughout the world is on there, which should help you to end the misery in your own country and with the prosecutions of Stromberti and Abdul Karim.

'Despite all our efforts we have, up to this moment, been unable to trace the whereabouts of Thompson, although it is odds on that Moushtak has him somewhere in the vicinity of Heathrow, and intends to use his life as a bargaining tool. The unknown quantity in all this are the Wilding brothers who are out there somewhere, keeping a low profile, and are very heavy duty.

'Then we have the fish out of water, the Phillips family. They are stepping up well out of their league and God only knows what their reaction will be when the proverbial happens. Up to now we have had no problems in following Sharon Dennison and, as the meet's at Chigwell with a destination at Heathrow, one assumes it will be motorway all the way. This will make our lives a lot simpler as we can change the tail frequently, but what happens to the lorry driver when it is all over is a major concern for us.

'We have to surmise at this point that he will become expendable, depending on whoever takes control of the load, but he is almost certainly an amateur and how he behaves under pressure could be the most important factor in all this. Before we go into today's plan of action I will briefly tell you that there are records for everything to do with the Karims on Thompson's discs, including the bad news as far as we are concerned.'

The murmuring started then, as they all realised what was coming next; they were expecting it, but it always came as a shock.

'This is not the time or the place to go into specifics but suffice to say that, yes, there are some of ours listed, although I hasten to add that they were not from this nick. In addition there are the names of prison officers and members of the judiciary who were on the take, and a lot of high-ranking people who were being blackmailed. Not only do we have the entire drug network on there, there is also a vast paedophile ring involving some very well known names.'

Martin Carlisle shuddered at the thought. Just how many members of a club that was supposed to be the pillar of British society were involved alongside Rees-Jones?

'In conclusion, I would like to congratulate Liam Jameson and Sergeant Mackenzie on this discovery. This find will remove a lot of the filth from our streets, although the repercussions will be far-reaching for a long time to come. Right, let's get down to today's business.'

*   *   *

305

Sharon hardly recognised her three brothers when she entered the kitchen of the family council house. They were dressed in their Sunday best and she smiled approvingly.

'Right. We've discussed this over and over and you all know how we are going to play this. I don't want any cocky gun-toting behaviour, especially from you two!'

Eric and Stuart looked at one another, their faces a picture of innocence, as Sharon continued; 'I mean it. You have a chance to grow up finally and get some respect, don't blow it. Kevin, you drive, and I want you all to keep your eyes open. I'm still not sure about the opposition and there are a lot of whispers along the river.'

'They are just leaving now. Kevin's driving with Sharon in front and they are heading north.'

'Give it fifteen minutes then come away, we have you covered.'

This was the pattern for the next hour, as the Phillips clan crossed the river at Dartford and, seemingly unaware of a tail, headed for Chigwell.

51

He'd been up all night, but at least he felt better about life as he made his way to the meet. No matter what happened now he was committed and, if it all went wrong, he at least knew that he had tried.

Despite the butterflies Tommy was hungry so, parking the lorry where he could keep an eye on it, he entered the café. Thankfully, there weren't too many in there, and no one he knew, as he ordered his breakfast and sat by the window. The doubts began to creep back into his mind again as he finished his meal and glanced at his watch: there was still time to unhitch the trailer and drive away from this lunacy. Too late, the mobile began singing in his pocket, bringing Tommy back to reality.

'Is yours the plain white rig?'

'Yes.' His heart was pounding now as he realised that there was no going back.

'Take the M25 direction Heathrow. We will identify ourselves nearer the destination. No funny business, and if we get separated we will call you.'

It was that women's voice that frightened Tommy more than anything else. Hard and cruel, he thought he would rather mix it with a gang of blokes than have to face her wrath.

His body was black and blue, his lips and eyes swollen, and the pain running through his body unlike anything he had ever experienced before, as he slowly regained consciousness. The barely discernible shapes of two men were hovering menacingly over him as he heard a door open and footsteps approach. He lifted his head, trying to force his eyes open, as Moushtak Ahmed stared down at him with a menacing grin spread across his face.

'My dear Gerald, this is getting beyond a joke. As I keep telling you, all we want are the goods – you can keep the territory, although I doubt if it will be for too long, knowing the credentials of your new workforce.'

The others laughed as he tried to get his senses together. What was he trying to prove by resisting any longer? Why not limp back to Charlton and let the money roll in from the off-shore account – Sharon and her brothers could take over the rest. He had thought of trying to talk a deal, but got the impression that Moushtak was not that sort of man and he would end his life as soon as he had told them the destination of the lorry.

'Up to now, Gerald, my men have been behaving like ladies. It is time they started acting like men, unless you tell us what we want to know, now.'

Quite what took place next he wasn't sure of, everything happened so quickly, but the front wall of the building suddenly caved in and armed men swarmed into the workshop before his captors could react. They opened fire on Moushtak and his men and, grabbing hold of him, managed to drag him outside just before the roof caved in.

There was chaos everywhere as he was bundled into the back of a four track, which then roared out of the yard, scattering the gathering crowd. Through half-closed eyes he watched in horror as his captors drove through one red light after another, narrowly missing buses and cars, before turning into the car park of a boarded-up pub. They drove around the back where there were two more cars full of people, and he was hauled out, collapsing on the ground. Huge hands grabbed hold of him, forcing him to his feet, then the pain returned as he felt the hammer blows in his stomach. 'What's the address, Mr Thompson?' This one had a different accent, but sounded just as vicious.

'You'll never find it, I'll take you there.' He braced himself, expecting more sickening blows, but instead they pushed him back into the four track, at least he had bought himself some time and a chance to think. There were at least a dozen of them, which would make it impossible for Sharon and her brothers to rescue him: he would have to come up with another solution.

'New Scotland Yard, how may I help you?'
'Detective Chief Superintendent Carlisle, please.'
'Your name, sir.'
'That doesn't matter, just put me through to him.'
'DCS Carlisle.'
'The stuff you are looking for is in the old Wonderglass factory on the A12 at Brentwood.'
'Mr Hughes. You're travelling down the M25 towards Heathrow with a bunch of armed thugs in tow, and you've emptied the trailer.' Carlisle was momentarily speechless, and had difficulty not bursting out laughing.
'How do you know all this and how do you know my name?'
'Mr Hughes, we know it all. The problem now is how do we protect you, what's your angle?'
Once again Tommy found himself out of his depth, his plan had been so simple and now he was confused again.
'Mr Hughes, I cannot applaud your action enough, I just wish you had done this sooner. You are heading for all sorts of trouble unless you tell me what your intentions are.'
'I've still got a few boxes on board and after they had given me my money I was going to tell them where the rest were. You would be there waiting to pick them up, and me and the missus could start a new life in Spain – it seemed so easy to me.'
Nothing is ever easy in this life, thought Carlisle as he tried to find a quick solution.
'Tommy, this is what we are going to do. We are going to pull you over, then escort you off the motorway. When your people phone tell them it's a regulation check and you'll call them back.'

'She won't buy that, Mr Carlisle, this is one clever lady.' Tommy was starting to panic again, that woman's voice was haunting him and the thought of facing her anger didn't bear thinking about.

'Tommy, calm down and just follow my instructions. We know the lady, and we will protect you, but we need to buy some time, OK? I'll be in touch.'

No sooner had Carlisle put the phone down than it rang again.

'Sir, we've just received a report from the Southall police. Someone has driven a breakdown truck through the wall of a garage workshop and murdered Moushtak and five of his heavies.'

'The Wilding brothers, Inspector?'

'Can only be, sir. I don't think there are any other players in this one. If they are that serious it changes everything, and puts the lives of not only our men but everybody else in extreme danger. What we must do now is get the special squad involved, but we don't have the time.'

'I've just bought us some time, you get it organised.' Carlisle then went on to tell him about Tommy Hughes and the empty lorry.

Kevin was getting impatient. Despite Sharon's insistence that everything was going fine, he was bored with driving at a steady 60 mph and longed for some action. When it came though it caught him totally by surprise, as two police Land Rovers, with lights flashing and sirens wailing, came down the sliproad straight out in front of him. Thinking they were for them Kevin panicked, they were tooled up and couldn't afford to be stopped so, before Sharon had time to take control of the situation, he pulled into the outside lane.

As the police reports came in, Martin Carlisle wondered just how many more people had to die before they could finish this. There were at least two dead: Kevin Phillips and the as yet unidentified driver of the other vehicle. The three other members of the family were in a critical condition, as was the driver of a third vehicle involved.

'What a mess, Inspector. Have we had a sighting of the Wildings yet?'

'No. They haven't shown up at the warehouse and I've told all units not to show themselves until they hear from me, no matter what.'

'Where are the special squad now?'

'About ten minutes from the lorry.'

'I'll phone our Mr Hughes and tell him what we propose.'

Tommy sat at the side of the road a gibbering wreck, the events of the past ten minutes vividly going round and round in his mind, and he still could not come to grips with what he had witnessed in his wing mirror. When the mobile rang he expected that cruel female voice and was somewhat relieved when it was Carlisle.

'Tommy. That was your paymasters who have just bought it on the motorway, and they were going to stiff you anyway. We have recovered from the boot of the wreckage a holdall full of cut, blank paper with fifty pound notes top and bottom. I don't know what you were asking, but I can assure you that you wouldn't have got very far on this lot.'

Tommy was speechless now, trying to comprehend how he could have been so naïve and, facing a prison sentence, his life now lay in tatters.

'Mr Hughes, are you there? Mr Hughes, will you talk to me? It's important?'

'Will I be going to prison, Mr Carlisle?' The question was from a broken man, Martin Carlisle sensing that no matter what he had done this man would not survive five minutes in a prison, and that he would be punished enough on the outside.

'All drug-related crimes, Tommy, carry severe prison sentences and I cannot guarantee you anything. However, your intentions to help us will be taken into consideration, and I will personally intervene on your behalf. That's the best hope I can offer you at this moment.'

'Thank you, Mr Carlisle. What happens next?'

'We are going to take your unit and trailer on to the meeting place, except you won't have to drive it, OK? You will be charged with knowingly conveying narcotic substances, but we won't oppose bail and you can go home very shortly.'

As they received the news, Paul and Liam's first thoughts were for Michelle, and how the injustices of life can repeatedly deal the nicest of people the hardest of blows.

'At this rate, Sergeant, if we sit around long enough they will all destroy one another.'

Paul realised that the little man's humour was a poor front for the awful task he would have to face later today when he confronted Michelle.

'At least the stuff won't reach the streets now, Liam. It's all over for the time being, although no doubt there will be a next time.'

'Unfortunately, that's what pays our wages, Paul – hang on pal, we've got visitors.'

'Three vehicles with ten to twelve persons on board have entered the estate and are cruising the area, Inspector. They're now taking up positions within the vicinity of the warehouse and whoever turns up will be caught in a three-way crossfire.'

'All units, keep your heads down until I give the order. Liam, the trailer's loaded with special forces and being driven by one of them, is there any chance we can take them by surprise?'

'No chance, sir. This bunch are very professional and strategically placed, it would be impossible.'

'What do you suggest, Liam?'

'Shit! Either they're calling our bluff or are not certain of what's going on, but they've turned Thompson loose. He's in one hell of a state, Inspector, and staggering to a point outside the warehouse covered by all three vehicles.'

'We'll make them wait a bit longer and see what they decide, but I don't think we'll be able to save Thompson. He'll be the

312

first to go when they realise there is no lorry. Stay in position, I'll get back to you.'

Gerald Thompson could barely stand, the cold pouring rain bringing some respite to his pain-wracked body, as he stood there wondering what could have gone wrong. The lorry was over an hour late now and every conceivable reason for this was flashing through his mind when the silence was broken by a loud-hailer, although he couldn't understand a word of what was being said. Then he heard car engines start up, and shots rang out as the area filled with men in black firing on the advancing vehicles. He felt more pain in his body and fell to the ground, aware that there were cars coming towards him but unable to do anything about it as he slipped into unconsciousness.

'Mr. Thompson, have you been shot?' He could hear the voice but couldn't focus on the face, and then he felt something sharp penetrate his arm and the pain began receding from his body. This relief, though, was only momentary, the previous pain quickly replaced by another of a different sort as the realisation that he had lost everything, including his freedom, sunk in before he slipped again into unconsciousness. The area resembled a war zone with burning cars and bodies lying on the ground, not all of them dead, as Liam and Paul went to help their colleagues disarm and arrest those still alive Fortunately, there had been no police fatalities, and as the Wilding brothers were taken into police custody the adrenalin began to subside and the two men embraced, thankful that this nightmare was finally over and that they were still alive.

313

52

The squad room was in a jubilant mood as the two men rejoined their colleagues to celebrate their success. It was hard for Paul to believe that he had only been in London a little under a month, so much had been achieved but, underneath the pleasure of a job well done, there was sadness lurking.

Stay in London or return to Africa: it was decision time now and although he had discussed it with his friend and mentor, Michael Mamtoba, and had spent many hours lying awake at night turning it over in his mind, he was still uncertain of which direction to take. Two totally different worlds and cultures – he had wondered if he could somehow embrace the two at the same time, but knew that that was only a pipe dream

There was nothing for him to return home to, no family, no girlfriend, but his conscience was telling him differently. Despite a black government in power, apartheid still reigned, the country was still divided and the poverty, crime and violence, that was the lot for the majority of his fellow countrymen would always exist. There was an immense challenge awaiting him back there and surely he owed it to his country to try and help build a better world for its people.

Then there was England, the place of his boyhood dreams, and although he hadn't seen much of the country, he felt an affinity with it already. The shadow of David would always be with him, wherever he lived, but he felt he could find happiness here.

Just then, the deciding factor entered the room, breaking his train of thought. DCS Martin Carlisle was almost back to his old self, although Paul knew that this case had taken its toll on him. There were a lot of skeletons still to be unearthed, friends and acquaintances of his, and he would have many difficult months ahead of him. Still, the smile and the charm had returned as he shook his men's hands and patted them on the back.

'Well done, Sergeant, this is a great day for the Met, but I have a nasty feeling you are going to ruin it for me.'

How could he turn his back on this man who would need all the support in the world over the coming months:? He owed him that in the very least.

'I'm afraid, sir, that you are going to have to put up with me for a long time yet, after I return from the trials.'

London, February 2004

It was the last place in the world he wanted to be in, but he had had no other choice. He had been unable to get a direct flight and, rather than hang around the airport, had caught the train into the city. Hailing a cab, he headed east along the river as the inexplicable force of the past months pulled him towards his destination.

Sister Mika gasped as she opened the door. Despite the years and her failing sight there was no mistaking the young man that stood before her.

'Matthew.' The tears welled up in her eyes as she embraced him. 'Come in and wait here, I'll fetch the Mother Superior.'

Nothing had changed much since the last time he had visited here with his mother, the calm and serenity of the retreat still all-enveloping, and the warmth and kindness that emanated from the sisters was something he would always remember. They were much older now, frail-looking, but he observed as Sister Ruth Bartok came towards him, they still had the desire and the love in their souls.

315

'My dear, Matthew, you have made us old ladies very happy: come and talk to me in my office, I'll send for some tea.'

As he sat there the news of his arrival had spread like wildfire, various sisters coming to see the Mother Superior on some pretence or another and, as if by chance, there was the young Duke visiting. When the tea arrived it was on a trolley pushed by a woman who shuffled painfully into the room, her once beautiful face contorted with pain, her hands and feet heavily bandaged. Clearly in agony with the effort of it all, the trolley her crutch, their eyes met and held. Matthew had to break the contact such was the intensity, and as he rose to help the woman serve the tea Sister Bartok intervened.

It was some two hours later that Matthew left the retreat, his mind and body a turmoil of mixed emotions, but at least now he knew the whole truth. The whole truth: it was something that had never bothered him, never given him sleepless nights and he knew that it wouldn't in the future. Maybe he would return here one day, maybe not, but for now he had a plane to catch.

Jamaica, February 2004

Another country, another chase, another kill. Matthew felt his being come alive once more as the 747 descended through the cloud base and the iridescent blue waters of the Caribbean rushed up to meet them as they came into land. The time spent in the desert had confirmed what he already knew, that this was his way of life until he made a mistake or his masters decided to silence him, that there was no other world for him. He was a sacrificial pawn in an endless game of chess that was played across the globe by people of wealth and power seeking to satisfy their never-ending greed, and their needs were his life blood. The events of the past forty-eight hours hadn't softened his resolve but at least now he understood why he was as he was. It was in his roots.

316

As he descended the steps of the plane a chauffeur-driven limousine came across the tarmac and pulled up alongside him. A well-built, suited man of his own age got out of the rear of the car and approached him.

'Welcome to Jamaica, sir. This route cuts out all the red tape and we thought you would prefer it that way.'

It transpired that although the British High Commission in Kingston was not acting officially on orders from London, they had been informed of his visit, and had laid on a car to collect the fifth Duke of Rushtington from the airport and put at his disposal the facilities of the Commission should he need them.

Matthew was supposed to be there on holiday and would have liked a much lower profile but was assured by his 'bodyguard come guide' that it would be more prudent to be accompanied around the city. For Matthew the last thing he needed was any involvement with the police, so he graciously accepted the hospitality, although he suspected that his companion was more than just a Third Secretary at the Commission.

He was a pleasant young man called Angus Fraser, whose Scottish grandfather had married a local girl, a heritage of which he was very proud. To all and sundry they were just two friends, young men from the privileged side of Kingston life out to have a good time without making themselves conspicuous, as they cruised the streets and visited the bars and clubs. All the time Matthew was learning about the island, where to go and where not to go, who were the crime lords and drug barons: Angus Fraser was the most knowledgeable Third Secretary, further convincing Matthew that he was part of this vast clandestine web that encompassed the world.

After three nights Matthew decided to make his move, informing his new-found friend that he was getting bored and it was time for him to move on and explore the rest of the island. He was not surprised at Angus's lack of reaction, only the sequence of events that followed as, instead of taking Matthew back to his hotel, Angus left the lights of Kingston Town behind them and headed in the direction of Spanish Town. It was Angus who finally broke the silence as they went through Spanish Town and turned towards Old Harbour Bay, confirming what Matthew already suspected.

'I know I don't have to tell you this but from here on in you are on your own and as far as the High Commission goes you do not exist. There will be a cruiser called the Catalina Belle waiting for you in Montego Bay which will take you to the Cayman Islands. There is an open ticket awaiting you and the arrangements have been made for you to fly out on your Italian passport.'

'How long have I got?'

'The Captain is under instructions to wait five days from this morning unless there is a hint of trouble, in which case he is to put to sea immediately. If this happens you have one last chance to rendezvous at St Ann's Bay in the north of the island.'

Angus turned off the road into some trees and stopped the car. Motioning for Matthew to follow him, they went down a track towards the sea, the full moon lighting their path.

'That's yours over there.' Angus indicated towards an old Ford pick-up, partly hidden in the trees, as they carried on down the path which led them finally into a tiny inlet. A small cruiser was gently bobbing at its moorings and Matthew could see, even in this light, that it had seen better days, its former green and white paint practically non-existent.

'She may not look much but, believe me, she is as sound a vessel as you will ever see and very seaworthy.' Angus had noticed the look of dismay on Matthew's face.

'There are charts on board, should you have to make your own way to the Caymans, as well as all your belongings and the other things you have asked for. Good luck and goodbye.' He shook Matthew's hand and was heading back up the path before Matthew could reply.

On closer inspection even the varnished interior hadn't seen a coat in years, but the big surprise came when he lifted the engine hatch. Crammed into the tiny space was an almost new diesel, the power of which, Matthew calculated, would be more than enough for a vessel four times this size. Reassured by this find he then surveyed the rest of the boat, discovering, after a lengthy search, his neatly packed suitcases behind a false bulk-head in the cabin, together with the weaponry he had requested.

Although hidden from the shore, Matthew decided to refrain from switching on any lights. The dawn was only a couple of hours away, so he pulled the canvas awning over the cockpit and settled down on the bunk in the cabin.

There were lights everywhere, people shouting and yelling – their words meaningless – and all around him there was fire, its heat all-consuming, his body burning, and he had to escape but in which direction. He sat bolt upright, his body a river of running water as the flames extinguished, the voices in his head ceased their cacophony of sound, and slowly the reality of life returned.

Glancing at his watch, Matthew saw that he had been asleep for six hours and he sat there a while listening out for signs of life. Getting up, he gently pulled back the awning to find himself all alone in a tiny bay of paradise, the only sounds being the gentle lapping of waves on the shore.

Diving over the side, he began to swim vigorously back and forth, exorcising the nightmare and revitalising his body. Back on board in the small galley he found the cupboards and gas fridge packed with enough food to last a siege – whoever was pulling the strings on this one had made sure of his every need. He lifted the cover over the gas rings and found a large white envelope which contained a photograph of a completely bald-headed man of European extraction, an Ordnance Survey map of the island, sea charts and two addresses.

As with the boat, the pick-up appeared to have entered its final stages of life but, again, under the bonnet was something else – Matthew fired the V6 engine and made his way out of the trees and on to the main road. Studying the map, he saw that in fact

319

it was the only road in these parts and he followed the first route marked out in red, turning off after a couple of miles on to a pot-holed track which took him up into the mountains.

The old Ford creaked and groaned but the V6 was making light work of the climb when, suddenly, he came upon streams of people, some with children strapped to their backs, heading in the same direction. They appeared to be very poor, the warm Jamaican smile missing from their faces, as they struggled with the effort of the climb. Then, without warning, his destination leapt out at him, so unexpected and incongruous a sight that he nearly ran into the thickening mass of people.

Set in the hillside was a huge building constructed of glass and steel with tarmac roads leading up to it and beautifully mani-cured lawns and gardens. 'The Foundation' was proclaimed in giant red letters across the front of the third floor, but what caught Matthew's eye were the number of armed personnel everywhere and the security cameras which surrounded the place.

He'd made a big mistake coming here but it was too late to turn back, so he carried on up, hoping that the track didn't just peter out. He only had a small handgun hidden under the dash-board: if they came after him he wouldn't have a chance, although he could probably outrun them with this engine.

Luck appeared to be on his side: the map showed the track winding its way to the centre of the island where it met another road but, to be sure that he wasn't being followed, Matthew stopped the pick-up and switched off the engine.

The welcoming silence that greeted him was a huge relief and, after waiting several minutes, he restarted the engine and continued his ascent of the hill. What he did not know was whether the target lived here all the time and rarely left the sanctuary of this armed fortress, or whether he only came here now and again and lived at the other address. It was odds-on that the truck had been captured on camera but whether they would check it out was a gamble he would have to take.

At least he had established one thing: the kill was going to be impossible up here, the terrain was far too restrictive, so he decided to try the second marked route. This took him to the other side of the island and, exercising more caution this time, he left the truck hidden in the undergrowth and proceeded to cut a path through the trees.

He found himself climbing high above the winding road, the trees thinning out as he reached a plateau overlooking a forested valley. Sweeping the terrain with the sight, he spotted a man-made clearing with a large mansion house which faced out to sea. The grounds were immaculate and, on closer inspection, he saw that there was a large security presence: armed men patrolling the area with dogs and the various antennae on the roof signifying computerised electronic surveillance. This had to be the place, but again the man was too well protected, and the range far too great for the rifle; he would have to find an alternative solution.

For three frustrating hours Matthew lay scanning the house and surrounding countryside, searching for an answer, when the unmistakeable sound of a helicopter reached him on the wind. He took refuge in the sparse cover that was available to him as the chopper passed directly overhead and proceeded to land. Crawling his way back to the edge, he watched as two armed men descended from the aircraft with a third person between them, his bald head unmistakeable even at this distance. Matthew had the answer to his problem.

Uncertain as to the daily movements of the target, he returned to the plateau before dawn next day and was relieved to find the chopper still on the ground. Time was not on his side, he had only two days left before his escape route off the island was cut off and he would be left to his own devices, so he settled down for a long wait and prayed that lady luck would smile on him. She didn't let him down. Within an hour the man appeared, flanked as before by two heavies, and the helicopter kicked into life. Taking off, it hovered momentarily before heading out to sea and Matthew thought he had lost his chance. Then it turned

321

back inland towards him and, as the undercarriage loomed large in the sight, he fired. Instantly, the chopper exploded as the bullet hit the fuel tank, and it crashed in a giant fireball into the valley below.

It would take months of investigation before the cause of the crash could be determined so, not being in any immediate danger, Matthew calmly drove his way back to the cruiser. As he approached the turning to The Foundation he was waved down by a very distressed-looking young lady standing by her equally distressed-looking motor car and, pulling over, Matthew knew before he had stopped that there was nothing he could do for her car, the rising steam said it all.

'Can I give you a lift somewhere? I'm afraid there's nothing I can do about your motor, that will need towing in.'

'Thank you, but no. I daren't leave it here, it will be gone by the time I get back.'

Matthew hardly heard her words, his eyes transfixed. She was one of the most stunning women he had ever seen, and all his plans for his escape were abandoned as he thought of how he could spend the day with her.

'I'm a tourist, I'm afraid, and I don't know the area – what do you suggest?'

'Work's out for the day, that's for sure, and I'll have to get the car towed in somehow. There's a garage about three miles up the road who could repair it.'

'If I leave you here and go and get them for you, will you be safe?'

'I'll be fine, but would you really do that for me?'

'In exchange for the pleasure of your company for lunch. I don't know this part of the island and would appreciate a local guide.'

Lunch turned into dinner, day into night, as Matthew found himself sitting on the deck of his boat with Frances still by his side. The two of them had shared a day to remember, both unsure of how it was going to end, and both not wanting it to finish.

She had told him everything about herself and he in turn had told her one half of his life story but did not feel guilty about omitting the other, certain that the time and place would come. All the hate and loneliness that was his being was evaporating in the heat of the sultry night air, and the closeness of this woman. The contract, the Sheik, all of his past life had been banished to the furthest corners of his mind, the only thoughts he had were for this beautiful woman and how he could stay with her.

'How do you fancy cruising around the island tonight and, tomorrow, you can show me more of your adored Jamaica?'

'I can't take another day off, Matthew. There are too many people on this island who need help and The Foundation is short of personnel.'

'I won't take no, Frances. If we don't go anywhere tonight, will you at least stay here on deck with me watching the stars and the ocean?'

She did not reply, her mind was in turmoil, not believing the feelings that were coursing through her body once again. She shivered as the cool of night descended and Matthew got up and went below returning with blankets and pillows. Arranging them on the deck he motioned for her to join him. Frances did not hesitate.

53

London, February 2004

Instinctively, she walked the kerb once more, oblivious to the snow settling heavily around her. Her hair, brunette streaked with fading blond and now flecked with snow, was untidily tied at the back with an elastic band and her make-up, liberally applied, did nothing for her ravaged features. The clothes she was wearing, or lack of them, were not suited to the freezing temperatures, but all she could sense and feel were the internal dictates of her body. She was reaching the point of no return once again. Sonny would be here shortly with her 'medicine' so she had to turn a trick soon or face another beating if he didn't get his money. Fighting back the craving, she glanced up and saw car headlights coming slowly down the street towards her and she stepped off the kerb into its path.

Another lost night had passed and Amanda awoke as the withdrawal symptoms started to kick in – she needed a fix. Her skeletal body was trying to tell her other things, but she was feeling too sick to read the signs. Just reaching the toilet in time, her first thoughts were that she had injected some dirty heroin, then, as she sat slumped on the lavatory floor, the truth slowly dawned on her – she was pregnant. She burst into tears as the hopelessness of her situation enveloped her, she needed help and there was no one to turn to, her only friend had deserted her. Crawling back to her bed, the tears still falling, she was reaching for her mobile when the door burst open and an angry Sonny stood in the doorway.

He realised immediately what was wrong with her and flew into a wild rage, hitting her defenceless body until he was exhausted, then he stripped the flat of all her possessions and threw them down the stairs, dragging Amanda out on to the landing before locking the door behind her. No one came to her assistance as, half naked, she stumbled down the stairway frantically retrieving pieces of clothing and her meagre possessions.

Homeless, and without a hope of finding the succour her body was crying out for, she took out her mobile once more and redialled the number in one last desperate attempt for help, and got the answerphone again. Where was her black knight in shining armour when she needed him most? He'd not contacted her in months despite all the messages she had left.

Totally desolate, she dragged her now screaming body onto Hungerford bridge and, with her last vestiges of strength, mounted the steel girders. Voices were yelling at her, hands grabbing her legs and feet, but she lashed out, freeing herself from the restraints and hurled herself into the fast flowing murky water.

Father Alistair had spent the morning as he often did, walking the streets of London looking out for those in need, and had been one of those who had tried to stop her and failed. Quickly disrobing, he dived in after her fast disappearing body. He was a strong swimmer, but the icy water combined with the fast current were more than he had bargained for as he surfaced and struck out for the now frantically waving hand as it rose and sank below the waves.

Diving under the water he immediately realised the hopelessness of his task, visibility was zero but, instead of resurfacing, he went down deeper, frantically kicking out as the air in his lungs expired. He did not fear death but failure was something he could not accept, although the time had come to admit defeat or die! As he began to lose consciousness he felt something material brushing his face and, lashing out to free himself from this encumbrance, quickly realised that there was a body attached to it. It was the girl. Although very weak, his will to survive kicked in and, with his lungs bursting, he dragged the dead weight upwards as he slipped into unconsciousness.

Bright lights blinded him as he struggled to open his eyes, and tender hands quickly shielded them as an angelic voice came to him, easing his mounting fear.

'It's all right, Father, you're safe and sound, just lie quietly.'

'Where am I?'

'Charing Cross hospital.'

Then the pieces of the jigsaw fell in to place and he tried to sit up as the picture formed in his mind, but she gently restrained him.

'Easy, Father, you'll be able to go home soon.'

'And the girl.'

'She's barely alive but still fighting. She was dead but the medics brought her back, but there are other complications. Not only has she had a miscarriage, she's on heroin and cold turkey is setting in.'

'Can I go to her?'

'Let's sit you up and see how you go.'

She swung his legs over the side and, as his feet touched the floor, Alistair Sullivan re-closed his eyes as everything started to revolve in front of him, the nurse holding on to him tightly as he began to fall.

'It's still too soon, Father, let's lie you down again.'

'No, I'll be all right, just give me a minute.'

The twitching sedated body was painfully thin, a sight he was used to, although he didn't recognise the girl as one of his flock. Beside the bed the life-support system was sending out its all important message: somehow, she was still on God's earth. Taking her frail hands in his he sat and prayed silently for her and for all the thousands of others like her. Then his thoughts drifted to the burnt, deformed women living not five miles away who was responsible for so much of this suffering and he shuddered. He knew that no one could ever eradicate the evil monster that now encompassed the world, but Father Alistair Sullivan vowed that he would fight to his dying day this invisible enemy that threatened to destroy all of mankind.

Jamaica, February 2004

Matthew awoke first and, turning, lay and contentedly watched a sleeping Frances beside him until his awakening mind suddenly brought him back to the reality of his situation. Carefully extracting himself from the bedding he rose and went to the stern of the boat. Diving into the welcoming cold blue water he began swimming vigorously away from the vessel, his mind a maelstrom of conflicting thinking when, suddenly, he felt something underneath him – it was Frances. She surfaced laughing, her smiling happy face tearing him apart as he realised that he had placed her life in tremendous danger by this involvement.

Breathless with excitement she just clung to Matthew as they made their way back to the boat and, exhausted, they fell to the deck together as all their feelings resurfaced and everything else became a blur. How long they lay there he did not know, but every second spent here increased the danger so, with the responsibility of Frances weighing heavily on his shoulders, he suddenly sat up.

'Matthew what's wrong?' She tried to pull him back down to the deck but he resisted. Turning to face her he could see the fear in her eyes, the trembling of her naked body, and he was swamped with guilt. He put out his hand, which she grabbed immediately and he pulled her up into his arms and held on to her tightly.

'Frances, for the moment all I ask is for you to trust me.' He caressed her still damp hair and kissed her gently before continuing. 'My way of life is such that, for the moment, I cannot tell you everything. All I know is that for the first time ever I want to share my life with someone and not run away from them.

However, I must leave the island immediately and leave you behind – believe me, it's for your own good. You have not seen me or spent any time with me and as soon as I possibly can I will send for you, OK?'

She pushed herself away and, kneeling in front of him, took his face in her hands and stared intently into his eyes, a multitude of fears running through her body. Silently they remained like that for what seemed an eternity then a smile broke across her face and she nodded and kissed him.

'No matter what, no matter where, no matter how long, I will wait for you, Matthew.'

She could sense the urgency in him and, without a further word being said, got up and went below to dress. Matthew was the lone mercenary once again as he left the vessel and climbed the footpath to the truck, all the while scouting the terrain for the tell-tale signs of unwanted guests. As he neared the vehicle he realised his senses hadn't let him down, the white envelope tucked behind the windscreen wiper, and flapping in the breeze, confirmed his fears. There was no explanatory note inside, only a ticket for the France/England rugby international at Stade de France in five days' time. He was trapped in the web once more.